"There's someo[illegible] ... [illegible]t Sally said as I walk[illegible] ... [illegible]r traditional spandex[illegible] ... blue suit that actua[illegible] ... [illegible]e way around. Someti[illegible] ... [illegible] few weeks, her wardrobe had undergone a major change. I wasn't sure why, but I liked it. She was even wearing fewer layers of eyeliner.

"Who is it?"

"He told me it was a surprise . . . said he's an old friend."

"No business card?"

She shook her head, and I sighed. She might look more professional from a sartorial standpoint, but she was still less than ideal as an assistant.

I straightened my jacket and headed for my office, wondering what "old friend" had turned up. I took a deep breath as my hand touched the knob—and froze.

"Something wrong?" Sally asked.

Yes, something was wrong. Very wrong. Unless my nose was deceiving me, Sally had let a werewolf into my office. But I wasn't about to tell Sally that.

"Next time somebody comes to visit me," I said, "would you please have them wait *outside* my office?"

She shrugged, and I resisted the impulse to snarl at her. Instead, I turned a[illegible] door.

He was sitting at my desk.

Also by Karen MacInerney

On the Prowl
Howling at the Moon

Leader of the Pack

Tales of an Urban Werewolf

KAREN MACINERNEY

BALLANTINE BOOKS • NEW YORK

Leader of the Pack is a work of fiction. Names, characters, places, and incidents are the products of the author's imagination or are used fictitiously. Any resemblance to actual events, locales, or persons, living or dead, is entirely coincidental.

A Ballantine Books Mass Market Original

Published in the United States by Ballantine Books, an imprint of The Random House Publishing Group, a division of Random House, Inc., New York.

ISBN 978-0-345-49627-0

Cover illustration: © Gene Mollica

Printed in the United States of America

www.ballantinebooks.com

9 8 7 6 5 4 3 2 1

For my sister, Liza Potter, with love

One

Most of the time, I'm not too crazy about being a werewolf. For so many reasons: the compulsory and inconvenient transformations, the excessive reliance on Lady Bic razors . . . not to mention the difficulty explaining to potential mates that our children would probably grow a natural fur coat and tail every twenty-eight days or so. Maintaining a normal relationship—much less a career—is a hairy proposition when you tend to sprout fangs every time someone pops *Moonstruck* into the DVD player.

But there are compensations. The lightning-fast reflexes, for example. The ability to scare the pants off of would-be muggers and rapists. The deep, almost carnal enjoyment of a rare prime rib at Ruth's Chris. And, as was currently the case, the ability to smell every nuance of a gorgeous spring day.

It was a warm mid-March afternoon in central Texas, and I was on my way back to Austin from a meeting with my favorite client in San Antonio. The radio was playing full blast and the windows in my M3 were wide open, letting in the mingled scents of fresh earth, new grass, cows, and a complete and total absence of werewolves, which was fine by me. The cows, however, were making me hungry. Lunch had been a long time ago, I realized as I gulped back a mouthful of saliva and reached for my tumbler of wolfsbane tea.

I was mentally reviewing the more intimate details of my

meeting with Mark Sydney, CEO of Southeast Airlines. He was my client, to be sure—and landing the Southeast Airlines account had recently netted me partnership—but most of the afternoon had been spent at a romantic River Walk restaurant staring over a giant margarita at my client's deep blue eyes. I was reviewing our good-bye kiss when my cell phone rang.

I flipped it open as the M3 rolled past another tasty-smelling herd of cows. "Sophie Garou."

"So, how did your 'meeting' go?" It was my best friend, Lindsey.

"Fine," I said. "We did some strategic planning and talked about general accounting practices. Everything's great."

"Are you dating yet?"

"Not officially. We're kind of keeping things quiet; I'd rather Adele didn't know." I didn't want to know what my boss thought of my mixing business with pleasure. And boy, was it a pleasure . . .

"Mark's a good match for you. I liked Heath, but he just didn't have the same . . . I don't know. Zing?"

Lindsey was right about Mark—he was all about zing—but my heart still wrenched a little at the mention of my ex-boyfriend. Heath had asked me to marry him on Valentine's Day, about a month ago, and I'd had to decline. Partly because I wasn't sure how he'd take the whole "I'm a werewolf" announcement, of course. And partly because I suspected he was sleeping with his gorgeous associate Miranda. But even without those rather significant mitigating factors, things just hadn't been right between us for a long time. It was a hard decision, but I was pretty sure it was the right one.

"For the record, Mark and I are not dating," I repeated. Even if we had enjoyed a few—okay, more than a few—steamy episodes together. "He's my client," I reminded her. But Mark was also something else—something even stranger than I was. About a month ago, when I'd gotten into trouble with a pack of deranged Mexican werewolves, he'd appeared out of nowhere wearing wings and what looked like a full-body coat of liquid napalm. Which was convenient—as was the fact that he knew I was a werewolf—but enough to give me pause when I thought of becoming involved with him long-term. It was bad enough that my children would have intermittent episodes involving a full coat of fur and a tail. A full coat of fur doused in napalm would be a bit much. Particularly if it occurred while I was giving birth.

Still, I had to admit Mark was absolutely fabulous in bed. I squeezed my legs together just thinking about our last episode, which had taken place between acts at the Zachary Scott Theater . . .

"Is he up for this weekend?" Lindsey asked.

"What?" I asked, pulling my mind up out of the gutter. Or, in this case, the coat room at Zach Scott.

"The Howl. Aren't you going?"

I'd blocked it out of my mind so thoroughly I'd almost forgotten about the upcoming inter-pack meeting, which was scheduled to start Friday in Fredericksburg, an hour or two west of Austin. Since I wasn't affiliated with any pack, I didn't feel too inclined to attend, even though Wolfgang, the leader of the Houston pack, had asked me to poke my nose in. To which I'd said a polite no thank you. As far as I was concerned, the less I had to do with the werewolf world, the better. "God, no," I said to Lindsey.

"Since you're not officially *dating*, why don't you drop in and leave Mark behind? You might meet a cute single werewolf."

Like Tom? I thought before I could stifle it. Tom was perhaps the most intoxicatingly handsome werewolf I had ever met. Granted, I hadn't met a whole lot of werewolves over the last twenty-eight years—I'd been "undercover" for most of that time—but I'd seen enough to know that Tom was something pretty special. He had long blond hair, chiseled

Nordic features, shimmery gold werewolf eyes, and a tanned body I just couldn't stop staring at. And then there was his smell, which was enough to reduce me to a quivering puddle of lust . . .

But Tom was dating Lindsey, which meant he was strictly off-limits—even if we had, in a weak moment, acknowledged a rather powerful mutual attraction. Still, his unavailability wasn't necessarily such a bad thing; if my father was any indication of werewolf quality on the mating front, a werewolf was the last thing I needed on my dating resume.

Twenty-nine years ago, my mother had had the bad fortune to fall—quite literally, since she tripped stepping off a tour boat—for a werewolf in Paris. According to my mom, it was Romeo and Juliet all over again, only with gypsies and werewolves instead of Capulets and Montagues. Despite extreme family disapproval, my mother and her lover continued to see each other in secret—at least until I came around.

Romance or no romance, the arrival of a bouncing baby werewolf was too much for Luc Garou: He sent my mother and me out of the country. My mother still claimed it was "for our protection"—the story had always been that the pack would kill us both if they found us there—but since we hadn't seen hide nor hair of him for almost twenty-eight years, I suspected my well-being wasn't my father's primary motive in shipping us overseas. I still carried his surname, Garou, but that's all I had to do with him. Other than the whole werewolf thing, of course.

"No, I think I'll just kick back this weekend. Maybe use my Lake Austin Spa Resort gift certificate. It's been a busy couple of weeks; I could use some R & R."

"Do you think I could talk Tom into letting me go to the Howl?" Lindsey asked.

I closed my eyes for a second. Then I remembered I was driving and jerked them back open, swerving a split second before my BMW slammed into the trunk of an Intrepid. "No."

"Why not?"

"It's a bad idea." In fact, Lindsey having anything to do with Tom at all was a bad idea, but I'd given up trying to convince her of that.

She hmmphed, and said something else besides, but I missed it because my phone started beeping.

"I've got to go," I said. "My phone's dying."

"Come see me when you get back to the office," she said. Since she worked right down the hall from me at Withers and Young, it wouldn't be much of an effort.

"I will," I promised, and hung up a moment later. Lindsey's fascination with werewolves—werewolves in general, not just Tom Fenris—was worrisome. Ever since she'd discovered my lupine identity last month, she'd been badgering me to "share my magic" with her. Personally, I didn't understand why anyone in their right mind would want the burden of compulsory transformations, excessive hair growth, and a need to drink gallons of wolfsbane tea, which was anything but a taste sensation. True, there were some benefits—a few extra centuries of life, for example—but in my opinion, the cons definitely outweighed the pros. Lindsey kept asking about it, though, and it wouldn't shock me if she showed up with a hypodermic needle and attempted to do an impromptu blood transfusion in the coffee nook one morning.

I was considering calling Tom to ask him to dissuade her when the phone rang again. The battery light flashed as I picked it up: It was my mother.

"Sophie, darling, I have some big news." She sounded breathless.

"You finished getting your tax paperwork together?" As a CPA—and auditor—I did the taxes for Sit A Spell, my mom's magic shop, every year. It wasn't my favorite job—my mother is not the most organized witch on the planet—but I soldiered through it anyway, because I loved her.

"Oh, nothing like that," she said. Then she said something else, but I lost it because of the beep.

"What?" I asked.

". . . coming to see you. It's amazing."

"What's amazing?"

"Your . . ." Her bright voice trailed off.

"What?"

The phone was dead.

I folded up the phone. Whatever it was would have to wait until I could call her from my office. Or till I swung by tonight for another package of wolfsbane tea. Thanks to my thrice-daily infusions, I'd managed to minimize the compulsory transformations to full moons that fell near solstices and equinoxes, which came only four times a year. But the spring equinox was coming up, which meant it was time to up the dosage—and to plan my quarterly trip out of town.

I set cruise control, played with the radio until I found a Red Hot Chili Peppers song, and took another deep breath of spring air, enjoying that rare feeling that all was right in the world—even if the pollen did make my nose run.

Of course, if I'd had any idea what was waiting for me at my office, I would have turned around and driven straight to Mexico.

"There's someone to see you," my assistant Sally said as I walked past her desk. In lieu of her traditional spandex, she was dressed in a flattering blue suit that actually covered her midriff all the way around. Sometime in the last few weeks, her wardrobe had undergone a major change. I wasn't sure why, but I liked it. She was even wearing fewer layers of eyeliner.

"Who is it?"

"He told me it was a surprise . . . said he's an old friend."

"No business card?"

She shook her head, and I sighed. She might look more professional from a sartorial standpoint, but she was still less than ideal as an assistant.

I straightened my jacket and headed for my office, wondering what "old friend" had turned up. I took a deep breath as my hand touched the knob—and froze.

"Something wrong?" Sally asked.

Yes, something was wrong. Very wrong. Unless my nose was deceiving me, Sally had let a werewolf into my office. But I wasn't about to tell Sally that.

"Next time somebody comes to visit me," I said, "would you please have them wait *outside* my office?"

She shrugged, and I resisted the impulse to snarl at her. Instead, I turned and opened the office door.

He was sitting at my desk.

Adrenaline pumped through me as I closed the door firmly behind me. The mystery werewolf stood up and smiled at me, exposing a line of pointy teeth. He was tall—well over six feet—with red hair and the golden shimmery eyes of a born werewolf.

"Who are you?" I said. "And what are you doing in my office?"

"Sophie," he said in a strange accent. "You're beautiful."

I backed toward the door as he rounded the desk in one fluid move. His smell was strong—overpowering, almost, even under the heavy cologne—and somehow, familiar.

"Who are you?" I repeated.

"Don't you know me?"

"I have never laid eyes on you in my life."

"Oh, but you have," he said, moving closer. "How about a hug?"

"I think you must be deranged," I said, pressing myself against the wall. Adrenaline pulsed through me, and it was a struggle to keep from transforming. "I don't know who you are, but I want you out of my office." When he continued to stand there looking at me, I clarified my position. "Out. Now. Before I have to call security."

He paused, arms extended, and looked a little bit hurt. He was a handsome man, probably in his late thirties, with a mane of reddish hair and a smile that was charming, even with the pointy teeth. “As if security could do a thing to stop me.” He had a point, but I wasn’t about to concede it. He didn’t give me a chance, anyway. “You really don’t know me, do you?” he asked.

“Nope.” I shook my head. “Now please leave.”

“But Sophie,” he said, hands extended. “I’m your father.”

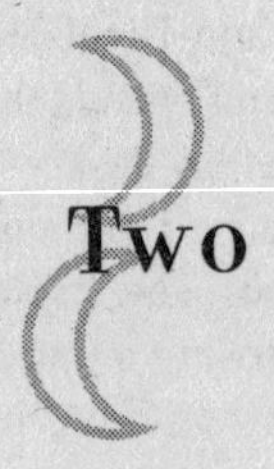

Two

I blinked at him. “You’re my *what*?”

“I’m your father,” he repeated, grinning slightly, and my stomach sank to the vicinity of my Prada pumps.

He was telling the truth. The reddish hair, the shimmery gold eyes, the familiar smell. The dimple in the right cheek when he smiled.

That didn’t mean I had to admit it, though. “I don’t have a father,” I said.

“Sophie, darling. I know how much pain I’ve caused you, how hard it must have been growing up without a pack, or your sire. It was a tragedy that I was unable to be there when you were just a pup,” he said, stepping forward to stroke my cheek with his hand. His scent washed over me, and I felt the hairs stand up on my arms. From some distant recess of my past, I recognized his smell. He continued talking as I struggled with some emotion I couldn’t name. “And then,” he said, "once you left, I couldn't find you. You and your mother just vanished."

"Yeah, right," I said, snapping myself back to the present. "Look. I don't know what makes you think you can waltz right back into my life after disappearing for the first twenty-eight years of it, but you're wrong. You're too late. I'm no longer interested."

He smiled at me, tenderly. "You *do* know me. You remember." Then he clapped his hands and did something like a jig, right there in the middle of my office. "This calls for a celebration! How about filet mignon and a bottle of Dom Pérignon?" He paused mid-dance to ask, "Are there any decent restaurants in Austin?"

"Of course," I said, crossing my arms. "But I'm not visiting any of them with *you*."

He looked crushed. "But Sophie, *chérie*, you must let me explain! I know it seems that I . . . well, that I *abandoned* you. But I swear to you, there were factors beyond my control."

His gold eyes were so sincere it was hard not to believe him. But twenty-eight years is a long, long time. And it's not like I went into the witness-protection program or anything. Heck, I hadn't even changed my last name.

"And I want to hear all about you," he continued. "Carmen has filled me in on some of the details, but I've missed so much . . ."

"You've seen my mother?"

"I just came from her charming little shop. How do you think I found your office?"

No wonder she'd called me earlier. I stared at him, still trying to grasp that he was related to me. Genetically, anyway. "If you're my father," I said, "how come you look only ten years older than I do?"

His smile faded. "Am I looking that old?"

"I'm only twenty-eight," I said.

"Elise tells me I don't look a day over thirty."

"Who's Elise?"

"Maybe I'll tell you when you come to dinner with me," he said with a sly grin.

"But I'm not going to dinner with you."

"Oh, but you must! I'll call Georges, he'll arrange everything. What's the best steak restaurant in town?"

Steak? My mouth started watering again. "Well, there's Fleming's," I said grudgingly. "And Ruth's Chris, of course."

"Which has the better wine list?"

"Ruth's Chris, I think."

"I'll have Georges make reservations. Will six thirty work for you?"

"I told you I'm not going to dinner," I said.

"Wonderful. Let's say Ruth's Chris. Shall I have Georges pick you up, or will you meet me there?"

"I'm not going," I said.

He reached forward and grabbed my hands, then kissed me on both cheeks. Something melted in me, just a little bit.

"I'll see you at Ruth's Chris at six thirty," he said in his low, suave, slightly growly voice. "I'll have them ice the champagne, and we'll buy the biggest, rarest filet mignon we can get. I think a nice Bordeaux would be good, too—perhaps a Château Lafite Rothschild?"

"But . . ."

"Now, *ma puce*, I would love to stay, but before we meet, I have one more errand to attend to. Georges will pick you up in front of the building at six fifteen. You look stunning in that suit—no need to go home and change." He kissed me on the cheek again, his bristly cheek brushing mine, his smell enveloping me, dredging up old memories. "I'm so looking forward to it," he said. "An evening with my daughter, to catch up on all we've missed. What could be better?"

Before I could answer, he swept out of my office, said a few words to Sally, and was gone.

And I hadn't even had to call security.

* * *

"Why didn't you tell me he was here?" It had taken me fifteen minutes to regain my equilibrium. When I finally succeeded, the first thing I did was call my mother.

"I tried, sweetheart. I called your cell. The phone died, remember?"

"You could have left me a message at the office!"

"I did."

I glanced at the phone; sure enough, the message light was blinking.

"So," she said. "What do you think? Isn't he charming?"

"Not particularly," I lied. "But he wants to have dinner tonight."

"I know. He invited me to come along, but I thought it would be best if you two got to know each other without me. He still looks wonderful, doesn't he?" my mother said.

"You're not considering getting involved with him again, are you?"

"Me? I've got Marvin now." I still didn't understand my mother's attraction to an attorney who could be a body double for Danny DeVito. But even Danny DeVito was better than a werewolf, I supposed. "I wouldn't want to leave you to go back to Paris with him anyway." She paused for a moment, then added, "Plus, I did a reading. The cards advised against it."

So she *had* considered it. Which was understandable, really; Luc Garou might be a piss-poor father, but he was a good-looking man. Even if he did look twenty years younger than my mom. "I'm not going," I said.

"Why not?"

"I don't want to get involved. My life is finally getting straightened out. I've got a good job, I've worked out a truce with the Houston pack, and everything's going smoothly. I don't need any complications."

"Darling, you should go. Just to talk to him; he'll be able to give you advice on all the things I wasn't able to help you with while you were growing up. Besides, he's quite high up in the werewolf hierarchy these days, I understand. He'd be a good ally to have."

"What do you mean, werewolf hierarchy?"

"He's the alpha of the Paris pack."

Alpha of the Paris pack? He'd evidently been moving up in the world. "So what? I live in Austin."

"Have dinner with him," my mother said. "For me."

"I'll think about it," I said.

"Don't think about it; just do it."

"We'll see," I said.

"A cosmopolitan, please. A big one."

As the waitress headed for the bar, I sank back into the couch and eyed the door to Ruth's Chris. After debating it all afternoon, I'd decided it wouldn't hurt to at least hear out Luc Garou. Besides, I had to admit I was curious. It's not every day you get a chance to talk with your long-estranged father.

The waitress appeared a few minutes later with a big, frosty glass of cranberry-laced vodka. I thanked her and sucked down a third of it; I needed all the courage I could get, even if it did come with a wedge of lime.

Six thirty came and went. So did six forty-five. I busied myself fiddling with my lime wedge and watching the other patrons. And becoming increasingly pissed. Against my better judgment I'd agreed to have dinner with my father—only to be stood up.

At six fifty I drained the rest of my cosmo, left a ten on the table, and grabbed my purse, feeling like an idiot for being taken in by the jerk who called himself my father.

I was halfway down the street and heading toward the parking garage—I hadn't waited for Georges, whoever he was, to pick me up—when I heard my name.

"Sophie!"

I hesitated for a moment, then picked up the pace. I'd

given him his chance; it wasn't my fault he couldn't manage to show up on time.

And then he was beside me, his hand on my arm. "I'm so sorry I was late. I was . . . detained."

I turned to give him my iciest look. Luc Garou's red hair was wild, as if he'd been running, and something that looked like a scratch mark trailed down his cheek.

He smoothed his hair down and adjusted the lapels of his sportcoat, fixing me with his shimmery golden eyes. Eyes that looked exactly like mine, right down to the flecks of green speckling the irises. "Please," he said in a thick French accent. "Georges has confirmed our reservation, and the staff has already set aside a bottle of Dom Pérignon for us." He gently grasped my elbow. "Forgive my tardiness. Won't you join me?"

And before I knew it, he was guiding me back toward the restaurant. I was addled again by his scent—it brought back such strong associations. Memories that danced just out of reach—just flashes, really. I took a deep breath and willed myself to stay calm. "What happened to your face?" I asked as he opened the door to the restaurant a moment later.

He cocked an eyebrow. "What do you mean?"

"You have a scratch," I said. "Right along your cheek-bone."

He touched it with his fingers, tracing the line, and shrugged. "I do not know."

I couldn't swear it, but it looked half-healed already. As I stared at the scratch, Luc smiled at the hostess, who blushed prettily and then led us to a secluded table in a corner of the restaurant. She shot me an envious glance as she handed me a menu. *If she only knew*, I thought.

He asked the young woman if she would bring out the Dom Pérignon, and she nodded, blushing to the dark roots of her blond hair. As she hurried to the bar, he reached across the table and squeezed my hands in his own. "Sophie." His voice changed; it was husky with what might have been emotion. "I have missed you so much," he said, devouring me with his eyes. "But I am *enchanté* to finally meet you. Your mother has done a wonderful job raising you. And you are strong, very strong; you and me, we are cut from the same cloth."

I wasn't sure I agreed with him—I liked to think I was a bit more reliable, for starters—but I didn't challenge him. For now, anyway. "After you sent us out of the country, why didn't you bother to track us down?" I asked.

"I tried," he said, shrugging. "But it was not possible. You and your mother, you simply vanished."

"You didn't have any trouble finding me today," I pointed out.

"That is because you reestablished contact with our world," he said. "I wasn't sure it was you—I feared it was nothing but a rumor—but the moment I heard a whisper of your name, I came to find out for myself." He smiled that toothy smile again. "And here you are. Gorgeous, smart . . . perfect."

I ignored the flattery. "*Our* world?"

"You know what I mean," he said, and at that moment, the waitress arrived with an ice bucket and two flutes.

He smiled up at her, flashing that devilish grin, and like the hostess, she melted. I resisted the urge to roll my eyes: my father, the werewolf Casanova. "Thank you, my dear," he said to the young woman after she poured a bit for him to sample. When we were both supplied with glasses of bubbly, he nodded at the waitress in approval. "Perfect. Now, for an appetizer, we will start with an order of the mushrooms, if you would be so kind." Then he turned to me. "Sophie, *ma chérie*, I propose a toast."

"To what?" I asked.

"To our reunion," he said, and I grudgingly clinked glasses with him. I wasn't sure I was on board with the whole reunion thing, but the champagne was fabulous. "Now," he said, turning to the menu. "Have you decided what you desire?"

What I desired, really, was that Luc Garou had never turned up on my doorstep, but it was a little late for that. So I went for an order of rare filet mignon instead. When the waitress disappeared, the werewolf across the table—my father, I reminded myself—focused on me again. "I recently learned that you and your mother were living here, and that you have been in contact with Wolfgang, in Houston."

"You know Wolfgang?"

"Oh, yes. Herr Graf and I have a long history," he said wryly. "I think he will be less than delighted to discover my presence here, but it is no matter." He gave me a Gallic shrug. Then his gold eyes bored into me again, oozing sincerity. "I know your mother has told you this, but if there had been any way—any way at all—for you to stay safely in Paris, I never would have let you leave."

"Oh?" I said frostily. "I hear you're a bigwig over there now. Alpha of Paris and all."

"Yes," he said, puffing his chest out slightly, reminding me of the silverback gorillas on Animal Planet. "I have risen through the ranks. As will you, of course."

I held up a hand. "Nope. Not going there."

"But my darling," he said, reaching across the table to squeeze my hand. *My darling*. Like we'd known each other for twenty years, not twenty minutes. "You cannot avoid it. It is your destiny." He smiled smugly. "Wolfgang must brace himself; he will lose a second time."

"I don't have a clue what you're talking about."

He nodded sagely. "Of course you don't know our history. He wouldn't have told you, would he?"

"Told me what?" I asked, taking another sip of champagne. The flavor was incredible—pears, vanilla, and even a bit of plumminess—and my wolfie senses were overwhelmed for a moment by the complexity.

"Does it meet with your approval?" Luc Garou asked.

"It's delicious," I said, still half-overcome by the flavors. Was that a note of apple in there? *Sophie*, I told myself sternly. *Stop thinking about the champagne.* I forced myself to set the glass down and focus.

Luc gave me an approving smile and continued. "You come from a very powerful family, my dear. And Wolfgang Graf was formerly the alpha of the Alsace territory."

"What does that have to do with anything?"

"The position of alpha in Strasbourg is currently being filled by your aunt, Marguerite Garou, and her consort, Bertrand." Once again, he puffed his chest out a bit.

"So in other words, your sister beat out Wolfgang for some French province a hundred years ago."

"A hundred and fifty, actually. And it was accomplished with some assistance from the Paris pack, I'm happy to say."

"And I have an aunt," I said. It was strange to think of some French werewolf being my aunt. Then again, it was strange to think of some French werewolf being my *father*.

"You have many relations," he said. "All of whom, I'm sure, would be delighted to make your acquaintance."

"Oh? Whatever happened to the old ethnic purity thing?" I could feel anger welling in me. "You know—the whole reason you kicked my mother and me out of France? Or was that just a convenient excuse so you could continue being Don Juan?"

"Don Juan was Spanish, not French," he corrected me.

I rolled my eyes. "Whatever."

"Certain things have changed over the past quarter century," he said. "*Et bien sur*, if you were a weakling, or had not inherited the gift, it would be a completely different issue."

The *gift*? Being born a werewolf was considered a *gift*?

Luc ignored my incredulous expression and continued. "But with me as your sire, and your fortitude . . ." he shrugged again. "It would be, how shall I say? Academic. And they will be even more welcoming when you have achieved the status of alpha."

"I'm sorry. What did you just say?"

"You will, of course, be taking over the Texas packs."

I took a deep werewolf-and-champagne-scented breath. "Look," I said. "I think we need to get something straight. I am not planning on going to France to meet relatives who wanted nothing to do with me when I was born, just because my mother wasn't a werewolf. And I have no desire—absolutely none at all—to join a pack, much less fight somebody for the position of alpha."

"But you are a Garou," he said, as if that made any difference whatsoever.

"My last name may be Garou," I said. "But I am a partner in a prestigious accounting firm, with a fully human identity. An identity I'm not interested in giving up, thank you very much." I paused to take another sip of champagne, and wavered. If being part of the Paris pack meant ready access to Dom Pérignon, maybe it wouldn't be such a bad idea to join up after all. Or at least pay them a brief visit . . .

Then my father's voice pulled me back to reality. "Sophie. *Ma chérie*. Can you not see that it is your destiny to wrest control of the pack from Wolfgang? It would not do for a Garou to be a subject of a Graf."

I put down my champagne and stared right into those shimmery golden eyes, ignoring the jumble of feelings that was swirling around somewhere deep inside me. "Let me get this straight," I said. "You came all this way just to tell me you expect me to overthrow Wolfgang and take his place as alpha?"

"But you are a Garou," he repeated, not seeing the problem. "Of course that is what you want. It is your birthright." He shrugged. "I am simply offering to help you achieve it. After all, I could not be there in your formative years, but I can offer you my assistance now."

"Sorry," I said. "But I'm not interested." I stood up and retrieved my purse.

"Where are you going?" he asked, looking mildly surprised.

"Home," I said.

"But we've got Château Lafite coming out at any second. And your filet . . ."

But my willpower remained strong. With a last wistful glance at my champagne flute, I turned on my heel and marched to the door.

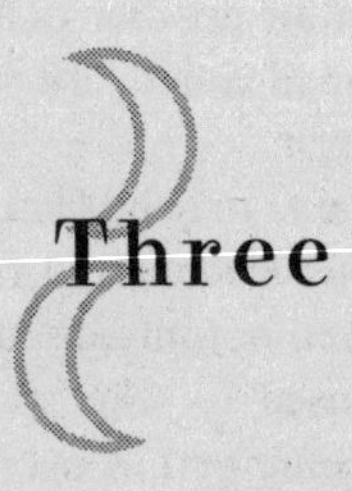

Three

"How did it go?"

"Poorly," I told my mother, cradling the phone between my ear and my shoulder as I reached in the pantry for my stash of Valrhona dark chocolate. It was French chocolate, which wasn't ideal—right now France wasn't exactly my favorite country—but it was still chocolate.

"Oh, I'm so sorry to hear that, darling," my mother said.

"The whole reason he came back is that he wants me to do my 'family duty' and move up the werewolf ranks."

"Sweetheart, I'm sure that's not the only reason."

"Actually, I'm pretty sure it is. And now that he's decided I'm not some weird hybrid mutant he should be ashamed of, he's ready to take me back to France so he can parade me around to all the relatives."

"See?" she said. "It's not all about your position with the pack; he wants to take you back into the fold. He mentioned that they'd loosened up the rules on cross-species matings. Isn't that fabulous news?"

I knew my mom was a Pollyanna, but this was taking it a bit far. I took another bite of chocolate and said, "Of course, he wants me to kick Wolfgang and Elena out and make myself Houston's alpha first." Since the former female alpha, Anita, had been exposed as a traitor—she had been plotting with the Mexican packs to take over Texas—she'd been replaced by another female werewolf, Elena. Like her predecessor, Elena hadn't exactly taken to me; I seemed to be more popular with the males of the species.

My mother was quiet for a moment. "I'm sure he was joking."

"Don't think so," I said through a mouthful of Valrhona. "Apparently my aunt beat out Wolfgang for control of some European territory a long time ago. I gather that's why he's now in charge of Houston instead of Strasbourg."

"What does that have to do with you being an alpha?"

"Luc Garou seems to think the Garous should repeat history here in the New World. For the family honor."

"Oh. Hm." She was quiet for a moment. "What did you tell him?" she asked.

"What do you think I told him?"

"That you'd think about it?"

"No!"

She sighed. "Well, then, at least that's settled. What else did you talk about?"

"We didn't," I said. "I left."

"I'm so sorry, honey."

I swallowed a mouthful of chocolate and said, "Me, too." And to my surprise, I *was* sorry. I'd never expected to see my father—but I guess secretly I'd always hoped that if I did ever find him, it would be a warm, loving reunion. Instead, despite the sugary words, the whole meeting had been about Luc Garou, and the family name. Which, based on his track record to date, shouldn't have been a surprise.

But it was certainly a disappointment.

"He's planning to stay in the Austin area for a while," she said. "Is there any way you would give him a second chance? There's so much you could learn from him."

"Mom, could we talk about something else?"

"Of course, darling." She was quiet for a moment. Then she said, "Are you going to the Howl?"

Which was not exactly what I had in mind when I said "something else". "Have you been listening to *anything* I've said, Mom? Of course I'm not going," I said.

"Is Tom going?"

"If Lindsey has anything to say about it, he is."

"Is she still asking to be turned?"

"Unfortunately, yes."

"So you're not considering it."

"Of course not. She's my best friend."

"It would be a very special gift," she said.

"Mom, if I could give it back, I would. It's not something I would wish on anyone, especially my best friend."

"But isn't it her decision?"

"She has no idea what she's asking for," I said.

"I suppose you know what's best," she said in a tone of voice that implied just the opposite.

I was finished with the bar of chocolate and had plowed through half a jar of maraschino cherries—I hadn't been shopping for a while, and was short on options—when the phone rang again. I picked it up guardedly, half expecting it to be my mother again. Or Luc. Thankfully, it was neither.

"How's the hottest auditor in the state of Texas?"

"Mark?"

"Were you expecting someone else?"

"No," I said, leaning back against the pillows of my bed. After my dinner of chocolate, cherries, and champagne, I was feeling bloated, and had been debating putting in an exercise video to work off some of it. Not to mention to take my mind off of my aborted meeting with the asshole who claimed to be my father.

But a phone call from Mark was an even more welcome diversion.

"Good," he said. "So, when are we going to the Howl?"

"Why on earth would we go to the Howl?" I asked. "And how do *you* know about the Howl?"

"Just one of my little secrets," he said.

"Some of them aren't so little," I said, thinking of his ability to magically appear and disappear. And make big, scary werewolves run off yelping with their tails between their legs. Not to mention the knack he had of sprouting wings and fire.

"I'll take that as a compliment," he said with a low, sexy chuckle that sent a current of lust zinging through me. "When can I see you again?

I rolled over onto my stomach. "How soon can you get up here?"

"I can't make it tonight, although I'm dying to see you. How does tomorrow night look? No hot dates planned?"

"Let me check my calendar," I teased.

"No second thoughts about Heap?"

"Heath," I corrected him, feeling a flash of irritation. "And no. Nothing's changed."

"Good," he said. "I hear he's been seeing someone anyway," he said.

Despite the fact that I was the one who had broken things off, I felt a flare of jealousy. I'd only broken up with Heath last month. Was he over me that quickly? "Oh, really?" I said lightly. "Who?"

"I think it was that associate of his—Miriam, or something. The blonde one you introduced me to that day at Romeo's."

I cringed, remembering the day Mark and I had run into Heath and his new associate, Miranda, at a romantic little Italian restaurant. I had suspected that something was going on between Heath and the gorgeous blonde, who looked like a life-size version of Career Day Barbie. "Oh," I said shortly. "Good for him."

"Anyway, I'm sorry to bring that up. We were talking about dinner tomorrow, weren't we? How about Ruth's Chris?" he asked.

"No," I said quickly. That was the last place in the world I wanted to go.

"Not in the mood for steak?"

"Of course I am. I'd just like to try something different. How about Sullivan's?"

"Everything all right, Sophie?"

"Fine. Why?"

"I just had a feeling earlier tonight that you might be upset."

I had been, of course—who wouldn't be? I glanced down at the ring Mark had given me a few weeks ago, wondering if it had forged some sort of psychic connection between the two of us. I was pretty sure it had let him know when I got into trouble. Was it somehow transmitting other information, too?

Still, regardless of its potential occult properties, the band was gorgeous, made of a silvery metal that didn't burn me, with a full-moon inset of some kind of opalescent stone on the front. My mother still hadn't figured out what it was, but she didn't like it one bit; which was the same way she felt about Mark. The problem was, the ring was stuck to me like glue—even when I transformed. Not for the first time, I wondered exactly what its properties were.

"Everything's hunky-dory," I lied.

"Good," he said. "Sophie, you know you can talk to me."

"I know," I said, suddenly anxious to get off the phone. "But I'd better get some shut-eye. I've got a meeting tomorrow morning at seven."

"Any client I should be jealous of?"

"She's a grandmother, Mark. She runs a garbage disposal company."

"Then I guess I'm okay. Shall I swing by your office tomorrow afternoon? Make sure Adele knows what excellent service you're providing?"

"Just don't lay it on too thick, okay? I think she suspects something already."

"I'll be the model of propriety," he said.

"I hope not," I said, feeling another little tingle. When I hung up the phone a few minutes later, I was feeling a lot less upset about the crappy dinner with my father—and very excited about my date tomorrow night. Dinner at Sullivan's, maybe a trip to the Elephant Room . . . who knew? With Mark, you *never* knew.

Which was more than half the fun.

I didn't hear a peep out of Luc Garou the next day—not that I expected to, of course—and as pleased as I was not to have to deal with him, I found myself a tad put out that he hadn't tried at least a *bit* harder.

But at least I had an exciting evening with Mark to look forward to. I had just brewed myself a big mug of wolfsbane tea and settled in behind my desk when Lindsey appeared in my office. Closing the door behind her, she eased into one of my visitors' chairs.

Lindsey was dressed in a clingy charcoal suit that hugged her curves like it was competing in the Indy 500, and her bee-stung lips were freshly glossed. The resemblance to Angelina Jolie was striking, as usual.

"Big date tonight?" I asked.

"Tom's taking me out after the opening ceremonies are over at the Howl," she said. "You're lucky—I can't go because I'm human."

"I'd trade with you in a heartbeat," I said.

"Likewise." She pressed her full lips together. "I don't know what your big hang-up is. You're a werewolf. So what? Why are you so worried about me wanting to take the same path?"

"It's not a path. It's a pain in the ass."

"Whatever," she said. "I still don't get what the problem is."

"The problem is that you seem fascinated with it. And once you do it, you can't undo it." Which wasn't entirely true; Tom seemed to have the ability to "unmake" werewolves. But since I didn't know exactly what that entailed—for all I knew, it could involve vivisection or eating eye of newt and wing of bat—I wasn't about to tell Lindsey that.

"Why would I want to undo it?"

"Because it's a curse!" I said.

At that moment there was a knock at the door; a moment later, Mark walked in, filling the small room with his smoky, erotic aroma. "Did someone mention a curse?" he said, blue eyes glinting. He closed the door behind him and walked over to my desk, giving me a quick, hot kiss that set my heart to pounding.

When I'd caught my breath, I filled him in on the conversation so far. "Lindsey wants to be a werewolf," I said.

He sat down in my other visitors' chair and leaned back. "Oh. Is that all?"

"Is that all?" I crossed my arms over my chest. "It's a pretty big decision, don't you think?

He shrugged. "Why do you care if Lindsey wants to get in touch with her animal nature?"

"Because she doesn't know what she's getting into," I said. "I'm trying to protect her."

His eyes roamed up and down Lindsey's curvy figure. "She looks like a big girl to me."

"Whatever," I said, exasperated.

"Are you and Tom going to the Howl tonight?" he asked Lindsey.

"I wish I could. But since I'm not officially one of the club, he's taking me out when he gets back."

I turned to Mark. "Did you talk to Adele?"

"Oh, yes," he said. "I told her how . . . *delighted* I've been with your services." His mouth twitched up into a wicked smile, and I felt the heat rise to my face.

"I think I've got some work to do," Lindsey said, winking at me as she headed for the door.

"What *are* we doing tonight?" I asked.

"It's a surprise," he said, grinning. "I've still got a few things to do this afternoon. Shall I pick you up at your place at, say, six?"

"How should I dress?" I asked.

He grinned more deeply, making his blue eyes glint. "If I told you that, it wouldn't be a surprise, now, would it?"

He gave me one last kiss, pressing his lean body against mine, his fingers sliding up under the front of my camisole to graze the edge of my bra cup. I sucked in my breath as his fingers circled my breast, touching my nipple lightly.

"Have you ever done it in your office?" he whispered.

"Uh-uh," I managed to respond. And I wasn't sure I should; as hot as Mark was, my office wasn't exactly the ideal place for a tryst. And there'd been a lot of talk of me "belonging to him" lately—I'd been meaning to address that. Although perhaps now was not the time . . .

"Want to?"

Before I could answer, he reached back and locked the office door. Then he peeled my jacket off and slid the straps of my camisole from my shoulders. He traced the lace trim on my bra, just barely touching my nipples, and then slid his warm hands around my back and unhooked it so that I was standing half-naked in my office. So much for self-control.

As my fingers fumbled with the buttons of his shirt, he lifted me to the top of my desk, his hands sliding up to the tops of my stockings. I shivered as his fingers touched the top of my thighs, parting them gently. He pushed my skirt up until it was around my hips; then his fingers eased up to the waistband of my bikini panties. He hooked one finger under each side and tugged them down, sliding my panties down to my ankles in one swift movement.

"Having fun yet?" he said in that sexy, ironic voice. My hands groped his flat abdomen, pausing briefly as my fingers touched the rough crescent moon on his chest—it matched almost exactly the moon tattoo on my shoulder.

Then he lowered his head between my legs, his tongue lapping at me, gently at first, then more urgently, until he thrust it inside me. I was on the brink of coming when he stood up suddenly and unbuckled his belt.

"Ready?" he asked.

But just before he could thrust into me, there was a knock at the door.

"Sophie?"

It was Adele.

"Ignore it," he whispered.

And as she knocked again, he plunged into me. I had to bite his shoulder to keep from gasping out loud. His mouth was on my breasts, and his thrusts were almost knocking me off the desk. Waves of pleasure rippled through me, pulsing as he pounded into me, his tongue on my right nipple, and then my body exploded into an orgasm that left me limp on the desk.

"Sophie?"

Mark's eyes, dark with desire, focused on me then; he raised one finger to his lips. "Shh," he said. Then he finished with one last deep thrust that echoed the pulsing inside me. "I told her the service was exceptional," he whispered, and I bit my lip to keep from giggling.

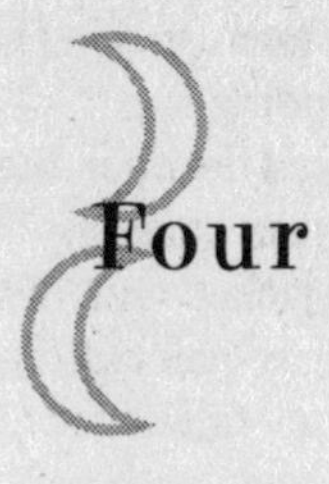

Four

At five forty-five, I was applying a final coat of mascara and checking my legs to make sure I didn't need to do a last-minute touch-up with my Lady Bic. I had no idea what I was dressing for, so I'd settled on a black pencil skirt and a lacy camisole, made decent by a curvy suede jacket I'd picked up at a Nordstrom sale a few weeks ago. I'd added dark red lipstick and smoky eyeliner to the mix—I was going for the sexy look—but my hair was not cooperating. Thank God for hairspray and curling irons, though; with a half hour of heavy effort, I'd managed to curl and spritz it into submission. When I was satisfied, I hurried to the kitchen to nuke a mug of water. If I was going to make it through the evening without a natural fur coat, it was time for another cup—particularly with the moon waxing.

At five to six, there was a knock at the door, and a delicious shiver of anticipation shot through me. *Mark.* What was it about him that was so irresistible? As hot as he was—and despite the fact that he was my biggest client—I really did need to tell him to tone down the whole possessive thing. Perhaps tonight . . .

I gulped down the rest of my wolfsbane tea, paused to touch a bit of Euphoria to my wrists—and between my breasts—and hurried to answer it. The building was supposed to have a doorman, but I'd long ago given up on Frank, who was more interested in HGTV than the parade of people visiting the building.

When I opened the door, the smile died on my lips.

Luc Garou was standing there, dressed in an expensive black leather jacket and designer jeans that looked like they'd been spray-painted on. It was almost embarrassing, really. He was my father, for God's sake! At least in name . . .

"What are you doing here?" I asked, arching an eyebrow.

"You look stunning. May I come in?"

"No," I said. "I'm on my way out. Did you need something?"

"I came to apologize," he said, shifting from foot to foot. "I'm afraid I may have been a bit . . . forceful in my desires yesterday."

I said nothing.

"Of course I'm proud of you, and of course I want big things for you. But it was thoughtless of me to try to push you too fast."

"Thank you," I said stiffly.

"Will you have dinner with me tonight? And promise to stay past the appetizer?" He gave me a wry grin. "I had to finish that entire bottle of Dom Pérignon by myself."

"The waitress didn't join you?"

"Well, maybe for a sip or two," he admitted. "I didn't want to let it go to waste."

I'll bet not. "I appreciate the offer," I said, "but I have plans."

"Ah," he said, glancing down at my rather form-fitting skirt.

He was about to say something else when the elevator door opened, and Mark's smoky smell joined my father's rather more animal bouquet.

"Sophie!" Mark was dressed in the same charcoal slacks and white dress shirt he'd worn earlier.

I could sense my werewolf father's hackles rising. "Who is this?" he asked me, gold eyes burning.

"My client, Mark Sydney," I said. "Now, if you'll excuse me, I have a . . . a meeting to attend."

He arched his right eyebrow. "A meeting?"

"Yes," I said. "A dinner meeting."

"Dressed like that?" Luc's eyes raked me up and down, lingering disapprovingly on my rather low-cut camisole.

"Who is this?" Mark asked, placing a protective arm around my shoulders, which only made Luc Garou's eyebrow rise higher.

"An old friend," I said.

"Luc Garou," he said, thrusting out a hand and staring hard at Mark. "I am Sophie's father."

I cringed as Mark turned to me with a look of surprise. "I thought you weren't in contact with your father."

"I wasn't," I said, "until yesterday. He's in town for the Howl, and dropped by to say hello." I tried to mask the welter of emotions coursing through me. Luc Garou was a jerk—that was beyond all doubt—but he was my father. Genetically, anyway. Was there a chance that we might get along after all? Perhaps—but this wasn't the time to find out. I turned to Luc. "Maybe another time. Now, if you'll excuse us . . ."

Luc Garou was still studying Mark. I could see him sniffing, and my face heated up at the thought of what he must be picking up. I'd had a chance to shower since our afternoon encounter, but I was betting Mark hadn't had the opportunity.

"Where are you taking her?" my werewolf father asked.

"To dinner," Mark said mildly. The tension between the two men was rising, and I was afraid if I didn't get out of there soon, they would come to blows. "Unless there's a problem with that?"

Luc Garou growled slightly and sniffed again. "What are you?" he asked.

"I'm the CEO of Southeast Airlines," Mark said calmly, ignoring the real question. Despite the reasonable voice, I could see tension in his shoulders. "Now, if you will excuse us, we have dinner reservations that we don't want to miss. Pleased to meet you," he said, holding out a hand.

My werewolf gene donor took it, and their eyes bored into each other as they shook. Firmly. In fact, I'm pretty sure I heard the crack of knuckles before they released each other. Luc glowered at Mark, and Mark shot a steely gaze right back at him.

"Take care of my little girl," Luc Garou growled.

As if he had *any* right to be protective of me, after abandoning me all those years ago.

"I can handle myself," I said in a chilly tone of voice. Then I turned on my heel and strode with Mark down the hall, glad to be getting out of there. Thankfully, the elevator came almost instantly; I'm not sure I could have stood a longer wait. Still, I'm pretty sure I heard a low growl as the elevator door slid shut behind us less than a minute later.

"No wonder you were upset last night," Mark said as the elevator descended toward the lobby. "What made your father decide to get in touch with you after all this time?"

I sagged against the mirrored wall. "He's in town for the Howl, I think, and decided to look me up. Wants to pretend the last twenty-eight years didn't happen, I guess." I tried to keep the bitterness from seeping into my voice.

"You resemble him," he said.

I turned to look at myself in the mirror. Mark was right: I was almost a carbon copy of Luc Garou—only female. I closed my eyes, trying to banish the image of my father's strangely familiar face. "I know," I told Mark. "I'm trying to forget."

"It's not necessarily a bad thing," Mark said. "I think your father must be where your sexy wildness comes from."

I turned to him. "You think he's *sexy*?"

"Not to me personally, of course. You know I have eyes only for you," he said, grinning. "But I can see how women might find him intriguing."

If Luc's effect on the women at Ruth's Chris was anything to go by, Mark had a point. "That's how he seduced my mother all those years ago." I shook myself. "But let's not talk about that. Where are we going?"

"If I told you, it wouldn't be a surprise, would it?"

"Am I properly dressed, at least?"

"You look ravishing," he said, leaning down to kiss me. Heat shot all the way through me—as always, Mark's body temperature seemed to be running a few degrees above normal. "Perfect. And even if you weren't 'properly dressed'," he continued, "would you really want to go back upstairs to change?"

"Excellent point."

As the elevator doors slid open, Mark slipped an arm around my waist. "Now, for the rest of the evening, I want you to forget all about Luc Garou and enjoy yourself," he murmured into my ear. His lips brushed my earlobe, and I shivered. "I've got all kinds of things in store for you," he said.

"Like what?" I asked.

"You'll just have to wait and see," he replied. The lobby doors slid open, and a moment later, we swept past Frank the Doorman, who was avidly taking notes on sponge painting, and escaped to the luxury of Mark's limousine.

The limo hadn't even left the curb before Mark had a glass of Conundrum—my favorite white wine—in my hand. "To relax you," he said, walking two fingers up my leg.

"If you're trying to relax me, that's not going to help," I said.

"But I can't resist."

"Good things come to those who wait." I squeezed his hand, halting its northward progress, and glanced at the back of the chauffeur's head. As hot as Mark was, I wasn't sure I was ready to strip down with nothing but a pane of glass to shelter us from Ben's eyes. Besides, as much as I hated to admit it, the little tête-à-tête with my father had dampened my ardor. How long ago had he taken over the Paris pack? How many other werewolf relatives did I have? Did they all look like me? If I visited Europe, would they really welcome me with open arms? *Stop thinking about it, Sophie.*

I turned to Mark and banished thoughts of European furballs from my mind. "So, where are you taking me?"

"I thought we'd try something new tonight."

"I guessed as much," I said. Usually we went downtown—it was close to home—but tonight, Ben was headed west, away from central Austin. "Like what?" I asked.

"If I told you, it wouldn't be a surprise. Just relax," he said, refilling my wineglass—even though I'd only had two sips. I leaned into him, enjoying the heat of him through my suede jacket. His fingers stroked my arm, and as I took another sip of wine, the moon ring he'd given me flashed in the reflected headlights.

"What exactly *is* this ring you gave me?" I asked, holding my hand up to admire it. "It's not silver. And it doesn't come off."

"You don't like it?"

"I think it's beautiful," I said. "I was just wondering what it was, and why it seems to be stuck to my finger." I glanced from the ring to Mark, who was staring at me from those deep blue eyes. "My mother isn't a big fan of it, to be honest. She thinks it's got some kind of magical properties." What I didn't tell him is that she was so anxious to get it off me that she'd tried cutting it with hedge clippers. It hadn't gone well; once the two metals touched, there had been some kind of weird explosion. We hadn't tried a second time.

"Your mother doesn't like me, either."

"Maybe because you're a bit on the possessive side. You know, the whole 'you belong to me' thing?"

He grinned at me. "Who wouldn't want to possess you?"

I sighed. "That's not the point."

"Actually," he said, staring at me with those smoky blue eyes, "I think it's that she considers me a bad influence." He leaned down, pushed my wine aside, and kissed me, his fingers plunging into my lacy camisole.

"She may be right," I gasped a moment later, pointing to the glass partition, through which I could see the back of Ben's head. "Is there any way to get one of those that's black?"

"I'll have one installed next week," he said. "But can you ignore it—at least for now?"

"I don't know," I said. "I'm not much of an exhibitionist."

"Will this help?" he asked, reaching over me; a second later, the interior of the limo went dark.

"Subtle," I said, but I didn't have a chance to say anything else, because Mark's arms were around me, and his hot mouth pressed down on mine.

A half hour later I had reapplied my lipstick, arranged my clothes to make sure everything was covered, and sat down at a table across from Mark. His surprise destination turned out to be Hudson's on the Bend, an Austin institution in an old farmhouse about twenty minutes west of town—and a perfect choice, since it specialized in wild game. After all, there's nothing like fresh feral pig to get a werewolf's salivary glands going.

And Mark seemed to know it. "When I heard they served wild game," Mark said after ordering yet another glass of Conundrum for me—and a scotch on the rocks for himself—"I knew I had to take you here."

I found myself swallowing back drool as I viewed the menu. Wild boar, American bison, venison sausages . . . it was a carnivore's delight.

"Appetizer?" Mark asked.

"Why not?"

"I think we'll skip the salad, though," he said.

"Good plan. Although there is one with a hot pig vinaigrette."

The next hour was a gourmand's fantasy. A meat-eating

gourmand, anyway. I had worked my way through a delicious plate of venison wellington and was debating between desserts—a difficult decision, since raspberry chocolate intemperance, crème brûlée, and a yummy-looking chocolate-dipped caramel pecan pie were all on the menu—when my cell phone jangled. I checked the caller ID and flipped it open.

"Who is it?" Mark asked.

"Lindsey," I mouthed. He rolled his eyes as I answered. "I'm debating desserts at Hudson's on the Bend right now," I told my friend. "This had better be important."

Her voice was oddly strained. "Sophie, I know you don't want to go to the Howl . . ."

"You're right."

"But I think you're going to have to."

"I can't think why I would."

She took a deep breath. "Tom just called me from the Howl. There's a guy there named Luc Garou—he says he's your father."

"I know," I said. "I saw him this evening. Is that the reason?"

"I wish it were, Sophie," she said. "But there's a problem. They've charged him with murder."

Five

I gripped the phone. "What?"

"I just got off the phone with Tom. He said some of the Houston pack members found a werewolf with his throat torn out last night, on Fourth Street," Lindsey said. "They think Luc Garou's responsible." The venison wellington I'd just eaten turned over in my stomach. I knew Luc had been downtown last night; we had almost had dinner together. "It was a guy named Charles," Lindsey continued. "He was pretty high up in the Houston pack, apparently, and someone saw him arguing with your father earlier that evening."

"But he was at my office," I said, wondering why Tom hadn't called me directly. "And then we went to dinner." Of course, dinner hadn't lasted more than ten minutes—and my father was late—but that was beside the point. He had had a scratch on his face, too, come to think of it. Was that because he'd just ripped someone's throat out? I gripped the phone hard. *No*. He couldn't have. My father might be a pretty crappy parent, but I was relatively sure he wasn't a murderer.

Or was he?

"It couldn't have been him," I said.

"You don't have to convince *me*," she said. "It's the judges who need to hear it."

"What judges?"

"Wolfgang, probably Elena, since she's in line to be made alpha. And a few other muckety-muck werewolves from around the country, according to Tom."

"I'm pretty friendly with Wolfgang," I said. "Maybe I can talk to him." Elena, of course, was a different story—last time we'd met she'd been less than cordial—but I'd deal with that as it came. Besides, now that she was about to be alpha, maybe she'd view me as less of a threat.

"I hope so," Lindsey said. "Because according to Tom, the penalty is kind of draconian."

I closed my eyes. "Do I want to know?"

"Sophie . . . I'm so sorry to have to tell you."

That didn't sound good. "Spit it out, Lindsey."

"Okay." She sucked in her breath, then said, "They stake him to death."

I sucked in a breath of my own, feeling like somebody had punched me. Even though I wasn't exactly on wonderful terms with my long-estranged father, I didn't want to see him spitted on a wooden stake before we'd even had a chance to *share* a steak. "Please tell me you're joking," I said, all thoughts of chocolate raspberry intemperance dissolved. I'd just managed to get my mother off the hook for murder six months ago. Now I had to deal with my father, too?

"I wish I were. Apparently the dead werewolf was a bit of a bigwig, which is why they're taking it so personally. It doesn't help that your dad isn't overly popular with the Houston clan."

"So I gather," I said, remembering our little discussion about Strasbourg, and my Aunt Marguerite. "He told me a little about it yesterday."

"I think you should head out there, see what you can do. You know, like you did with your mom."

"I don't know if I'll be able to do anything," I said. "But I doubt anyone else is going to be leaping to his assistance, so I guess you're right."

"Tom seems to think he'll need all the help he can get."

I let out a long sigh and looked at Mark. "How far is Fredericksburg from here?" I asked.

He shrugged. "An hour, maybe?"

"We'll head over now," I said. "Do you know exactly where it is?"

"Tom gave me the street address," she said, and I jotted it down on the back of an old receipt.

"What's wrong?" Mark asked as I flipped the phone closed a moment later and tucked it back into my purse.

"I'm afraid we're going to have to skip the crème brûlée," I said.

"And the port?" he said, looking mournful.

"Yup." I took a deep breath. "My father's been arrested for murder."

He raised his eyebrows. "By the police?"

"Worse. The werewolves."

"So you're running to his aid?"

"What else can I do? If I don't," I said, "there's a good chance he'll end up dead."

"You know, whatever happens, you're safe with me," Mark said as the limo hurtled west toward Fredericksburg. His finger traced the crescent-moon tattoo on my shoulder.

"Even if a pack of pissed-off werewolves decides I'd make a nice midnight snack?"

"I've protected you before," he said. He was right; he had come to my aid once. "You're mine, remember?"

"I appreciate the thought," I said, "but I like to think I belong to myself."

Mark just smiled enigmatically.

"You've never told me exactly where this . . . *power* of yours comes from," I pointed out.

"I kind of enjoy being a man of mystery."

"Even my mother isn't sure what you are," I said.

"She doesn't like me much," he said.

No, she didn't. Which was a bit unsettling, because in

general, my mother was nothing if not open-minded. I mean, she ran a magic shop, for God's sake. "I think she just wants me to be with one of my own kind," I said.

"With someone like Tom?" he asked. I felt an involuntary shiver just thinking about Lindsey's Nordic werewolf boyfriend.

I shrugged.

"I'm right, aren't I?"

What, was *he* psychic, too? "Maybe." I looked up at him. "But I'm still not sure I should be involved with someone who won't tell me what he is."

"You weren't exactly forthcoming, either," he reminded me.

"Forgive me if I don't make a habit of announcing that I'm a werewolf. Besides," I pointed out, "you already knew."

"True."

"So, don't you think you should come clean?"

He reached down and removed the wineglass from my hand, then lowered his mouth to mine. The heat of his kiss pulsed through me, and I could feel my body straining to meet his. Some time later, he released me, and I gasped for breath.

"Do you really want to know?" he asked, staring at me intently.

"Yes."

He paused for a moment, and I braced myself for his revelation. But all he said was, "I'll think about it," which was an *incredibly* unsatisfactory answer. The limo was slowing down, though, so I didn't get a chance to hound him about it further. Not then, anyway.

The glass partition rolled down two seconds later. "Are we there?" I asked.

"This is the address," Ben said. The headlights illuminated two massive limestone pillars flanking a big-ass gate. *GRAF RANCH*, read the wrought-iron sign arching up between the pillars. Ben pulled into the short drive, stopping next to the intercom, and looked back at his boss. "What do you want me to tell them?"

"Tell them Sophie Garou has arrived," Mark said. Ben nodded and rolled down the window, letting a gust of chilly, smoke-tinged air into the limo's plush interior.

"At least I'm arriving in style," I murmured to Mark, trying to still the butterflies that had taken up residence in my stomach.

Ben said a few words into the intercom, and a moment later the heavy gates swung open. As the limo purred through them, limestone chunks pinged off the undercarriage. I winced at the clunks, but Mark seemed unconcerned by the damage. Having ready access to a gazillion dollars will do that for you, I suppose.

The Graf Ranch was huge. The caliche road wove through at least a mile or two of scrubby oaks and cedar trees before we saw any signs of civilization, and I was beginning to wonder if there were any buildings at all when a large cluster of farmhouses appeared on the road before us. A short distance to the right of them, in a clearing, a group of people—correction, *werewolves*—was gathered around a bonfire that leapt toward the sky.

"Must be s'mores night," Mark quipped as I scanned the group around the fire. I didn't see anyone I recognized, which wasn't a big surprise, since I'd only ever met like ten werewolves. *Where were they holding my father? Would they take their anger at him out on me?*

Not with Mark at my side, I realized, reaching over to grab his hand. As if reading my mind, he said, "Don't worry—I'll look after you." Ben parked the limo at the end of a long line of BMWs and Mercedeses; a moment later, he held the door open for me, and I stepped out into the cool night with trepidation, trying to use my nose to get the lay of the land.

The place was crawling with werewolves; the sheer number made it nearly impossible to make out individual scents. "Ready?" Mark asked, putting a proprietary arm around my shoulders.

"I suppose so," I said, and as Ben got back into the limo—lucky Ben—Mark and I walked toward the inferno, since that's where all the werewolves appeared to be.

Hundreds of them were clustered around the leaping fire, and although I was worried about my father—not to mention myself—I couldn't help staring at them. Even though it was a werewolf get-together, everyone in attendance was in human form. For the time being, anyway. As we approached, a few werewolves turned toward us, shooting Mark appraising glances from their golden eyes. Other than Ben, who had stayed with the car, he was the only non-werewolf in attendance—at least according to my nose—so I guess I shouldn't have been surprised. I straightened my back and put on my best confident look as two werewolves, one of whom topped out at just over four feet, detached themselves from the group and approached us. Both wore jeans and brown leather jackets, but that's where the resemblance ended. Except for the gold eyes, of course.

"Miss Garou?" the short, roundish one asked. I recognized his rather taller partner from an unpleasant encounter in my loft; he was one of Elena's henchmen. Last time we met, he and his partner, who wasn't in evidence tonight, had been wearing pleather pants; ever since, I'd thought of them as the pleather boys.

"That's me," I confirmed.

The short werewolf, who reminded me of an Oompa-Loompa, glanced at Mark. "I'm afraid I'm going to have to ask you to leave," he said in a low, rumbly voice. "This is a private gathering."

"I don't think so," I said. "He's with me. Plus, Wolfgang knows him; he's helped him in the past."

The short werewolf hesitated. "It's against the code . . ."

Mark's smoky smell intensified suddenly; I glanced at him; his eyes appeared to be flickering. "I'm staying," he said quietly.

The two werewolves shot glances at each other, but something in Mark's voice—or perhaps it was the almost literal fire in his eyes—convinced them not to press their case. Despite the fact that my father was being held on suspicion of homicide—or wolficide—I had to fight to suppress a smile.

After one more uncomfortable glance at Mark, the Oompa-Loompa werewolf seemed to decide the wisest course was to ignore him. "I'm Franco," he said with a polite smile and extended a hairy hand. I reached down to shake it, then turned to Franco's partner, who had about three feet on him. "And this is Boris," said Franco. Boris didn't bother to extend a hand; he just gave me a curt nod.

"I believe we've met," I said, remembering how he and his werewolf boss Elena Tenorio—who was now about to be one of Houston's alphas, I reminded myself—had broken into my loft and tried to intimidate me a few months ago. "Where's your pal Dudley?" I asked.

He didn't bother to answer.

"Where's my father?" I asked, addressing the Oompa-Loompa. "I mean, Luc Garou."

Franco's round little face tightened a little bit. "He is in the garden cottage."

The garden cottage? Well, that didn't sound so bad. "I want to see him."

"I'm afraid I'll have to clear that first," Franco said, reaching up to tug at his earlobe.

"Then take me to Wolfgang," I said. "I need to talk to him."

"Unfortunately, I can't do that right now; you'll have to wait until after the opening ceremonies." He tugged harder at his earlobe and nodded toward the fire, where the werewolves were now doing something that sounded like a cross between singing and howling like sick dogs.

"I understand Luc Garou has been accused of murder. So I need to talk to Wolfgang. *Now*."

There was a murmur of voices behind Franco and Boris; a second later, Tom emerged from the crowd, the flames glinting off his long blond hair. His shoulders were broad in a black leather jacket, and even in the dim light, his golden eyes shimmered. I felt a tug of longing deep within me. *Stifle it, Sophie.* This was definitely not the time to indulge my repressed werewolf crush. Or to think about that one illicit kiss we had shared . . .

"Sophie," Tom said in a quiet voice. His golden eyes might make me quiver inside, but the tone of his voice made my blood run cold.

"Where's Wolfgang?" I asked, sounding a bit strained even to my own ears.

"He's conducting the opening ceremonies right now," Tom said, glancing at Mark.

"Can you take me to Luc Garou?" I asked.

Tom glanced at the two werewolves who had come to greet me. "Ms. Elena said it wasn't possible," Franco started.

Tom cut him off, focusing on me. "I'll take you to him."

The Oompa-Loompa pulled his earlobe so hard I was afraid it was going to pop off. "But . . ."

"Enough," Tom said shortly, and beckoned me to follow him.

Franco spluttered for a moment, and Boris the pleather boy looked kind of huffy, like he was considering telling Tom where to get off, but he must have had second thoughts. Instead of trying to stop us—or come with us—the two of them scuttled off, to report to Elena, no doubt. I just hoped she was too busy conducting the werewolf choir to be disturbed for a few minutes.

"Why the death sentence?" I asked as I hurried after Tom, whose long strides ate up the narrow trail. Mark was at my side, emanating heat, like always. Tom was headed away from the bonfire, but the howling still grew louder. But not, alas, more in tune.

"The victim was high up in the Houston pack," Tom answered. "And the murder happened during the proscribed time."

"The proscribed time? What the heck is that?"

"It's the period of time surrounding a major werewolf assembly. From three days prior to three days following the Howl, the penalties for attacking another werewolf are far more serious," he said. "Werewolf packs have a natural tendency to engage in rough play," he went on to explain. "Without harsh consequences for infractions, an inter-pack meeting would be a bloodbath."

"That would make one heck of a party," said Mark. "Nothing like a supernatural dogfight to liven things up."

"So any fighting is a capital offense?" I asked, ignoring Mark.

Tom shrugged. "Only if somebody ends up dead."

I didn't have a chance to ask anything else, because Tom had stopped at a small wooden house, the perimeter of which was absolutely devoid of vegetation. I could only guess that the "garden cottage" title heralded from an earlier, more botanically diverse era on the Graf Ranch.

In place of the rose bushes I had been expecting, the door was flanked by two large, unpleasant-looking werewolves who evidently shared both a fondness for the gym and an aversion to dentists. I could tell because they were baring their teeth.

"We're here to see Luc Garou," Tom said quietly.

"No entry allowed," said the larger of the two, giving me a full view of his brownish canines. "Elena's orders."

"Elena is not an alpha," Tom said. "Do you really want to argue with an enforcer?"

Enforcer? I knew Tom worked on contract to help packs deal with problem werewolves, but I had no idea he had a title. "Unlock the door," he continued in that soft but deadly voice. "Now."

Evidently the word *enforcer* had an impact, because the werewolf with the brown teeth acquiesced, and a moment later we were face-to-face with Luc Garou.

My father was dressed in the same embarrassingly tight

jeans I had seen him in earlier that evening, only now, he was chained to a chair in the middle of a room. Mark stuck close behind me; his smoky aroma was comforting.

"Sophie!" Luc said, gold eyes lighting up. His hair was a bit rumpled, as was his jacket, but other than that he looked undaunted. Like he was waiting for somebody to bring out another bottle of Château Lafite. "How sweet of you to come and visit!"

"Did you kill someone?" I asked. I wasn't in the mood for small talk.

"Of course not. A little misunderstanding," he said, shrugging. "I'm sure it will all be cleared up presently." His eyes flicked to Tom, and hardened. "Why are you here with her? And where's your little feathered appendage?"

"I am Sophie's friend," Tom said dryly, "and Hugin is back in Norway for the mating season. Thank you so much for inquiring after him." I realized I'd missed seeing Hugin, the raven who usually accompanied Tom everywhere. Hugin was almost like Tom's familiar; the two had a psychic connection, and were able somehow to communicate.

Luc turned to me. "You associate with this . . . this Nordic *chien bâtard*?" He eyed Tom with contempt.

I wasn't sure what a *chien bâtard* was—it hadn't made it into my French vocabulary lists—but I could tell by Tom's reaction that it wasn't flattering. God, my father was a jerk. If he ever got out of here, I was definitely investing in a fresh copy of Emily Post for him.

I could sense Tom's irritation, and admired his restraint. Mark, on the other hand, appeared keenly interested in the whole scene. "Look," I said to the chained-up werewolf whose face eerily mirrored my own. "Knock off the xenophobia, *Dad*. Without Tom, I wouldn't even be here."

"But . . ."

"But nothing," I said. "Everything was fine until you showed up. You stayed out of my life for twenty-eight years. Now, within twenty-four hours, you've managed to get yourself accused of murder." For a moment—just a moment—I wished Heath and I were still together. He was an incredible trial attorney. On the other hand, part of the reason we broke up was that he didn't know I was a werewolf. It would have been a bit of a challenge asking him to help defend my father before an ad hoc werewolf tribunal.

Luc Garou shrugged. "It is a misunderstanding."

"Well, you'd better start clearing it up fast," I said. "They say you ripped some guy's throat out on Fourth Street."

"It is a lie," he said tossing his red mane like he was some kind of supermodel. "I would never . . . how did you say it? 'Rip his throat out?' So uncivilized."

"Well, civilized or not, unless we can prove that someone else did it, I don't think the powers that be are going to let you off," I said.

"They cannot touch me," Luc said, raising his chin. "I am the alpha of the Paris pack. I am above the rules of some petty New World werewolf pack."

Great. My father was Marie Antoinette reincarnated. Only male, and with a lot of excess fur. Come to think of it, though, Luc Garou was probably already wooing helpless young women when Marie told the peasants to eat cake . . . "I don't think it matters too much what you think of the Houston pack," I said, eyeing his chains.

Luc surveyed the motley group around me: Tom, Mark, and the rather uncomfortable-looking guards. "Leave us," he said in an imperious voice.

Tom gave me a questioning look, and I sighed. "Go ahead. I'll be fine."

"I'm not going anywhere," Mark said quietly.

"Just stand outside the door for a minute or two, okay?" I raised the hand with the ring slightly. "You'll know if I need you."

To my surprise, they all acquiesced, leaving me alone with Luc. When the door clicked shut, I hurried over and examined his shackles, which unfortunately were secured with three separate, very large, padlocks. I took a deep breath, and once again, the familiar animal scent of my father stirred up a host of long-dormant feelings.

Before I could begin to sort them out, Luc leaned forward and spoke in a quick, low voice. "Sophie," he said. "I haven't got long. You need to get in touch with my assistant, Georges. My brother—your uncle, Armand Garou—will come to my aid. I'm in the governor's suite at the Driskill; if you go there, Georges will know what to do."

"So you really did kill that guy on Fourth Street."

"Sophie," he said, golden eyes warm. "I have done many things I am ashamed of, not least of which was abandoning you when you were nothing but a pup. But I did not kill that werewolf."

Well, that was something. "If Georges does get in touch with him, what exactly is Armand going to do?"

"He can be very persuasive," Luc said with a glint in his eyes.

I wasn't sure I wanted to know what that meant. "So you didn't kill the guy on Fourth Street," I said. Just to be sure.

Luc shook his head emphatically. "I swear on my honor that I did not touch that despicable creature."

"Despicable creature?"

He shrugged. "He was a traitor. I would not sully my paws with his like."

"Traitor," I repeated. "Care to elaborate on that?"

"It is a story for another day," he said. "We do not have time now. But you must believe me; I did not murder him."

"I want to," I said. "But I'm having a hard time." I glanced at the almost-healed scratch on his cheekbone. "Besides, if you didn't kill him, where did the scratch on your face come from?"

Before he could answer, the door burst open behind me.

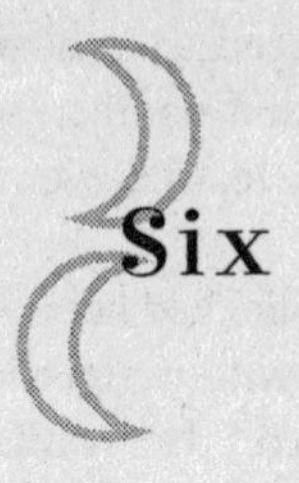

Six

It was Elena, looking spiffy in a pair of designer jeans and a very expensive DKNY blazer. Behind her glowered Boris. "You are not authorized to be here," she said, narrowing her golden eyes at me.

"I am the one who brought her here," Tom said as he stepped in behind her. "Sophie is blameless."

"I'm not so sure about that." A wicked little smile played across Elena's lips. "Dudley," she barked. "Get another chair, and another set of chains. Since Miss Garou wanted a little quality time with her father, I think we should indulge her."

"No," Tom said quietly.

"No?" Elena said, arching a dark eyebrow. She straightened her back and tried to look down her nose at Tom, but since he was more than a foot taller than she was, it didn't work out too well. Despite the obvious vertical challenge, she managed to inject a good bit of ice into her voice. "Mr. Fenris, last time I checked, you were not alpha."

"Miss Garou has committed no infraction," Tom said coolly. "According to the Code, you have no authority to hold her here."

Elena's nostrils flared a little bit, but evidently the code was on Tom's side, because she didn't pursue it. Even though I knew she was dying to. "Put it away," she said to Dudley, who had managed to produce an uncomfortable-looking wooden chair and another set of chains. As he dragged everything back to wherever it came from, Elena turned to me. "Get out."

"Why?" I challenged her.

"Only those with permission from an alpha may speak with the accused." Her smile broadened. "And you don't have my permission."

"You're not alpha," Tom said quietly.

"The ceremony is imminent," she said. "And it is merely a formality."

"But a formality that has not yet been observed," he pointed out. She pushed her lower lip out, but said nothing.

"I'll talk with Wolfgang, then," I said.

"Be my guest," she said, shrugging.

I turned to my father. "I'll be back. In the meantime, don't do anything stupid." Not that he'd be able to do much, since he was chained to a chair. On the other hand, he wasn't gagged, so there was really no telling what he might manage to accomplish. Like further pissing off the people, or should I say werewolves, who were already selecting wooden stakes for his impending execution.

Luc Garou looked at me fondly. "You're everything I hoped you would be. *Comme père, comme fille*, I suppose."

"Whatever," I said. My eyes strayed to the now virtually invisible scratch on his cheek. I fervently hoped my father was wrong, and that he and I were nothing alike.

Particularly if the allegations about him were true.

"So what do I do?" I asked Tom as we traipsed toward the singing werewolves. Whatever they were howling, it wasn't Kumbaya. It was in a language I didn't understand, and the whole effect was kind of mournful and chilling. Funereal, really, which wasn't the mood I was looking for just then, particularly with a death sentence hanging over my father's head. Mark was a reassuring presence next to me, even though I could almost taste the tension between him and Tom. The smell of testosterone was enough to fell an ox.

"Well, this is certainly turning out to be an interesting evening," Mark said.

"I think it would be wise to talk to Wolfgang," Tom said.

"Luc called Charles a traitor," I said in a low voice. "Do you know what he was talking about?"

"Charles used to belong to a Garou pack," he said. "That is no longer the case."

"He switched sides?"

Tom nodded.

I let out a low whistle. "No wonder Luc didn't like him."

"Now," Tom asked, "do you want to speak to Wolfgang?"

"Do you think it will help?"

"I don't know," he said. "You probably aren't aware of it, but your father has a rather stormy history with the Grafs."

"No, I wasn't aware of it, but I can't say I'm surprised. He's not exactly the Dale Carnegie of werewolves."

He sighed. "No, he's not. In fact, your father's rather turbulent history is probably why Wolfgang didn't automatically extend pack membership to you when you helped break up the Mexican alliance." Tom was referring to a situation that had occurred about a month ago, when I'd somehow managed to . . . well, let's call it *neutralize* . . . the leader of the *Norteños*, a Mexican pack that was trying to "reclaim" Texas. In exchange for my services—including enabling the rescue of one of their important pack members—Wolfgang had given me permission to live in Austin without any disturbance from the Houston pack. Which was all I really wanted, in truth. He hadn't been overly effusive in his thanks, and certainly hadn't gone as far as to invite me into the fold with open arms. I wouldn't have taken him up on it anyway, though, so it hadn't bothered me.

"What's this *history* you keep referring to?" I asked.

"You've heard of the province of Alsace?" Tom said. Mark was still beside me, listening intently.

"It's in France, right? My father was talking about it the other night."

"It is now," he said. "But it used to belong to Germany. And, at least as far as the werewolves are concerned, to Wolfgang."

"One of the Garous has it now, right?" I asked as we paused about ten yards away from the ring of singing werewolves.

"One of your aunts," Tom said. "Marguerite Garou. She recaptured the province from the Grafs, with your father's help, well over a century ago. Which is why Wolfgang is now the leader of the Houston pack instead of the Strasbourg pack."

Well, that certainly explained why Wolfgang hadn't rolled out the red carpet for me. Still, I was having a hard time believing that my father had been involved in a battle for a French territory that had evidently occurred sometime in the 1800s. What Tom said made sense, though—and unfortunately didn't look good for Luc Garou's immediate future. Time might heal all wounds, but even after a century or two, I imagined Wolfgang must still be pretty sore about losing a whole province and having to pack up and move to Texas.

"So Luc's family ousted Wolfgang's family?"

"Yes. The Garous bested the Grafs, and your father was instrumental in making that happen. I believe Wolfgang still holds a bit of a grudge."

"More than a bit, I imagine." I could feel my stomach sink. "So I'm guessing begging isn't going to help. No wonder Luc asked me to get in touch with his brother."

Tom's head whipped around. "Did he? Which one?"

"Armand."

"I'm not sure that's a good idea," Tom said quietly. "If a French contingent shows up, it could result in a bloodbath."

Great. "So you think I should try to talk Wolfgang into letting Luc go, instead?"

"You could try it, but I don't imagine you'll have much success. And even if you did, Wolfgang is only half of the equation," Tom reminded me. "His counterpart was ready to slap you in chains a moment ago, if I recall."

"But she's not alpha."

"Not officially, but she will be soon."

I sighed. "Elena's never been overly fond of me," I said.

"She views you as a threat," Tom said.

"I have no idea why. It's not like I'm after Wolfgang or anything." Both males bristled slightly.

"Well, that's a relief," Mark said. He'd been listening to our conversation intently.

"So there's not much I can do to help my father, then," I concluded. Other than getting in touch with his Parisian relatives, that was. Provided I was okay with potentially starting the War of the Werewolves, right here in central Texas.

"I'll do what I can to intercede," Tom said, "and it can't hurt to petition Wolfgang in person."

I groaned. "Why didn't Luc Garou just stay in Paris?"

"At least you got to meet him," Mark said.

"Great. Of course, odds are he'll be dead in a week."

I glanced back toward the garden cottage, where my father was chained to a chair—and probably finding new and creative ways of mortally offending his captors. "Thank God I'm nothing like him," I said. "He's kind of a pain in the ass, isn't he?"

Tom made a sound that resembled choking as Mark pointed to the circle of werewolves. "Looks like the shindig's breaking up." He was right; the awful howling had stopped, and the werewolves were starting to mill around.

"I'll go see if I can set up an audience," Tom asked, nodding his head toward Wolfgang, who was standing on a platform on the far side of the bonfire. He was dressed in pressed blue jeans, a chambray shirt, and a leather jacket with fringy things on it, and was deep in what appeared to be a somewhat strident conversation with a tall, black-haired werewolf I didn't recognize.

"That's Jean-Louis, one of the New Orleans alphas," Tom said, following my gaze. "They are considering an alliance, but there seems to be some friction."

Fascinating though they might be, Louisiana–Texas pack relations were not at the top of my priority list at the moment. "How can I find a way to meet with Wolfgang?"

"He'll probably return to his quarters shortly. I'll see if we can meet with him there. We'll have to hurry, though," Tom said. "The first hunt starts in a half hour."

"What's the hunt?"

His canines glinted as he gave me a toothy smile. "Exactly what it sounds like. Stay here; I'll be right back."

As Tom wove through the werewolves toward Wolfgang, Mark put an arm around me. "It's never a dull moment with you, is it?" he asked.

"Unfortunately not," I said, grimacing. "I could use a little boredom right about now."

"You had no idea about your family history?" he asked.

I shook my head. "My mother didn't know any of it, and we left Paris when I was just a baby, so it's all news to me." I sighed and leaned into Mark. "Maybe I should just let my father deal with this himself."

"He did ask you to talk with his assistant. Georges, was it?"

"Right. And start another werewolf war?"

"He *is* your father," Mark reminded me.

"I know," I said gloomily. "I know." We lapsed into silence, watching the werewolves. A few were heading toward farmhouses—doubtless to lose their clothes before donning their natural fur coats and chasing armadillos—and I could hear snatches of several languages. Most of the group appeared to be European in origin; I saw only a few with the shining black hair and caramel-colored skin of Mexican werewolves.

When a few of the males gave us speculative looks, Mark put a proprietary arm around me, which kind of precluded them from trotting out werewolf pickup lines.

Tom came back a few minutes later, shouldering through the crowd. "Wolfgang will meet with you in ten minutes, at the main house. But you'll have to be brief. He and Elena have only a few minutes before the hunt starts."

"No way to get rid of Elena?" I asked.

He gave me a crooked smile that showed a few of his gleaming canines. "Unfortunately not."

"Oh, well. Thanks for setting it up," I said.

"Follow me," he said, leading us toward the largest of the farmhouses.

"You know, I never asked: Is there a point to the Howl?" I asked as we followed Tom. "Or is it just some kind of were-wolf glee club?" None of whose participants would *ever* make it past the first round of *American Idol*, I thought, remembering the awful bonfire chorus.

"It's hosted by different packs at different times," Tom said. "It's one of the most important social events; it's where alliances and matings are approved and ratified."

"You're joking. Matings have to be *approved*?" I asked.

He nodded. I was tempted to find out if Tom would have to ask permission to, well, *you know*, with Lindsey, but decided it would be tacky to ask. Since he didn't belong to a particular pack, the rules probably wouldn't apply to him the same way anyway. "It's also a way to meet suitable mates," he said. "Usually it's hard to meet werewolves from other packs, since territory rules are so stringent."

"So it's kind of like a werewolf singles night," Mark said.

"Usually, yes," Tom said. "But at this particular Howl, there will also be meetings of several of the border packs, to discuss recent events with the *Norteños*. At least six of the southern alphas are in attendance."

"The *Norteño* thing is probably why Wolfgang asked me

to come," I said, glancing at my watch. "Eight minutes to go. What should I say to him?"

"Ask him if he can order an inquiry. I doubt Luc Garou is the only one who had cause to kill Charles."

"Really?"

"Charles was very connected, politically, and was excellent at . . . how do you put it? Excavating information?"

"You mean digging up dirt on people?"

"Exactly," he said. "Which is why I think someone may have used your father's presence as an excuse to get rid of him."

"Like who?"

"That's what we need to find out," he said.

Wolfgang might have faults, but his choice of interior decorators wasn't one of them, I thought as we were escorted into the living room of the main farmhouse a few minutes later. The Houston pack enclave might look like a Mexican villa, but this house looked like it had been lifted from the pages of Country Living.

Wolfgang and Elena were enthroned in big leather chairs flanking a limestone fireplace; when we entered, Wolfgang rose to his feet, but Elena just crossed her designer-jean-clad legs and swung a boot in irritation.

"Thanks for taking a few minutes to see me." I addressed Wolfgang, ignoring Elena. "I know you're very busy right now."

"I'm glad you decided to attend the Howl," Wolfgang said formally, then turned to Mark. "And it is a pleasure to see you again, Mr. . . ."

"Sydney," Mark supplied.

Wolfgang nodded. "Sydney," he repeated. Elena narrowed her eyes at Mark, but Wolfgang seemed unperturbed by his presence and turned back to me. "Sophie, I am delighted to see you participating in the Howl. It is a wonderful time to make connections with others of our kind. And I do hope you will consider taking part in the border talks tomorrow. Your firsthand experience would be of real benefit."

His golden eyes bored into me, and I felt my body stir in response. I chalked it up to my animal nature; after all, Wolfgang, like Tom, was tall, blond, and exceedingly fit, with a smell that—also like Tom—exuded werewolf sexiness. Being in a room with two very masculine werewolves, smoky-scented Mark, and a pissed-off Elena at the same time, not to mention the mixed bouquet of a couple hundred other werewolves in the background, was distracting, to say the least. But I forced myself to ignore my nose and focus on the business at hand: saving my father's skin. Or trying to, anyway.

"I'd love to attend the talks," I lied, "but I'm here because there's another problem."

"She's talking about her father," Elena interjected in a flat voice.

"You're here on Luc Garou's behalf?" Wolfgang asked politely, as if he were surprised to hear it. "I understood you were estranged from your sire."

"I am. I mean, I was."

His blond eyebrows rose. "Has something changed?"

"I just met him the other night for the first time," I said. "And now I hear he's been charged with a capital crime."

Wolfgang shrugged, his muscular shoulders rippling under the chambray shirt. "I appreciate your concern, but I'm afraid I will have to allow justice to take its course."

"But how can you be sure it's justice?" I protested. "I mean, have there been any inquiries?"

"It is a busy time for us," Wolfgang said, shrugging again.

"So the answer is no," I replied shortly.

He opened his hands wide. "Your father was seen arguing with Charles less than an hour before the body was found. Now, unless you can account for that time . . ."

"I can," I said quickly.

"Can you?"

"We had dinner together."

"At what time?"

"Six fifteen," I blurted. "At Ruth's Chris." Of course, my father hadn't shown up until six fifty, but how would Wolfgang know that?

"How odd," Wolfgang said, a furrow appearing between his bushy blond eyebrows.

"What?"

Elena answered for him. "That your father should be in two places at once."

"What do you mean?" I asked, with a sinking feeling in my stomach.

"Six fifteen was when he was spotted arguing with Charles Grenier. Several blocks away from Ruth's Chris," Wolfgang clarified.

"Surely there's a mistake," I said.

"Like maybe you need to learn to read a clock?" Elena said snarkily. I resisted the urge to shove one—or both—of her expensive cowboy boots down her throat.

"Sophie," Wolfgang said gently, although something in his eyes was disturbingly cold. Old grudges died hard, I supposed. "I understand your desire to protect your sire. But all the evidence points to his involvement."

"You should consider yourself lucky that the old rules don't apply," Elena said, still jiggling a boot-clad foot.

"What do you mean?" I asked.

"According to previous versions of the code," Wolfgang explained, "a murderer's descendants were also held accountable for actions taken during an official Howl."

"So you're saying . . ."

"You're fortunate that you won't be joining your dad on the stake," Elena said with a wicked smile.

I swallowed hard. "I still think there needs to be an inquiry. I understand Charles Grenier wasn't the most popular werewolf in Houston. Maybe somebody got rid of him, and framed Luc Garou."

Wolfgang glanced at his Rolex. "I know this issue is near to your heart, but I'm afraid I have another engagement. You will consider attending the border talks tomorrow?"

"I'm sorry," I said stiffly, "but I'm afraid I have another appointment." I stared at Wolfgang, giving him my most imploring look. "Are you sure you won't reconsider the inquiry?"

"I'll see what I can do," he said in a less-than-encouraging tone of voice, "but I can't make any promises."

Elena smiled slightly, and my stomach sank. I'd done what I could, but it wasn't enough to keep my father alive. It was obvious that no inquiry would be forthcoming. "Thank you for your time," I said to Wolfgang. "I'm sure we'll be talking again—very soon."

"Good," said Wolfgang impassively. "Now, if you will excuse me, I must prepare for the hunt. You wouldn't care to join us?" He lifted an inquiring eyebrow.

"No, I'm afraid I'm not up to fun and games tonight."

"Good night, then," Wolfgang said. "I'm sure our paths will cross again soon."

I gave him a strained smile. "I'm sure they will."

Seven

"God, what a night," I groaned as the limousine rolled back toward Austin. So much for our perfect date. The evening had certainly been a surprise, but it wasn't quite the stuff dreams were made of. Okay, well, nightmares, maybe. Despite the rather dire circumstances, I still regretted missing dessert at Hudson's; I could have killed for a double helping of chocolate raspberry intemperance right about now. And a bottle or two of muscat to wash it down.

Instead, I took deep breaths of clean, werewolf-free air. Mark and I had parted ways with Tom right after my audience with Wolfgang and Elena, and I was still trying to come to terms with everything that had happened since our cozy pig-and-deer dinner was so rudely interrupted.

"It's not totally hopeless. I might be able to set your father free for you," Mark offered, rubbing my shoulders.

I glanced back at him. "What are you going to do, grow another napalm bodysuit and burn the garden cottage down?"

He laughed. "That would be one way. But I was thinking of a slightly less invasive approach. After all, I'm a man of many talents."

"Other than seducing innocent werewolves?"

His hot lips brushed my ear, and I shivered. "I'm glad you consider that a talent," he murmured. "But that wasn't what I had in mind in this case, no matter how good-looking your father might be. The problem is, if I did set him loose, you'd probably have the entire Houston pack nipping at your heels again. And I'm not sure that's what you want."

"God, no." I shuddered. "What I'd really like to do is find a way to prove Luc Garou is innocent."

"You think he's innocent?"

"I'm going to operate under that assumption." Luc *had* been thirty-five minutes late to dinner, and I still hadn't gotten a good explanation for the scratch on his cheekbone. But I decided to stick with the innocent-until-proven-guilty thing for as long as possible. "I wish I could talk to Heath."

Mark halted the massage for a moment. "Why Heath?"

"He's a trial attorney. Defending people is what he does for a living." I closed my eyes as Mark started rubbing again. "Unfortunately, it would be a little tough explaining the circumstances."

"What, that your werewolf father is scheduled for execution by a werewolf tribunal?"

"Exactly."

"You could always get in touch with James, or whatever his name is, and have him contact your uncle."

"Georges," I said. "I could do that, I guess. If I wanted to start the War of the Werewolves."

"At least you wouldn't be involved," he said.

"Maybe. But I'm still a Garou, and I live in central Texas, so maybe not."

"You could always let me whisk you away to Tahiti," Mark said, his lips brushing my ear. Despite the bleak circumstances, I felt a quiver run through me at his touch. "They'd never find you there," he whispered. "And the mai tais are terrific."

"Sounds lovely," I said, "but it probably belongs to another pack already. Besides, I'm guessing the career path for auditors is kind of limited in Tahiti."

"I could always move the Southeast Airlines account to

your new firm," Mark offered. "You could be president. Garou and Partners. Has a nice ring to it, don't you think?"

"Thanks," I said, "but I think I'd prefer to stay in Austin." I sat up straight in the plush leather seat. "There's got to be a way to get Luc off. We need to find out more about Charles—and who wanted him dead."

"Sounds like a great plan. But the trial is in a couple of days," Mark reminded me. "And you're not particularly connected with the Houston pack."

"Thanks for the pep talk," I said. "Got any more wine in that fridge?"

They always say things look brighter in the morning, but the sun did very little to lighten my feeling of impending doom. And Lindsey's arrival in my office sporting what looked like a bite mark on the right side of her neck didn't help much, either. Had Tom spent the night at her place?

"What, did somebody mistake you for a feral pig last night?" I asked.

"Not exactly," she said, pulling up her collar.

I held up a hand. "Say no more."

"I wasn't planning on it," she said, plopping down in my visitor's chair and crossing her long legs. I tried not to look at her neck as she continued. "How was the Howl?"

"I didn't see much of it." I gave her the rundown of what had happened.

She let out a low whistle when I finished. "So what are you going to do about your dad?"

"He's not my dad."

"Okay, fine. Your gene donor. Whatever you want to call him."

"Gene donor sounds great," I said. "Anyway, I've decided that what I need to do is prove that he wasn't the one who did it."

Lindsey nodded. "Sounds reasonable."

I sagged back into my chair. "The only problem is, I have no idea how to go about doing that."

"Maybe you should talk to Heath," Lindsey suggested.

I'd had exactly the same thought last night, but there was still a big problem with that approach. "And tell him what?"

Lindsey shrugged. "I don't know. The truth, maybe?"

"No way," I said, crossing my arms. "He'd never believe me."

"*I* believe you," she reminded me.

"I know. But the thing is, in order for you to believe me, I had to sprout a fur coat and a tail," I said. "And there is no *way* I'm doing that in front of Heath."

"Why not?"

Did I need to spell it out for her? "Because it's gross, that's why."

"I don't think it's gross," she said. "In fact, I think it's kind of cool."

"I haven't slept with you," I pointed out. Then I remembered she was dating a werewolf, so obviously it wasn't a big issue for her. In fact, she for some reason was coveting the ability to sprout fur herself. No accounting for taste, I suppose . . .

"I still think you should talk to Heath," she said.

"What about Hubert?" I asked, sounding only a little bit desperate. Hubert was a rather scholarly member of the Houston pack. I was confident he'd be a font of information. Besides, he owed me a favor, since I'd helped rescue him from an operation involving the rather forceful removal of his still-beating heart not too long ago. "After all, he said he was in my debt. Maybe he could help me out, do a little sleuthing."

"He's a bright guy," Lindsey said, "but I don't think he's too big into gossip. He's a bit on the bookish side."

She had a point. If I wanted to know more about the ancient mating practices of Sumerian werewolves, Hubert was probably my go-to guy. Unfortunately, however, I doubted he was a font of juicy tidbits regarding the dating practices of his more contemporary counterparts.

"Do you think Tom could ask around for me?" I asked.

"Maybe, but the pack knows you two are friends, so I'm not sure how much he'd be able to find out. Why can't you go by yourself?"

"Because I'm Luc Garou's daughter. Who's going to want to talk to me? I mean, Luc isn't the most popular guy in town. I'm surprised they haven't strung him up already."

"I thought you generally had to use a stake or a silver bullet to kill a werewolf," Lindsey said.

I shuddered. "Thanks for reminding me. The thing is, if it weren't for him, Wolfgang would still be back in the motherland."

"I think Germany's called the fatherland," Lindsey pointed out. "But anyway, you're right; a lot of them probably wouldn't be overly chatty with the daughter of the guy who helped overthrow them, even if it was like two hundred years ago."

"Stupid grudges." I sighed. "So it's a dead end."

"Not necessarily," she said. "Not everyone in the pack goes back to the old country, I'll bet. Besides, what if they didn't know you were his daughter?"

"My last name's Garou," I reminded her. "It's not exactly a common name."

"That's why I think you should go incognito."

I touched my hair. "Since I look like Luc Garou's clone, that's going to be tough."

She shrugged. "Change your hair, wear different clothes. Change your name."

I thought about her idea for a moment. It was interesting, but I wasn't sure it would work. "What about my scent?" I asked. "I can't hide that."

"Yes, you can. Remember? No one can smell you if you don't want them to. That's why the Houston pack asked for your help when Hubert was missing."

"Oh, yeah." That was how I'd gotten to know Hubert, who was Wolfgang's cousin. The pack had sent me to track him down earlier this spring, and we had spent a good bit of time bonding—in shackles. We were still friends.

"I'll bet Hubert could say you were a friend of his, in town from . . . I don't know. Topeka? Anchorage? Zimbabwe? Something far away."

"What about Wolfgang? And Elena?"

"You'll just have to stay away from them, I guess."

"It's a crazy idea," I said. "It would never work."

"You could always get in touch with your uncle, then." She cocked an eyebrow. "Or Heath."

In other words, I was screwed. "All right. I'll give it a shot."

"Good," she said, glancing at her watch. "I've got a meeting in ten minutes, so I've got to go. Call me and tell me what happens, okay?"

"Will do," I said.

"I'll close the door behind me," she said.

"Thanks." The last thing I needed was to have Sally overhear my conversation with Hubert.

When the door clicked shut, leaving only a trace of Lindsey's signature perfume—Beautiful—I picked up the phone and dialed Hubert's cell phone number. He picked up on the third ring, and listened politely while I outlined our plan.

"I wish I could help you," he said, "but I'm afraid I won't be at the Howl tomorrow evening."

"What do you mean, you won't be at the Howl?"

"I'll be there for the morning talks, but afterward . . . I'm not much of a social animal, I suppose."

"Couldn't you make an exception?" I gripped the phone. "Hubert, I *need* you."

"Why don't you ask Tom?" he suggested. "I think it's an excellent idea; it's just that I'm not the person to help you. Even if I were to attend, it would raise eyebrows to have a female accompany me. I'm engaged to a young werewolf from Bratislava."

"Bratislava?"

"We met while I was researching ancient pack-mating rituals in Slovakia."

"Ah."

"I would recommend you contact Tom; he is unaffiliated, and is known to have a wide circle of female acquaintances."

"Is that so?" I asked.

"Oh, yes. He has quite a reputation among the females of the species."

"I had no idea," I said, wondering if Lindsey knew about Tom's reputation. Probably not.

Hubert kept talking, interrupting my private speculation regarding Tom's evidently quite colorful romantic history. "If he said you were a friend from one of the northern territories, it could work. Maybe the Minneapolis pack, or one of the smaller organizations."

"Sounds like a plan," I said. Not a very good one, of course, since I knew absolutely squat about Minneapolis. But since I couldn't come up with anything better, I kept my mouth shut and tried not to think of what the pack might do to me if they discovered I was a wolf in sheep's clothing. Or someone else's clothing, anyway.

I pushed morbid thoughts of rabid, stake-wielding packs from my mind and adopted a bright tone of voice. "What's the schedule this evening?"

"A deer run," he said.

"What's that?"

"It's kind of like a hunt, where everyone competes to take down the largest animal. The wild hunt will be in a couple of days. This is kind of a warm-up."

"Everyone hunts in wolf form, I presume?"

"How else would one hunt?"

I don't know. With a gun? At least I wouldn't have to worry too much about my wardrobe. "What time?"

"It starts at seven."

"I'll call Tom now," I said. "Thanks for the tip."

I hung up a moment later and flipped through my card file, my fingers lingering on Tom's cream-colored business card, which bore his name and a phone number. After a minute of deliberation, I took a deep breath and dialed.

"Hello." His voice was deep and throaty, and even that one word was tinged with one of those tantalizing European accents that make American women weak at the knees. Or maybe it was just me.

"Tom," I said.

"Sophie." Hearing him say my name sent a tingle through me. Which I ignored, of course.

"I need a favor," I said.

It took a bit of convincing, but when I pointed out that it would look a little weird for *him* to be asking questions about the pack, he relented. "It's risky, but I admit the options are limited. You have a knack for disguising your scent," he said, "but even so, we'll have to avoid Wolfgang and Elena. And you should change your human appearance as much as possible."

"What about my wolf aspect?"

"That would be a challenge. But fortunately, I am the only werewolf who has seen you in your lupine form," he pointed out.

"I hadn't thought of that."

"I'll meet you at your place at five," Tom said. "That should get us there by seven."

"Looking forward to it," I said. And it was actually true, which made no sense, since it wasn't exactly a dream date or anything.

He chuckled, sending another little tingle through my nether regions, and said, "That makes two of us."

Even if I did end up sporting a few silver bullets, I thought, at least I'd have spent the evening in good company. Of course, Lindsey would probably decapitate me when she found out, but I figured I'd cross that bridge when I got to it.

I had just hung up the phone and was still wearing a goofy

smile when it rang again. I grabbed the receiver. "Sophie Garou."

"How's my favorite party animal?" The voice was low, and undeniably sexy. Mark.

"I've had better days," I confessed, feeling guilty for looking forward to an evening with Tom.

"Any progress on dear old dad?"

"Not so far, but I'm working on it." For some reason I wasn't inclined to tell Mark I was going to be posing as Tom's date tonight.

"I'd ask if you're free this evening, but I imagine you have other plans."

"I do."

"Ah, well. We'll just have to save the intemperance for another night."

"Good things come to those who wait," I said, remembering his smoky smell. And the heat of his skin . . .

"Anything I can do to help?" he asked, jolting me from what was rapidly morphing into an X-rated fantasy. "I can spring your dad if you need me to."

"Thanks for the offer," I said. "I'll keep it in mind."

"What happened to your hair?" Tom asked when I answered the door at five thirty. Hubert was with him, but he seemed to fade into the wallpaper next to Tom, whose werewolf scent was particularly musky tonight. Either that or I was just feeling sex-deprived.

I forced myself to stop staring at Tom and turned to Hubert. "Are you going, too?"

He shook his head. "I'm just here to help prepare you. Tom asked me to come." He stared at my hair.

"What do you think?" I asked, reaching up to touch my head.

"It's certainly distinctive," Hubert said, diplomatic as always.

"It's a disguise," I explained. "Do you think it will work?"

When I told Lindsey I'd need help going incognito, she'd told Adele we both had a client meeting and escorted me directly to the hair-color aisle of CVS. We repaired to my loft shortly thereafter, armed with a bottle of something that looked like shoe polish but promised hair the color of "Midnight Satin."

"You have to tell me everything," Lindsey had said after ruining three towels with streaky dye and turning my hair a dull black that was not ideal for my skin tone. In fact, it made me look like I was suffering from an advanced case of jaundice. "And don't worry about your hair," she added. "It says it will wash out in ten shampoos."

"I'm more worried about what happens to it when I transform," I said, staring at my ghastly reflection in the bathroom mirror. If it was this bad when I was human, I could only imagine how I would look with a reddish-gold fur coat and a black mop on my head.

"I hadn't thought about that," Lindsey said. "We could always dye the rest of your hair, I guess."

"No," I said quickly, snatching the bottle of dye from her hand.

"Are you sure I can't come with you?" she asked.

"I'm going to a multi-pack werewolf hunt, Lindsey. And you're a human. Does that sound like a good idea?"

She bit her lip. "I hadn't thought of it in those terms. Well, perhaps an evening in wouldn't hurt."

And thankfully, that was the last I'd heard of it.

Now I was wondering if I wasn't insane for trying to make it through the Howl undetected. The hair-color change had sounded good at the time, but since I'd noticed black streaks on not just my towels, but the backs of my new couches, I was starting to question the choice of temporary dye. Maybe a wig would have been better.

As Tom and Hubert stood eyeing my unfortunate appearance, I touched my hair self-consciously and said, "It was Lindsey's idea."

"And that . . . aroma?" Hubert asked.

"Calvin Klein's Euphoria," I said. I'd sprayed about a gallon of the stuff on, just in case my weird scent-shielding power was on the fritz, and after sitting in the loft with myself for almost twenty minutes, I was convinced my nose was permanently damaged.

"It certainly is . . . intense," Hubert said, wrinkling his nose and taking a step back. Hubert's thin face resembled his cousin Wolfgang's—pale, Nordic skin, sharp eyes, and strong cheekbones. Only without all the alpha male stuff going on. Hubert looked a little monkish, really—kind of like a werewolf ascetic. He gave me a polite, if slightly worried, smile. "It's certainly . . . a change."

Tom, although obviously trying to avoid sniffing through his nose, looked like he was trying not to laugh. I ignored him and focused on Hubert.

"Enough of one to disguise me, do you think?"

"You've certainly disguised your natural features," Hubert said as he and Tom stepped into my loft. In addition to my new inky black 'do, Lindsey had applied black liquid eyeliner, raccoon style. Not to mention so much mascara that my eyelashes kept sticking together.

"Can I get you guys something to drink?"

"Perhaps a quick aquavit?" Tom asked hopefully.

"Sorry. I do have Macallan, though." A relic from my time with Heath.

"Thanks, but no," he said. I had to agree with him; scotch smelled like turpentine to me. Although I had doused myself with so much perfume, tonight it might be just fine.

When Hubert, too, declined a drink, I cut to the chase. "What's my story?"

"Hubert's got it all worked out," Tom said.

"I did some research on common werewolf names, and where they originate. Your name is Inga Lindholm," Hubert said, his eyes darting to the window, which I suspected he was wishing was open. "You come from a small pack outside of Minneapolis," he continued. "You and Tom met on a business trip, and he invited you to join him at the Howl."

"So are we . . . together?" I asked.

Hubert shifted uncomfortably. "That would not be permissible, not without pack approval. Let's just say that your presence at the Howl would be . . . a sign of mutual interest."

"So we're kind of dating," I clarified.

"Essentially, yes," he said.

I turned to Tom. "I hear you've been with quite a number of werewolves."

"I *have* been on the dating scene for several hundred years," he pointed out, golden eyes glimmering with something that looked suspiciously like suppressed amusement.

"Does Lindsey know about that?"

"Does Lindsey know you and I are going to the Howl together?" he countered.

"Not exactly," I conceded.

I forced myself not to think about the extremely erotic kiss Tom and I had shared less than a month ago, right outside my loft. Would we be going to the Howl on his motorcycle? I wondered. I forced myself not to think of what it would feel like to be pressed up against Tom for an hour and a half, and turned to Hubert instead. "Will I meet any long-lost relatives at this thing?"

"I certainly hope not," he said. "That is why I selected a small pack as your family. Your parents are originally from Sweden, but you've been here for many years, and don't remember all the details of your heritage."

"I'm Swedish?" I asked.

"For tonight, you are."

I wished I'd known that when Lindsey and I were cruising the hair-color aisle at CVS that afternoon. "Are you sure I can't be Italian, or something? I mean . . ." I gestured toward my hair.

Hubert bit his thin lip. "That is a point I hadn't considered. Perhaps your mother had some Spanish blood."

"That would probably be a good idea," I said. I turned back to Tom, who was studying my new look with marked interest. "What?" I asked.

"It's an interesting look," he said. "I'm still adjusting to it." His eyes traveled down to the brief but rather snug miniskirt I'd donned for the occasion. "I'm particularly fond of the hemline."

"Thank you," I said primly, adjusting my short skirt and trying not to blush. All business, that was me. "What's our story?"

"You and Tom met while he was doing a little work up north. You decided to come south to get away from the cold."

"How come Tom gets to move all around the country, and other werewolves don't, except when there's a Howl?" I asked.

Hubert and Tom exchanged glances. "I provide an unusual service," Tom said.

I looked at him. "The werewolf unmaking thing?" Tom's claim to fame—or at least one of them—was his unusual ability to turn werewolves into humans.

He nodded.

"No one else can do it?"

"Not in this generation, no. And to make problems disappear . . . it is a useful talent."

"And tends to inspire a healthy dose of respect," Hubert added. "Besides, he's of a very old lineage."

"From Norway. The old country and all. Right." I adjusted my skirt. "So, is this a casual relationship, then?" I felt my cheeks heating up as I asked the question.

"I think that would be a prudent assumption," Hubert said.

Huh. "Okay. Any werewolf protocol I should know before going in?"

"Ideally," Hubert said, "we'd be able to give you a briefing on who is who, but we are short on time, and we have no photographs. Tom, will you fill her in on the important players as you go?"

"Of course," he said.

"Any general rules I should know?" I asked.

Hubert looked pained. "Werewolf society is very hierarchical. Don't volunteer much information, and be respectful. Defer to anyone you don't know, just in case."

"In other words, defer to everyone."

Tom gave me a wry grin. "If you can manage it."

"Will we all be in human form the whole time, or wolf?"

"Human for the first part of the evening, but we will assume wolf form for the hunt."

"Tell me more about this 'hunt'," I said.

"There is not much to tell," Tom said. "The pack gathers and then hunts together. As always, deference is given to superiors; the hosting alphas make the first kill. After that, it is fair game."

It sounded like the best thing to do would be to hang back and let everyone else do the hunting. Not much chance of pumping werewolves for information when they were out trying to sink their teeth into feral pigs, or deer, or whatever it was they hunted. "Got it."

"Now, when we get there, can you point out anyone I should talk to?" I asked, suddenly feeling very nervous about this whole endeavor.

"Of course," he said.

"The Houston werewolves will probably be the most informative," Hubert pointed out.

"Anyone in particular we should look for?"

"Charles Grenier was friendly with several of the males of the pack—but he was also courting a woman named Kayla," Hubert said. "She might be the best source of information. Tom, do you know what she looks like?"

"I can identify her," Tom said.

"What do you know about her?" I asked.

Hubert shrugged. "Very little. She occupies a different level of the pack hierarchy; our lives did not intersect very often."

"You don't know her either, do you?" I asked Tom.

He shook his head. "Like Hubert, our lives have not intersected much."

There's that old werewolf elitism again, I thought. "Surely you knew Charles, at least. He was pretty high on the totem pole, wasn't he?" I asked.

"Totem pole?" Hubert asked, a furrow in his brow.

"It's a saying. A totem pole is a tall thing, kind of like a carved tree, that the Indians used to make, with pictures on it." I made a few illustrative gestures with my hands.

"How does a carved tree relate to pack politics?" Hubert asked, looking puzzled.

"I guess if your picture is near the top, you're important or something," I said. "Anyway, what I meant was, Charles must have been high up in the pack."

"What an interesting expression," Hubert said. "Do you know what tribe was responsible for the totem pole?"

Enough about the stupid totem poles, already. "Haven't a clue. But back to Charles," I said, trying to shift Hubert off the whole Indian tangent. "Wasn't he a mover and a shaker?"

"You are correct in that. He was one of Wolfgang's closest advisors, in fact. And he was very well connected."

"I'm surprised he didn't end up with someone of his own, well, pack level."

Hubert sighed. "It would have been preferable, and Wolfgang strove to dissuade him from choosing Kayla as a mate, but he was staunch in his assertions that she was the right choice for him."

"Let's just hope he told her enough that she'll be able to suggest an alternate suspect," I said, feeling a bit overwhelmed. I had only a short time to infiltrate the Howl and see if I could find out something that would prove my father innocent, and the foundation of my plan was chatting up a werewolf named Kayla. And I wasn't even sure Luc Garou *was* innocent. I looked at Tom and Hubert. "You've both had dealings with my father in the past, am I correct?"

They shared a glance. "Yes," Tom said. "We have had many interactions with your father over the years."

"Really?" I asked, my curiosity piqued. "What kind of interactions?"

Tom sighed. "Someday, when we have a few hours, I'll give you the whole history. Why are you asking this now?"

"Because I want to know. Do you really think my father murdered Charles?"

Hubert furrowed his brow, which made him look suddenly, disconcertingly, old. Not as old as he probably was, of course—since Wolfgang had had his portrait painted in the 1600s (I'd seen it once in Houston), I was guessing Hubert, too, had a couple of centuries on me—but the change was unsettling. "All signs seem to point to his guilt," Hubert said, "but I cannot say with certainty." He turned to Tom. "What do you think?"

"I do not know," Tom said. "Wolfgang, of course, is convinced he is guilty, but he and your sire have tangled in the past. Their history may be clouding his judgment."

Lovely. "So we know where Wolfgang stands. I'm curious about the trial, though," I said. "What's the procedure? Will my dad—I mean, Luc—have a lawyer or anything?"

"No." Tom shook his head, but his eyes were steady on mine. "Although he is not prohibited from appointing a representative, it would be highly unusual. This country's litigious bent has not yet filtered through to the werewolf community."

Normally, I would consider fewer lawyers a benefit, but in the current circumstances, it wasn't exactly what I wanted to hear. Especially considering my father's rather outspoken, and decidedly unflattering, opinions regarding the leader of the wronged pack.

"Each side makes its case to the judges," Hubert added, "and then the judges decide."

"The judges. Wolfgang and Elena?"

Tom nodded. "The other alphas will be asked to preside, of course, but they are primarily in alliance with Wolfgang."

"What about the Louisiana pack alpha?" I asked, remembering the tall, dark-haired werewolf I'd seen talking to Wolfgang. "He's not necessarily an ally, is he?"

"No," Tom said, looking pained. "But I doubt we can count on Jean-Louis's support."

"Why not?"

"His uncle was the previous alpha of the Paris pack."

"You mean the one my father took over from."

Tom nodded. "Were it not for your father's intervention, Jean-Louis would have set aside his weak cousin and ascended to the rank of alpha."

My stomach sank a few notches lower, which was a surprise—I hadn't known it was possible. "So half the jury has a vendetta against my father, and the rest of them are their allies," I clarified. "Sounds *completely* unbiased."

"The system does have its faults," Tom admitted.

"Does *anyone* like my father?" I asked. "He seems to have pissed off just about every werewolf I've ever met."

"He has had a stormy history," Tom acknowledged.

"And he's about to go out with a bang," I said glumly.

"There is one other approach to a trial of this type—much more primitive," Hubert said tentatively.

"What do you mean?" I asked.

"I do not know if it is a possibility in this case. It has fallen out of favor, but it was the prevailing method for centuries, particularly in the Old World."

"Let me guess. Stoning to death? Vivisection? Holding defendants underwater till they drown?"

Tom gave me a lopsided smile that made me wonder if those had in fact been considered viable options at one time. Then again, since humans did it, why should I be so shocked if werewolves joined in the fun?

Hubert moved into scholar mode as he explained the system to me. "In the past, a duel was considered a viable approach to testing innocence," he said. "Probably a way of ensuring the survival of the fittest from a biological perspective. I'm still researching the practice; it was common in the German states in the 1300s, as well as some of the Scandinavian countries . . ."

I cut him off. "A duel between whom?"

"Between the accused and the alpha of the wronged pack. It was probably a way of ensuring that the alpha really was the strongest individual, since the pack leader would be making the largest genetic contribution. But with the advent of modern society, the practice has fallen out of favor."

"But it's still considered kosher?"

"The code still allows it, if that's what you mean," he said.

"Hmm," I said, mentally sizing up Luc Garou and Wolfgang. If I somehow managed to convince them to try the dueling approach, could my father take him? Evidently he had once before, back in the old country . . .

"I seriously doubt that Wolfgang will agree to it, though," Tom said, bursting my fantasy bubble.

"Unfortunately, I believe Tom is right," Hubert said. "A duel has not been recorded in this country for at least a century. The last occurrence I am aware of transpired in New Orleans, in 1883."

"But it's still in the code," I said.

"Yes," Hubert confirmed. "It's still in the code."

"I still think it would be wise to mount a legal defense," Tom said. "Wolfgang is hardly likely to agree to a duel."

I took a deep breath. "And to mount a legal defense, we need to find out what's going on."

"That's generally how it works," Tom said. "I'll see what I can find out, but I'm limited in the questions I can ask. Since you're an outsider, you'll have more leeway."

"So, it's off to the Howl we go?" I said.

"Are you sure you want to go?" Tom asked. Something in his golden gaze made my stomach flutter a little bit. Probably nerves.

"What do I have to lose?" I asked, feeling like Little Red

Riding Hood about to enter a forest crammed to the gills with big bad wolves.

He fished in his jacket pocket and pulled out a little vial of capsules, shaking two of them into his hand. "Before we go," he said, "swallow this."

"What is it?" I asked, staring at the two brown horse pills.

"Fenugreek," he said.

"What's it for?"

"Your scent is already shielded, but consider it an insurance policy," he said. "Just in case something goes wrong."

"How does it work?"

"You'll see."

I poured myself a short glass of wine—I know, you shouldn't mix herbs with alcohol, but I needed a shot of courage—and downed them. Then I straightened my skirt and gave the two werewolves a bright smile. "Ready when you are!"

Eight

Before I knew it, I was bumping down the road to Werewolf Central on the back of Tom's motorcycle. I was having mixed feelings about my choice of wardrobe—the short skirt made riding on the back of a motorcycle a rather risqué endeavor—and trying to ignore the fact that my body, including my crotch, was pressed right up against Tom.

The ride, I must confess, was anything but boring.

We made it to Fredericksburg in record time, and I was a little sorry to have to dismount, so to speak. Tom glanced away as I scuttled off the motorcycle, yanking my skirt down so that my smiley-face cotton undies were under cover once again. When I was no longer in flasher mode, he turned to me and took my arm, sending a pleasant tingle through me.

"We're together, remember?" he murmured.

"Of course," I said. I couldn't have forgotten if I'd *wanted* to.

Even with the rather heavy aroma of my perfume, the mixed bouquet of a gazillion werewolves was overpowering. As, strangely, was the smell of maple syrup.

"Is there a pancake supper tonight or something?" I asked. "I thought it was a hunt."

"The maple smell is from the fenugreek," Tom informed me.

"You mean the pills you had me take?"

"Exactly."

"Oh. So instead of smelling like a werewolf, I smell like a short stack of pancakes?"

"I don't know about short," he said. "Maybe a statuesque stack of pancakes?"

"Compared to you I'm a midget," I pointed out. Even though I was five-eight, he towered above me. "What's the protocol tonight?" I asked, rather enjoying the feel of his arm through mine. If my goal hadn't been to interrogate pack members and get my father off murder charges without being discovered by a bad-tempered alpha werewolf, I might have found the prospect of a few hours on Tom's arm rather pleasant. Even if it was in the company of a couple hundred other werewolves.

I glanced in the direction of the inappropriately named garden cottage, straining to pick up a whiff of my father's scent, but there were too many werewolves to isolate it. Unless they'd beefed things up over the last twenty-four hours, there were only the two guards at the doorway. Would they decrease security during the hunt? If so, perhaps I could slip in and set Luc Garou free. Assuming I could co-opt a car, we could be out of here in no time flat. We weren't that far from the airport; if all went well, he could be on a plane back to Paris before the night was out.

Unfortunately, however, even if I did manage to spring my father, I would still have to convince him to get out of Dodge. And something told me that skipping town and hopping on a plane wouldn't come anywhere close to the top of his to-do list.

"We'll mingle a bit," Tom said, reminding me that my goal tonight was not to break my father out of jail, but to find a way to get the werewolves to drop the charges and set Luc Garou free. "There's usually a happy hour and some light dinner before the hunt begins. A good chance to start meeting people."

"And even better if they've sucked down a few margaritas," I said, sniffing at my arm. My stomach gurgled; my personal pancake aroma was making me hungry. "So I need to talk to Kayla. Is it safe to assume you know what she looks like?"

"I'll point her out to you. It will probably be best if we part ways; she will be likely to talk more to you than to me."

"What happens after happy hour?" I asked.

"When they ring the bell, we'll move to one of the changing rooms to transform. If we get separated, meet me near the site of the bonfire, and I'll show you where to go."

I stared at him. "You're kidding me. They really call them *changing* rooms?"

Tom grinned at me. "Can you think of a more appropriate term?"

He had a point. As we approached the festivities, which centered around the big farmhouse in the middle of the compound, but spilled out into the surrounding fields, I gripped his arm tighter and murmured, "Any last helpful hints?"

"Ever been to Minnesota?"

"Nope."

"Then I probably wouldn't start reminiscing about your golden childhood."

I rolled my eyes. "Thanks for the tip. What I meant was, are there any weird werewolf conversational conventions I need to know about?"

"None that I can think of," he said. "Just tell whoever you're talking to that you're new to this part of the world; since you're from a small pack, they should forgive your ignorance."

"Gee, thank goodness for that."

Moments later, we joined the group of werewolves milling around the grounds. Despite the casual setting, the area was swarming with jacket-and-tie-clad waiters—werewolves, I noticed, probably pack underlings—toting around trays of longnecks and piles of plump little venison sausages on toothpicks. The starched uniforms were incongruous, to say the least—I'd never thought of beer and barbecue as a particularly formal cuisine. Aside from the waiters, the dress code tended toward blue jeans, with a smattering of miniskirts, which made me feel quite at home. As did the number of rather hairy limbs I spotted. It was comforting to know that if my recent appointment with my Lady Bic wore off, I'd have plenty of company.

As we made our way through the crush on the porch, Tom greeted several werewolves with a handshake or a clap on the back. I don't know what I'd expected from a werewolf get-together—maybe raw-meat-ripping contests, or lots of bared teeth and unrestrained howls—but aside from a little excess body hair, a rather strong animal bouquet, and a preponderance of shimmery gold eyes, everyone in attendance seemed downright, well, *human*. Tom traded pleasantries with many of them, tossing around names I'd never heard of and introducing me as his Swedish "friend" from Minnesota. The introductions frequently elicited knowing looks, and even a few guffaws—invariably followed by a few off-color remarks and a barrage of questions directed at me—my pedigree, my age (Tom and I had decided on a youthful fifty, which to me felt just ancient), and how long I'd known Tom (our story was we'd met a few months ago, which was true). I found myself raising my eyebrows at Tom on several occasions, wondering exactly how many women he'd trotted out to previous Howls. He ignored my glances, of course, and I resolved to question him with more intensity later on.

After shaking paws with at least twenty rather buzzed werewolves who showed a disturbingly strong interest in the Swedish werewolf from Minnesota, I found myself desperately trying to turn the conversation to anything but me. Tom seemed to be a pretty popular guy, and not just with the female contingent. Which surprised me a little bit; I guess I'd always thought of him as something of a lone wolf.

The smell of beer and werewolves almost knocked me over when we squeezed through the front door into the main room of the house. The Shiner Bock had apparently been flowing for a while, which—despite the preponderance of supernatural predators—gave the entire get-together a relaxed, rather boozy feel that suited me just fine. There were little packs of werewolves jammed in everywhere, cradling beer bottles and swapping hunting stories. As I followed Tom through the crowd, I overheard a trio of werewolves with big gold belt buckles and fancy boots discussing last night's excursion. "Did you see how Graf took that buck down?" one of them was saying. "I wouldn't want to meet *him* in a dark alley."

"I wouldn't want to run into his consort, either."

"Oh, I don't know. Depends on the circumstances," the first werewolf said. "She's got a good-looking tail, if you know what I mean."

I resisted the urge to roll my eyes as we passed them by. Although I picked up a few familiar smells among the crowd of werewolves, many of whose noses twitched a bit at my perfume-and-syrup-scented passage, I didn't see anyone I recognized. "Have you seen Kayla yet?" I whispered to Tom as he snagged a fifth sausage from a passing tray. Either he hadn't eaten in days, or he was blessed with an excellent metabolism. I limited myself to one miniature link, even though the juicy taste left me drooling for more.

"She's over there," Tom murmured into my ear. The feel of his breath on my earlobe was so delicious it took me a moment to register that he was pointing in the direction of the kitchen. I spotted her a moment later: a frizzy blond werewolf in too much eye makeup, tight jeans, and pink rhinestone-studded cowboy boots, leaning against the wall and peeling the label off her Shiner Light. She even *looked* like she belonged in a bad country song. "Shall we?" Tom asked, and I trotted after him, struggling to keep up with his long strides.

"Hello, Kayla," he said in his rumbly, sexy voice. Her eyes gleamed a little as she looked up from her beer bottle.

"Tom Fenris, right?" she asked, with a deferential—and rather flirtatious—head dip.

"I'm so sorry to hear about your loss," he said in a voice that would have melted butter. Kayla looked like she might be feeling a little moist herself.

"Thank you," she simpered.

Tom turned to me. "Kayla lost her promised mate in a terrible accident last week."

"It wasn't an accident," Kayla said, chin stuck out.

"I'm sure they'll get everything worked out," Tom said soothingly. "Are you holding up?"

"Kind of," she said in a tone of voice that indicated just the opposite.

"If there's anything I can do, don't hesitate to ask," he said gravely. "For now, though, I have a favor to ask of *you*."

"Really?" she asked, eyes widening in anticipation. I felt kind of bad for her—from the light panting, she seemed to be expecting an opportunity to do a little one-on-one two-step a little later on.

Her disappointment was obvious when he revealed the rather more pedestrian nature of his request. "Would you be so kind as to entertain Inga for me for a little while?" he asked. "I have one or two things to do before the hunt, and I don't want to bore her."

"Sure," she said with a faint east Texas drawl, turning to inspect me with interest. Her snub nose wrinkled slightly as she picked up my perfume-and-pancake scent, and she took a small, involuntary step back. I couldn't blame her.

"Nice to meet you," I said, thrusting out a paw. I was glad I'd never really picked up a Texas accent. I didn't know what a Minnesota accent sounded like, and I was hoping Kayla didn't, either.

"You, too," she said, with obvious reservations.

"I know I'm leaving you in good hands," Tom said to me with a smile and a slight warning look. I resisted the urge to stick my tongue out at him. "Thanks, Kayla," he said, turning a full-wattage smile on her.

"Sure," Kayla said, looking less than thrilled by the assignment. I couldn't blame her; my liberal application of Euphoria was curling my own nose hairs, and I'd had a couple of hours to get used to it.

"I will see you both soon." Tom gave me an intense look from his golden eyes before disappearing into the jeans-clad throng. It was just Kayla and me now.

"So," she said, reaching up to pry her eyelashes apart. The golden eyes shimmering behind the gloppy black mascara marked her as a born werewolf. The made werewolves' eyes—most of whom were toting trays of sausages, I noticed—had the shimmer, but not the signature whiskey color. She raked me with an appraising up-and-down look. "How do you know Tom?"

"We met a few months ago," I said.

"Huh," she said. "I didn't know Tom had a girlfriend."

"I'm not his *girlfriend*, really," I said, hoping to dampen her curiosity. "We're just . . . getting to know each other," I continued. "Nothing official."

"He's cute," Kayla said, watching him weave through the crowded room. "Plus he's got that royal blood, and those special powers of his . . . he's got carte blanche to go anywhere he wants. A real catch. If you manage to hold onto him, anyway." She looked me over a second time, with a hint of disdain. Which was pretty rich, considering her own personal makeup regimen consisted of half a tube of mascara per eye. "I wouldn't have guessed you were his type, really. No offense."

"None taken," I said dryly. And then, because I couldn't help myself: "Does he *have* a type?"

"I've seen him with a lot of different chicks," she said, and my heart plummeted a bit. "But none of them dressed like you."

"What do you mean?"

"Well, they were all a little less . . . well, they were classier, I guess. No offense," she said again.

Of course not. Granted, my ensemble tonight was more Britney Spears than Hillary Clinton, but still . . . "Well, maybe he's looking for a bit of excitement, then," I suggested, trying for a salacious grin.

"Maybe," she said, giving me a dubious glance that suggested he would have better luck spending a few hours in a pit full of vipers.

I decided it was time to turn the conversation toward what I really came here to find out about. Which was not Tom's dating habits, fascinating though they might be. "Here we've been going on and on about my love life, when you . . ."

Her face clouded.

"I'm sorry about your loss," I said. "Tom told me something had happened to your fiancé, but he didn't say what."

Kayla's golden eyes misted up a little bit, and she spoke in a low voice. "My promised mate was . . . was murdered a few days ago."

"Oh, how awful! You poor thing."

"Yeah," she said, her voice tinged with sadness. "We were going to be joined next month." I felt kind of bad for bringing up the subject—her face had paled, and although it was hard to tell through the mascara, her eyes seemed a bit hollow.

But duty calls. I drew in my breath and feigned shock. "Oh, how awful," I repeated, reaching out to give her arm a sympathetic squeeze. "What happened?"

She turned her head away. "He . . . he had his throat ripped out by some savage French werewolf."

Nine

I resisted the urge to roll my eyes. Luc Garou, the savage French werewolf with a weakness for undersized designer jeans. Yeah, right. "How dreadful!" I said. "And to have seen it *happen* . . ."

She gave me a scornful look from under her gloppy eyelashes. "*I* didn't see it. I was at my sister's house, out in Galveston, for a couple of days."

"Still," I said, studying her face and searching for a change in expression under the pancake makeup. "To hear about it from someone who *did* see it—that must have been terrible."

Kayla gave me a suspicious look. "What are you talking about? Nobody actually *saw* it happen," she said.

"Nobody saw it? Then how the heck do they know it was a French werewolf?"

She rolled her eyes, her grief evidently swamped by a wave of annoyance. "*Everybody* knows it was Garou. He's wanted to kill my Charles for a century—he was just waiting for the opportunity. Dudley saw them arguing just before it happened, and when Boris found him, he could smell the guy all over him."

"Who are Boris and Dudley?"

"Elena's guards," she said. "Boris is really cute—wears these leather pants that make him look *totally* hot."

Ew. Unless wearing synthetic leather was common among werewolves, she was describing one of the pleather boys. And evidently, just because her beloved was dead didn't mean she was; despite her bereavement, Kayla appeared to be already back on the prowl. But did she really think that Boris was *hot*?

Kayla sniffled dramatically, distracting me from an unpleasant mental picture of Boris's pleather-encased backside. "Anyway, I'm so glad they've got that awful French werewolf locked up," she said, wiping away an eyeliner-laden tear. "I just wish they could bring my Charles back."

"I don't get it. Why would a French werewolf want to kill your boyfriend?" I asked. "Wasn't your boyfriend a member of the Houston pack, too?"

She shot me a suspicious look. "Why does it matter to you?"

"I don't know. It just doesn't make sense to me, I guess." And then there was the fact that the accused was my father, of course. "Maybe somebody else was mad at him," I suggested. "Or maybe someone was jealous that he was seeing you, or something. I mean, I'm betting you're a pretty hot ticket around here."

Unfortunately, my flattery didn't work. "I told you, it was the French guy," she said haughtily. "He's had it in for Charles for years."

"Maybe you're right," I said quickly, not wanting to alienate her. "But are you sure there wasn't . . . I don't know. A jealous would-be lover, or something?"

"No," she said flatly.

"It was just a thought," I said lamely. So far, not so good. I flailed around for something else to talk about. My gaze landed on a buck's antler-studded head, which was affixed to a nearby wall. "Are you going on the hunt tonight?"

"Of course," she said. "*Everybody's* going."

"I heard one of the alphas took a buck last night."

"Yeah, that was Wolfgang." Her eyes gleamed slightly. "He's really something, isn't he?"

Before I had a chance to respond, two male werewolves sidled up to us, their gold belt buckles flashing in the dim light. "Can I buy you a drink?" asked the taller one, who had long dark hair and a belt buckle that said BUD, as he sidled up to Kayla.

"Why not?" she asked, flashing him a flirtatious smile. Despite her recent personal tragedy, she was certainly resilient.

Bud's slightly shorter friend gave me a measuring look, and his nose wrinkled a little bit. He wasn't bad looking—medium-brown hair and a cute smattering of freckles on his nose—but he wasn't my type. "I haven't seen you around before," he said. "My name is Anthony."

"I'm Inga," I said.

"She's from Minnesota," Kayla said helpfully. "She's the one who's with Tom Fenris."

Both werewolves pricked their ears at this, and their twin golden gazes increased in intensity. What was it with Tom that just saying his name got everyone's undivided attention? "I'm not really *with* Tom," I clarified quickly. "We're seeing each other casually. I'm just in town for a dose of warm weather," I said. "How about you? Are you guys from around here?"

"We're down from Texarkana," Bud said.

"I'm from Houston," Kayla said, pushing her rather insubstantial chest out a bit.

"I'm afraid I don't know too much about the Texas packs," I ventured. "How big are they?"

"Houston's the biggest," Kayla said proudly. "I'm surprised Tom hasn't told you. Five hundred and fifty members strong. It's one of the biggest packs in the whole south. Texarkana's got a couple hundred, too." One over-tweezed eyebrow arched a little bit. "I thought everybody knew that."

I forced a laugh. "Oh, where I live is such a backwater, we never get any news."

"Where in Minnesota are you from?"

"Oh, a little town outside of Minneapolis," I said. "I'm sure you've never heard of it."

"Try me," Anthony said, eyes glinting. "I used to travel up there on business a lot."

Uh-oh. I stared at him for a moment, racking my brain for the name of a town in Minnesota. "Saint Paul," I finally blurted.

His eyebrows rose. "I thought you said you were from a *small* town."

"Well, everything's relative," I said, anxious to shift the topic from my fictional hometown. "I mean, compared to *Houston* . . ." There was silence for a moment, and then I plunged ahead. "So, what about you? Have you always lived in Texarkana?"

"Born and bred," Anthony said. "But it's so cool that you're from Saint Paul, although I can't believe you'd call it *small*. Who's running the pack these days? When I was there it was Gunther and Helga, but that was a few years back."

I grabbed a beer from a roving waiter and took a long swig, stalling for time. "Still the same," I said quickly, glancing at Kayla, who was now deep in conversation with Bud. Time for a subject change. "Did you hear about what happened to Kayla's promised mate?" I asked Anthony in a low, conspiratorial voice.

"The one the French guy killed?"

"I heard it might have been someone else," I said.

"I don't know who you've been talking to. Everything I've heard pretty much places him on the scene. It looks like an open-and-shut case." He shook his head. "Sad, really. I hear the guy just found his estranged daughter again, and then he has to act out during the Howl and get himself executed . . ."

I shivered and took another long swig of beer.

"You sure are thirsty. Want another one of those?"

"No, no," I said. "I'm good." I glanced at Kayla to make sure she was occupied, then asked in a low voice, "Why does everyone think the French guy did it?"

"History," he said sagely.

"Huh," I said, feeling more than a tad frustrated. Everyone in the world of werewolves was ready to consign Luc Garou to a stake, and he hadn't even had a trial yet. "But from what I heard, the whole thing happened like a hundred years ago. Don't you think that's a long time to wait?"

"I guess so," he said, shrugging. "But you know how werewolves are."

"What do you mean?"

"Short tempers and long memories," he said, giving me a toothy grin. "So, since you're not with Tom, you want to join me in the hunt tonight?"

"I'd love to," I demurred, "but Tom asked me to join him."

He laughed, a low, guttural sound that made goose bumps rise on my arms. "You'd be better off with me, sweetheart. He doesn't have the longest attention span, if you know what I mean."

"We're just friends," I said quickly.

He studied me for a second. "Yeah, right."

Before I could respond, there was a loud gonging noise.

"What's that?"

"Time for the hunt," he said. He held my eyes for a long moment. "Sure you don't want to join me?"

"I can't. But thanks."

"Good luck," he said. "And if you change your mind . . ."

"I'll remember you," I said. He conferred briefly with his friend before heading to the door. Bud lingered, shooting alternate glances at both Kayla and me.

"Can you find Tom on your own?" Kayla asked in a low voice, picking a clump off of her eyelashes.

"Yeah," I said.

"I'm gonna go with Bud then, if that's okay." She edged closer to her companion's oversize belt buckle.

"Go for it," I said. "Nice to meet you, and thanks for keeping me company."

"No problem," she said, walking off with her new interest and leaving me to finish my beer alone.

As I swigged down the rest of the Shiner and followed the pack out into the cool evening, I felt a wave of despair wash over me. I'd just "interrogated" my most likely source of information, but all I'd managed to find out was that my father's guilt appeared to be a fait accompli. And then there was the unsettling disclosure that Tom's romantic history was, well, less than consistent. Or rather, consistently changing.

Which wasn't my problem, I reminded myself. It was Lindsey I should be worried about.

I spotted Tom near the ashes of last night's bonfire, scanning the crowd. Even with the olfactory load of hundreds of werewolves, his musky, wild scent was unmistakable, and as I approached him, his eyes swiveled to fix on me with an unsettling intensity.

"Did you learn anything?" he asked as I followed him into a stand of cedar scrub and gnarled oaks.

"Not much in terms of my dad. Other than that he's already considered guilty as hell by the entire werewolf community."

Tom made a small sound.

"But I had no idea you had such a reputation," I said, my

heels sinking into the soft, springy earth. The air had a wild smell to it—like a storm was brewing.

"What do you mean?" Tom asked.

"You're evidently known as quite the Casanova," I said. His back stiffened slightly in the twilight.

"I was for a while," he admitted. "At a different time in my life."

"So you've mended your ways?"

"I had no idea my love life was of such interest to you," he said, stopping in his tracks to turn and look at me.

"It's not," I said quickly. "I mean, not to me personally. But you *are* dating my best friend," I pointed out.

"So there's no . . . personal interest?" he asked, eyes steady on mine. They glowed slightly in the fading light from the sun.

"Of course not," I said, looking down. "There can't be, can there? You're with Lindsey, after all . . ."

"And you are with Mark," he reminded me.

I gave him a wry smile. "So there we are, then."

"There we are," he repeated. He stared at me for a moment, during which all sorts of declarations bubbled up inside of me, only to die in my throat. After a moment, he turned and continued down the path, with me stumbling along in his wake, trying not to break off one of my heels. I fiddled with the ring Mark had given me as I stepped over a fallen tree limb; it was uncomfortably warm on my finger.

"Here we are," Tom said, stopping next to a line of canvas tents. Small groups of werewolves loitered outside of each; as I watched, a lean, dark gray wolf slipped out of one of the farther tents and vanished into the trees. "Remember. . . the alpha takes the first kill."

"Got it. Keep the teeth sheathed." I glanced at the line of tents. "These are the changing rooms?"

"What were you expecting?"

"I don't know. I guess I was thinking they might be something more . . . permanent."

"Sorry to disappoint you," he said as we joined a short line a few tents down. We stood in awkward silence as the two werewolves before us—a stout redheaded man and an equally stout, platinum-blonde woman—slipped into the tent and emerged a few minutes later as a chunky reddish wolf and one that was almost blindingly white. Which made me wonder all the more how the whole hair-dye thing was going to translate.

"Ladies first," Tom said, indicating that I should precede him into the little canvas room. Which was a relief—I had been wondering whether we were supposed to go in at the same time.

As the flap closed behind me, I unzipped my skirt and slid it over my hips, folding it and tucking it into one of the canvas cubbies that lined three walls of the tent. I followed it with my shoes, which was a relief, because they were really pinching my toes. Within seconds, I was naked in the tent, very aware that Tom was a mere couple of feet away.

Then I took a deep breath and let the change pass over me.

It started as a rippling sensation under the skin, a feeling of surrender. I closed my eyes and let the sensation wash over me, feeling a tingle as fur grew on my arms and the slight cramping sensation that accompanied my body's reconfiguration. As always, the world around me took on extra dimension—the slightly mildewed scent of the canvas was so sharp I could practically taste it, and the woodsy perfume of the cedars enveloped me. Of course, so did the smell of Euphoria, maple syrup, and several hundred werewolves with varying levels of personal hygiene, so the transformation wasn't quite as pleasurable as it normally was, but the sudden expansion of sensation was always a lovely little shock.

I slipped through the tent a moment later, looking up at Tom, whose golden eyes had widened a hair at my exit.

I gave a gentle woof that I hoped meant, "What?"

"It's your fur," he said. I did my best wolfie version of

cocking an eyebrow, waiting for him to explain. "You've got this big black tuft on your head—it kind of looks like a beret," he said.

I woofed again and dropped my tail between my legs, utterly embarrassed.

"It's certainly distinctive," he said, which helped not at all. Then he disappeared into the tent, leaving me wishing I had a full-length mirror, and glad that the remaining wisps of light were fading fast.

It wasn't until Tom had transformed into a huge, gorgeous golden wolf—I had been standing outside the tent sniffing squirrels and trying not to think about Tom peeling his shirt off, exposing his muscled torso—that I realized my oversight. I'd been so taken aback by the discovery of Tom's Don Juan reputation that I'd completely forgotten to ask what the hunt protocol was. Or if there was one.

Well, it was too late now.

After his rather regal exit from the tent—he was downright majestic, with those broad, powerful shoulders and iridescent golden eyes—he gave me a little nudge with his nose and indicated I should follow him into the scrubby oaks. Which I did, reveling in the crispness of the world—even in the dim light, every blade of grass was sharply drawn, and I could see the reflection of the waxing moon on the oak leaves' shining surfaces. If I wasn't careful, I might lose myself staring at the bark of a tree . . . or the play of the moonlight on Tom's shining coat as he leapt nimbly over a stray boulder.

I followed Tom away from the tents and farmhouses, away from civilization. As we padded over last season's dead leaves, I found myself sniffing to detect what animals had passed by—already I sensed a pair of armadillos digging for grubs, a feral pig on the hunt for acorns, and a female werewolf who had recently used Nair. I was aware of the wolves padding silently through the underbrush around me. In fact, there were so many of us that I wondered exactly how this "hunt" was supposed to go. With the concentration of werewolves in the area, I'd be amazed if there was any game within a five-mile radius.

We climbed a gentle hill, weaving through chunks of moonlit granite and clumps of bluegrass, cresting in a big, hilltop clearing ringed by werewolves. In the center were two werewolves I recognized, even though I'd never seen them in wolf form before. Wolfgang was on the left, looking powerful and massive, the tips of his blond fur gleaming in the moonlight; beside him, sleek and black, was Elena, her long nose—as usual—high in the air.

I expected we'd just park on the fringes where we came in, but instead found myself following Tom as he circled around the group, finally stopping at a spot on the far side of where we'd come in. It wasn't until a breeze brought us the mixed bouquet of the alpha couple that I realized why he'd chosen this spot; we were now downwind of the dynamic duo.

Despite the hundreds of werewolves converging on the hilltop, the night was soundless, save for the whisper of the wind and the droning chirp of crickets.

Tom waited attentively, as did the rest of the werewolves. It was hard to believe that the rather eerie group of silent wolves had been wearing jeans and swilling longnecks not twenty minutes ago. What were they waiting for? I wondered, suddenly aware of exactly how much I had missed by being raised among average humans. Well, maybe not average—my mother the psychic witch was hardly what you'd consider run-of-the-mill—but you know what I mean.

The crickets were growing increasingly annoying, and I was ready to start yipping just to break up the monotony when it finally began.

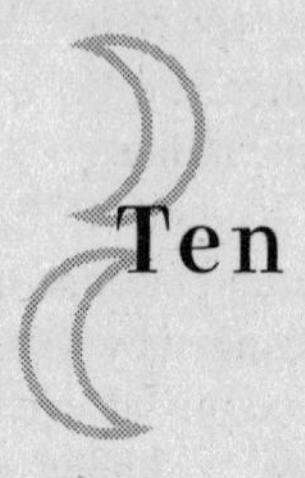

Ten

Wolfgang tipped his head back and let out a low, throaty howl; a moment later, Elena joined in, soprano to his bass, making a counterpoint to the melody that sent chills down my spine. When the long notes died away into the silent night, the rest of the pack picked up the refrain, their voices mingling in an eerie howl so compelling that I found that I had joined in without realizing it.

The back-and-forth continued a few times—there were almost words in the howls, though I couldn't quite grasp them—before stopping as suddenly as it began. Then a small space opened in the circle of wolves, and Elena and Wolfgang leaped through it. The circle rejoined for a moment; then, as I stood watching, the ring of wolves melted away, disappearing into the trees.

I glanced at Tom, who indicated with a flick of his ears that I should follow. Which I did, wondering exactly what the whole point of this undertaking was. We'd met on a hilltop and exchanged some howls. Were we now officially on the hunt? Or just heading to another hill somewhere?

I took a deep breath and followed the big blond wolf, nose flared, scanning the landscape with all my senses. The game, as I had suspected, was long gone; I could smell a hawk roosting in a tree, and hear the flap of an owl as it swooped down through the branches. The woods were alive, and not just with the stealthy padding of werewolves, which was pretty much everywhere. The night world vibrated around us, and despite my concern for my father—and my extremely conflicted feelings about the huge blond werewolf in whose footsteps I was padding—I felt myself sliding into a primal role I had spent most of my life trying to hold at bay.

Predator.

I had hunted on my own before, of course. During the four times of year when the change was unavoidable, I rented a small cabin in the wilds of the hill country, shed my human skin, and did what wolves have always done.

Most of the time I had limited myself to tracking down jackrabbits, or spooking armadillos from their dens. The bloodlust had descended on me once or twice, when I disturbed a buck or doe, and I had run at least one of them to ground, slightly scared by the ferocity that had bubbled up in me. Although that same ferocity had come in handy once or twice when dealing with would-be car burglars.

But now, something about the night brought all that rushing back. I was no longer Sophie Garou, auditor. I was part of a larger organism, the breathing, living creatures that swarmed through the woods all around me, eyes shimmering gold in the faint light.

I dropped my nose to the ground, deciphering the tangle of scents crisscrossing the ground beneath me. A jackrabbit, a pair of squirrels. Nothing recent. My senses attuned to the night, the cedar trees dark and dense, the new leaves of the mesquite trees silvery in the moon's light.

Tom had just rounded a fallen oak when I caught a flash of movement, near to the ground. I glanced at Tom, but then my ears picked up the skitter of dead leaves, and my eyes followed it, searching for the source.

The temptation was too great. And after all, I told myself, this was a hunt, right?

I veered off the trail toward the small dark form, breathing in deeply. A rabbit—always fun to chase. I picked up the pace, following the flashing white tail through the trees.

Nothing existed suddenly but the animal racing in front of me—it was one of those big jackrabbits, with ears the size of banana leaves, and I could smell the adrenaline pulsing through its furry body. I dropped low to the ground, loping after it as it dashed through the trees. The gap was closing; I could almost taste the rabbit's scent, and saliva flooded my mouth in anticipation of the salty tang of its blood.

As I rounded a cedar, two paces from my prey, ready to pounce, the rabbit vanished.

I skidded to a halt, sniffing for my vanished prey, but all I found was a big hole in the ground.

I padded around the gap in the earth, thrusting an experimental paw down it, but it was too deep. Unless I spent the next hour digging, I was out of luck.

With the rabbit no longer in range, the predatory instinct faded, and I looked up and around, trying to orient myself. I couldn't smell the werewolves as strongly—they must have gone in a different direction—but the scent of ashes wafted to me on the wind. The rabbit must have led me back toward the compound.

And Luc Garou.

I sniffed again. I had lost Tom when I'd gone down my rabbit trail; there was no trace of his scent. Should I try to find him? I wondered. If I went back to hang with the other werewolves, the conversational opportunities would be somewhat limited by our nonhuman form, so I wasn't sure how beneficial that would be. If anything, it would greatly increase the likelihood of my running smack into Elena and being outed.

My father, on the other hand, was merely a few hundred yards away. And even if I couldn't spring Luc Garou from the garden cottage, it wouldn't hurt to scope out the area—just in case the whole trial thing didn't work out and I ended up having to break in and try to gnaw through his shackles. The night breeze brought another whiff of ashes with it; the bonfire was definitely off to my right. After a final check to make sure I was alone, I padded toward it, all my senses on high alert.

Within minutes, I had found a trail back to the compound and was heading to the small building that housed my father.

I paused next to a bush about twenty yards away, using my nose and ears to get the lay of the land. I could make out the faint odor of my father—and since he evidently hadn't had access to running water, odor was definitely the mot juste. What I didn't smell, though, were the guards. Had they left him unwatched during the hunt?

I padded closer to the house, alert for any movement. Aside from the rustle of the breeze through the grasses, though, the place was dead.

So dead, in fact, that for a moment I was afraid they'd moved Luc Garou elsewhere. Or perhaps dispensed a bit of vigilante justice prior to the trial date. But then a particularly strong breeze brought a clear whiff of his pungent bouquet, and my fears were assuaged.

I studied the door, a flimsy wooden thing with a shiny brass lock. It wouldn't be hard to get in; there was no security system, and it wouldn't take much to break a window.

I hesitated a few yards from the door. Did I dare take the time to retrieve my clothes?

Since the alternative was to chat with my estranged father in the buff, I decided it was a risk I was willing to take. Naked with fur was fine, but I didn't want to turn up in human form looking like I'd just signed up to join a nudist colony. I turned away from the little cottage and headed back into the woods; it was only a matter of minutes before I found the tent where Tom and I had stripped down. I slipped inside, switched back to human form, and tugged on my clothes, including my highly impractical stiletto heels. The downside of my transformation, unfortunately, was that I was at a disadvantage when it came to detecting other werewolves. My sense of smell and hearing might still be better than the average human's, but I was operating at less than half of my wolf capacity. I had no idea how long the hunt was supposed to last; to be on the safe side, I decided it would be wise to keep the family visit on the short side.

Thanks to the shoes, the trip back to the cottage took twice as long. I found myself startling every time I stepped on a dead branch, convinced I'd turn the corner and plow right into a pack of annoyed werewolves. But I made it back to the cottage unmolested, and although I was disappointed that they hadn't left the door unlocked, I was feeling pretty good about the way the evening was shaping up.

Ideally I'd be able to slip in and out without anyone knowing I'd been there, but a quick circuit of the house's exterior indicated that wasn't really an option. So I found a big rock, heaved it at one of the back windows, and took cover behind a large bush as the glass shattered, sounding about as subtle as a plane crash. I was amazed that the entire Houston pack didn't come bounding up to see what had happened, but after a few werewolf-less minutes, I decided the coast was clear and crept up to the side of the cottage. A volley of French invective met my ears as I reached inside, fumbled for the window's lock, and eased the frame open.

When I didn't answer, my father grew silent. Then, in a hopeful tone that was disturbingly vulnerable, he called, "Armand?"

"Nope," I said. "It's just me." I pulled the window shut behind me—why, I don't know, because the glass was rather conspicuously absent—and walked across the small, dilapidated kitchen toward the doorway to the main room.

"Sophie?" My father looked up as I entered, something like joy—or triumph—lighting his gold eyes. Then his brow furrowed. "What is it that you have done to your hair?"

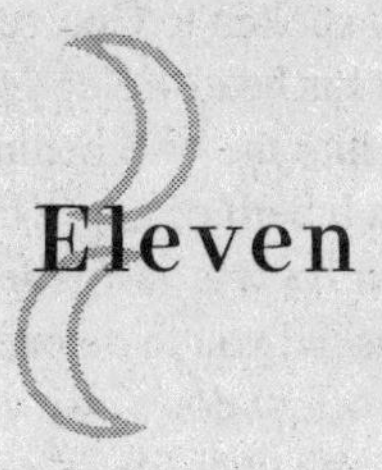

Eleven

Unbelievable. I had risked life and limb to see my father and he was criticizing my *hair*? "It's a disguise," I said.

"That color does not suit you at all," he said with obvious distaste. "Not to mention that smell," he added. "Like American waffles. And you're wearing too much perfume."

His nose wrinkled delicately. Which, in my opinion, was pretty rich coming from a werewolf who smelled like he hadn't bathed in a week.

"You're not exactly fresh as a daisy yourself," I said, perhaps a bit tartly. When I explained that Tom had given me an herb to help disguise my scent, Luc's bushy eyebrows rose.

"Fenris assisted you?"

"He's my friend," I said. "Remember? He was the one who got me in to see you yesterday." I glanced nervously at the front door, listening for the sound of oncoming werewolves. "Look. I don't know how much time we've got, so let's make the most of it." I hurried over and examined his shackles; they were decidedly gnaw-proof, and the key was nowhere in sight.

"Right, right. Excellent thinking." As I searched the room for the key, Luc looked at me expectantly. "Did Georges get in touch with Armand?"

I sucked in my breath. "Not exactly . . ."

"What does that mean?"

"I haven't spoken to Georges yet, actually," I said.

He shook his head violently, rocking his chair back so that it slammed into the wall behind him. His chains jangled like cowbells on a herd of angry cattle, and for a moment, I was kind of glad he was restrained. "This is insupportable," he barked. "I asked you to do one simple thing . . ."

I cut him off. "I don't owe you *anything*."

"You owe me your life."

Oh, please. Maybe I owed him a sperm, but my life? That was pushing it. "What you're asking me to do would start a war in central Texas," I said calmly. "Forgive me if I'm not too excited about that."

His gold eyes were fiery. "So you'd rather see me die like a stuck pig than cause an altercation?"

"I thought it might be nice to at least try and prove your innocence before we started calling in the reinforcements."

He snorted. "Obviously you are unfamiliar with the Grafs. You are being completely naive, Sophie. This is not about guilt or innocence, *chérie*. This is about revenge."

I gave up on the key—wherever it was, it wasn't here—and took a deep breath through my nose, wishing my father was a little less pungent as I did an olfactory sweep of the room, sniffing for other werewolves. Even though Luc's rather assertive animal odor and my Mrs. Butterworth bouquet were enough to mask just about anything—including two-week-old Limburger—it seemed we were still alone. For the moment, anyway. I returned my focus to my father. "Where were you that night, before we had dinner?"

"What night?"

"The night Charles died."

He shrugged. "I do not remember."

"You were late," I reminded him. "You showed up with a scratch on your face. What was that from?"

He shifted in his chair. "I caught it on a branch."

"So you didn't catch it on Charles's claw? Prior to, say, ripping his throat out?"

"No," he said, looking affronted. "I told you; I would never resort to such barbaric practices. Why won't you believe your own father?"

"You don't exactly have a stellar track record for me to draw on," I pointed out.

"Touché," he said. "All right, Sophie. I will be honest with you." He looked up at me from haunted eyes. "I did have an altercation with Grenier before we met that night. I was still angry over his betrayal, and I did not hide that fact. But I did not kill him," he said.

"Why not?"

He shrugged. "What benefit would it have? Other than satisfying my thirst for revenge, of course—but I was not that parched. Certainly, his betrayal of the Garous, particularly since he was a member of the family—a distant branch, to be sure, but still . . ."

"What exactly did he do that was so awful?"

"He was a spy. He reported our plans to the Grafs; it was almost our undoing at the battle of Colmar." He thrust out his chest. "Nevertheless, we prevailed."

"So you're not still pissed enough to kill him," I clarified.

"Of course not. He is in a new, weaker pack now, and he is not even alpha. What worse punishment could I contrive?"

Clearly we had different opinions on what constituted punishment, but I let it go.

"I was angry that he had jeopardized the family, and the cause," Luc continued. "And I will confess that for a time, I would happily have dispatched him. But I swear to you that I did not kill him."

"And the scratch on your face?"

Luc sighed. "I will admit that he did take one swipe at me, and I failed to duck in time. I had recently imbibed a Pernod, and my reaction time . . ."

"He scratched you, but you didn't retaliate?"

"Well, perhaps I did respond," he said sheepishly. "One cannot let an insult such as that simply pass by, you know."

"Of course not," I said, crossing my arms across my chest. "And how exactly *does* one respond to such an insult?"

He stared at me frankly from those golden eyes. "Sophie, my darling. Perhaps I dealt him a few light blows, just to make my point. But I did not rip his throat out."

"Glad to hear it," I said, wondering why I needed him to keep telling me that. "The problem is, someone did. And unless we can come up with a reasonable alternative, the werewolf community at large seems quite content to shove a stake in you and call the case closed."

"It is an unfortunate coincidence that we were together prior to his demise, but alas, I have no information to help you apprehend the murderer."

I resisted the urge to beat my head against the nearest wall. "Let's go through the whole evening, just in case there's something we missed. Where did you meet with him?"

"I ran into him on Second Street," he said.

"It wasn't a planned meeting?"

"Of course not," he said.

"Was he by himself?" I was beginning to feel a bit like a professional interrogator.

"At that moment, yes. But he had recently been with a woman," he said. "I could smell her on him."

"Werewolf, or human?"

"A *lupin*, of course."

He said it with a disgusted curl of his upper lip, as if the alternative would be roughly equivalent to engaging in sexual congress with a banana slug. This despite the fact that he and my human mother had obviously once been rather closer than "just friends." Not for the first time, I found myself questioning why I was bothering to help him.

"Any idea who it might me?" I asked.

He shrugged. "I am not familiar enough with the Americans to say."

"What did you say to him?"

"The truth," my father said simply.

"Meaning?"

"That he was a lying, traitorous bastard who did not deserve to live, of course. What else would I say to him?"

Gosh. I couldn't imagine *why* the pack thought he was guilty. I stared at the wild-haired, smelly werewolf before me, thinking how astonishing it was that this man had been successful in politics. Clearly there was a bit of a difference between the werewolf world and the human one I'd grown up with, at least where the political process was concerned. "And then you beat him up a little bit and walked on?" I asked, feeling very tired suddenly.

He gave another one of those Gallic shrugs, making his chains clank. "*Oui*."

I sighed. "You didn't see or smell any other werewolves?"

"None at all."

"Well, that's less than helpful," I said. I racked my brain for other questions to ask, but came up blank. I stared at Luc, still trying to come to terms with the fact that the scruffy werewolf in front of me was my biological father. And that unless I was willing to risk an out-and-out war, there was an excellent chance he would be dead within a week.

"Why didn't you try to find us?" I asked quietly, almost involuntarily, feeling a tightness in my throat.

"Pardon me?" Evidently the subject change was a bit much for him to follow.

"When my mother and I left Paris," I croaked. "Why didn't you follow us?"

He let out a long sigh. "I wanted to, my dear. But I owed it to my family to stay."

"*We* were your family."

"Yes," he said. "And it is one of my biggest regrets that I was not there to guide you in your growth. But I did it all for you."

I blinked at him. "Excuse me? You're saying you drove us out of Paris and left my mother on her own for *my* benefit?"

"My dear," he said. "I am now alpha of the Paris pack. Don't you know what that makes you?"

"The daughter you kicked out of Paris and abandoned?" I asked, not really seeing the silver lining.

"You do not understand," he said, shaking his head. "Sophie, my darling. You are *royalty* now! The Paris pack is yours for the taking. Once I am gone . . ."

"No. *You* don't understand," I said. "I don't *want* the Paris pack."

"Why not?"

"I've built a life for myself here, in Texas." I shrugged, which made me feel irritatingly Gallic. "I have no interest in moving to Paris. Besides, my French sucks."

"I would be honored to instruct you . . ."

"That's not the point."

"Well then," he said. "The solution is clear. Take charge of the Texas packs."

As if all I had to do was walk up to Wolfgang and Elena, tap them on the shoulder, and inform them that I would be stepping up in their places. And that while I was at it, I was making myself supreme ruler of all the other packs, too. "I don't think so," I said.

"All you have to do is get in touch with Armand. The entire Paris pack will be at your disposal."

"Even though I'm half human, and they were ready to stake me as an infant?"

"All that is past," he said. "You are a strong, beautiful werewolf, with an obvious and striking resemblance to your sire."

I stared at the smelly, disheveled man in too-tight jeans who sat chained before me and thought, *Dear God, I hope not.*

But he was still rambling on. "Your destiny is clear now. You will be a credit to the pack."

"Forget it," I said. "Forget I asked. I'm going to do my best to get you off. Then, maybe, if we get really, really, lucky, we can have a quick celebratory dinner. After which you can get on the first plane back to Paris, and I'll consider sending you a Christmas card."

He looked pained, and I don't think it was just because his shackles were tight. "But . . ."

"Shh," I said, closing my eyes and straining my ears. Adrenaline shot through me, and my hackles stood up at attention. "There's something outside," I whispered. "I have to go."

"Contact Georges," he said in a low, urgent voice. "Do it tonight."

But I was already headed for the window. "I'll be in touch," I said, as if we'd just had a nice chat over a couple of caramel macchiatos at Starbucks. Ten seconds later, I leaped through the glassless window, fumbling at the buttons of my blouse as I sailed through the air and hoped I wasn't aiming for a prickly pear. As I hit the thankfully cactus-free ground, there was a flurry of activity from a small patch of oak trees. Before I knew it, I was in full wolf form, tugging at my skirt with my teeth and taking a deep, long whiff of the cool air. There were werewolves, all right. And another scent . . .

I had just managed to get my left shoe off when something exploded into the clearing beside me.

What I should have done, particularly after Tom's repeated admonitions, was to turn and run as fast as my stiletto-less paws could go. But when a beautiful buck with a rack the size of a small crape myrtle burst into view, instinct and adrenaline took over. I leaped forward and sank my teeth into its neck, bringing the huge animal down with a startled grunt.

Naturally, that was the moment when the rest of the pack came thundering into the clearing, Wolfgang and Elena at its head.

Twelve

I looked around at the group of assembled werewolves, the buck's neck still firmly attached to my fangs, and attempted something like a smile. Which is a challenge when you're (a) not in human form and (b) hampered by a large mouthful of flailing, rather bloody deer.

Elena glared at me, widening her nostrils, and I broke out into a cold sweat, hoping my special scent-shielding power was still in full force and worrying that the fenugreek had worn off. A worry that was allayed a moment later as a strong whiff of eau-de-Waffle-House reached my hypersensitive nostrils.

Wolfgang stared at me impassively for a long moment, as if memorizing every feature of my blood-stained, dyed-hair wolfie countenance. Then he turned and stalked off, nose in the air. After one last cold glare, Elena followed suit, with the rest of the werewolves in her wake.

Suddenly I was all alone in the clearing again. Well, not completely alone, really—the deer was still kicking a bit, making awful grunting sounds as its lifeblood seeped out onto my face. I managed to detach myself from the huge animal, feeling kind of bad about the poor thing, hoping no one had recognized me (fat chance, with my hairdo), and wishing I'd just kept my mouth shut—and deer free.

At least one werewolf had identified me. I was busy wiping my face on the grass, trying to get the sticky blood off, when Tom appeared in the shadow of a short oak tree.

Never have I found myself more frustrated by an inability to talk. While I stood there covered in deer blood, thinking all kinds of questions at him, he just gave me a long, sad look. Then he gave me a quick head jerk—kind of a "follow me" gesture—and loped off into the direction of the changing tents.

Since I had my skirt and top right there with me—half-hanging off of me, in fact—I took a few more swipes at my face, then took a moment to slip into the nearest bush and reassemble my human persona. Then I trotted after him, hoping I was correct in guessing his destination.

When I got to the line of canvas tents, my left ankle twinging from where I'd twisted it on a tree root, he was standing, jeans-clad, outside the tent we had changed in earlier, arms crossed across his broad chest.

"How bad is it?" I asked in one breath, suddenly conscious of the blood I knew was still smeared across my face. I was not exactly at my best just now, and next to Tom's Nordic perfection, I was all too aware of it.

He grimaced. "Where did you go? I thought you were going to stay with me."

"I followed a rabbit down here, and then the buck came . . ." I trailed off. He stared at me, silent.

"So, it was a pretty big faux pas?" I asked.

"You could call it that."

"Well, what do I do now?" I asked, feeling miserable.

"I think it would be best for us to leave," Tom said, gold eyes sweeping over my disheveled self. Maybe my father and I resembled each other more than I liked to admit, I thought, my cheeks burning. We certainly did at that moment.

"Okay," I said, prepared to follow him down the path. I took two steps toward him, wincing at the pain in my ankle. When I grabbed a tree branch for support, Tom stepped forward and put an arm around me. "Lean on me," he said quietly.

"Are you sure? I'm kind of messy." I gestured toward the liberal splatters of deer blood that decorated my neck and arms.

"Just let's go," he said, and we walked down the path toward his motorcycle with me clinging to him for support.

As we made our way toward the parking lot, he turned and looked at me. "By the way, why were you so close to the garden cottage?"

"I stopped in for a quick family visit."

"You saw your father?" Tom asked, pulling me closer as I stumbled over a rock. A tingle went through me as my body pressed against his.

"Yeah," I said, trying to sound calm and reasonable and not like I was trying to keep myself from burying my face in his chest and wrapping my arms around him.

"How did you get in?" he asked.

"I broke a window."

"Of course," he said, as if it was the most natural thing in the world. "Let's hope they don't connect the window with your location when you took the buck down."

"Oh. I hadn't thought about that."

He was quiet for a moment, thinking what I hoped were charitable thoughts about my enterprising behavior. Finally, he asked, "What did he say?"

"He still wants me to get in touch with the Paris pack." Not to mention take over the entire Texas werewolf world.

"And will you?"

"I don't know," I said. "I'd like to prove his innocence, but if there's no other way . . ." I shivered. "He's not my favorite person in the world, but he's still my father. I'd have a hard time watching them stake him and knowing I could have done something to prevent it."

"I understand," he said softly.

"He seemed surprised that you and I are friends," I said.

"He would be," Tom said.

"Why?" I asked, picking my way over a particularly rocky area and vowing to wear flats next time I came out to the ranch. If there was a next time. After what had happened tonight, it was unlikely Inga would be received with open arms in the future.

"Your father is surprised because I have historically sided with the Grafs," Tom said, tightening his grip on me as I leaned against him. "Against the Garous."

"Then why have you been so nice to me?"

He shrugged. "You aren't a typical Garou, I suppose. You haven't been raised among them, so you lack certain of their . . . prejudices." He hesitated for a moment, then said, "My sister was married to Wolfgang once."

"That's right," I said. "What was her name . . . Astrid?"

He nodded.

"She died, didn't she? How?"

Tom glanced down at me, his eyes shimmering in the moonlight. "Your uncle Armand killed her."

I pulled away, horrified. My own uncle had killed Tom's sister. And *he* was the werewolf my father wanted me to contact for help. "No . . ."

Tom reached for me, pulling me back toward him. "It is not your fault, Sophie. It was in the heat of battle. You were not even alive then."

"But still . . . I'm so sorry, Tom. God. How can you stand to be near me?"

He shrugged. "Like I said, you were not raised among the Garous. And you are not your family."

Before I could ask any more questions, we turned the bend and were back in the parking lot. "We have arrived," Tom said. "Are you ready to head back to Austin?"

"I don't think I can do any more damage here," I said.

He chuckled, a low, growly sound that sent a ripple of lust through me. "Let's hope not."

As he climbed onto the motorcycle, I allowed myself one

last look at the garden cottage. Would I be able to find a way to get my father out of there? Or would I have to resort to calling in the werewolf who had killed Tom's sister?

Then Tom beckoned to me, and I climbed on behind him, and suddenly I wasn't worried about anything anymore. The engine roared to life beneath us, and I leaned my head against Tom's back as he backed out of the spot and pointed the front wheel toward the exit. Breathing in his wild alpha-male scent, which was only heightened by the soft, leathery smell of his jacket, I pushed the less than productive—not to mention embarrassing—events of the evening aside, luxuriating in the feel of Tom's hard body against mine. Even if I wasn't exactly at my best—unless you're a vampire, bloodstains aren't particularly sexy, and I was pretty sure my mascara had smeared—Tom still made me feel incredibly hot. And there's nothing like a cheap erotic thrill to put things in perspective. Even if it *is* with a guy who's currently dating your best friend.

We were almost past the last farmhouse and I was shamelessly scootching up a little bit closer to Tom when something in the woods caught my eye.

It was a werewolf, still in wolf form, standing half-hidden behind a cedar tree. His golden eyes were trained on Tom and me, and despite the rather warm feeling I had from being this close to Tom, something in the intensity of the werewolf's gaze caused me to shiver. We were just passing him when a gust of wind brought me a whiff of a familiar synthetic scent.

Pleather.

"What do you think I should do now?" I asked when we had made it past Frank the doorman without him noticing that I looked like an extra from Night of the Living Dead. For the first time, I found myself thankful for Frank's obsession with HGTV; he'd barely spared us a glance as we scurried across the lobby.

"I don't know," Tom said as we stepped off the elevator a moment later and I fished for my keys. We hadn't had much of a chance to chat on the back of his motorcycle, what with the sixty-mile-per-hour winds and all, so we were just now catching up on the evening's events. "Did you find out anything from Kayla?"

"Not much." I unlocked the door to the loft and tried to smooth down my flyaway black hair. "She was in Galveston when the murder happened, and she's convinced it was Luc who killed him. As is everyone else," I added grumpily, remembering my conversation with Anthony. I flipped on the lights and turned to Tom. "Can I get you a drink?"

"Not right now, thanks. I promised Lindsey I would stop by to see her," he said. Suddenly, there was a huge awkwardness between us. Or maybe it was just me.

"Oh," I said. "Well, tell her hi from me." I'd figure out whether to share what I'd learned about Tom's reputation later. It wasn't like they weren't well matched; Lindsey didn't have a long attention span herself, and had cut quite a swath through the male population of Austin over the last few years.

Tom put a warm hand on my arm, and I suppressed a shiver. "What about your father? Was he able to tell you anything?"

"He admitted to having a scuffle with Charles, but said he didn't kill him." I snorted. "Said Charles's not being alpha was punishment enough."

"He said nothing else?"

"Wait," I said. "Maybe he did come up with something useful. He told me Charles had slept with a woman that day, a werewolf. He could smell her on him. But it couldn't have been Kayla, because she was in Galveston."

Tom's blond eyebrows rose. "Interesting. Are you thinking he might have been killed by a jealous lover, then?"

"I don't know. What's the take on monogamy in werewolf packs?" I asked, feeling the blood rise to my cheeks as I asked the question.

"Prior to making a commitment, it is not required," he said. "But once a couple is promised, it is expected that they will refrain from consorting with others."

"Ah." Tom and Lindsey weren't "promised", I thought, shooting a sidelong glance at the tall, lean werewolf with golden hair and eyes to match. Did that mean he was seeing other people? Kayla certainly seemed to think he liked to play the field. I glanced down at his hand, which was still resting lightly on my arm. Was it possible he might be interested in seeing me? I'd kind of gotten that impression a few weeks ago . . .

Don't go there, Sophie. "So if he was . . . er . . . *with* someone else that night," I confirmed, "it wouldn't have been kosher."

"If what you are suggesting is that it was improper," Tom replied, "you would be correct."

Werewolf society might have some ethically questionable takes on what constituted acceptable behavior—it might have several of them, in fact—but evidently free love wasn't among them. "Do you know if there was anyone else he was interested in?" I asked. "Or what he was doing in downtown Austin that evening?"

"I do not know. Many werewolves were in Austin prior to the Howl—even Wolfgang and Elena stayed in town for a couple of days before moving to the ranch. But as for Charles's romantic interests . . ." He shifted from foot to foot, looking a little bit uncomfortable. "Perhaps I may be of some assistance in that matter."

"How so?"

"It happens that I am on familiar terms with one or two of his former flames," Tom said, staring with intense interest at a spot on the wall above me.

"Oh, really? My, you *do* get around," I said.

His golden eyes dropped from the wall to me. "I did not say that I had been *with* them," he pointed out. "I merely said that I was on familiar terms with them."

"Familiar enough to find out if one of them was still sleeping with Charles?"

"We shall see," he said. He gave my arm a little squeeze,

then released me, eyes lingering on mine. His voice was a bit husky when he spoke again. "As exciting as my time with you has been, I'm afraid I have to go."

"How bad was tonight's faux pas?" I asked as he turned toward the door. I had been afraid to ask, but I needed to know before he left.

He looked back at me. "The buck killing?"

I nodded.

He sighed. "It was an unfortunate occurrence."

"Was it bad enough that I won't be able to go back as Inga?"

He hesitated. "I'm not sure. What you did was a breach of etiquette, to be sure, but it is not a punishable offense. You may return as Inga, certainly—you were successful in cloaking your true identity—but your reception may not be warm."

"So my odds of getting people to talk with me are pretty much slim to none."

He nodded. "I wish it were otherwise, but that is probably so. Still, there is hope; tomorrow, I will apologize, tell them all of your embarrassment, and explain again that you come from a small town."

In other words, sorry about my girlfriend the hick. "What's tomorrow?"

"It is largely devoted to border talks; there will be some touring of Fredericksburg, but no major events. I will call you if anything comes up."

"You think I shouldn't go?"

He hesitated "I think it would be wise to take a day off. I will do my best to excuse your behavior as innocent enthusiasm; then, if tensions aren't too high, you can attend the interpack assembly the next day."

"Great," I said, feeling like someone had punched me in the stomach. "That's like a third of the time I've got to get my father off, and I can't use it."

"All is not lost, Sophie. I will smooth things over, and will ask what questions I can. As I said, the small-town angle may help explain your lack of familiarity with pack rules. And we all know what it's like to be gripped by bloodlust."

If he meant that to be comforting, it wasn't working. I bit my lip. "Oh, and by the way, on the small town thing? You might want to know I told someone I came from St. Paul."

He winced. "Really?"

I nodded, and he sighed. "I will do my best," he said, one hand on the doorknob.

Tom was halfway out the door when I realized that although it was true that the evening hadn't been exactly what I had envisioned—not only had I not found proof of my father's innocence, but I'd managed to piss off the entire pack—I was being a tad churlish. The truth was, even though Tom had a long-standing feud with the Garous—my uncle had murdered his sister, for God's sake—he was taking risks to help me free my father. And here I was, being grumpy.

I closed the gap between us in three steps and touched his arm. "I'm sorry I'm so frustrated tonight. I'm really thankful for everything you're doing to help me."

Tom turned to look at me, and I could feel the heat of his eyes all the way down to my toes. "You're welcome," he said. Then he leaned down and kissed my forehead, very lightly. His eyes burned with something—repressed desire?

I was about to throw all caution to the wind and ask him to stay when the phone rang.

"Better get that," he said.

"Oh. Yeah. You're probably right," I said, flustered.

"I'll call you tomorrow to let you know what I've discovered," he said, and closed the door behind him.

As I ran to get the phone, I felt an emptiness where he had been moments before. My breath was still coming in rapid bursts when I picked up.

"Sophie?"

It was Mark.

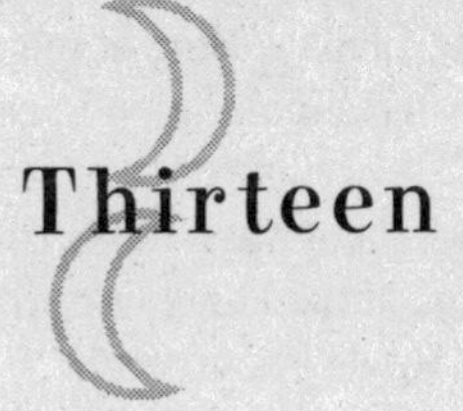

Thirteen

"Mark," I said, still eyeing the door. "Hey."

"Where were you? I tried your cell, but you wouldn't pick up. I was worried about you."

"I was doing some investigating," I said, collapsing on the couch. It had been a long night.

"At the Howl?"

"Exactly. I went with a fake identity."

"Ah. As Tom's girlfriend?"

A shiver went up my spine. "Sort of," I said, wondering exactly how he knew.

"What does Lindsey think of that?"

"I haven't spoken with her."

He chuckled. "I'll bet not. Find out anything interesting?"

"Maybe," I said, running a hand through my abused hair. "Apparently Charles was with someone other than his girlfriend the day he died."

Mark clicked his tongue. "Naughty, naughty," he said. "So you think the perpetrator was a jealous lover?"

"I don't know yet. I kind of made a little error tonight, so Tom's going to try and smooth things over."

"What did you do?"

"I killed a deer."

"You're a werewolf," he said. "Isn't that what you're supposed to do?"

"Not before the alphas have a shot at it." I shuddered,

remembering that awful moment—the deer hanging from my mouth, Elena staring at me with utter disdain, the rest of the werewolves looking on in scorn . . .

"Oops."

I sighed. "Anyway, Tom's going to try to smooth things over for me at the Howl tomorrow, and see what he can find out about Kayla's boyfriend."

"Just give me the word, and I'll break your dad out. Then you won't have to go through all of this charade." He was quiet for a moment. "Assuming it is a charade."

"What do you mean?"

"Tom is an attractive male werewolf."

"So?" I said, glad Mark couldn't see the blood burning in my cheeks. I took a deep breath. "He's my friend's boyfriend. And we're working together to save my father." This jealousy issue—even if it wasn't entirely unfounded—was starting to bug me. Mark, as attractive as he was, was exhibiting some serious symptoms of controlling boyfriend. And I didn't like it one bit.

"You know he's not serious about her."

"How do you know?"

His voice was calm, but it had an edge. "I know many things, Sophie."

A shiver ran down my spine. "You know, Mark, sometimes you're kind of spooky."

"I prefer to see myself as mysterious and intriguing," he said playfully.

"What exactly are you?" I asked, feeling goose bumps rise on my arms. "You were going to tell me the other night, but you never did."

"If you'll let me take you out tomorrow night, and if you're, very, very good," he said seductively, "or maybe very, very bad . . . perhaps you'll be able to wring it out of me."

My first instinct was to refuse—after all, every hour was precious right now, since there weren't very many of them between my father and his appointment with a sharp wooden stake—but the truth was, since I was unofficially banned from the Howl, what else was I going to do? Besides, as usual when I was around Mark, my body was overruling my brain. He just seemed to *do* something to me. "Okay," I said, feeling totally conflicted.

"Such enthusiasm."

"It's been kind of a rough week," I said.

"I'll distract you for a few hours. Where would you like to go?"

"I don't know." I closed my eyes and leaned up against the wall. A little diversion—particularly a diversion that involved my tall, dark, and very handsome client—might be just the ticket right now. Besides, it might give me a chance to bring up some of his rather medieval attitudes toward dating. "Surprise me," I said.

"Always, Sophie," he purred in a voice that made me almost instantaneously moist. "Always."

As it turns out, Midnight Satin did not wash out in ten shampoos. Nor, in fact, did it wash out in twenty shampoos. I would have kept going, but was afraid if I did stop, I'd be dye-free but bald. I tried to look on the bright side. My hair might look like crap, but at least I no longer looked like I'd been frolicking in a slaughterhouse.

After staining yet another set of bath towels with streaky black dye and putting the kettle on for a mug of wolfsbane tea, I grimaced at a strand of my blotchy hair and thought back to Tom's departure. His masculine, wild scent still filled the loft, even though he'd left more than an hour ago, and I felt a pang knowing he was probably with Lindsey right now.

Mark had said Tom wasn't serious about Lindsey. And Kayla seemed to think he was a bit of a playboy. Should I warn Lindsey?

It's not your business, Sophie. I mean, if Lindsey didn't know Tom was a werewolf, that would be one thing. But she was well aware of his animal nature—in fact, she was rather anxious for him to pass some of it on to her. And as far as his dating history was concerned, it wasn't like she was naive; the streets of downtown Austin were littered with her discarded lovers. So why was I so bothered by their relationship?

Because you want Tom for yourself, something inside me whispered.

No, I told the voice. *He's a werewolf with a spotty dating history, and he doesn't even live here. Besides, I would never betray my best friend that way.*

Oh no? the voice replied. *What about that kiss?*

A moment of weakness, after a traumatic experience, I thought, trying to banish the memory of how he tasted, how his body felt pressed up against mine . . . *Besides, I have a date with Mark tomorrow night. He's a much better option.*

But he's your client, the voice whispered. *He sprouts wings, and flames, and gives you weird jewelry that won't come off. And you don't even know what he is.*

I'll find out tomorrow, I told the voice. *If you'll go away and leave me alone, I'll find out. I promise.*

Just to make sure I didn't have any more split-personality moments, I poured myself a small glass of wine and then hit the sack. The day had been long enough already. I'd deal with my hair—and that annoying little voice that kept bringing up unpleasant topics—tomorrow.

"There's another French guy in your office," my assistant Sally informed me as I passed her desk the next morning with my skinny latte in hand.

I stopped short, almost spilling my latte, and whirled to face her. "Why is he in my office?" I asked.

"He said he was a friend." She adjusted the lapel of her sober black suit, and again I found myself wondering what had prompted her wardrobe transformation. I hadn't seen either her rather ripply midriff or anything made of spandex in two weeks.

"Name?" I asked tartly.

"Don't know," she said, shrugging and giving me a funny look. "What happened to your hair?"

My hand shot to my blotchy-looking locks. I'd tried pinning them up, but it only seemed to accentuate the uneven, and frankly unflattering, discoloration. "My hair is . . . well, it doesn't matter what happened to my hair. We're talking about the guy in my office."

"What about him?"

I let out a long breath. "In the future," I said, "would you mind waiting until I'm actually *in* my office before you escort strangers in? And, perhaps, if it's not too much trouble, finding out their names? I've got sensitive documents in there, you know."

"Okay, chief." She glanced at her watch. "It's almost nine. You're late."

"That's not the *point*," I said.

"You've been coming in late a lot lately. Adele mentioned that the other day."

"I'm a partner now," I reminded her, glancing at my office door and taking a deep breath. Yup. Werewolf. Probably Georges, who was *not* on the list of people I really wanted to see today.

"Junior partner," she reminded me.

"Look, Sally. We'll talk about this later. For now, do not let *anyone* in my office without talking to me first."

"Whatever," she said, and returned her attention to her computer.

I did not, I am proud to report, dismember her right there in the middle of the office. Instead, after privately resolving for about the four hundredth time to talk to Adele about finding better help, I straightened my shoulders and prepared myself to prevent my father's assistant from calling in the French werewolf army. Which, unlike the human version, apparently was a force to be reckoned with.

I steeled myself and opened my office door.

When my father had visited me, he had made himself at home behind my desk, but Georges was sitting respectfully in my visitor's chair, looking kind of like a boy who has been sent to the principal's office. Only with thinning hair and a rather natty double-breasted gray suit.

"Hi, Georges," I said, closing the door behind me.

He shot to his feet. "Ms. Garou." His eyes flickered to my hair, but unlike Sally, he was polite enough not to mention that I looked like I was wearing a calico cat on my head.

"Sit down," I said, rounding the desk to plop down in my own chair. I set my latte down and stole a glance at the hike-and-bike trail, which beckoned greenly from twenty stories down. For a brief moment, I found myself wishing I was down there watching the ducks that were tooling around the lake's green surface. Or chasing them. Although in truth, I would have been glad to be just about anywhere but here right about now.

"Have you heard from Mr. Garou?" Georges asked, leaning toward me, his thin face drawn.

"When was the last time you talked with him?" I asked.

"Two days ago. I escorted him to a bar on Sixth Street—Shakespeare's, I believe it is called. He told me he would be back at the hotel that evening, but he never returned." Dark circles ringed his gold eyes. "Of course, at first I imagined he had met with a lady friend, but now . . ." He opened his hands.

Always the lady friends. Dad was quite a Casanova. *Just like Tom.* "You haven't heard from him since then," I confirmed.

"No. And without him, I am not feeling comfortable attending the Howl. There is bad blood there, you see . . ."

"I know," I said, taking a fortifying swig of latte. "I've heard all about the family history."

He sighed. "Then you understand my concern. I am thinking that perhaps I should call Armand."

"No," I said, almost spilling my latte.

He looked puzzled. "Why not?"

"Luc is fine." Of course, "fine" was relative, and perhaps even extremely temporary, but Georges didn't need to know that. Not yet, anyway.

Georges's eyes lit up—he looked a little like a spaniel who had just been offered a nice, crunchy Milk-Bone. "You have spoken with your father?"

"I met with him just last night."

"Where is he?"

"He's . . ." Where? At a spa resort, having his toenails painted? I decided that honesty was the best policy. Partial honesty, anyway. "He's at the Howl," I said.

Georges stood up quickly. "Why did he not take me with him? I must join him there immediately."

"No," I said. "No, no. That would be a very bad idea. And not what Luc wants at all." I gave Georges my most winning smile. "With all the excitement, I forgot to get in touch with you, so I'm really glad you're here. Luc asked me to tell you to lay low for a while."

"Lay low?" he asked, a furrow appearing in his unwrinkled brow. How old was he? I wondered. He looked to be in his late forties. If my father was anything to go on, though, I was guessing I was talking to a werewolf who was at least 500 years old. I was still having a hard time getting my mind around that.

"Wait for him to contact you," I said firmly. "He is undergoing some delicate business." Like being chained to a chair and pissing people off.

"Without my assistance? *C'est impossible*. I *must* be with him. I am *always* with him."

"He forbids it," I said.

He blinked. "Pardon me?"

"He forbids it," I repeated. "He needs to be alone right now. And he needs you to be ready, so that when orders come . . ." I gave him a knowing look.

"So you are in communication with him," Georges said, looking slightly mollified.

"Of course I am." Or at least I had been. After last night's fiasco, my chances of a second chat session with Luc Garou weren't very good, but once again, that was more than Georges needed to know. What had the werewolves made of the broken window? I wondered. I was guessing they wouldn't be leaving him unguarded again.

"Oh," Georges said, gold eyes glinting. "I think I understand now. You are plotting to overthrow the Texas packs so that Paris will have a little southern colony."

"Something like that," I said, thinking, *over my dead body*. Which was, come to think of it, entirely possible.

"Please tell him to call me," Georges pleaded. "I will act with the utmost discretion, as I always have. And certainly Mr. Garou will want his French cousins to come and assist with the coup. Do you have any idea when he is planning the action? I will call them and ask that they prepare . . ."

"Wait," I said quickly. "Let's wait a day or two. I'll talk to him . . . tomorrow. And when I do, I'll get in touch with you immediately. You're at the Driskill, correct?"

"Yes," he said. "Room four hundred and thirty-four. I will be there day and night, awaiting your call."

"Good," I said, meaning it. Because if Georges was at the Driskill, that meant he wasn't finding out all kinds of bad things at the Howl. Which bought me at least a little more time.

"Now, if you will excuse me," I said formally—he seemed to like the formal thing, found it comforting somehow—"I have a meeting to attend."

"Of course, Ms. Garou. Thank you so much for your time."

"My pleasure," I said. "And don't worry. I'll be in touch."

He gave me a flourishy little bow. "I am at your command."

"Excellent," I said, standing up and walking him to the door. He gave me another little bow before heading down the hall with a new spring in his step. I watched him all the way to the elevator.

"Who was that?" Sally asked as soon as the doors slid shut behind him.

"None of your business," I said.

"That's not what you told me ten minutes ago," she pointed out.

I didn't bother responding. But it was definitely time to talk with Adele about finding a new assistant.

At six o'clock, I was putting the final touches on my outfit—a swingy little blue dress I'd picked up on sale at Nordstrom—and trying to do something with my hair. Four more washes had dimmed the splotchiness, but not eliminated it, and unless I wanted to wear a headscarf, there was no real way to hide it.

The depressing thing was, if I was going to go back to the Howl tomorrow, I'd have to dye it black all over again.

As I headed to the kitchen to fix myself a last-minute cup of wolfsbane tea, I glanced at the phone, willing it to ring. Tom hadn't called me with an update yet, and I was on pins and needles.

I still hadn't gotten around to telling my mother what was going on, either. She'd left me five messages over the last couple of days—since she was psychic, it wasn't a surprise that she suspected something was going on—and I hadn't returned any of them. Because if I did, what was I going to tell her? That her ex-lover and the father of her only child was scheduled to be executed unless I called in the French werewolf army?

The teakettle had just begun to whistle when the phone rang. I fumbled to turn off the stove and raced to the phone, heart pounding. *Please God, don't let it be my mother.*

"Sophie?"

It wasn't my mother. It was my ex-boyfriend. "Heath," I croaked, my heart in my throat.

"How are you?" he asked.

"Fine," I lied. "Just fine." And I guess that apart from the whole father-about-to-be-executed thing, everything was going okay. At least my client was happy. That could be because I was sleeping with him, but that was beside the point. "How about you?" I asked in my best light conversational tone.

"Doing great," he said. "Business is really going gangbusters."

"And I hear you and Miranda are hitting it off well," I said, because I couldn't help it. It's not that I wanted to be back together with him. It's just that his recovery time was awfully quick for a guy who'd asked me to marry him six weeks ago.

"We've been seeing a bit of each other, yes," he said coolly. "And I understand you and your client have been rather friendly, too."

"Um, I guess so." If by *friendly* you meant making passionate love several times a week. Touché.

"Anyway, that's not why I called," he said smoothly.

"Why *did* you call?" I asked, glancing at my watch. The client in question was due to arrive at any minute now. "I mean, it's lovely to hear from you and all . . ."

"Lindsey gave me a ring tonight," he said. "She told me you might need some help."

"What?" I barked.

"She mentioned you had reunited with your father."

Dear Lord. What had Lindsey been *thinking*? "I'm not sure if I'd call it *reunited*," I said.

"And that he's had some legal trouble."

"Some legal trouble," I repeated, realizing that the next time I saw my so-called best friend, I might have to kill her. I took a deep breath. "It was sweet of her to think of me, but it's nothing too major."

"That's funny," Heath said. "She told me he's up for homicide."

I blinked. "She *what*?"

"The thing is, though, I looked for it in the papers, and the court records—I know you told me his last name was Garou—and I didn't find anything."

That's because he was charged with homicide by a pack of *supernatural creatures*, I thought. *Shit, shit, shit*. What now?

"Sophie?"

"I'm thinking," I said.

"She told me you wouldn't be thrilled to hear from me," he said, and I could hear a note of disappointment in his voice.

"It's not that," I said. "It's just . . ."

"Sophie, what's going on?" he asked.

I groaned. "If I told you, you wouldn't believe me."

"Try me," he said.

At that moment, thank God, there was a knock on the door.

"Someone's at the door, Heath. I have to go."

"I'm not going to stop calling you until you tell me what's happening. We may not be . . . *together*, but I still care about you."

"Heath . . ."

"Call me when you get in. I don't care how late it is. I'm worried about you."

"Fine," I said. I'd agree to just about anything to get him off the phone. Whoever was at the door knocked again. "Thanks for calling. I'll talk to you later."

"You'd better," he said, and hung up.

Fourteen

I took a deep breath, rearranged the neck-line of my dress, and headed to the door. I knew before I opened it that it was Mark; his smoky smell was already curling up underneath the door.

"Sophie," he said, his blue eyes roaming down and then up me, coming to a rather abrupt stop on my hair. "Wow. That's a new look for you."

I raised a self-conscious hand to my head. "It's temporary. I hope."

"I brought this for you," he said, pulling a single red rose out from behind his back.

"Gosh. Thanks," I said, burying my nose in the red petals. The bloom even smelled good, which was unusual for a store-bought rose. "Come on in, and I'll find a vase."

"Don't mind if I do," he said, following me into my loft and closing the door behind him.

"Did Frank just wave you up?" I asked.

"Sort of," he said. "To be honest, I'm not sure he noticed me." Mark came up behind me as I stood at the sink, filling a vase, and nuzzled my neck in a way that sent all kinds of sensations zinging through me. "So," he said, nibbling my ear, "what's the scoop with your dad?"

"Haven't heard anything yet today," I said, feeling myself tense up just thinking about it. I tucked the rose into the vase, admiring the bloodred petals. "But I'm planning on taking my cell phone tonight."

"Why?"

"In case Tom calls," I said.

"You certainly are dedicated," he said dryly. "Who were you on the phone with just now?"

"Heath."

"Heath? The ex-boyfriend?"

I nodded.

"I thought he was history. After all, from what I've heard, he and Miranda have been pretty hot and heavy lately."

I turned to look at him. "How do you know about his love life, anyway?"

He didn't argue. Instead he gave me a wicked, sultry smile and slid his arms around my waist, pulling me closer.

His lips touched mine—they were hot, as always—and an answering heat welled up inside of me. His warm hands explored my back, running over the smooth fabric of my dress, toying with the clasp of my bra. Already he was hard against me.

I pulled away suddenly, and he opened his eyes, pupils dilated with desire. "What is it?" he asked hoarsely.

"We haven't even had dinner yet," I pointed out, trying to catch my breath. "And besides, you promised you'd tell me what you are tonight." Plus, I had vowed to do two things before I slept with him again: first, address his rather archaic attitudes toward dating; and second, make him tell me exactly what made it possible for his skin to burst into flames on command. I was planning to bring both subjects up during dinner, after a glass or two of wine.

"I didn't promise," he said teasingly, a smile tugging at his mouth. "I said if you were very, very good, you might be able to persuade me."

"What about very, very bad?" I asked, allowing my hand to stray down his flat abdomen. *What are you doing, Sophie?*

What was it about Mark that made my better judgment fly out the window?

He sucked in his breath. "That might work better, actually. I've never been a big fan of Goody-Two-Shoes."

"Good thing," I said, once again wondering where my willpower had gone, and kissed him again. Then, exercising incredible restraint, I pulled away. "Let me go fix my lipstick, and we'll head downstairs. Where are we going?"

"I thought you might be in the mood for steak," he said.

"Only the nonwooden kind," I said. "And only if it's rare."

"Done," he said. "Now, go do what you need to; Ben is waiting downstairs."

Unfortunately, the only place Mark could get a reservation was Ruth's Chris, which wasn't ideal for putting my father's rather unfortunate situation out of my mind. I checked my phone to make sure the ringer was on and ordered a glass of cabernet, trying to push the memory of my father out of my head. When we'd met for dinner, we'd sat just two tables over. Had it really been only a few days since he showed up on my doorstep?

As Mark drank down two martinis, I told him about my faux pas of the earlier evening.

"So you dyed your hair black, took something that made you smell like maple syrup, pretended you were a Swedish girl from Minnesota, and then accidentally stole the big hunting prize from Wolfgang and Elena?"

"In a nutshell, that's it," I said, taking a fortifying swig of wine. It hadn't been a good couple of days.

"Need another?" he asked when I put down an almost empty glass.

"Evidently," I said.

Mark grabbed the bottle and topped it off for me. "But you talked with your father. Is he well?"

"As well as he'll ever be," I said, and told him about Georges's visit to my office this morning.

"So what are you going to do?" he asked, running a long finger around the rim of his glass and staring at me from those deep blue eyes.

"The plan hasn't changed. I'm going to try and prove him innocent. If I can't manage it, I'll consider other options."

"You know my offer stands."

"I know," I said, wondering why I didn't just take him up on it. "And thank you."

He nodded. "What does your mother think?"

"I've never gotten around to telling her," I confessed.

He raised a dark eyebrow. "You didn't tell her about your father?"

"She knows he's here, but . . ."

"She doesn't know he's been charged with murder."

As if on cue, my phone rang. I grabbed my purse and yanked the phone out, hoping it wasn't my psychic mother again.

"Sophie Garou," I barked into the mouthpiece.

"Sophie, It's Tom."

Thank God. "What's going on?"

"I think you're safe to come back tomorrow," he said. "Like I said, I explained that you come from a rather . . . provincial background."

"Provincial?" It wasn't exactly the most flattering explanation, but at this point, I'd probably be okay if he told everyone I was a nymphomaniac who had recently escaped an X-rated circus act. I sighed. "Did you find out anything else about Charles?"

"I did, and it may be helpful . . . but there's something else you need to know."

"What?"

"Elena moved the trial up."

"To when?"

"The day after tomorrow."

Fifteen

"The day after tomorrow? That gives me no time at all." I gripped the phone.

"I think we should meet tonight," he said.

I glanced up at Mark, whose dark blue eyes were intense. He wouldn't be thrilled if I cut our date short, but surely he'd understand. "When?"

"How about an hour? It will take me that long to get back into town."

"My place?"

"I'll see you there."

"What's going on?" Mark asked as I flipped the phone shut and dropped it into my purse.

"Tom needs to meet with me. They've moved the trial up to the day after tomorrow."

"Ouch."

"I told him I'd meet him at my place in an hour."

"What about our date?"

"My dad is going to be perforated with a stake in two days if I can't find a way to prove him innocent. I think that qualifies as extenuating circumstances."

He sighed. "I guess we'd better eat fast, then."

We arrived back at my loft almost an hour later, after speed-eating our way through two strip steaks and an order of sautéed mushrooms. Conversation, unfortunately, had not been particularly stimulating. In part because most of the time we'd been stuffing steak into our mouths, but largely because Mark was obviously less than thrilled that I'd be meeting Tom in about an hour.

"Is everything okay?" I asked as I let us into my loft.

"Fine," he said shortly. "I'm hoping you will at least let me stay until your friend arrives."

"Of course," I said. "Can I get you a drink?"

"What are my options?"

I gave him the rundown—beer, lots of wine, vodka, and a bottle of scotch that I used to keep for Heath. A moment later, I poured him some of Heath's leftover Macallan 12 and myself a small glass of Conundrum, and the two of us sat on the loveseat together.

And waited.

Although conversation between us was usually fluid—not to mention filled with sexual innuendo—things were a bit tense, and we didn't talk too much. I made a few halfhearted attempts to pry into his true identity, but he didn't rise to the bait, and with Tom due to stop by at any moment, sex wasn't a good option. So we sat there watching a rerun of *What Not to Wear* while Mark worked his way through his Macallan. The man must have a cast-iron stomach, I thought as he poured himself a third. He'd had two martinis at Ruth's Chris, too, but he didn't seem even tipsy.

At seven thirty, I couldn't stand waiting anymore, and pulled my phone out and dialed Tom's number. He didn't pick up.

"That's weird," I said.

"Not answering?" Mark asked.

As I shook my head, the phone in my hand rang. I answered it without looking at the number. "Tom!"

"Sophie?"

It was my mother.

"Hey, Mom." I hit the mute button just as Stacy sent a snakeskin bra swan-diving into the trash.

"I didn't know you and Tom were talking. Has anything changed?"

"No," I said. Meaning that Lindsey and Tom were still together, and I was still not interested in dating werewolves.

"That's a shame. But that's not why I called. Why haven't you been returning my calls?" she asked sharply. "Is everything okay?"

"It's been a little . . . busy," I said. "What's up?"

"I've got a bad feeling about tonight. I wanted to make sure you were okay."

"I'm fine," I said. "You worry too much."

"Well, *stay* fine. And don't go anywhere if you can help it. There's something in the air tonight . . ."

I shifted a little on my love seat, but said nothing.

"What about your father?" my mother asked. I *knew* she'd ask about him. Having a psychic parent can be a real pain sometimes.

"What about him?" I asked lightly.

"What do you think? Are you two speaking? Is he getting on with the Texas packs? Has he been able to fill you in on all the things you missed? I'm surprised I haven't heard from him. Although maybe I shouldn't be," she said, and I caught a hint of bitterness I hadn't heard before. I guess if you spent almost thirty years building up someone's memory in your mind and they show up and turn out to be a schmuck after all, it can be a bit of a letdown.

"He's gotten himself into a little bit of a political trouble," I said vaguely, watching as Stacy held up a hot pink tube top, "but I'm sure he'll come out unstaked. I mean *unscathed*."

Mark snorted beside me, and I elbowed him hard.

"Sophie. What's happening? What's going on?"

"Apparently there's some history between Luc and the leaders of the Houston pack," I said. "They're working out a few issues."

I could hear her sigh of relief. "Thank the goddess he's okay. And you. But I'm just *sure* something awful is going to happen. I did a reading, and the Devil and the Death cards were extremely prominent. I even did a second spread, for clarification, and the same two cards kept turning up."

"Didn't you once tell me that the Death card meant change?" I suggested.

"Not in a spread like this," she said ominously.

"I'll be very, very careful," I promised, wondering if the cards in the reading were somehow related to my father. *Should* I call in the French werewolf brigade?

"You'd *better* be careful," she said. "I don't want to lose you. And you never did stop by to pick up your wolfsbane," she reminded me.

"I know," I said. "Sorry. I'll swing by as soon as I can."

"Don't do anything rash, sweetheart. If I lost you . . ." Her voice swelled with love.

"You won't," I assured her.

"I wish I could be sure of that."

Just then, there was a knock at the door.

"Mom, there's someone here to see me. Can I call you later?"

"Don't go out if you can help it!" she said.

"I won't," I said, and after telling her I loved her, I flipped the phone shut, turned off the TV, and headed for the door.

It was Tom.

"What took you so long?" I asked, breathing in that wildly erotic scent of his. Only there was something different about it tonight. Something coppery, like blood . . .

He gave me a lopsided grin, then turned to the side so I could see what was left of his jeans on the right side of his leg. "The motorcycle hit an oil slick," he said. "So I was a bit delayed."

I stared at the hamburger-like consistency of his leg and the hole in the elbow of his gorgeous leather jacket. "That must have been some fall. I'm glad you didn't get yourself killed."

"So am I," he said, gold eyes glinting.

"Shouldn't we be taking you to the hospital?" I asked, staring at what was left of his leg. Strips of bloody denim hung around it, and the muscle was exposed in several places. "God, that looks awful."

"It will heal quickly," he said. "If you'll let me use your bathroom to clean up . . ." He broke off what he was saying and raised his head sharply. A moment later, Mark stepped up behind me, and the smile faded from Tom's tanned face. "Oh," he said, and I could sense him bristling. "I didn't realize you had company."

"It's okay. Come on in," I told Tom. "Mark won't bite." I glanced at Mark, who had a strange smile on his face. "Will you?" I asked.

"Not unless provoked," Mark said lightly.

Despite the fact that his right leg looked like it had fought—and lost—a battle with a meat grinder, Tom gave Mark a long, measured look before limping to my bathroom. He refused my offer to help him pick out the gravel. "Just show me where the alcohol and the gauze are, and I'll be fine," he said.

I raided the first-aid kit and laid out what he'd requested on the bathroom counter. "I'm a little short on gauze—do you want me to run and get some?"

"I'll be fine," he repeated.

I glanced at his leg, not convinced. Shreds of denim were embedded in the flesh, as were a number of rather large chunks of gravel. "So you rode the rest of the way here like that?"

He nodded.

"Ouch." I watched as he picked the first piece of gravel from his leg. "Are you sure I can't help you?" I asked. Not that I had much experience picking gravel out of hamburger meat, but I felt I should offer.

Tom's eyes strayed to Mark, who leaned against the doorway of the bathroom as Tom lowered himself onto the side of the bathtub. "It will be all right," he said quietly, his eyes fixed on my client.

"Let me know if you need anything else," I said, suddenly very uncomfortable.

"I wouldn't mind an aquavit, actually."

"Fresh out of aquavit, I'm afraid." As if anyone who hadn't grown up in Norway stocked the stuff. "How about a beer, or some scotch?"

He grimaced and dug another piece of debris out of his thigh. "Better make it scotch."

"Got it." I walked past Mark and poured a large glass of the medicinal-smelling liquid, trying not to breathe in the fumes. I'd had the bottle around for almost a year now, but at this rate, it would be empty before the night was through.

"Maybe he needs to go to a defensive-driving class," Mark said as we sat down on the love seat a minute later. He slung an arm over my shoulder and drew me closer to him, which normally would have been enough to set off an explosive chemical reaction in me. And I did feel a stirring, as I always did when he touched me. I looked up into his deep blue eyes, wondering what it was about him that made me so wanton. And wondering what exactly he was, come to think of it.

But with Tom digging bits of road out of himself in my bathroom—not to mention my rather tenuous family situation—it wasn't the best moment to indulge my carnal impulses. When Mark leaned over to nuzzle my earlobe, I pulled away a little bit.

"Mark," I said, reaching over to squeeze his leg gently. "I was thinking, maybe we should just get together another night. It's hard to be romantic with . . . company," I said, pointing toward the bathroom door.

He stared at the closed door for a moment. "You want me to leave you here with Tom?"

"It's not what I *want*," I said.

His eyes flickered. "Are you certain?"

"Of course, Mark!" I said, feeling flustered. "It's just that under the circumstances . . ."

"Call me Ash," Mark said urgently.

"Ash?"

"Ashmodei," he said, his voice strange.

"Ashmodei," I whispered, and my whole body flushed with heat, which seemed to be emanating from—or centering on—the ring Mark had given me. The moment I spoke the name, Mark stood in a fluid movement, eyes burning with barely suppressed desire. He pulled me up after him and pressed my body to his, igniting a wave of lust that—Tom or no Tom—had me wanting to rip his clothes off and push him right back down onto the love seat.

He looked down at me and ran a finger along my chin. Slowly, seductively, so that I couldn't help wanting him to take it further . . . "I will accede to your request," he said formally, his voice with a hint of an accent—which was strange, since I hadn't ever noticed it before. "But remember," he continued, staring at me from those incredible eyes, "that you belong to me."

There's that whole possessive thing again, some distant, disconnected portion of my mind whispered. But my body was in the driver's seat; and it just didn't care. Mark's smoky smell intensified, kindling a matching response deep inside me, and for a moment I thought I saw a blue flame flicker in those dark, dark pupils. Then he lowered his mouth to mine and kissed me with an intensity that left me gasping for breath.

As I stood by the love seat, panting, he bowed slightly, his eyes never leaving mine. "I will call you tomorrow," he said. "In the meantime, as your mother said . . . be careful."

"I will," I whispered, desperate for him to stay, to keep touching me . . .

But after one last kiss, he strode to the door and was gone.

Sixteen

By the time Tom emerged from the bathroom with a giant wad of gauze poking out from under what remained of his jeans, I was halfway through a mug of wolfsbane tea and had managed to regain my composure. Or at least most of it.

"Doing better?" I asked.

"I've been worse," he said. "If I could trouble you for another scotch—and a couple of ibuprofen?"

"Coming right up," I said. Normally, I was cautious about mixing drugs with alcohol, but from what I'd seen of his leg, Tom needed all the medicinal help he could get.

"Where's your friend?" Tom asked, sniffing the air and looking around as I retreated to the kitchen to refill his glass.

"He left," I said.

"I'm surprised."

"Why?"

"He seems quite possessive of you."

I couldn't argue with him there. "So, you hit an oil slick," I said, anxious to change the subject. "It's a good thing you weren't killed."

"We werewolves are tougher than we look," he said. "It was strange, though—I know I hit something slick, but afterward, when I looked at the road, I saw nothing. And I have never had an accident before."

"Maybe it was just a little bit of gravel," I said. "There was certainly enough of it embedded in your leg. Did you get it all out?"

"I think so," he said, taking another swig of scotch. "It should be healed in a day or two."

"Seriously?"

"Like I said, we werewolves are tougher than we look." He stood in the living room, seeming to take up half the space. I struggled to catch my breath.

"How did the Howl go?" I asked. "Am I still totally on the outs?"

He chuckled. "It took a bit of persuading, but they didn't totally ban you. I just explained that after years in a small-town pack, the excitement of a big Howl kind of clouded your judgment. You can come back, but you'll have to be on your best behavior."

I let out the breath I had been holding. "That's something, at least."

"They're suspicious of you, though. They found the broken window in the garden cottage. If it weren't for me vouching for you . . ."

"Thanks," I said.

"Just be sure to stay away from it next time. Don't even look at it, if you can help it. I think Elena's on to you."

"I'm not surprised," I said. Elena seemed destined to be a thorn in my side.

"I also discovered a few things about Charles," he said, lowering himself onto the love seat where Mark had been just twenty minutes earlier. His biceps bulged impressively, and the gauze on his elbow stretched and threatened to pop off. I forced myself not to stare at him. After Mark's kiss, my sex drive was still in high gear. And Tom's musky werewolf smell, overlaid with what remained of Mark's smoky scent, was doing all kinds of things to my hormones.

"Oh?" I asked.

"Apparently he wasn't quite as devoted to Kayla as he should have been."

"That's what my father said. What was going on?"

"Rumor has it that he was involved with another woman. A powerful woman, although no one seems to know exactly who. Some say she is from Louisiana."

Men, I thought. Well, men and male werewolves. I sat up. "Do you think Kayla killed him because he was having an affair?"

Tom's eyebrows rose. "I thought you said Kayla was in Galveston."

"Maybe she wasn't. Maybe it was just a cover story."

"It's worth looking into."

"The problem is, how?" I slumped into the love seat, my desire fizzling at the reminder of my father's tenuous situation. "I don't even know where to begin."

"Do you want to go back to the Howl tonight?"

"Is it a good idea? I mean, the whole buck thing is pretty fresh."

He shrugged. "Today, tomorrow—what difference will a night make?"

"Good point," I said. "But how are we going to get there?" I pointed to his leg.

"You do have a car, don't you?"

I nodded. "But if I'm going as Inga, it's a problem. It's got Texas plates. Besides, my hair is still splotchy; I'd have to redye it."

"Then we will wait until tomorrow, then. Hopefully by then my leg will be healed."

"I hate to lose the time, though. Besides, I think your leg will probably take longer than a day to heal," I said.

"Maybe. Or maybe not." He raised his glass. "May I have another scotch?"

"Absolutely," I said, getting up to refill it. "How can you stand to drink that stuff? It makes my nose hairs curl."

He laughed as I handed him his refilled glass. "Years of

practice," he said as I settled into the love seat with my own glass, which I'd topped off with wine. After all, I wouldn't want my guest to have to drink alone.

"So," I said, reclining into the cushions across from Tom and taking a deep breath of his werewolf aroma. Despite the circumstances, there was something delightfully intimate about having him in my living room, and my body was very aware that only a short expanse of leather loveseat separated us. I took a sip of wine. "While I've got you here, I've been meaning to ask a few questions."

"Shoot," he said, with a hint of challenge in his golden eyes. The light gleamed on his golden hair; he looked like central casting's top pick for the leader of a Norse pantheon.

I took a long, deep breath. "I've got lots of questions, really. Like, how come you're not part of a pack? You seem to be one of the only werewolves I've met who's solo. And how was it that your sister was married to Wolfgang?"

The glint went out of Tom's eyes, and he swirled the scotch in his glass. The amber liquid was almost the same color as his eyes. "It is a long story."

"If we're not going to the Howl, I've got nothing but time," I said. "Besides, I'm curious about how the whole werewolf world works. Maybe I'll learn something that will help me get my father off." I toyed with my own glass. "Tell me about your family. Do you have any brothers or sisters? Other than Astrid, I mean?" I said quickly, remembering that my uncle had dispatched her personally.

"I have one brother," he said slowly, staring at the contents of his glass. "His name is Svend Fenris."

"Is he in one of the Norwegian packs?"

"He is the alpha of the Oslo pack, like my father before him."

"Wow. So your family is kind of high up in the rankings, too," I said.

He nodded. "The Oslo pack is one of the oldest and most powerful; it is very large, and encompasses most of Norway."

"What made you decide to leave?"

He looked up at me with an intensity in his eyes that made it hard to look away. "Do you know anything about how alphas were traditionally chosen?"

"No. I always assumed it was a lineage thing."

"To some extent, it is. It used to be more so, particularly in the old country. The aristocracy passed down through the blood, but that has changed over the last hundred years."

"So it goes to the oldest son, like in the human aristocracy?"

"It goes to the son, or daughter," he said. "But not necessarily the oldest. The strongest."

"Oh."

"In most cases there is a battle for supremacy," he said.

"What about your case? Did you have to fight your own brother?"

"No," he said quietly. "I stepped aside and left the pack."

"Wow. He'd turned down a chance to be alpha. "Why did you do it?"

A muscle twitched in his cheek, and I could smell the tension in him; it was obvious that although this had happened quite some time ago, the pain was still pretty fresh. "If we had fought, I would have had to kill him. He would never have given up the role of alpha; he would sooner have died."

"So if you won, you'd lose a brother."

He nodded. "I stepped aside. And I do not regret my decision."

I leaned toward him a little, wanting to comfort him somehow. But I couldn't. "Honestly?" I asked.

Tom shrugged, sending a ripple through his muscular back. "To be alpha? That was never my calling. But . . ."

"But what?"

He sighed. "The role of alpha was not the only thing lost to me."

"What do you mean?"

He grimaced. "Her name was Beate."

"Oh," I said, feeling something turn in my stomach. I knew Tom and Lindsey were dating, but this was somehow . . . different. "You lost your girlfriend because of it."

Tom looked away. "She was more than that, really. We were betrothed."

Ah. "How exactly did you lose her?" I asked, suddenly afraid that the answer would be that one of my relatives dismembered her, or fed her mistletoe, or drove a wooden stake through her heart.

"She did not die," he said, as if reading my mind. "She is still alive, and in Norway."

"What happened?"

"Our plight was trothed; the joining was scheduled. Then my parents both died during an outbreak of distemper. They caught the disease at our summer den, in Trondheim. My siblings and I were at my aunt's home in the north at the time, and the disease did not reach us."

I drew in my breath. And I thought I had it bad because my father abandoned me. "Jesus. I'm so sorry."

"It was a long time ago."

"They died of distemper? I didn't realize that was a big issue for werewolves. I mean, I thought you could only kill them with a silver bullet, or a wooden stake. Or ripping their throats out," I said, remembering the unfortunate Charles.

"Oh, yes. Distemper can be fatal, and before the vaccines, it was a real problem. It's a terrible disease. Very painful." As he spoke, I started to worry. I'd been hanging out with tons of strange werewolves, and although I'd gotten my MMR shots, I'd never asked my doctor to give me a distemper vaccination. Somehow it had just never come up during my routine (and nerve-racking—after all, I wasn't entirely human) checkups. Would my human genes be enough to prevent me from catching it?

I suddenly realized that Tom was still talking. "I'm sorry. The whole distemper thing kind of threw me off. Could you repeat that?" I asked.

"I was saying that with my parents' deaths, the issue of succession arose."

"Between you and your brother. Why wasn't Astrid involved?"

"She was already plighted to Wolfgang, and would reign as the alpha in Strasbourg."

"So it was up to you and Svend, and you stepped aside rather than kill him."

"Yes. But there were consequences to my actions. When I abdicated, Beate's mother considered the betrothal null. She had only agreed to it with the understanding that I would reign as alpha. I was always larger and stronger, so the outcome was assumed."

"Why couldn't the two of you run away together?"

"We considered it. But where would we have gone?"

"I don't know. America? Everything seems to be a bit more loosey-goosey here."

He gave me a wry smile that tugged at my heart. "But Sophie, my dear, you forget. All of this happened a long time ago. The New World hadn't been discovered yet," he said.

Hadn't been *discovered* yet? *Dear God.* "Exactly how long ago are we *talking*, Tom?"

"Just over six hundred years."

"Six hundred years," I repeated, having a hard time believing he was telling me about an ill-fated love affair that had occurred more than half a millennium ago. I mean, I considered my first high school crush, which was only thirteen years ago, ancient history. Granted, we'd never gotten engaged or anything, but Steve Barclay's defection to a perky member of the cheerleading squad had been a pretty big deal at the time. We were talking six hundred years here. And Tom was still carrying a torch?

"What happened to her?" I asked. "To Beate?"

Tom's lips twisted into a wry smile. "She joined with Svend, of course, as her mother told her to. They've been a happy family ever since. Lots of pups to fight for the right to succeed them."

I winced. "Ouch. I can see why you decided to leave home."

"I'm glad you understand," he said wryly.

"So where did you learn all these special skills of yours?" I asked, hoping to move to a less sensitive subject. "You know, the werewolf-unmaking and all that?"

"Svend, Astrid, and I were all trained in the old ways by our Aunt Freya," he said. "She was a very powerful werewolf; she could easily have taken the role of alpha if she'd wanted to. But she preferred to live alone in the woods, providing her services to the pack when required."

"And training the three of you," I said.

"She tried, yes. We spent several summers under her tutelage. But I was the only one who really had the talent."

"Kind of like my mom," I said.

"In what way?" he asked.

"The magic. She's got it."

"As do you," Tom said.

I snorted. "Hardly. The most magical thing I do is transforming a few times a year, and everybody does that." Everybody who is a werewolf, anyway. "But I have another question. It seems like you and Wolfgang have been allies for a long time, even though you're not from the same pack. Is it just because he was married to your sister?"

"In Europe," he said, "there are individual packs within each country, but they ally in larger groups. In the north, Scandinavia, Germany, and Switzerland are allied. There is another bloc in the Slavic countries, and in the south, Spain, France, and Italy tend to support each other."

Wow. I had no idea werewolf politics were so complicated. "So you were lending assistance not just as a brother-in-law, but as a political ally."

"Yes," he said. "But there is more to it than that. We are also cousins."

"Wait a minute. If *you* were cousins, that means your sister and Wolfgang were cousins, too. Isn't that illegal or something?"

"Cousin marriage has always been common in aristocracies," Tom pointed out. "Both *lupin* and human."

"You call them *lupins* too?"

He nodded. "Sometimes. We go by many names: *varulv*, loup-garou, *vukodlak, kveldulf, nagual* . . ."

"Sounds better than werewolf, at least," I said, rubbing my temples and trying to absorb what Tom had told me. After a few moments, I gave up and took another swig of wine. "So Wolfgang's beef with my dad has got the whole historical ally thing going on. Plus he's still pissed about losing Alsace."

"Correct."

"Which means my father's chances of escaping execution are just about nil."

"Unless you want to call in the French and start a war, you may be right," he said softly.

"Don't you think they're going to want to avenge him if he dies anyway?"

"Perhaps," he said, giving me a pointed look. "Although that would depend on who succeeds him."

"What?"

"It would depend on who succeeds him," he repeated slowly.

"Oh," I said, suddenly realizing the implications of what he was suggesting. "You mean . . . *me*?"

Seventeen

"Yes," Tom said. "You would be the natural heir to your father's position."

I shook my head. "No way."

"No? Why not? Many werewolves would kill for the opportunity. It is a very prestigious position."

"You turned it down," I reminded him.

"Yes, I did. Because I didn't want to murder my own brother. But you have no sibling to battle with."

"Even so. I've never even *been* to France. And how can I be alpha of the Paris pack when I barely speak French?" I mean, I knew what a croissant was, but after three years of foreign language classes, that was about all I remembered. That and prêt-à-porter.

Tom shrugged. "Astrid did not speak German until she went to Strasbourg. If you choose to take the position, that obstacle can easily be overcome."

"The Paris pack wanted to kill me when I was born!"

"They didn't know about you," he pointed out calmly. "And things have changed substantially over the last fifty years."

"And what about the current female alpha?" I asked, realizing I'd never found out if there was one. "She's not going to want to step down for me, so it's a moot point anyway. Luc said something about someone named Elise; she must be the alpha, right?"

Tom shook his head. "Your father has never partnered with anyone."

"And how did my father become alpha, anyway? Isn't there some kind of succession thing?"

"He was part of the royal family," Tom said, "but rather distantly related, and not in direct line. When the previous alpha died, he had only a weak son to replace him—he had suffered an accident that left him mentally disabled."

"So what happened?"

"Your father challenged him. And won."

"And they just handed the position to him?"

"He had, of course, been gaining political allies for some time. Your father is a very intelligent man."

"Intelligent werewolf," I corrected him.

"Werewolf, then."

I sighed. "So there are no other children in line."

"Correct."

"Won't someone else just step into his shoes, then?"

"They will ask you first."

I took another swig of wine and set the glass down with a bang. "I'm not interested."

"Are you certain?"

I turned to look at him. Was he serious? "Of course I'm certain."

"Certain enough to renounce all rights, eternally?"

"I guess so. Why?"

"Because if you do not take the mantle, that is what your father's successor will require of you. Either that, or death."

I swallowed hard. "Wonderful."

We were quiet for a moment, each lost in our own rather unpleasant reveries. Then Tom spoke. "I brought you something. It is why I wanted to meet tonight."

"What is it?"

"It's in my jacket pocket. Over by the door."

I retrieved the jacket for him—our fingers touched as I handed it to him, sending a pleasant little current through me—and watched as he dug in the left-hand pocket and pulled out a small book. He tossed it to me. "Take a look."

I caught it, along with a hefty whiff of dust. The cover was leather, and the pages were yellowed with age. Embossed on the front, in gold letters, were the words *Codex Werwolfarius*.

I opened it up to a random page; it was filled with dense text that looked like it was in German.

"What am I supposed to do with this?"

"Turn it around and upside down," he said.

I did. On the back, in the same faded gold ink, were the words *The Code of the Werewolves*. Goose bumps rose on my arms as I touched the soft leather.

"Where did you get this?" I asked.

"I retrieved it from Wolfgang's farmhouse," he said. "There are very few in print, and they are jealously guarded, lest they fall into the wrong hands."

Human hands, I thought.

"I figured you needed it more than he did," he continued. "That's why I wanted to see you tonight. If you're going to defend your father, it will help to know what the rules are."

So the infamous "code" was an actual document. And one that had been around the block a few times, from the look of it. I flipped to a page at random. *Rules Concerning the Hunting of Humans,* it read. Yikes. "How up to date *is* this, exactly?"

"Some of the sections are antiquated," he said. "This is an older version; some of the hunting rules have changed in newer editions."

"I hope so," I said, reading further. Apparently women and children were verboten, at least.

"But the rules regarding the Howl—and the trial protocol—are still in force."

I was still staring at the entry in the book. *Packs must limit their human kills to two per month.* Good lord.

"Please tell me they don't hunt humans anymore," I said.

"No. And it was never particularly common, thankfully, but since the advent of forensics, it's been strictly forbidden."

I'd like to think it was more than the risk of being caught that would prevent my fellow werewolves from running down and tearing apart humans, but what the hey. "How old is this book?"

"I think that's the 1850s edition. It was printed in two languages specifically for the Anglo-German population in Texas."

"So it was still all right to hunt people then," I said. "Even here, in Texas."

"It was legal, but it wasn't done much," he said.

Even so, a shiver ran down my back. Many of the Texas packs had made their fortune rustling cattle, Tom had once told me. Did that include hunting down the cowboys who guarded them? Tom could probably tell me, but I wasn't sure I wanted to know.

I flipped through the pages of the *Codex*. It was thrilling, somehow, to see the mysterious "code" in actual black and white—even if parts of it were downright repulsive. I closed it and set it gingerly on the coffee table. "I don't know how to thank you, Tom. When do you need it back?"

"I did not request permission to borrow it, so it would be best if you returned it to me tomorrow. I suggest you make a copy and return it to me when I come to pick you up for the Howl."

I'd almost forgotten; I'd have to have another session with my bottle of Midnight Satin. Would I have any hair left by the end of the week? Not that my hair was my first priority, of course, but I didn't want to have to attend my father's execution bald. "What's on the agenda tomorrow, anyway?" I asked, almost afraid to hear the answer.

"It's the night of the assembly," he said.

"What's that?"

"Kind of an inter-pack council, where things like matings,

alliances, and inter-pack issues are brought up before the alphas and voted on."

"The alphas get to vote on matings?"

He shrugged. "Werewolf society is very hierarchical," he said.

"A bit too hierarchical, if you ask me." Despite the fact that my father was bound to be on the agenda—and my feelings in general with the rather feudal way werewolf society appeared to be run—I found myself curious about the proceedings. It was bound to be more interesting than the annual auditor conferences I attended, in any case. "Are you sure you'll be up to going?" I asked, eyeing his leg.

"Absolutely. It's a minor wound."

If what had happened to his leg was minor, I didn't want to imagine what he considered major. Amputation?

He finished the rest of his scotch and glanced at his watch. "I should leave you now," he said, levering himself up out of my couch.

"Do you need a ride to . . . to wherever you're staying?" I didn't want to ask if it was at Lindsey's place. "You had a lot of scotch"—half the bottle, in fact—"and after that motorcycle accident . . ." I took a deep breath, inhaling his musky, wolfie scent. "You know you can always stay here."

"Oh?" His eyebrow rose jauntily, and the level of pheromones in my living room just about tripled. There was what I guess you'd call a pregnant pause, then he said, "What a tempting invitation."

I felt my cheeks flush with heat. I'd never been with a werewolf before, and I often found myself wondering all kinds of things about Tom, in particular the fit body beneath his leather jacket, jeans, and now, wads of gauze. The stolen kiss we had shared stirred something deep, deep inside me—I might go so far as to call it something animal. What would it be like to have him in my bed? To feel his warm lips on my skin? To wake up with my head on his muscular chest?

To explain to Lindsey that I'd slept with her boyfriend?

Stupid reality—always interfering with my fantasy life. "On the couch," I finally said. I was nothing if not a good friend.

"Pity." Our eyes locked for a moment, and all kinds of images flashed through my head. Me running a hand across his chest, tasting his salty skin. His mouth trailing down my neck, pushing aside the fabric of my blouse . . .

Down, girl.

"Ah, well," he said, slinging his jacket over his shoulder. "Perhaps another time. I imagine Mark wouldn't approve anyway."

No, he wouldn't. "Lindsey wouldn't be too excited about it either," I reminded him, watching as he limped to the door. Even with the wound on his leg, he had the grace of a predator at the top of his form. "Speaking of Lindsey, is she still bugging you about becoming a werewolf?" I asked.

His lips twitched into a smile. "Constantly."

"What are you going to do about it?"

"I will have to make a change. Soon."

I drew in my breath. "And by 'make a change,' you mean exactly . . . what?"

"I haven't decided yet," he replied.

Was Tom thinking of making her a werewolf? Or breaking up with her? He *did* have a reputation as a womanizer, after all. "Would you do me a favor?" I asked.

"What?"

I took a deep breath. "Please don't make Lindsey a werewolf."

He cocked an eyebrow at me. "Is it so bad, then?"

"It hasn't been the thrill of a lifetime, no," I confessed. Sure, I might have great skin into my nineties—or even longer. But I wasn't sure it was worth all the inconvenience. Not to mention the cost of razors.

"I'll take your concern into consideration," he said. "I will pick you up tomorrow. Can you be here by five?"

"No problem. I'll leave work a little early," I said.

When the door closed, I sank back into the love seat, trying to take it all in. Centuries-old European werewolf wars, fiery, wing-sprouting boyfriends, hot, forbidden werewolves, impending executions, antique human-hunting rules . . .

At least I couldn't complain that life was dull.

Eighteen

I'd barely sat down behind my desk the next morning before Lindsey was in my visitor's chair, looking fetching as always in a navy pantsuit and low-cut red blouse. Her long brown hair shone in the light from the window, and I found myself wondering if she'd spent the night with Tom.

"What's going on?" she asked.

"Have you talked with Tom?"

"I called him last night, but I haven't heard back. No one tells me anything!"

I'm ashamed to admit it, but hearing that Tom hadn't slept at Lindsey's made me feel better. "He had a motorcycle accident last night," I told her.

Her gray eyes grew round. "Oh, my God! Is he okay?"

"He's fine. His leg's a little torn up, but it will mend."

Then her eyes narrowed. "How come you know about it and I don't?"

"Close the door," I said. As Lindsey walked to the door, I

reached into my briefcase and pulled out the book Tom had given me last night, dropping it on the desk. A little puff of dust blew out of it. "He brought me this," I said.

She picked it up gingerly. "*Codex Werwolfarius*? What's that?"

"Turn it over," I said.

"*The Code of the Werewolves*," she read, then sucked in her breath. "Wow . . . how cool! I didn't know it was an actual book. I thought it was just . . . I don't know. Understood."

"So did I."

She leafed through it, touching the pages with something like reverence, and looked up at me. "Did he drop this off at your loft last night?"

I nodded, and her gray eyes narrowed.

"Why?"

"It's to help me defend my father. It lays out the basic werewolf laws," I said as she flipped through the pages.

"Yikes. Rules for hunting humans?" she asked, reminding me why werewolves were rather cautious about the book's distribution. Perhaps if Lindsey spent some time going through the gorier aspects of pack rules and regulations, it would be a nice little werewolf prophylactic, if you know what I mean.

"I have to make a copy and return it to Tom tonight," I said. "If you want, I'll make you one, too, so you can read it. And decide if this is something you really want."

She flipped a few pages and made a face. "Ick. You have to get approval from the pack leader to mate?"

"Like I said, the whole fur-and-fangs thing has its drawbacks."

"Surely this is outdated," she said. "When was this printed, like the 1700s or something? It looks ancient."

"It's from the 1850s, according to Tom. And some of it may be out of date," I confessed. "But not all of it. The sections on Howl rules and on trials are all supposedly current.

And I know the mating approval thing is still in force, at least here."

She thought about that for a moment, then returned her attention to the book on her lap. "How about this human-hunting-rules thing? Is that still on the books?"

"Not so much," I admitted. "But only because I think they're afraid of being caught."

"That makes sense," she said, nodding.

Makes sense? It didn't bother her that the group she was dying to join spent so much time killing people that they needed to *regulate* it? Not outlaw it, mind you . . . but *manage* it? It was like reading the Texas hunting code, only replacing *deer* with *person.*

"This should help us with your dad's defense," she said, flipping through the section on the Howl rules. "He can appoint someone to represent him, it looks like."

"Speaking of appointing people," I said. "Who appointed *you* to tell Heath about my father?"

"Oh," she said in a small voice. "He called you, then."

"Yes," I said, "he did. And oddly enough, he couldn't find any reference to my father's murder trial in the court records."

"That *would* be a challenge," she admitted.

"Lindsey," I said. "This whole werewolf thing may seem like a game to you, but it's not. If the wrong people find out about me, I don't know what would happen. They might kill me, or stick me in a cage for observation for the rest of my life."

"But . . ."

Before she could say anything more, there was a firm knock at the door, and it swung open.

It was Heath.

"Sophie," he said, walking in and shutting the door behind him. He looked good enough to eat, as always, in khakis and a brown-striped oxford that picked up the chocolate color of his eyes. The smoky scent of Miranda clung to him, along with the more familiar aroma of CK1 and laundry starch;

either they were sharing the same office these days or Mark had been right about Heath's increasingly intimate relations with his lovely associate.

For a long moment, I sat there staring at my ex-boyfriend, unable to think of a thing to say. Unfortunately, that was what Lindsey was doing, too, which wasn't a very good plan, because what she should have been doing was finding somewhere to put the *Codex Werwolfarius*.

"Heath," I said in a strangled voice.

"What happened to your hair?" he asked.

"It was an experiment that didn't work," I said vaguely, finally finding my voice. I darted a glance at Lindsey and attempted to communicate telepathically. *Hide the book, you idiot!*

But of course she didn't. "What brings you here?" I asked Heath.

"I told you I wasn't going to stop bothering you until you told me what I could do to help," he said. His eyes alighted on Lindsey. "And you're here, too. Great."

"Yes," I said feebly.

"What's that?" he said. And then it happened, in what seemed like slow motion. Heath reached down and plucked the book from Lindsey's hands. She made a small squeaky sound as he looked at the cover. "*Codex Werwolfarius*? Weird title."

"It's nothing," I said, standing up and making a grab for it. But before I could pry it from his hands, Heath flipped it over and saw the English title.

"*The Code of the Werewolves*? Lindsey, what *is* this?"

"It's . . . it's . . ." As I stood tongue-tied, watching him in horror, he started flipping through the pages. Had I spent the last year of my life struggling to keep my true nature under wraps, only to have him discover it six weeks after we broke up? "Mating customs, ruler succession, dueling . . ." He looked up at me. "What is this, some kind of joke book?"

"Sort of," I said.

But he had stopped on a page near the end. "Execution procedures," he read. "The prescribed methods are impalement with a wooden stake or shooting. If shooting is the selected method, it must be undertaken with ammunition containing at least fifty percent silver to ensure effectiveness." He looked up at me. "What the hell is this?"

"It's nothing," I said, finally finding my voice. "Lindsey found it in a secondhand store the other day, and thought it was cool."

He read further. "This looks *real*."

"It does, doesn't it?" I asked lightly, then glanced pointedly at my watch. "I hate to break things up, but it's not the best time. It's great to see you, but can we get in touch later? I've got a meeting to go to."

"Sophie," he said, looking at me levelly. "Why does it make you so uncomfortable that I'm looking at this book?"

"I'm not uncomfortable," I said, while promising myself that I would never again consent to dating a trial attorney. Cross-examination was Heath's specialty—and cross-examination was the last thing in the world I wanted to deal with just now. "I'm just a little stressed, that's all. About my father," I said, because I couldn't think of anything else to say.

"Why do you have this book?"

"Um . . . it's not mine. Lindsey found it. At Half Price books."

"I didn't know you two were into weird stuff like this. Then again, with your mother's magic shop, maybe I shouldn't be surprised." He shrugged. "But that's not why I'm here. I want to help you, but I need some more information. I can't find your father's name anywhere in the records."

"That's because . . ." Lindsey said, and stopped when I shot her a furious look.

"Because what?" Heath said. "Because he's a werewolf?"

Lindsey just sat there with her mouth open.

Oh my God. This couldn't be happening. Couldn't be. Heath had been *joking*. And Lindsey, sitting there gaping like a fish. She might as well just go ahead and let the cat—or in this case the wolf—out of the bag.

"Don't be ridiculous," I said quickly.

Heath looked at the book in his hands. He flipped through the pages, squinting at the text. "This isn't a joke book, is it?" Heath asked quietly.

"Of course it is," I said.

He turned to Lindsey then, disbelief on his handsome features. "You think Sophie's father is a werewolf," Heath said.

Nineteen

Why, oh why had I dated a man with such excellent courtroom instincts?

Neither of us said anything, and after a rather awkward couple of seconds, he turned to me. "What's going on, Sophie?"

Lindsey finally found her voice. "You need his help, Sophie."

"No," I barked. "Not that much."

"He deserves to know," she said.

I closed my eyes. Was she right? Or would he totally freak out if I told him?

"What do I deserve to know?" Heath asked. Even though

my own eyes were closed, I could feel his just about burning a hole through me.

Well, what did I have to lose? The worst that could happen would be that Heath would think I was a crackpot. On the other hand, if he believed me and was willing to help, I might have a chance of getting my father off the hook.

Desperation won out. My eyes still closed, I said, "My father is a werewolf. He's been arrested by the Houston pack, and is on trial for his life."

Heath snorted a little bit. It seemed the crackpot scenario was winning out. "Where are they holding him? The Houston zoo?"

"In Fredericksburg," I whispered, finally daring to open my eyes.

"Fredericksburg? But they converted the jail to a restaurant." He looked at me with something like shock. "You *are* serious." He looked down at the leather-bound book in his hands, then back at me. "This thing is *real*."

Now what? I didn't know what to say, so I just sat there, silent.

But Heath was still thinking. And studying me as if I were a paramecium in a petri dish. Or a defendant on the witness stand. "But if your *father's* a werewolf, that means . . ."

I decided to exercise my rights under the Fifth Amendment—you know, that anything-you-say-can-be-used-against-you-in-a-court-of-law thing—and kept my mouth shut. I'd like to say it was because I was being savvy, but the truth was that I couldn't think of a single thing to say. My mind was blank.

As it turns out, though, it didn't really matter, because Heath's legal mind was busily fitting the puzzle pieces together. "Those nights that you disappeared. All the shaving you had to do."

I spoke almost involuntarily. "You noticed that? But I was so careful!"

He shrugged. "I just figured you had a hormonal imbalance. Evidently I wasn't too far off the mark." Heath ran a hand through his dark hair, obviously agitated. And who could blame him, really? "All those nights you didn't show up. Like on our anniversary. I'll bet that was a full moon, wasn't it? And those trips you took from time to time, without telling me where you were going." He barked out a bitter laugh. "I can't believe I asked a werewolf to marry me."

I jerked back in my chair, stung. "Would it be so awful?"

"At least I could say my wife was an animal in the bedroom," he said, shaking his head. "I can't believe this. A werewolf. I was dating a freaking fairy-tale creature." He turned on me. "Why didn't you tell me?"

"Why didn't I *tell* you?" I shook my head. "Isn't it obvious? I mean, how exactly was I supposed to bring it up? 'Oh, by the way honey, I won't be there this weekend; it's the full moon, and I have to transform into a wolf'?"

Lindsey shrank into her chair, looking like she wished she could be absorbed by the upholstery. But I hadn't forgotten about her. Not at all. "This is your fault," I hissed at her.

"It's her fault you never told me you were a werewolf?" Heath asked. "I don't think so, Sophie. And how come you could tell Lindsey and not me?"

"I didn't tell her. She found out," I said.

"How? Did you suddenly sprout fangs over roast beef sandwiches at Subway one day?"

"Of course not," I said. "I'm more careful than that." Even though it had been touch and go with Heath while we were watching *Pirates of the Caribbean* last year. When the Kraken burst on the screen, the adrenaline rush had knocked my defenses right down, and it had been all I could do to control the fangs. "She followed me one night. I didn't know she was there until it was too late."

"When was this?"

"About six weeks ago," I said. "There was a big werewolf problem out near Round Top."

"Round Top? Isn't that where your office retreat was?" he asked. "Wait a minute. Is your boss a werewolf, too?"

"No!" I said. "That was a coincidence." I thought of everything that had happened last month—the ancient Aztec sacrifice ritual; my paw-to-paw battle with the leader of the *Norteños*; and last but not least, Mark's surprise cameo performance, for which he arrived looking like a recently lit Duraflame log with wings attached—and decided not to elaborate. Finding out I was a werewolf was enough of a shock for one day. "It's a long story," I said lamely.

"When exactly were you going to tell me?" Heath asked. "I wanted to *marry* you, Sophie. I wanted to have *kids* with you. Were you planning on waiting until our baby woke up with a tail sticking out of its diaper?"

I crossed my arms across my chest. "So now that you know, you're no longer interested?"

"You were the one who broke it off," he reminded me.

"And this is why," I shot back. "Think about it, Heath. How were we going to explain it to your mom and dad? 'I know it's a bit unusual, mom, but think of the benefits—like being able to claim minority status on her Harvard application!' " I took a deep breath, then kept going. "And we both know you have political aspirations. Skeletons in the closet are one thing, but werewolves in the cradle? That's a little tough to keep quiet. I mean, do you have any idea how hard it was for my mom to raise me? She spent the first ten years of my life paranoid I was going to sprout fur and bite the arm off one of my schoolmates."

"That's beside the point," he said.

But I wasn't done yet. "No, it's not. You can't control the change until you're older—not unless you want to risk feeding your children wolfsbane tea all the time. And wolfsbane's poisonous to humans, you know."

He blinked. "That's what's in that herbal tea you're always swigging down?"

I nodded. "It works for me—but I'm half werewolf." The

words sounded strange coming out of my mouth. Was I really saying this to Heath? "Our kids would only be a quarter, though—it might kill them."

"Look, guys," Lindsey interrupted. "I know you have a lot to talk about, and this is all kind of a shock, but Sophie's dad is on trial for murder—or werewolficide, or whatever you want to call it. Can we focus on getting him out of the werewolf pen? Then, later, I'll buy you two a bottle of wine and you can hash everything out."

We both looked at her, and Heath sighed. "You're right. I'm sorry. It's just . . . a bit to take in, that's all." He looked at me for a moment, brown eyes filled with something like hurt. Which made me feel just awful. But honestly: What choice had I had?

Just when I thought I couldn't stand it anymore, Heath broke eye contact with me and opened the leather-bound book. "I guess we'd better start by learning the code, then."

"You'll still help me?" I asked. "Even with . . . well, you know?"

He looked up at me, and his gaze was cool. "Like Lindsey said, we can discuss our personal issues later. The first priority is to get your father out of jail. I presume they're keeping him in a jail?"

"Actually, they're holding him in a place called the garden cottage."

His eyebrows shot up. "The garden cottage? What the heck is that, a potting shed? Or a tea room?"

"More of a guest cottage with guards, really."

"Doesn't sound like a high-security facility."

"Secure enough. There are guards, and they've got him chained to a chair. Plus the building is in a compound that belongs to the alpha of the Houston pack," I said.

He blinked. "I'm sorry, I didn't quite catch that. It belongs to whom?"

"The alpha of the Houston Pack," I repeated, suddenly tired.

"Wait a second. You mean there are actual werewolf packs, right here in Texas?" he asked. "And they have alphas?"

"It was news to me, too. I just found out about it last year."

"Christ. Exactly how many werewolves *are* there in this country?" Heath asked.

"I'm not really sure," I answered, doing a rapid mental calculation. If there were 500 in the Houston pack, and there were other packs all over the country, there must be quite a few. "Thousands, I guess. Maybe tens of thousands. I have no idea."

He turned to Lindsey. "Tom's one too, isn't he?"

She nodded. "How did you know?"

"The eyes," he said, turning back to study me in a way that made me a little uncomfortable. Less like I was the former girlfriend he was longing for and more like I was sitting in a cage next to the monkey house. "He and Sophie have the same eyes. Kind of shimmery." He paused, still staring at me, and I felt my face heat up. Then he asked, "Who else is one?"

"No one you know," I said. "Well, there's Koshka, one of the auditors downstairs. Only she's a werecat, not a werewolf."

"A werecat?" Heath asked, running a hand through his rumpled hair. "Jesus. You mean to tell me there's more than just werewolves?"

"No wonder she always smells like cat pee," Lindsey said. "How come you didn't tell me?"

"It never came up, I guess. But we're kind of getting off topic here," I said, trying to steer them back to the matter at hand. Lindsey had been right; this wasn't the ideal time to discuss the subtleties of the werewolf world—or, for that matter, the werecat world. Which I knew squat about anyway. "Heath," I said. "Thank you for your offer to help. If you're still willing, I'll take you up on it."

"I'm willing," he said, with a smile that made my heart ache.

"Thank you." At least there was a trained attorney on the case. Now if only I could find a way to trade in the jury . . .

Heath raised the *Codex*. "I'll need a copy of this to get started, though."

"No problem. You just have to swear you'll keep it hidden."

"It's not exactly something I'd leave lying around on my desk," he said, with a pointed glance at Lindsey.

"It wasn't on my desk, it was on my lap. And you just barged in," she retorted. I didn't point out that she hadn't been too quick to shove it under a folder or anything. "Can you make a copy for me, too?" she asked.

"I guess so. But you have to keep it secret," I said, hoping that some more in-depth reading on the habits and predilections of werewolves might put the kibosh on her I-want-to-be-a-werewolf campaign.

"What are we up against?" Heath asked as he thumbed through the book.

"He's charged with murdering a werewolf here in Austin," I told Heath. "The victim is a werewolf who double-crossed him back in Europe, and the judge and jury are friends of the victim and sworn enemies of my father."

"That's encouraging," he said dryly.

I sighed. "I know. My dad's probably going to be found guilty. And I only just met him three days ago."

"What's the penalty?" he asked.

"Death."

Heath paled. "Sophie. I'm so sorry."

I pointed to the book in his hand. "It's because it happened during the proscribed time—during the Howl. That's why it's so punitive."

"What's a Howl?"

"It's kind of a werewolf convention, where a bunch of packs get together and meet," Lindsey said, once again acting like she'd known all about this stuff since birth. I wouldn't be shocked if she signed up to teach courses on werewolf protocol at the local community college. "This year, they're getting together to talk about pack relations with Mexico," she said.

I could see by Heath's rising eyebrows that we were moving into another fascinating topic for him, but I steered him back on course. "Because of when it happened, the sentence is death. And according to the book in your hand, the penalty is execution with a silver bullet. Or wooden stake."

He cringed. "God. That's awful. And to think people complain about lethal injections being inhumane."

I pushed aside an image of my father being spitted like a rotisserie chicken. "As you can imagine, any advice would be greatly appreciated."

"Talk about a hostile jury," he muttered. He opened the *Codex* and shifted into attorney mode; you could almost see the transformation. "Do we have alternate suspects?" he asked.

"One or two," I said, and briefed him on what I knew about Charles's affair.

"So it could be a spurned lover. Or maybe even Kayla."

"She was supposedly in Galveston," I said.

"It's within driving distance. Does she have a solid alibi?"

"I don't know," I said.

"Do we know the name of the woman Charles was seeing on the side?"

"Uh, no."

"We need to find that out. Also, I was thinking: Is it possible that one of the alphas could be involved?" He shook his head. "Alphas. Did I really just say that?"

I couldn't help smiling. "I know, Heath. I still have a hard time with it myself." Unlike Lindsey, unfortunately. "But in answer to your question, I don't know. Why would the alphas be involved?"

"You said that one of them was a sworn enemy of Luc Garou."

"Then why not just kill *him*?" I asked.

"It was just a thought," he said. "It may or may not have merit, but we have to consider all the possibilities."

"I do know that the woman he was seeing was a werewolf," I said, trying to be helpful.

He sighed. "Well, that knocks out the human population, anyway. When is the trial?"

"You see, that's the sticky part," I said, stomach sinking. "It's the day after tomorrow."

He ran a hand through his dark hair. "Jeez. That's no time at all. Why didn't you call me sooner?"

I glanced at the book in his hand. "Isn't it kind of obvious?"

"I guess you're right. Now, here's what we need to do. I need you to find out who Charles was seeing and track down Kayla's alibi. We need to see if we can pinpoint the location of the two alphas, too. Is there anyone else who might have wanted him dead?"

I sighed, thinking of my father's rather assertive personality. "There's probably a waiting list."

"What opportunities do you have to meet with these people?"

"Werewolves," Lindsey reminded us. We both ignored her.

"Everyone's been at the Howl, out in Fredericksburg. I've been going undercover—that's why my hair looks weird."

"Why not go as yourself?"

"My last name is Garou. If everyone thinks he's guilty, why would they want to talk to his daughter?"

"Good point," he conceded. Then he cocked his head to one side. "What exactly do they do at a werewolf convention?"

"Just werewolf stuff," I said, although I had no idea what that entailed. I suspected tonight's assembly would be rather educational, though. "I'll tell you what. Why don't I go make a few copies of this, and I'll deliver them at lunch."

"See what you can find out tonight, and in the meantime, I'll look for loopholes in the code."

I reached out and touched his arm; to my relief, he didn't recoil. "Thank you for your help."

"You're welcome," he said stiffly. "But once this is over, you have a lot more explaining to do."

I shut the door after them a moment later and leaned against it, feeling utterly drained. I was glad to have Heath's help—and relieved, in a way, that my big fat hairy secret was finally out in the open. But it was unsettling how quickly my secret was slipping away from me.

Twenty

I left the office at three thirty, which was a tad early, but still barely enough time to redo my dye job in preparation for the evening's festivities. If you could call them that. While I was headed to the Howl, Lindsey and Heath were planning to spend the evening together with the *Codex*, in hope of finding a technicality that would help my father's case. The two of them had been closeted with it—and each other—all afternoon. I just prayed that tonight's little foray would result in some information they could use in my father's defense. Provided, of course, he hadn't pissed someone off so much with his Garou superiority complex that they'd already dispatched him.

Hope springs eternal, I guess.

Sally had shot me yet another nasty look as I shouldered

my briefcase and hustled past her. As I waited for the elevator, hoping Adele wouldn't pick that moment to round the corner, I thanked my lucky stars that I had (a) made partner and (b) was . . . well, to be quite frank, sleeping with my client. Because my work product over the last week had been less than stellar.

On the not-so-bright side, however, relations with my star client weren't exactly at their zenith right now. Mark usually took every one of my calls, but I hadn't made it past his assistant that morning. And when he'd finally called me back late in the afternoon, I'd had to endure another cross-examination—only this time, the subject was Tom.

"So, are you going out with him again tonight?" he'd asked.

"I'm not 'going out' with him," I said. "He's helping me do reconnaissance work, so I can prevent my father's execution."

"I still don't see why you're going to all of this trouble. I've told you I could get him out of there in a heartbeat."

"Yes, I know. And it's lovely of you to offer," I repeated for what felt like the millionth time. "But I'd like to see if I can do it legally, so there aren't any long-term repercussions." Like angry packs of werewolves pounding down my door, inviting me to take my father's place on a sharpened stake.

"So, you and the dashing Tom will be back at the Howl again tonight."

"Yup. That's the plan."

"When will you be home?"

What was he, my mother? "I don't know."

"Call me when you get in," he said, and the ring on my finger heated up, just a little bit.

"I will . . . Ash." On impulse, I used the name he'd given me the other night. Even with miles of distance between us, I could feel him respond.

"I'll wait for your call," he said in a voice that thrummed with desire, and as I hung up, I felt an answering twinge deep inside.

Now, though, I had to face yet another evening of werewolves. Whatever happened, I told myself, it was only two more days. If I could just make it to the end of the week and get my father off the hook, everything would be fine. Or, if not fine, at least over.

I had just finished blow-drying my poor, abused, reblackened hair when there was a knock at the door. I knew before I opened it that it was Tom.

His musky, wild scent filled the room as I opened the door, making me just a little bit weak in the knees. Speaking of knees, his no longer seemed swathed in gauze. "How's your leg?" I asked, glancing down at his jeans. From what I could tell, there was no bandage under the denim at all—just a long expanse of muscular thigh. Mmmm.

"Almost healed," he said, stepping into my loft.

"How come I don't heal that fast?" I asked.

"You're not as old as I am," he said. "Give it time."

"How old *are* you?"

He grinned. "Older than you." He eyed my hair. "That's not a good color for you, you know. I much prefer it auburn."

"You and my father agree on something, at least." I touched my hair self-consciously. "I know it's awful. I'm hoping this is the last time I'll have to use it."

"I like the outfit, though," he said, his eyes roving from my form-fitting jeans to the rather plunging neckline of my Banana Republic wrap top. "And I definitely approve of the top. Though I must confess that I do miss the skirt."

"Should I wear something different?" I asked, trying to ignore the heat in my cheeks. "I mean, what's the protocol tonight?" I'd made the mistake of not asking once; I wasn't going to do it a second time.

"Jeans are fine," he said. "Dinner will be barbecue tonight, so you'll be right in line."

"What else is on tap for the evening?" I asked.

"Tonight is the assembly," he said. "The packs will gather

under their banners. Wolfgang will announce his intention to mate with Elena, and they'll do any other pack business that needs to be attended to before the full-moon ceremony tomorrow." He touched my hand. "Your dad will be there, too.

"What? Why?"

He took a deep breath. "Sophie, you have to prepare yourself. At the assembly, they'll officially indict him."

I closed my eyes and swallowed, overcome with emotion. When I was able to speak again, I croaked, "And jeans are appropriate for an indictment?"

"Trust me, you'll be right in line with everyone else," Tom said. Tears sprang to my eyes, which was a big problem, because I was wearing several ounces of eyeliner. I reached up to wipe them away.

Tom's voice was low and reassuring. "Don't worry about your dad, Sophie. They won't do anything but set the trial." He paused for a moment, and his voice took on a teasing tone. "Besides, you're supposed to be an unsophisticated werewolf from a small town. You're not supposed to look put together."

I barked out something like a laugh, lifted my chin, and gave myself a good shake. This was not the time to fall apart. "Anything special I need to do tonight? Other than grovel and act mortified?"

"Poor Sophie," he said, reaching out to touch my hair. "Hopefully, your Swedish alter ego will soon be a thing of the past."

"No kidding," I said, taking a shaky breath. Best to get this over with. "Let me just get my jacket and we'll go."

Ten minutes later, Tom's muscular body was wedged between my thighs. Of course, it was because we were on the back of his motorcycle, but it was still a very pleasurable experience. I scootched a little closer to Tom and wrapped my arms tighter around him, trying to blot my worries out of my mind. We were close enough that I could feel his heart beat under the leather of his jacket as the rolling Texas hill country unfurled before us, the bluebonnets and Indian paintbrush mirroring the purple-orange hues of the sunset flooding the sky.

All too soon, we were back at the Graf ranch, bumping down the caliche road and into the crowded parking area. Several torches lit the area around where the bonfire had been a few nights earlier, and a dozen picnic tables laden with food dotted the field. I sniffed the air, and my salivary glands kicked into action. Brisket, ribs, and sausage, unless I was mistaken, along with several bottles of Shiner Bock. And, of course, werewolves. Lots of them.

Tom was right; casual was the word for werewolves tonight. In fact, the preponderance of khakis and jeans made the gathering look like a bunch of professionals getting together for an al fresco happy hour on casual Friday. Only by the strong animal aroma—and the legions of shimmery eyes—could I tell it was otherwise.

I leaned forward, putting my lips close to Tom's ear. "So is this where the assembly happens?" I asked.

"No," he said. "The assembly will occur in the clearing where the hunt started."

He pulled in next to a black Mercedes, and I climbed off the motorcycle and attempted to fix my hair. "This whole werewolf thing isn't exactly what I was expecting," I said.

Tom unzipped his leather jacket; beneath it, he wore a black T-shirt that stretched tight across his muscular chest. "No? Why not?"

"It's too . . . I don't know." I surveyed the casually dressed crowd, groping for the right word. "Normal?"

He chuckled, a deep, growly sound that made me shiver inside. "It hasn't begun yet, my dear." Something about the way he said it made the hairs stand up on my arms. I rubbed them, feeling a shiver pass through me, then shuddered as I caught a glimpse of myself in the tinted window of a Mercedes.

"Dear God."

"What?"

"I look like the bride of Frankenstein," I said, and made him stop while I did my best to tame it. Once I'd done what I could to tame it, Tom took my arm and walked toward the field, where the werewolves were grouped in bunches, digging into the brisket and talking in low voices. I could sense the tension in the air as Tom greeted several of them with a pleasant, slightly toothy smile. I kept my head down and moved a little closer to Tom, who put a protective, musk-and-leather-scented arm around me.

Although none of them actually bared their teeth and threatened to rip my throat out for my bad manners—for the first time, I found myself thankful we were in the "proscribed time"—the hostile looks sure didn't bode well for me sniffing out more information. I soon found myself wondering if it might not have been wise to choose a different dye color—and yet another identity. After all, with Tom's apparent Don Juan reputation, chances were excellent no one would have turned a hair.

As we rounded another clump of werewolves, I glanced almost involuntarily toward the garden cottage, where I hoped my father was still imprisoned. I was heartened to see burly werewolves flanking the door. Although another family gathering was probably out of the question, the presence of the guards meant Luc must still be alive and kicking. And doubtless offending everyone within hearing range.

We had almost reached the meat-laden tables when I realized that the mug of wolfsbane tea I'd downed before leaving had made its way to my bladder. I also needed a break from the sea of golden eyes that was focused on me with more than a bit of hostility. "Is it okay if I just run into one of the houses and use the bathroom?" I asked Tom.

"Sure," he said. "They should all be open."

I was about to ask him if there were any I should avoid when a trio of burly werewolves walked up. "Hey, Tom.

Heard your little honey got herself into trouble," the largest one said, shooting me a scornful look.

"She's in touch with her animal impulses," he said, grinning salaciously. "That's what I like about her."

"Not just on the hunt, eh?"

He squeezed me tight, and I looked up to see desire in his golden eyes. I felt a response stir deep inside me; if he was acting, he deserved an Oscar.

"I can't complain," he said in a low growl that set my body on fire. His buddies looked me over again in a way that was distinctly, well, carnal. Cheeks burning, I excused myself and hurried over the shorn grass toward the nearest farmhouse, anxious to escape the werewolves' staring eyes.

Unfortunately, the inside of the house was hardly a respite, because evidently the farmhouse I had chosen was occupied by Elena. Her scent, and the synthetic-textile aroma of her guards, just about bowled me over when I opened the door and stepped inside.

I had assumed Elena was bunking with Wolfgang, but that didn't appear to be the case. Maybe they were waiting for her alpha status to be made official before taking up residence together. Or maybe I'd been wrong about the whole alpha-alpha relationship thing. I mean, just because they were both alphas didn't mean they were, well, sleeping together. Did it?

The sound of a familiar, gravelly voice jerked me out of my speculation. "What do you think's gonna happen tonight?"

It was one of the pleather boys. The sound of his voice made my heart start pounding in my chest—and not in a good way. I debated closing the door and walking right back outside, but then I remembered I was here to gather information. Besides, I really did need to pee.

So I thought every protective thought I could and crept toward the bathroom, which I'd spotted down a little hallway to the left. The floorboards creaked beneath my feet as I tiptoed over to it, but evidently the pleather boys weren't paying very good attention, because they didn't seem to notice. I eased the door shut behind me and pressed my ear against the wood, trying to ignore the urgent distress signals from my bladder.

"I don't know." I recognized the second voice, too: Elena's other guard. Their voices were growing louder; they must be moving in my direction. "It's a sticky situation. He's got to come up with some way to avoid the alliance."

"Can't he find some way around it?"

"Not without causing trouble. If he agrees to it in front of the assembly, it'll be tough to renege later."

"Even if he does have to go through with it, is he still going to back us?"

"That's the agreement," said the second voice. "Otherwise, no Beaumont."

I clenched my legs together—God, I needed to pee—and pressed my ear to the bathroom door. Who wanted to avoid an alliance? How did Beaumont enter into this? And was Beaumont a person, or the town in east Texas? And—most important—did this have any bearing on my father's impending trial? "It was touch and go the other day, with Wolfgang," the gravelly voice continued. "Put Miss Elena in a tight spot when he saw the Grenier guy leaving her hotel room."

My pulse picked up another notch. *The Grenier guy?* Did they mean Charles?

"It's a good thing Garou turned up. Do you think he's the one who got rid of him?"

"I don't know, but it works out fine for us. Hard for him to answer any questions now. And Miss Elena's got Wolfgang calmed down."

"I'm still worried about good old Wolfi. Miss Elena says he's fine, she's got him under control. But he's not stupid."

"Think that's why Miss Elena isn't at the big house?"

"After the ceremony she will be. He's just waiting for it to be official. You know the Germans—*alles in Ordnung*."

"Yeah, and Wolfgang's gonna be real happy to get that Garou guy back in *Ordnung*. I just hope the Frenchies don't get pissy about their alpha winding up with a stake in him."

"Not our problem," he said. "Besides, if he broke the code, what can they do?"

There was another set of footsteps—lighter, but firm—and a woman's voice cut through. "Is there a problem?"

I drew in my breath. *Elena*.

"No, ma'am."

"What were you discussing?" she asked.

"Just talking about the trial."

"Garou is guilty," she said shortly. "There's nothing to discuss."

"Of course not, ma'am."

"Good." There was silence for a moment, then she spoke again. "Is someone else here?"

"Just us," said the gravelly voiced pleather boy.

"No," she said, and I could hear her sniffing. "There's someone else." Her footsteps came closer. I scuttled toward the toilet, jerked down my jeans, and was in the process of relieving my overfilled bladder when the door burst open.

Twenty-one

Elena stared at me for a moment, surprise in her golden eyes, then shut the door in a hurry. I congratulated myself on my quick action; I'd figured if she caught me with my pants down, it would help deflect suspicion.

It was a nice thought, anyway.

Once I'd finished my business, I washed my hands, using a bit of water to flatten down my hair, and steeled myself for another encounter. Three pairs of eyes bored into me when I stepped out of the bathroom a moment later. Elena stood with her arms crossed, radiating disapproval.

"It's the hick Inga from Minnesota," she said, her voice icy. Even though everyone else was dressed in jeans—except Boris and Dudley, who were sporting their signature pleather pants—she was all business in a beautifully cut black suit. "What the hell are you doing in my den?"

It looked more like a house than a den to me—I mean, for starters, it had actual working plumbing, not to mention an antique pitcher collection on the mantel—but I didn't bother to argue. "Um . . . someone told me there was a bathroom in here. Sorry to intrude."

"You're the yokel who took down the buck the other night. And was hanging around the garden cottage. Did you break the window?"

"What window?" I asked, trying to look puzzled.

She sniffed. "You smell different."

I shrugged. “I just came in here to go to the bathroom. I didn’t know it was a private house. I’ll get out of your hair now,” I said, and started inching toward the door.

“She’s here with Fenris again,” said the burlier of the two—Boris, I think—and Elena stepped in front of me, blocking my way. Despite the fear of imminent discovery, my eyes were drawn involuntarily to the shiny fabric stretched across his bottom half. Kayla really thought he was *hot*? I tore my eyes away and found myself staring right into Elena’s golden eyes.

“I remember when you had the buck in your mouth,” she said, staring at me like I was a bug she was about to crush. “You had a strong aroma last time—like maple, I believe—but now I don’t smell it.” *Shit.* I’d sprayed on Euphoria, but I’d forgotten the fenugreek.

She sniffed again. “I knew you were here because of your perfume. But there’s something familiar about you.” Her eyes bored into me. “Why are you in my house?”

I looked down at the floor, avoiding her eyes. “Like I said. I just needed to go to the bathroom. I’ll leave now. Sorry.” Any moment now, Elena was going to figure out exactly who I was. I was surprised she hadn’t pegged it already. From what everyone had told me, werewolves who were light in the scent department weren’t particularly common. “Can I go back outside?”

“I know you from somewhere,” Elena said, narrowing her eyes at me. “Maybe we should ask her a few questions,” she suggested, and I shrank away from her, praying I’d applied enough eyeliner that she wouldn’t recognize me. “Find out if she’s got connections to Garou we don’t know about. Maybe she’s a French spy . . .”

“Inga?”

Four heads swiveled to the door.

“There you are,” Tom said, stepping into the room. “I was starting to worry about you.” He nodded to Elena and the pleather boys and took my arm. “I think the assembly is about to start. Ready?”

"Absolutely," I said. I turned to my reluctant hosts. "Thanks for letting me use the facilities—again, I'm so sorry to bother you." And then, with Elena and the pleather boys boring holes in my back with their eyes, I followed him out of the little house, heart pounding. Talk about a close shave . . .

"What happened in there?" he asked. "I realized after you left that the closest place was Elena's house.

"Thanks for coming after me," I said. "I think Elena's onto me. I totally forgot the fenugreek, and she noticed the change in my scent."

He said something that sounded like a Norse curse, slapping his thigh with his hand, then winced; evidently he hadn't healed quite as completely as he'd let on. "I forgot to give it to you. And then I got distracted, and let you put yourself in danger."

"It's okay. After tonight, I'm hoping Inga can rest in peace. And I overheard some interesting things." I opened my mouth to tell him what I'd heard, but he put a finger on my lips.

"Shh," he said. "Let's go somewhere more private."

I followed him away from the crowd, toward a small grove of oaks. He drew me behind a tree as if we were lovers, then pulled me close. Despite the presence of a couple of hundred suspicious werewolves just yards away, I had an overwhelming urge to slide my hands into his leather jacket and let my animal nature assert itself.

"Tell me everything they said," he said in a soft voice. "But speak quietly."

My heart hammering in my chest—he was so close I could feel his warm breath on my face—I relayed what I'd heard of Boris and Dudley's conversation. The words tumbled out, ending with "I think they may have set my father up to take the fall for someone else."

"Perhaps," he said. "But who?"

"That's the million-dollar question. Maybe someone who

was jealous of Charles? Or maybe it had something to do with that alliance they were talking about. Maybe Charles knew something he shouldn't have." I bit my lip, trying to piece what I'd heard together. Tom's presence made it hard to think clearly. "Is there a werewolf named Beaumont here?"

Tom shook his head. "Not that I know of."

"So they're talking about a place. But what does a town in Texas have to do with anything?"

He shrugged. "Unfortunately, I cannot help you with that."

"Whose territory is it in?"

"It is in east Texas?" he asked.

I nodded.

"Houston, probably."

"What about the guy leaving Elena's hotel room? They said his name was Grenier. Was that Charles? Or are there other Greniers here?"

"The Greniers are a large family, but most of them are still in France," Tom said. "Charles was the only one I know who was in Texas. And he was here because his family disowned him."

"So Luc wasn't the only one angry that he double-crossed his family." A new possibility emerged. "Do you think a family member might have killed him?"

"It is possible," he said, but he didn't look convinced.

"You don't think so?"

"I think they would have done it long ago, if they were intending to. It's been over a hundred years."

"But the Houston pack still thinks my father killed him," I pointed out.

"*They* do. I did not say that *I* do."

I sighed. "Maybe Heath can bring in the whole hundred-years-ago thing when he's putting together a defense."

Tom looked startled. "Heath?"

Oh, yeah. I'd forgotten to tell Tom about Lindsey's little faux pas.

When I filled him in, his face grew still. "Sophie, that was not wise. And to share the *Codex* . . ."

"It was an accident. And they promised not to say anything about it."

"Still. To have it in circulation, and to have two humans know of your existence . . . You may be compromised."

"Lindsey knows about you, too," I pointed out.

"But my home is not in Austin."

I had to admit he had a point. "I know, I know. It's not good. It wasn't what I wanted—I mean, I dated Heath for over a year without telling him—but I can't change it now. Besides, I could use the legal help."

"Still . . ."

"Let's talk about it later—I've got enough to think about as it is." He nodded slightly, which I took to mean assent, and I plowed on. "Back to what Boris and Dudley were saying. They mentioned Grenier leaving Elena's hotel room, so maybe Elena's the person Charles was seeing on the side. But that doesn't make sense."

"Why not?"

"The thing is, would Elena take the risk? She's about to be alpha of the Houston pack. She's big into power, and as far as that's concerned, Charles had nothing to offer. I mean, unless he was phenomenally good in the sack or something."

"You are assuming they were intimate?" Tom said, his gold eyes burning into me.

I felt my face heat up, and I was keenly aware that only a few inches separated us. "My dad—I mean Luc—said he had been 'with' someone. A female werewolf."

He held my gaze. "That does not necessarily mean it was Elena. There were many werewolves in Austin that night, and I have heard rumors that Charles was involved with a woman from Louisiana."

"Okay, so maybe he wasn't sleeping with Elena. But he was still in her hotel room—and the pleather boys didn't want Wolfgang to know about it. They seemed relieved my father showed up. But the thing is, is it because Luc killed Grenier before Wolfgang could question him? Or is it because someone else killed him, and Luc is an easy suspect?" My father had sworn his innocence, but I still wasn't completely sure.

"Excellent questions," Tom said, his eyes steady on mine. "Unfortunately, I have no answers."

I sighed. "I wish werewolves were into forensics."

"It would be helpful," Tom conceded. "But we may learn some things tonight that lead us to the truth."

"When? During the assembly?"

He nodded. "At least we should know which alliance is in question."

"But even if we do, we only have a day to find things out," I said, feeling a rush of despair. "And who's going to talk to Inga the hick werewolf?"

"There are other ways," Tom said. "I will find out what I can."

"I just hope it will be enough," I said gloomily, thinking of the pleather boys and what they'd said about the French werewolves. Maybe I should get in touch with Georges after all; the way things were going, the situation was less than rosy for the alpha of the Paris pack. But if worse came to worst, there was always Mark's offer. Wouldn't it be better to have him free my father independently than to invite the whole Parisian werewolf army to avenge their alpha? But for some reason, I was reluctant to do that.

My stomach clenched at the thought of Luc Garou, chained to a chair in that little room, awaiting trial. If only I could prove that someone else had killed Charles—or at least that there were other possibilities. Did reasonable doubt constitute a defense in the werewolf world? Hopefully, Heath was at home with the *Codex*, busy figuring that out. *Heath*. I felt a pang just thinking about the hurt look I'd seen in his brown eyes. In truth, I was still reeling a bit—after all these years of silence, I hadn't come to terms with the fact that my secret was out of the closet. And that my carefully constructed cover had caused pain to a man I cared about . . .

Worry about Heath later, I told myself, pushing thoughts of my ex-boyfriend out of my head and focusing on Tom instead. Which was disturbingly easy to do, since he was just inches away from me, and his musky male scent was making my breath quicken. Among other things. "What about the alliance?" I asked, forcing my thoughts—with some difficulty—to remain rated PG.

"There are at least three alliances proposed among the southern packs," Tom said, shrugging slightly. "It could be any number of them."

"Are they planning on bringing that up tonight?" I asked. "What *is* the schedule of events at this assembly, anyway?"

"Mating approvals come first," he said. "Then alliances, then a presentation of any potential new alphas—in this case, Elena. After that, they will deal with disciplinary matters."

My stomach knotted. "Like Luc Garou?"

"That has not changed. It will be tried tomorrow, at the *Fehmgericht*."

"I'm glad we have another day's reprieve . . . but why the special trial?"

His voice was grim. "The *Fehmgericht* is convened only for capital crimes involving born werewolves. Tonight's proceedings will be for smaller infractions."

"Have you been to a *Fehmgericht* before?"

He nodded slowly.

"How did it turn out?"

"For the accused?" he asked.

"Yeah."

"Not well," he said, and something in his voice made my hopes sink further. Then he smiled gently. "But we do not have to deal with that tonight. Tonight is for other things."

I took a deep breath, trying to think positive thoughts, and said, "Like Wolfgang and Elena getting together." I recalled her beautifully cut black suit. Very nice, but not what I would have chosen for a wedding. "So after tonight it will be official?"

"Not yet. All of the matings and alliances will be formalized at the beginning of the wild hunt, in two days, just before the full moon rises."

"Didn't we do the wild hunt already?'

"That was a warm-up," he said.

"What's different about this one?"

"The prey," he said, and something about his voice made me shiver. My eyes strayed to Elena's farmhouse, which was barely visible through the low oaks. "When Elena is made alpha," I asked, "does that mean she and Wolfgang will, well, you know?"

"That they will mate?" Tom asked, grinning a little bit, so I could see his gleaming canines.

"Um, yeah."

"That is the custom," he said.

"Is it normal for them to stay apart before the . . . the wedding, or whatever you call it?"

"The handfasting."

"They call it *handfasting*? God, that's clunky. And why isn't it called pawfasting?"

He rolled his eyes. "The betrothed do not always stay separate, but Wolfgang is very traditional. And concerned for the lineage. If a pup was conceived, it would be better if it occurred when both parents held the alpha title and were officially mated. Although the odds of such a conception are very slim."

"Why?"

He gave me a considering look. "Has it struck you as odd that there are so many adult werewolves and so few pups?"

I glanced toward the gathering of werewolves, suddenly realizing that I hadn't seen any children. "I guess. I just assumed this was an adults-only gathering."

"Conception is very rare for werewolves," Tom said.

"Really? Why?" I had to admit that all this birds-and-bees talk with Tom was making me feel, well, moist.

He shrugged. "We'd have to submit ourselves to science to discover that. It is another mystery of our kind."

"Ah," I said, feeling Tom's magnetic pull on me. What was it about him that made me respond so deeply? Was it that we were both werewolves? But from what I'd seen of other werewolves, they didn't have this effect on me. I looked up at Tom, and my eyes were drawn to his mouth, thinking of how his lips would feel on my own lips, and on my neck, and other places . . . Heat rushed through me at the thought of it, and I was leaning toward him when a loud crack splintered the air above us.

Tom yanked me toward him, burying my face in his chest; a second later, I was sprawled in a thin bed of last year's leaves, Tom's body pressed against mine. Adrenaline pulsed through me, and I had to fight the urge to change as my eyes scanned the area, looking for the source of the cracking noise. When I found it, I shuddered. Where we had stood a moment earlier was a huge oak limb, its splintered end smoking slightly in the spring air.

"Jesus," I said. "What the hell was that?"

"I don't know," Tom said, rolling off of me and moving to inspect the fallen limb. It was huge—about eight inches in diameter—and solid enough to have crushed my skull. "It looks like a lightning strike," he said, examining the smoking, splintered end of the branch and then glancing up. "But there's not a cloud in the sky."

I glanced over toward the throng of werewolves. A few golden-eyed faces were turned in our direction, but most of them were involved in conversation. "They barely noticed it," I said. "And if it was lightning, where was the thunder? All I heard was the tree cracking."

Before I could ask more, there was a long, mournful howl. A chill ran down my spine as the note died away. "We'll have to work it out later," he said softly.

"What do you mean?"

"It's time for the assembly."

Twenty-two

As if on command, the werewolves drifted toward the edges of the clearing, disappearing onto the trails that led into the darkening woods. I glanced at the fallen tree limb again, shivering at how close we'd come to being crushed.

Tom reached for my hand. "Don't worry about it now. We have other things to deal with."

With one last look at the splintered branch, I turned and followed Tom across the clearing, behind the other werewolves. I stole a glance at Elena's farmhouse, wondering if Elena would emerge. There was no movement, though. My eyes swerved to the little house on the perimeter of the compound, where my father was imprisoned; despite the broken window I'd left the other night, the two werewolves who had flanked the door were gone. I briefly considered slipping back to see if I could free him, but abandoned the idea when I realized there was no way for me to chew through his shackles. If there were, he would have already done it anyway. Which brought me to another question—namely, what special powers did Mark have that would allow him to set my father free? Something told me it wasn't because he'd studied lock-picking.

I turned back to the trail. Tom's wide back was just a few paces before me. The murmur of voices in the clearing had quieted, replaced by the sound of hundreds of loafers crackling on dead leaves. The air was electric with anticipation—or maybe it was my own nervousness that made it seem that way.

It must have only been fifteen minutes, but it felt like we'd been in the woods an hour before we exited into the same clearing where the hunt had begun the other night. The area was unrecognizable.

A smaller version of the bonfire from the other night lit the center of the clearing, and the area was lit by a ring of flickering torches, which gave the spring air a smoky smell and cast long dark shadows over the uneven ground. Canvas tents in a variety of colors ringed the perimeter of the clearing, each bearing a fluttering banner with what appeared to be a coat of arms and a motto. Some were larger than others, with a bigger throng surrounding them, and as we moved farther into the clearing, I could see that each tent sheltered two thronelike wooden chairs, only a few of which were occupied. In the center of the clearing, a few yards from the bonfire, several werewolves gathered around a large, flat chunk of granite. It was topped with an ornate wooden podium that looked like a medieval pulpit.

Overall, except for the absence of women in leather bodices, men dressed like Jack Sparrow, and throngs of chunky suburbanites gnawing on smoked turkey legs, the scene resembled something you'd see at a Renaissance Faire. With one major difference—this was anything but pretend.

"What are the tents for?" I asked Tom as we entered the clearing.

"They're for the alphas in attendance," he said. "Each pack gathers at their tent."

"I can't believe they have coats of arms," I said. "How fifteenth century." I glanced at the words on the nearest one—they appeared to be in Latin. "What does that mean?"

"*Aut vincam aut periam*?" he asked, glancing up at the banner. The coat of arms above it depicted a wolf set against a yellow backdrop, its mouth dripping blood, standing on top of what appeared to be a stack of dead wolves. "*Win or perish*. I believe that's the motto of the Arkansas pack."

"Jeez. Whatever happened to 'The Land of Opportunity'?"

"I think that only applies if you win," he said.

As I watched, the werewolves distributed themselves among the tents, until Tom and I were just about the only ones who hadn't picked a tent. I now noticed that many of the werewolves had chosen to wear their pack colors; in fact, the array of gold and red polo shirts under the Arkansas tent made it look like a tailgate party for the Kansas City Chiefs.

Two tents down I recognized the Louisiana male alpha, Jean-Louis, whose co-alpha was a striking redhead who looked to be twenty but was doubtless a couple of centuries older. The pair was dressed more formally than the others, she in a royal blue sheath dress that sparkled with gems, he in a dark suit with a tie that matched his mate's attire. The fleur-de-lis figured prominently on the flag, which strangely featured no wolf references—only a couple of castle turrets.

"What's the alpha family name in Louisiana?" I asked Tom.

"De Loup," he said.

"You're kidding me." Unless my admittedly awful French had deserted me entirely, *de loup* meant 'of the wolf'. *Loup* was one of the few vocabulary words from French class that had kind of stuck in my mind.

I could spot the Houston pack's tent without any trouble, and not just because Wolfgang had taken up residence in one of its wooden thrones. It was at the top of the clearing, and was larger than the rest of them, thick with dark-blue and yellow stripes. The coat of arms bore a wolf that was somehow, despite the lack of opposable thumbs, clutching a bloodstained sword in one paw. Upon its head was a crown. "What's the Houston pack motto?" I asked.

"From the tooth a crown," he said.

"Not exactly pacifists, are they? Do the Garous have a motto?" I asked.

Tom gave me a sidelong look. "Yes."

"What is it?"

He smiled a little. "*Aspiro.* Or, *J'aspire.*"

"I aspire?" I thought of my father's grand plans for my ascension to the top of the Texas packs. Not to mention his own taking of the reins in Paris. "If the name fits. . . . Did my dad pick that one out himself?"

His grin widened. "No, it's centuries old—even older than he is. Perhaps ambition runs in the family."

"And what about the Fenrises?" I asked. "Does your family have a motto?"

The fire flared suddenly, making Tom's prominent canines gleam. "Death feeds the ravens."

I shuddered a little, thinking of his raven, Hugin. "Charming." If nothing else, I thought, this little gathering was proving mighty educational.

Suddenly, that eerie howl from earlier echoed in the clearing again, making all the hairs on my arms stand up. It was much louder this time, and appeared to be emanating from a tall, muscular woman wearing a long black ponytail and a black pantsuit. She stood behind the podium, clutching at it with both hands as she tipped her head back and howled again.

"Who's that?" I whispered.

"Isabella Murano." Before he could say more, there was a responding swell from the assembled werewolves, and any last vestige of resemblance to a Friday night drinks party disappeared. Tom drew me over to the side of the clearing, where a couple of other lone werewolves milled, and we stood near a small cedar tree.

"She's leading the assembly tonight," Tom explained. "She's an alpha from the Philadelphia pack; she's agreed to act as a neutral moderator."

"Why doesn't Wolfgang do it?"

"Because it is traditional to have a high-ranking alpha from an uninvolved pack to preside," he said. "To maintain neutrality."

"So she'll be the main judge at the trial, too?" I asked, feeling my hopes rise.

"Unfortunately, no. The *Fehmgericht*—the Fehmic Court—is different," he said. "Wolfgang will preside."

"But he's not neutral!" I hissed.

If Tom answered, I didn't hear it, because the dark-haired werewolf at the center began calling the assembly to order.

"Greetings, fellow *lupins*." The werewolves howled their response. Isabella extended a hand to the biggest tent, where Wolfgang sat on one of the two thrones, looking extremely self-important. Behind him, a little to the left, stood Elena and the pleather boys. "Herr Graf wishes me to extend special thanks to the alphas of the New Orleans, Texarkana, Dallas, and Oklahoma City packs for honoring us with your presence," Isabella announced. She then went through and named each pair of alphas; as they were called, they rose, glancing around at their audience as if they were royalty. Which, in a way, I suppose they were. Wolfgang was the only solo alpha named, and as he stood and nodded to his audience, Elena stood with a fixed smile on her face. When the introductions were completed, Isabella said, "Herr Graf—along with the rest of the American werewolf community—thanks you again for joining us, and hopes that the alliances forged during this Howl will go far in keeping the southern packs strong against the threat of the *Norteños*."

Another howl of approval erupted from the surrounding werewolves.

"And now," she said, intoning the words like a Catholic priest about to serve communion, "let us say the words of binding."

Words of binding? I glanced up at Tom, but he was focused on the werewolf at the podium. Isabella began to speak then, and the words echoed around me, but they were in a language I didn't understand. Latin, maybe? It sounded like a prayer, but there was something eerie about the rising chant around me, like it was a living thing that wound itself around me, pressing against me, swallowing up all the air. I pretended to chant along, even though I had no idea what anyone was saying, and was starting to feel a tad panicky when they stopped all at once. After several seconds of silence, as if on cue, the whole gathering erupted into another bone-chilling howl.

Then two werewolves in khakis processed toward the podium, carrying a cage containing a terrified brown rabbit. Bowing their heads, they presented the cage to Isabella, who flipped the lid open and pulled the poor creature out. The rabbit let out a squeak of terror as the werewolf raised the animal to her mouth and ripped its throat out.

I stifled a gasp, staring in horror at what had just happened. It was like we were at an Ozzy Osbourne concert or something, only without all the electric guitars.

Then, as blood poured down her chin, Isabella held the flailing little body up and intoned, "Let the assembly begin."

"Dear God," I murmured as the two khaki-clad werewolves retrieved the dead rabbit and returned it—rather unnecessarily, since it wasn't likely to hop away anytime soon—to its cage. Tom put one hand on my shoulder, and I glanced up at him. "What's next? Group maulings?"

"Unfortunately, that'll be all the excitement for a while. Now we go through the mating approvals, which usually take up half the night. After that, things will get interesting again."

A moment later, Isabella called for betrothed couples to approach the podium, and a line six couples deep formed in the center of the clearing. Despite the carnage that had recently occurred on the slab of granite, I could smell their excitement. Which made sense, I supposed, since they were getting married. Or mated. Or whatever it was the process was called.

They all looked to be in their twenties or early thirties, but who knew how old they really were? I glanced over at the Texarkana tent. Kayla stood there alone, looking glassy-eyed. This couldn't be easy for her. Nor, I suddenly realized, for Tom. I glanced up at him, but his face was masklike. I caught a flicker of something—pain, perhaps—and I wondered if he was recalling a lost moment with Beate. That wound might never fully heal, I realized.

As I studied Tom, I got the uncomfortable feeling that someone was studying me. I looked away from the Nordic werewolf beside me, my eyes sweeping the crowd until I found Elena. She and the pleather boys had located me on the sidelines, and her gaze was less than friendly. I gave her a quick, perhaps slightly strained smile and focused on the hopeful couples instead.

Tom was right about the mating approval process being a rather bureaucratic endeavor. I watched the first couple, a rather hirsute pair even for werewolves, with interest. She was evidently a sweet young thing of only 150 years of age, originally from Czechoslovakia, now in Chicago, whereas he was a mere 130 years old, and a native Texan from El Paso. As the waxing moon rose, making my skin itchy, we got to hear the history of their existing pack alliances, their family trees and pack alliances dating back five generations (to prevent excessive inbreeding, according to Tom), and the responses to a number of rather intimate questions. As in, had they been intimate to date (yes), was there a chance that a pup was already on the way (no), and which pack would they choose as their primary residence (Texarkana)? Then the parents, who strangely seemed to be the same age as their offspring, were called up to give their blessing to the happy couple, and then, as if that weren't enough, the alphas got involved. By the time the first couple had jumped through all the requisite hoops I was ready to start screaming—and there were five more to go.

This was all well and good, but my father was due to be tried tomorrow, and unless they got the show on the road, there was no way I was going to find out anything useful. I might get a chance to talk to him, though . . . if by chance the garden cottage was unguarded.

I turned to Tom. "While we're waiting for all this to finish up, do you think I could slip back and visit my dad again? Before they indict him?"

"No," Tom said.

"Why not?"

"He's already here," he murmured.

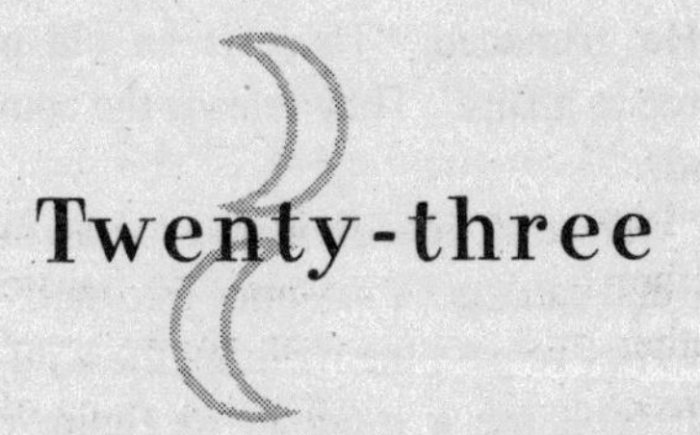

Twenty-three

"He's here? Where?" I took a deep breath, sniffing for him, but all I got was smoke, dead rabbit, and excited werewolf.

"Come with me," he said, and I followed him as he slipped out of the clearing, away from the flickering light of the torches, and headed into the dark woods. "They'll bring him out after they hear the case against the others."

"What others? I thought the big court date was tomorrow?"

"There are three made werewolves who are accused of hunting humans; they will be tried before the assembly tonight. They are not born werewolves, so it is considered minor business."

I shivered. "Not Fluffy, Stinky, and Scrawny?" I was referring to the three made werewolves who had prowled in Austin last fall. I'd rescued a sorority girl from them once in an alley off Sixth Street.

"No," he said. "They are no longer werewolves. Remember?"

"Oh, yeah," I said. "I forgot you used your magic unmaking thing on them." My thoughts turned back to the werewolves in custody. "So, if they're found guilty, what will happen? Will you 'unmake' them?"

"No," he said.

"What then?"

He grimaced. "There is an old punishment, known as 'Free as a Bird'. They release the convicted werewolves," he said.

"Well, that doesn't sound too awful," I said. "How come my dad can't get a sentence like that?"

"They release them during the wild hunt," he clarified.

It took me a moment to figure out exactly what Tom meant. And when I did, it was more than a little bit disturbing. "Wait a minute. Do you mean that . . . that they're the prey?"

Tom nodded sharply, and my stomach clenched. "Dear God," I breathed. "But what if they're found innocent? What will everyone hunt instead?"

"They won't be found innocent," Tom said with a chilling air of finality. "They are as good as dead, I'm afraid. Unless they can run very, very fast."

"And my father?"

He was silent for a moment. "I don't want to scare you, Sophie, but it is not promising. There is some hope . . . but not much."

Shit. Shit, shit, shit. "So the trial is fixed." My pulse started racing, and I could feel the sweat spring up on my body. I should have listened to my father, done what he'd asked. I should have told Georges right away, and told him to call Armand. The trial was tomorrow. Was it too late?

"The trial will not be fixed, exactly, but it will be rather heavily weighted against him."

"But why is my father being tried separately, in this—Famish Court thing, or whatever you call it?" I asked.

"The Fehmic Court," Tom said. "Your father is a born werewolf, and an alpha. Which means that different rules apply."

"But . . ."

"Shh," he whispered, pointing through a break in the cedar trees. "He's right over there."

Just then, a fresh gust from the south brought me a strong whiff of Luc Garou.

He stood motionless in the center of a small clearing, wrapped head to toe in chains and surrounded by four burly guards, two of whom held torches. A few feet away from him, chained together by their manacles, were the three made werewolves Tom had told me about. Teenagers, at least by the look of them—two lanky boys and a girl with cropped black hair. Their fear was acrid in my nostrils.

And so was my father's.

Despite his ramrod-straight posture, all of Luc Garou's cockiness was gone, his face grim. I was suddenly desperate to talk to him. If what Tom had told me was correct, this might be one of my last opportunities. But even if I could snatch a few moments alone with him, I realized with a sick feeling, the first thing he would ask was if I'd gotten in touch with Armand.

And I'd have to tell him I'd let him down.

I stared at my father for several minutes, guilt eating at me. After twenty-eight years, I'd been reunited with my father, only to lose him just days after our first meeting. I was still angry at him—that hadn't changed at all—but knowing that I'd probably see him executed was wrenching. I looked at my father one last time, trying to memorize his face. Then I touched Tom on the arm. "I can't stay here," I said.

He nodded, squeezing my arm lightly, and together we found our way back to the clearing. As the next couples went through the motions, I stood beside Tom in a daze, running through scenarios in my mind. As soon as I got home tonight, I'd go and see Georges, and tell him the situation was dire—that he needed to call in Armand immediately. If they left Paris tonight, they could be in Austin in time for the trial.

The question was, how soon could I leave? Just after the assembly brought Luc before them and indicted him officially, I decided. I wanted to hear all the charges, so I knew exactly what we were dealing with. Not that I held out much hope for the trial. I knew in my heart that even with a reincarnated Johnnie Cochran defending my father, he wouldn't have a chance.

I stood, lost in my thoughts, for a long time; suddenly, I realized the final couple was receiving the werewolf seal of approval, and we were about to move on to the next stage.

"What's next?"

"I think the petition for Elena to become alpha," Tom said, and sure enough, Isabella called both Wolfgang and his soon-to-be-paramour to stand before the pulpit. Wolfgang rose from his wooden throne and held out a hand to Elena, who took it regally and strode beside him, chin up, looking like the Queen of England as the pair approached the center of the clearing. Her blouse, I noticed now, was gold, to reflect the colors of the Houston pack's banner.

"Herr Graf," Isabella said formally, inclining her head slightly to Wolfgang, who dipped his head in response. It was clearly a meeting of equals. "Miss Tenorio," she then said, addressing Elena with only a trace of a nod. Elena's eyes flashed a little bit as she returned the Philadelphia alpha's greeting, dipping her own head just a fraction of an inch. Then Isabella returned her attention to Wolfgang. "I understand that you have selected a consort to share your reign," she said formally.

"I have," Wolfgang said, turning to address the crowd. He wore dark blue slacks and a starched white shirt, with a tie that was the gold of the Houston pack's banner. If I hadn't known he was a werewolf, I would have pegged him for a CEO. "I present Elena Tenorio, whom I have selected to reign with me as alpha of the Houston pack," he announced solemnly. "She hails from the Tenorio line of Andalusia." He spent a few minutes listing a long line of relatives, none of whom I recognized—werewolves in general seemed kind of hung up on genealogy, I noticed—concluding with a word about her more illustrious relations. "As many of you know, her grandmother Rosamaria was alpha of the Seville pack for more than fifty years, so nobility runs in her blood. Ms. Tenorio has served me faithfully since her arrival in Houston twenty years ago, and I very much look forward to welcoming her as my mate." Wolfgang's eyes moved among the tents, from alpha to alpha, as if searching for someone who might have a different opinion on the subject. "If anyone should object to her coronation," he intoned a moment later, "the time for words is now."

He looked slowly from face to face, lingering slightly at the Louisiana tent. Something unreadable passed between the New Orleans alpha and Wolfgang—I could see a slight tension in Wolfgang's jaw—before his gaze slid past Jean-Louis to the Arkansas tent, where he was greeted with a curt nod.

"If there are no objections," Isabella said when Wolfgang had made eye contact with the last alpha, "the coronation will proceed tomorrow, just before moonrise."

Applause rang out among the assembled werewolves as Wolfgang and Elena stepped down from the slab of granite and walked hand in hand back to their tent.

"That's it?" I asked.

"That's it," Tom said. "Now we go through the alliances."

Tom was right; a moment later, Isabella launched into an impassioned speech about solidarity and standing firm against our southern neighbors, the *Norteños*, who were trying to "rise like a phoenix from the ashes." I watched with interest as the alphas proposing alliances approached the center slab together, all looking like lions about to enter the ring. Boris's—or was it Dudley's?—words came back to me: *"If he agrees to it in front of the assembly, it will be tough to renege."* Were they talking about a proposed alliance between Wolfgang and another alpha? Who did they think might back out?

The first two alliance propositions went along just fine; Wolfgang renewed ties with Texarkana and formed new ties with Oklahoma, which ended with a lot of handshaking and gibberish. Then he and Jean-Louis faced off, and a stillness passed through the clearing. The red-haired alpha stood beside Jean-Louis, her face a mask.

"What's the deal?" I asked Tom.

"The Louisiana alphas are French."

"So?"

"Not a lot of love lost between the Germans and the French."

Despite their historical differences, though, they seemed to have gotten over it. Wolfgang had just agreed to forge a new alliance with his eastern neighbors, and Isabella had just turned to the alphas of the Louisiana pack to confirm that they were on board with the whole thing when there was a jangle of chains from the side of the clearing, and a familiar voice called out.

"*Jean-Louis! Comment va tout en New Orleans?* Or what's left of it, after your visit from *l'ouragan*."

The owner of the voice was, of course, Luc Garou. I cringed. I couldn't be a hundred percent sure, but I was fairly certain he was referring to Hurricane Katrina. Like I said, my father wasn't exactly gifted in the politics department.

A murmur rose among the tents as Jean-Louis's head whipped around. My stomach sank. "Traitor," Jean-Louis hissed. Then he turned to Wolfgang. "Why is he here?"

"He will be tried tomorrow," Wolfgang said. "For murder."

"He should be killed now! For treachery!" Jean-Louis thundered, the blood rushing to his cheeks.

Luc raised his head. "I took what was rightfully mine," he called. Then he looked at Wolfgang. "And Armand will take what is his—again. My daughter has already contacted him. I would not be astonished if they arrived tonight."

I shrank against Tom, willing my father to shut up.

Jean-Louis shot my father a venomous glare, then turned back to Wolfgang. "Until Garou is dead, there will be no alliance. You are harboring a traitor to my family."

"And to mine," Wolfgang reminded him.

"Then let us both avenge our families," Jean-Louis growled.

"No," Wolfgang said, his voice like steel. "We will convene the *Fehmgericht* tomorrow."

"He has not officially been indicted. It is not yet binding. So kill him now," Jean-Louis demanded, his eyes flaring in the firelight. "Only when he's dead will I accede to your alliance. As long as you harbor this *traître*, I cannot trust you."

"He is my prisoner," Wolfgang said. "Not my ally."

"He should be dead," Jean-Louis said.

Wolfgang seemed to be considering this logic. He turned to look at my father, who took that moment to say, "Armand will be so happy to see you, after all these long years. You must miss the wurst . . ."

I winced. What the hell had happened to all that fear I'd smelled on my father earlier? Why on earth couldn't he keep his mouth shut?

Wolfgang turned back to Jean-Louis. "Perhaps we could make an exception . . ."

"No!" I shouted before I even knew what I was doing. "It's against the Code! We're in the proscribed time!" As Wolfgang and Jean-Louis stared at me with something like shock, I bolted into the center of the clearing. The fire was hot against my skin as I faced the two alphas.

"Who is this?" Jean-Louis asked, looking utterly confused.

"That is my daughter," Luc announced proudly from his shackles on the edge of the clearing. "Sophie Garou."

Another excited murmur passed through the clearing. Wolfgang's eyes burned with cold anger as they met mine. "Why are you here under false pretenses?" he barked. Behind him, Elena bared her teeth and snarled.

"She's here with me," Tom said, striding up beside me and putting an arm around my shoulders. "And she is correct. If you fail to follow through with the trial, you, too, will be guilty of the same crime with which you have charged Luc Garou."

"But he is a traitor!" Jean-Louis bellowed.

"Tom is technically correct. Luc Garou is the alpha of the Paris pack," Wolfgang said. Although I was all in favor of what he was saying, the look in his eyes—not to mention the tone of his voice, which made liquid nitrogen seem toasty by comparison—paralyzed me with fear. I wasn't sure if Wolfgang had ever been someone I'd consider a friend, but he certainly wasn't now. "He must be tried."

"Sophie! When will Armand be here?" Luc Garou called from his spot along the sidelines.

I stared straight ahead, feeling guilt wash through me that I hadn't done what my father had requested. Was there enough time left? The murmur rose to a roar around us, and Isabella responded by hammering the podium-pulpit thingamajig with a big gavel. "Silence!" she bellowed. "At once! We will return to the business at hand."

She glared around the clearing, as if daring someone to speak. When no one volunteered, she returned her gaze to Wolfgang and Jean-Louis. "Am I to presume that the alliance will not move forward at this time?"

"Not until Luc Garou is dead with a stake in his chest," Jean-Louis said, then slowly turned to me. The look in his golden eyes froze me to the marrow. "Along with his mongrel whelp."

Twenty-four

My heart just about stopped in my chest at the poison in Jean-Louis's look. I'd never known what it was like to have someone want to murder me because of my parentage, and I can't say I enjoyed the experience. My eyes veered away from Jean-Louis and landed on my shackled father, which wasn't a vast improvement.

"Sophie has done nothing wrong," Tom said from somewhere behind me.

"She's called the Paris pack to attack," Wolfgang pointed out. "I think that qualifies, don't you?"

My face burned under the gaze of hundreds of werewolf eyes. Including my father's, which were blazing with misplaced hope. I hadn't, in fact, gotten in touch with the Paris pack, but I wasn't about to admit that in front of my father.

"You are bound by the code to try Luc Garou," Tom said evenly.

Wolfgang stared at Tom, his eyes cold, and I could sense the battle of wills. Then, quietly, Tom said, "Do it for Astrid." Astrid, Tom's sister—and Wolfgang's former mate.

Wolfgang's face didn't even flicker at the mention of his deceased beloved, but to be honest, I wasn't surprised. After all, Astrid and Wolfgang had parted ways a long time ago, and Wolfgang was about to get hitched to mate number three—that I knew of, anyway. There could be many more. But after a long moment during which I promised everything but my firstborn to whatever gods might be in the neighborhood if only the Houston alpha would relent, Wolfgang turned to Isabella. "Summon Luc Garou to the *Fehmgericht*," he said curtly.

I let out the breath I hadn't realized I was holding.

"But . . . what of the alliances?" Isabella said.

"I believe we have just concluded that portion of the assembly," Wolfgang said, glancing at Jean-Louis, who was still looking at me like he was deciding if the two-inch or the three-inch stake would be a better fit between my ventricles. Wolfgang continued, his voice quiet but deadly. "The alliance will progress no further until this other business is attended to. I ask you again: Summon Mr. Garou to the *Fehmgericht*, Frau Murano."

After a moment's hesitation, Isabella beckoned to one of the cadre of werewolves standing nearby, and he hurried up to the podium. As the werewolf underling scurried off, Isabella addressed Wolfgang. "The preparation of the document summoning Monsieur Garou to the *Fehmgericht* has not yet been completed," she said. "I propose that while we wait, we attend to the other outstanding issue."

When Wolfgang nodded, Isabella said a few words to the rest of the attending werewolves, who scattered to the tents. Then Isabella addressed the entire assembly. "I call all present alphas to preside at a criminal trial."

Each alpha howled assent, including Wolfgang and Jean-Louis, who were returning to their thrones as the three manacled werewolves were dragged to stand in front of the podium.

"State your names," Isabella announced. When they had done as she requested, she said, "You have been charged with the crime of attacking and mauling humans in an urban area. How do you plead?"

"Not guilty!" said the girl, whose fear was so strong I could smell it over the smoke of the fire. "Not guilty!" echoed the two teenaged boys flanking her, their voices quavering.

"Are there witnesses to the crime?" Isabella asked.

A woman from the Texarkana pack raised her hand. "I saw it," she said.

"Your name, madame?"

"Guinevere Morton of the Texarkana pack," she said. "Formerly of the New York pack."

"For the sake of the court, Ms. Morton, please state what you observed."

"I was in town for the Howl, out for an evening run, and I saw these three harassing a young woman in the Greenbelt."

"She was my friend!" the girl cried. "We weren't harassing her—we were just out for a hike!"

"Silence!" Isabella said, addressing the girl with an icy voice. Then she turned back to the born werewolf. "How were they harassing the human?"

"One of them had his teeth on her arm. They were pinning her down. They were about to rip her throat out, but I intervened."

"We were helping her up!" the girl wailed. "She'd tripped! We're innocent, I swear it!"

Isabella didn't even glance at the girl, who was on her knees now, begging for mercy. "Excellent, Ms. Morton. Thank you." The Philadelphia alpha looked around. "Are there any other witnesses for the prosecution?"

Nobody answered.

"All right, then. Are there any witnesses for the defense?"

"We didn't do it, ma'am. Honest, we didn't," the girl cried. "We were just trying to help!"

"The accused will remain silent," Isabella said.

"But please!" Tears formed in her eyes. "My mother would die if anything happened to me . . ."

"Any witnesses for the defense?" Isabella repeated. I was dying to speak out on their behalf—they looked so pathetic that even if they *had* been harassing a human I thought they deserved another chance—but was afraid that any word from me would only damage their case further. After a torturously long moment, Isabella said, "If there are no more witnesses, and no further evidence, I commend this case to the judges."

The girl wailed, but Isabella ignored her, and within a minute, the werewolves who had dispersed to the tents started returning to her with folded pieces of paper. When the final slip had made its way back to the central podium, which must have taken all of five minutes, Isabella reviewed the papers and then faced the three made werewolves. The two boys were trying to pull the girl to her feet, but her knees appeared to have given out on her. "Rise to hear the verdict," Isabella said, and they somehow managed to get her up onto her Keds. Her mascara made streaks down her face, and with her cheeks still slightly chubby with baby fat, she looked no older than thirteen.

"The assembly court finds you guilty of hunting humans in a manner that violates the Code," Isabella said in a flat voice. The girl screamed, a long wail that took a long time to die. "The sentence," Isabella continued, "is that tomorrow at moonrise, you, the condemned, will be 'Free as a Bird'."

The girl looked up in disbelief. "You're gonna let us go?" she asked, her voice quavering. She raised a hand to wipe her cheeks, but the chains held her back.

"You are dismissed until tomorrow at moonrise," Isabella said briskly, turning away from her. The jailers moved toward the trio.

"They're letting us go!" the girl said. "I can't believe it!" But when the burly werewolves made no move to unlock the padlocks and started pulling the three made werewolves back to the edge of the clearing, she looked confused. "But why are we still in chains? Are they just waiting till tomorrow? If we're going to go free, why wait?"

My heart plummeted all the way to my shoes as they led the three young werewolves out of the clearing. How long would it take for her to figure out what "Free as a Bird" meant? Would it be when Wolfgang ran her down?

I closed my eyes, feeling panic pressing in against me. If

what I had just witnessed was considered a fair trial, then Luc Garou was screwed.

While the tents buzzed with speculation, Isabella stood gripping the podium with one hand and smoothing down her black hair until finally one of the werewolves returned with a rolled-up document in one hand and a black case in the other.

Isabella whisked it from the underling's hand, then unrolled it. Gesturing for the underling to open the case, she directed her attention to the Houston tent. "Herr Graf, will you please approach the podium and apply the appropriate signature?"

"Of course," said Wolfgang, and strode to the center of the clearing. Isabella handed him a long, silvery knife and something that looked like a pen. To my shock, Wolfgang rolled up his left shirtsleeve and drew the knife across his forearm until blood started running down to his elbow. Then, to my utter disgust, he held the nib of the pen to the wound and applied the pen to paper. After three returns to the inkwell, so to speak, he finished his signature with a flourish and returned the document to Isabella, who read it to the assembly while Wolfgang stanched his wound with a cloth.

"Let it be known by this document," Isabella intoned as the torches flared around her, "that Luc Garou of the Paris pack has been called to trial by Herr Wolfgang Graf, reigning alpha of the Houston pack and *Freigraf* of the Texas *Fehmgericht*."

"What's a *Freigraf*?" I whispered to Tom.

"The leader of the Fehmic Court," he said.

Isabella continued. "The charge is the murder of a fellow werewolf during the proscribed time. The court date has been set for tomorrow, March twentieth, at sundown. Failure to appear will constitute an assumption of guilt, with the sentence appropriate to that verdict." With a flick of her wrist, she rolled up the document and handed it back to the underling, pointing at my father. "Deliver it to the accused."

The werewolf took the rolled-up parchment and crossed

the clearing to where my father stood in chains. Luc refused to take it, until two werewolves grabbed his arm and pried his hand open. My father growled, but was forced to wrap his fingers around the roll.

"The summons has been delivered," intoned Isabella. "The court will convene tomorrow evening."

"You'll be dead before it even gets started!" Luc called as they started pushing him out of the clearing. "My daughter will see to that! You'll all pay for this!"

He was still shouting when Tom took my arm and pulled me away from the crowd of shouting werewolves. "Let's get out of here while we still can," he said, leading me away from the fire. "They're not supposed to be able to hold you here, but with passions running high, we should leave as quickly as possible." I took a last glance back at the leader of the pack, who appeared to be barking orders to his underlings, before Tom and I sprinted through the woods, escaping to his motorcycle—and to the twenty-first century.

Twenty-five

"We have to go to the Driskill," I yelled as Tom revved up the engine of his Harley and we tore toward the Graf Ranch exit. I glanced over my shoulder as he gunned it; nobody had followed us yet, but I was afraid it was only a matter of time.

"Why the Driskill?"

"To see Georges," I said. "My father's assistant."

"You really want to involve the Paris pack?" Tom asked. "It's a dangerous move."

"What choice do I have?" I asked, but Tom didn't answer me. I liked to think it was because it was too loud to hear, but I was afraid that wasn't the only reason.

I spent the next hour and a half leaning into Tom and savoring the clean, cold, slightly exhaust-scented wind. After my evening of medieval hell, I'd never been so thankful to see technology before, and the neon-lit gas stations and tacky billboards I usually found so annoying were the most gorgeous things on the planet. Tom kept the speedometer around seventy-five, which was fine by me; I was anxious to put as many miles of blacktop as possible between me and Fredericksburg.

The reprieve was extremely temporary, though; I'd be back tomorrow, for the trial. And even though I'd managed to escape, at least for the night, both my father and the poor teenaged werewolves were still there, awaiting their awful fates.

I also knew that if Jean-Louis had his way, I would soon be joining them.

It was almost midnight by the time Tom pulled up outside the Driskill Hotel's grand exterior, but the Sixth Street crowd was still going strong, staggering in and out of bars and, from the smell in the air, occasionally disgorging liters of partially digested beer and margaritas onto the sidewalk. Tom parked along the street—one of the benefits of riding a motorcycle is that it's easy to find a place to put it—and I once again fought to resuscitate my hair as we headed into the old hotel's grand front entrance together.

"What room is he in?" Tom asked as we nodded to the bellhop and padded through the ornate entryway. The massive chandelier glistened comfortingly above us, speaking of civilization and normalcy. If it weren't for the smoky smell that clung to my hair and clothes, it would be hard to believe I'd watched Wolfgang cut his arm open by the light of a hundred torches just an hour or two earlier.

"He's on the fourth floor," I said.

Tom paused a few yards away from the elevator. "What are you planning on telling him, Sophie?"

"That my father's in trouble, and that we need reinforcements immediately."

"There are several hundred werewolves in attendance at the Howl," Tom pointed out. "That's an awful lot of plane tickets."

He had a good point; I hadn't considered the difference in numbers. Would the French reinforcements be enough? Or should I abandon the plan and just ask Mark to free Luc? Provided he really could . . . "I'm open to suggestions, Tom. I don't know what else to do. If tomorrow's trial is anything like tonight's, it doesn't matter if my father's innocent. It's going to be a sham."

Tom caught my arm. "Are you willing to risk a war for your father's life?"

"It seems the answer is yes," I said. "Otherwise I wouldn't be here."

His grip on my arm hardened. "Are you willing to risk your existence in Austin, and maybe even your life, for a man who abandoned you when you were just a pup?"

How could I explain what I was feeling? I wasn't sure I could; everything in my world had been turned upside down over the last few days. "I think my life's already in danger, to be honest," I said. "But I've thought about it, Tom, and the thing is, I can't just let my father die. He may have abandoned me when I was a child, but I won't do the same to him now."

Tom released my arm, but not my gaze. It was impossible to tell what he was thinking—those golden eyes seemed blank as mirrors to me. "It sounds like your decision is made, then," he said slowly. "I just want to make sure you've thought about the consequences."

I took the opportunity to voice a suspicion I'd been harboring all evening. "Is there another reason you don't want me to rescue him?" I asked. "Are you sure you don't still have a grudge against my father, for what happened to . . . to Astrid?"

"I'll admit that Luc Garou is not my favorite person," he said. "But my primary concern is you."

Something about the way he said it sent delicious feelings rippling through me. "Honestly?"

"Honestly," he said.

"Why?"

"Because it is," he said, and looked away.

A tension hung in the air, and I wasn't sure what to do with it. Finally, I broke it. "Are you coming with me?" I asked softly.

"I don't think so," he said. "Considering our families' history, I think it would be better if I stayed here."

"I'll meet you in the lobby then," I said.

Before I turned to head for the elevator, he gave me one last warning. "Tell him they're going to subject him to the Fehmic Court," he said. "Tell him they must come quickly, if they come at all." Something about the look in his eyes sent a pulse of heat through me—and a ripple of fear.

"Got it," I said, and pressed the up button on the elevator, which dinged and slid open a moment later. When the doors shut behind me, I sagged against the elevator wall. It had been a pretty big night, and it wasn't over yet.

I knew as soon as the elevator doors opened that something was wrong. Everything looked perfectly normal—the floral carpet, the wooden doors, an abandoned room service tray—but something was different. Something was wrong.

I approached Georges's door with caution, sniffing for clues as to what might await me. But someone had recently swabbed down the area with Lysol, which put me at a major disadvantage, although I thought I picked up the thread of a familiar scent.

Taking a deep breath, I raised my hand to knock. *If you survived the CPA exam, you can survive anything,* I told myself, though it didn't do quite as much for my courage as I would have liked. My knuckles had barely touched the wood when the door flew open, and two werewolves launched themselves at me.

The change ripped through me automatically; the bigger werewolf, whose teeth were on my neck, lost his grip as my body transformed. I took advantage of their surprise to bolt down the hallway toward the stairwell door.

The only problem was, I didn't have the thumbs required to turn the knob.

Since I had no other choice, I wheeled around to face my attackers, who were already barreling down the hallway toward me. They were large, dark, and smelled like pleather. Blood was thick in the air, too—Georges's, probably, I realized—but even that couldn't knock out the overpowering scent of synthetic textile.

And the acrid smell of my own fear.

As I struggled to disentangle myself from my jeans, the bigger one launched himself at my head, sharp teeth bared in a death's-head grin. I managed to duck out of *his* way, but the second werewolf was ready for me. He darted forward, mouth open, going for the kill. I backpedaled, but not in time; his teeth grazed my neck, and I could feel the gush of hot blood on my fur. *Tom,* I thought. *I need you!*

I stumbled down the hall, trying to escape the onslaught of tooth and claw, hoping I could get to Georges's room and shut the door. I didn't know what I'd do then—maybe call animal control and let them deal with it—but all I could think of right now was getting a big chunk of solid wood between me and Elena's pleather boys.

I was a few feet from the door—and relative safety—when a set of teeth sank into my tail, making me howl in pain. I whipped around, snapping at the wolf behind me, but he hung on, muzzle bloody from his first attack, eyes gleaming, waiting for his friend to come and finish me off. I tried pulling away, but his teeth dug in deeper, sending waves of agony through me. I struggled to think through the pain. Could I slip loose by transforming back to human form? It was a nice idea, but with the amount of adrenaline running through my system, changing into a human would be about as easy as changing into a camel right about now.

And I was out of time, anyway. The larger wolf advanced on me again, staring at my throat. As he crouched for the final pounce, I thought, *I'm sorry, Dad—I tried*—and closed my eyes, waiting for the pain to begin.

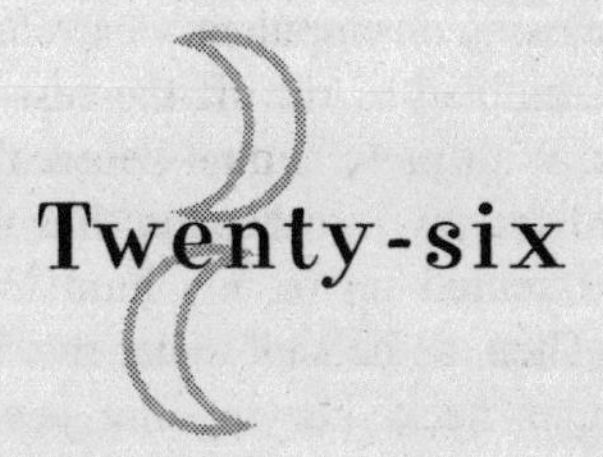

Twenty-six

But it didn't.

There was the ding of a small bell, and all three of us whipped around to face the elevator, whose doors were already sliding open. *Thank God*, I thought. I never dreamed I'd be thrilled to have a human catch me in wolf form at the Driskill Hotel. Now, however, I could think of few things that would delight me more.

Except for what *did* happen. Which was that a huge golden wolf leaped out of the elevator and launched himself at the werewolf on my tail.

The pleather boy on my tail released me, turning to face what amounted to a very large kink in the general plan to dismember me. But while Tom had the smaller one under control, I still had to deal with Boris. Or Dudley. It was hard to tell which was which.

As Tom shook the tail-biting werewolf around like a dead chicken, the bigger of the pair charged me, teeth bared and directed at my throat. I jerked to the right, but he was right there with me; and with my jeans still tangled between my legs, I was slower than usual. As he barreled toward me, time seemed to slow down. *I'm going to die on the fourth floor of the Driskill Hotel.*

But I couldn't. Not until I rescued my father.

Just before the werewolf's teeth clamped down on my neck, I rolled to the right. He skidded to a stop on the carpet, jaws closing on empty air.

I scrambled to rip off the rest of my jeans, freeing my limbs. With preternatural speed, the werewolf whirled and lunged for my throat again, but this time I was ready for him. I reared up on my hind legs, dodging him just in time. Then, as he shot under me, I snapped at his massive, muscular neck, burying my jaws in his wiry, pleather-flavored hide.

The werewolf howled in dismay, shaking hard to dislodge me, but I held on tight, despite the awful taste flooding my mouth. He bent his head around, snapping at my hindquarters, but I just bit down harder, until a gush of blood spurted out, splattering the wall and darkening the carpet under my front paws. I was vaguely aware of a door opening and then slamming shut somewhere, and the thought *you need to get out of here fast* floated through my mind. But that little detached thought just hovered around the edge of my thoughts, like an irritating gnat. My entire being was focused on the burly werewolf beneath me—and on staying alive.

My jaw ached as I clamped down, struggling to keep my

hold on him, but I didn't let go, even when he reeled sideways, slamming me against the wall. If I let go, I knew, I'd be dead.

Finally, just when I thought I couldn't hold him for another second—not only was my jaw aching, but he tasted just awful—the burly body grew limp in my jaws. I let the wolf drop to the floor, but refused to release him—if he was playing possum, I'd be toast. Only when Tom padded over to me, dragging the other pleather boy by the scruff of the neck, did I dare loosen my grip.

Tom's golden eyes were inscrutable, but he jerked his head toward Georges's open door. He'd seen the door open, too; we both knew it was only a matter of time before hotel security started sniffing around. The day had been long enough without ending it in the Town Lake animal shelter's version of doggie death row.

I started to pull the werewolf in my jaws toward Georges's door, but Tom stopped me with a short bark.

As I lifted a tuft of fur that functioned as one of my eyebrows, he dropped the smaller werewolf and sprinted into the hotel room, returning with a blanket clamped between his teeth; within seconds he had rolled the limp body of the larger werewolf onto it, and I followed suit with the second one. He dropped the remains of our clothing on top of the furry bodies, and together we dragged the whole kit and caboodle through the doorway. Boris's head took a nasty hit on the doorframe, I'm afraid, but since he had just tried to rip my throat out a few minutes earlier, I didn't feel too awful about it. I had just nudged the door closed behind us when I heard the ding of the elevator, and voices in the hallway.

I turned back to Tom, and what I saw took my breath away.

Tom was back in human form, stark naked, and looking even more perfect than I could have imagined. Even *with* the still-healing wound on his thigh. But his gorgeousness wasn't the only surprise—and the other was far less pleasant. Sprawled across the bed, a rictus of pain on his waxen face, was the body of Georges. Blood stained the flowered bedspread, and a wooden stake sprouted from his chest.

"You need to transform," Tom said, heading for the bathroom as he spoke. "When they come to the door, we'll both be in towels. We didn't hear anything—we were in the shower."

I dipped my head and padded toward the bathroom, where I waited until Tom left, a towel wrapped around his trim middle, before nudging the door closed and calming myself down enough to let the change course through me. Once I was in possession of opposable thumbs again, I rinsed the blood off my face and neck, splashed some water on my hair, and grabbed a towel.

"What do we do about these two?" I asked when I stepped back into the bedroom a minute later.

Tom's eyes raked me up and down, making my skin feel like it was on fire, but all he said was, "We'll put them in the bathtub. Out of sight."

"Are they . . . dead?" I asked.

"Not yet," he said ominously. "But I'm afraid your friend Georges didn't make it. I think he should go first. If you'll take the feet, I'll take the arms."

I did as Tom asked—what choice did I have?—but it was a gruesome process. The stake was entangled in the bedsprings, so we had to rock him back and forth a few times to get him loose. By the time we had levered Georges into the bathtub and piled the pleather boys on top of him, I needed a new towel, since mine was slipping off and covered in werewolf blood.

Tom left the bathroom for a moment as I exchanged my towel for a fresh one, and despite the pile of dead or wounded werewolves just inches away, I found myself very conscious of the fact that we were almost naked—and in a hotel room together. Alone, if you didn't count the unconscious werewolves. When I closed the bathroom door behind me a moment later, Tom was covering up the mess on the bed with pillows. I found myself staring at the dusting of golden hairs on his bronze skin, just above the towel. Then I realized he was watching me, and I jerked my eyes northward, to his face.

"Thanks for your help out there," I said. "Why did you get the blanket?"

"So the blood trail wouldn't lead here," he said.

"Good thinking," I said. My eyes strayed from Tom's tan, lithe body to the bloodstained bed. Poor Georges. "Why do you think they killed him?" I asked.

"Why do you think?" he asked.

"To keep him from getting in touch with Paris?" I thought about it for a moment. "And then they ambushed me, to eliminate all other contacts . . ."

"That would be my assessment," he said.

The smell of blood and werewolf made my stomach roil. "I feel awful—like it's my fault."

"What could you have done to change it, Sophie?"

"Maybe if I'd told him to call the Paris pack . . . told him that Luc was in trouble . . ."

"Do you think he'd be alive if you had?" Tom asked, moving closer to me. Despite the rather awful circumstances, I felt my hormones buzzing at his nearness; particularly when he put a warm hand on my shoulder. It was just a touch, but it was incredibly erotic.

"He would have gone to the Howl, confronted the pack, and the result would have been the same," I said, trying to control my voice—and my feelings, which were running haywire. "They would have killed him on the spot rather than let him get in touch with their enemies."

As a loud voice sounded from the hallway, he lifted his hand, breaking the spell. I glanced at the remains of my clothes, then back at Tom's golden eyes. "We're trapped, aren't we?" I said.

Before he could answer, there was a knock at the door. My eyes leapt to the door. "Now what?" I whispered.

"Answer it," he said softly. "Tell them you didn't hear anything—we were showering together. Ask what happened."

A second knock came. "Did I get all the blood off?" I whispered.

"You're fine," he said. "Just answer it."

Heart pounding, I tightened the towel around me and walked to the door, peeking through the peephole. Then I opened the door.

A chubby security guard stood there, stance wide. His nametag identified him as Alberto Sanchez. I peered behind him, a bit shocked to see the aftermath of our tussle. The hallway looked like an abattoir. "What's going on?" I asked.

"That's what we were hoping you could help us with, ma'am."

I blinked, trying to look perplexed. "What do you mean?"

"We had a report that there were four dogs fighting in the hallway a little while ago. Did you see or hear anything?"

"No," I said. "But we, I mean, *I* was in the shower," I said, reaching down to adjust my towel. Alberto's eyes flicked down to my towel, and a slow blush suffused his chubby face. "One of the other guests said she saw them head toward your room."

"I don't think so," I said, opening the door a little bit wider and hoping we'd managed to cover all the blood. "As you can see, it's just my boyfriend and me," I said.

The guard's eyes took in the scene behind me: a rumpled bed, with Tom sitting at the end of it, wearing only a towel.

"Howdy," Tom said, adopting an atrocious Texas accent and waving cheerfully. "Everything okay?"

"Just doing a little investigation, sir," the guard said. "There was a bit of a dogfight in the hallway a few minutes ago. Did you see or hear anything?"

Tom shook his head and gave Alberto a salacious grin. "No, but since we were, uh, occupied in the shower . . ."

The guard's face flushed a little bit at the sight of the disheveled bed and the near-naked man sitting on it.

"This is awful," I said. "Wild dogs in the hallway? What if I'd stepped out to get a drink or something? I could have been savaged! Where's the manager?" I added recklessly, figuring the best defense was a good offense. "Maybe I need to ask for a discount on the bill!"

"I'm sorry to disturb you two," the guard said. "If you think of anything, please let security know."

"Thank you," I said. "And please let the manager know we will be speaking to him shortly." Which was not in fact the truth—if anything, the manager would be wanting to speak with me once he'd seen what had happened to his rather expensive mattress. Not to mention the dead body in the bathtub.

"Of course, ma'am. Thank you for your help."

"You're welcome," I said, shutting the door firmly.

"Nicely done," Tom said from his spot at the end of the bed.

"Thanks," I said. "But what do we do now?"

"I don't know," Tom said, a sly smile on his face. He patted the bed beside him. "I can think of a way to pass the time until the pleather boys wake up."

I surveyed the bloodstained sheets, which were only partially covered by pillows. "You're kidding me, right?"

"Only partially, I'm afraid. Unfortunately, unless you can magically produce a wardrobe, our options are limited."

"I could call Lindsey," I said, then realized that since we were both essentially naked in a hotel room, it might be tough to explain. "Although that might not be the best idea, come to think of it. And besides, what about the pleather boys?" I asked, glancing at the bathroom door.

"We'll question them when they come to," he said. "If there's enough left of them to question, that is. You sure did sink your teeth into the big one."

"Was that Boris? Or Dudley? Whoever it was, he tasted awful. I still have the taste in my mouth."

"Boris," he said, getting up to peer out of the peephole.

"They've got the cleaning crew at work, at least. Which means they're not calling in the police."

"Thank God for that," I said, examining the remains of my clothes. My jeans were relatively intact, as was my bra, but my wrap top was stained with blood and torn into two pieces. My jacket had suffered some major damage, too. "I'm going to look like hell walking out of here, though."

"I left everything I had in the elevator," Tom pointed out.

"Oh, no, Tom. How are we going to get you out of here?" I considered the problem for a moment. "I guess I could pretend you were my dog, but after what just happened . . ." I stifled a smile at the thought of taking Tom the werewolf for a walk. "It's a shame. You'd look good in a collar," I said.

"Too bad you'll never get to see it," he said, standing up and smoothing out his towel. I tried hard not to stare, but there was something so magnetic about him, it was almost impossible. "Georges's whole wardrobe is here, but based on his size, I doubt they'll fit. Same with Elena's boys—they're large, but not tall."

Think, Sophie. We needed to get out of here, and without drawing attention to ourselves. We were surrounded by men's clothes, but unless Tom was comfortable strolling through downtown in the equivalent of capri pants, it wasn't going to work. If only we were in Luc's room . . .

"Wait a minute," I said. "That door over there"—I pointed to a door on the side wall—"I'll bet it connects to my father's room. You wouldn't fit into Georges's clothes, but you and my father are pretty close in size."

I walked over and tried the door. It was unlocked. I opened it gingerly, relieved to pick up the faint scent of my father. But the relief was quickly followed by a sinking feeling. This might be one of the last times I ever smelled him . . .

I pushed those thoughts out of my mind and headed for the closet, Tom behind me. "Will these work?" I asked, pulling a pair of jeans off of a hanger. He hung up his jeans? *Don't worry about it now, Sophie.* "They may be a little tight, I'm afraid."

"Your father does favor snug-fitting clothing, doesn't he?" Tom said.

"They'll be better than pleather pants, at least. Why don't you get changed here, and I'll try to get myself together in the other room."

"Seems a shame, really."

"What?"

"Oh, you know. A beautiful hotel room, a beautiful woman . . ."

"Not exactly the best time, though," I said.

"Would another time be better?" he asked.

"You know what I mean," I said, even though I wasn't sure *I* knew what I meant. As heat rose to my face, I decided to change the subject. "I never thanked you for coming up to help me, by the way. How did you know I needed you?"

"I don't know," he said, golden eyes shimmering. "It was like I heard you."

"But you couldn't have."

"I know," he said. Then he leaned down, eyes burning with something that I dared to hope was repressed desire, and kissed me, lightly, tenderly, on the forehead, his hands hot on my shoulders. "You're full of mysteries, Sophie Garou," he whispered.

I closed my eyes, savoring the slow burn of his touch. And then he released me, suddenly alert.

"What is it?" I asked.

"I don't know," he said. "Something tells me we should hurry. More may come."

I blinked. "More what?"

"Werewolves," he said, and something in his voice made the hairs stand up on the back of my neck.

Twenty-seven

Ten minutes later, we were fully clothed and back in Georges's bathroom again, along with the pile of werewolves. Although the jeans fit Tom better than they did my father, I found myself missing having a half-naked werewolf around. *Stop it, Sophie.* I drew my blood-streaked jacket closer around me and forced myself to focus on the werewolf Tom was hauling out of the tub.

Tom slung him over one shoulder and carried him to the bedroom, where he flung the lupine body onto a chair.

"Wake," he commanded, and to my surprise, the furry eyelids twitched a little bit, then shot open. I could smell the werewolf's wariness—and fear.

"Transform," Tom barked, and then, right before our eyes, his limbs lengthened, the fur receded, and a naked Boris—or Dudley, I could never tell which was which—stared back at us.

Tom tossed a towel over his nether regions, for which I was infinitely grateful, and proceeded to drill him with questions.

"Who sent you here?"

The werewolf just blinked at him, which was not the right answer, because Tom reached out and grabbed his arm. The werewolf yelped a little bit in pain, and when Tom drew his hand back, the skin he had touched was an angry red—almost blistered, it seemed to me.

"Who sent you here, Boris?" Tom repeated quietly.

Boris grabbed his arm, just below the wrist, and stared up at Tom, the whites showing around his eyes. "Elena," he whispered.

"Why?"

"Because . . . because she didn't want the Paris pack involved."

"That's why you killed Georges. But why did you attack Sophie?"

"She is a Garou," he said. "She's a threat to the Grafs."

"Did Wolfgang send you?"

"I don't know whose idea it was," he said. "Elena sent me. We never talk with Wolfgang."

"Why was Elena in Charles Grenier's hotel room?" Tom asked. The werewolf's eyes widened even further, which I hadn't thought possible, and the acrid scent of his fear threatened to overpower me.

"I don't know," he whispered. "I don't know."

"It had something to do with Jean-Louis's refusal to ratify the alliance, didn't it?"

Boris said nothing, but his eyes slid to me. He was figuring out where Tom's information had come from, I realized.

Tom reached out and touched Boris's wrist again, and the werewolf winced, his eyes jerking back to Tom. Tom's voice was slow and steady, and sent chills down my back. I was seeing a side of Tom I'd never experienced before—and to be honest, it was a bit unsettling. "Was Elena working with Charles to overthrow Wolfgang?" he asked.

Boris said nothing, but from the startled look in his eyes, it looked like Tom had come pretty close to the truth.

"So that was the plan, wasn't it?" Tom asked. "Once Elena was alpha, she was going to use Louisiana's backing to take over the Houston pack. That's why Jean-Louis wouldn't agree to the alliance; he knew he'd have to break his oath."

When Boris didn't say anything, Tom moved to take his wrist again. The werewolf jerked his hand away, stuttering, "It wasn't my idea. I was just taking orders."

"What was his reward going to be? A chunk of east Texas? Or was he going to be her co-alpha?"

"Just the territory," Boris whispered.

"Beaumont?"

Boris nodded.

"Who was going to be her co-alpha?"

Boris closed his eyes. "Once Wolfgang was . . . taken care of, Grenier was supposed to rule with Elena."

"So who killed Charles Grenier?"

"I don't know," he said. "I was told to arrest Luc Garou."

"Why were you told to kill Sophie? It wasn't just because of her connection with Paris, was it?"

"Elena said she was a threat," Boris said. "Our job is to eliminate threats."

"Did one of you kill Grenier? And pin it on Garou?"

"No," he said. "Like I told you—I don't know. They said it was Garou, so we arrested Garou."

Tom glanced at me. "I'm about out of questions. You have anything you want to ask?"

I swallowed hard. "Why . . . why does Elena think I'm a threat?"

"Because of your lineage," Boris said. Now that he'd spilled the beans about the alliance, he was becoming positively chatty. "And that thing that you did to Anita. And because Wolfgang . . ." he trailed off.

"What about Wolfgang?"

"I think Miss Elena was afraid Wolfgang would choose you instead of her," Boris said.

"What? But he hates my family!"

"I don't know about that," Boris said. "I'm just telling you what I've heard."

He looked back at Tom. "I'm sorry I tried to kill your girlfriend—it was business. You know?"

I waited for Tom to tell him I wasn't his girlfriend, but he said nothing.

"I've told you everything I know," Boris continued. "But

now that I've told you, could you keep it, you know, just between us? Because if Elena finds out I told you . . ."

"Actually, I'll need you to testify tomorrow," Tom said.

Boris's eyes bulged. "Testify? What are you talking about?"

"At Luc Garou's trial," Tom said calmly. I wanted to tell Tom that there wouldn't be a trial tomorrow, that unless I could find a way to bring in the French reinforcements, I was going to ask Mark to go in and rescue my father. Because as far as I could tell, that was my only hope of seeing Luc Garou survive the week. But since I couldn't explain how Mark was going to get into the compound and manage to set my father free, I didn't bother. Tom would figure it out tomorrow, when the prisoner didn't show up. I had to find a way to lose Tom and get in touch with Mark, I thought. Because if he was going to break my father free, tonight might be the last opportunity.

Boris was protesting Tom's idea. "I can't testify. If I do, they'll kill me!"

"But if you don't . . ." Tom didn't finish his sentence, but the ramifications were crystal clear. Boris's eyes widened, and the stench of fear grew even stronger. "Besides," Tom added, almost as an afterthought, "Wolfgang might reward you for protecting his interests."

"But what about the leader of the New Orleans pack?"

"I'm going to have to tell Wolfgang what you told me anyway," Tom said. "Wouldn't Wolfgang be more likely to extend his protection if you—out of loyalty—told him what Elena was up to?"

Boris swallowed hard.

"If you like, I can end it now," Tom said, "and then you won't have to worry about Jean-Louis."

"No, no," Boris gasped. "I'll do it. Please . . ."

"Do we have a deal, then?"

"Yes."

Tom grabbed his jaw, and the meaty werewolf flinched.

The Nordic werewolf's voice was glacial. "If you do not keep your promise, I will hunt you down."

"Okay," he said. "Okay. I understand."

"Do you give your oath?" Tom asked, his fingers still clamped on Boris's jaw.

"I swear it by the *Codex*," he said, his voice tinged with desperation. "I will testify tomorrow. Whatever you want, I'll do it."

"Good," Tom said, releasing him. "We'll be leaving shortly. When we do, please deal with the mess you created. We moved Georges into the bathroom, along with your compatriot."

"Of course, Mr. Fenris. Thank you for sparing me."

Tom nodded. Then he stood up, smoothed my father's shirt, and turned to me. "Ready to get out of here?"

"Not yet," I said. "I need to see if there's a way to contact Armand."

As Tom watched Boris, I rifled through Georges's drawers, looking for something that would help put me in touch with the Paris pack. I don't know what I was looking for—an address book, maybe, or a Day-Timer—but outside of an antique-looking grooming kit with nail scissors the size of hedge clippers, a slicker brush, a bottle of something called Brush and Shine Grooming Spray, and a pair of tickets to Charles de Gaulle airport, there was nothing to connect either Luc or Georges to the werewolf world. Or Paris.

After closing Luc Garou's dresser drawer in defeat, I returned to Tom, who was sitting on the edge of Georges's bed, facing Boris, who was eyeing him with fear. "Did you locate anything?" Tom asked.

"Nothing," I said. As I looked at Tom, I realized how little I knew about him—and how many sides he seemed to have. He'd been so cold just a moment before, when he was interrogating Elena's pleather boy; his calm demeanor had almost been scary. On the other hand, Boris *had* tried to kill me—and Tom. And Tom's motivation was to help me free my father. Even so, the whole episode had been disturbing.

Tom smiled at me then, and all the ice melted. He was the Tom I knew again. "Let's get out of here," he said.

"The sooner the better," I said. I glanced at the bed, feeling a pang once again for the werewolf who had faithfully served my father for so long. But I was glad to close the door behind me; the smell of pleather and dead werewolf was about to make me puke.

The cleaning staff was scrubbing at the bloodstains on the wall, and I pulled my jacket tighter around me, trying to hide the splashes of blood on my top. The elevator came quickly, thank God. And even though Tom's clothes appeared to be long gone, at least we didn't have company.

"How did you do that?" I asked Tom as the doors slid shut behind us.

"Do what?"

"Wake him up? Make him talk? Give him those little . . . blister things on his wrist?"

"My aunt taught me," he said, and before I could grill him further, the elevator dinged and the doors opened onto the first floor. We stepped out of the elevator, and Tom whisked me through the lobby and into the throngs on Sixth Street. As I climbed onto the back of his motorcycle, I glanced back up at the hotel's beautiful Victorian facade, suddenly remembering its history as one of Austin's most haunted buildings.

Would Georges's shade be joining them? I wondered.

As we left the crowds on Sixth Street. behind us, I leaned forward into Tom's broad back, wrapping my arms tighter around him. It was disturbing having my father's scent layered on Tom's musky, primeval male aroma. And despite the feeling of relative safety I had being with Tom, the reminder of my father made it hard to relax. Whether I wanted to or not, I'd have to break free from Tom tonight, at least for a while. Because I still had business to attend to, and I needed to do it alone.

I expected Tom to drive me to my loft, which was only a few blocks from the Driskill. But instead of turning onto Fourth Street, he crossed the river and headed into south Austin.

"Where are you taking me?" I asked as we stopped at the light on Barton Springs Road. I stared at Threadgill's, envying the happy, normal, non-werewolf people chowing down on cheese grits and pot roast behind the big plate-glass windows. Why couldn't I be one of them?

"Your mom's shop," he said. "Your loft isn't safe."

"But Boris and Dudley are, well, out of commission," I said.

"They're not Elena's only lackeys," Tom responded. I was about to suggest he take me to Lindsey's instead—I'd been less than forthcoming with my mother over the last week, and Sit A Spell was *not* the place I wanted to be right now—but before I could say anything, the light turned green and Tom gunned the engine.

All too soon, we were pulling up outside of the 1910 bungalow that housed Sit A Spell.

"Do we have to go here?" I asked. My mother still didn't know my father was on werewolf death row, and I didn't want to be in the same room with her when she figured it out. Which would be any minute now, unfortunately, because just being in the room with her would be enough for my mother's annoyingly precise psychic gifts to read me like an open book.

"Where else would we go?" he asked.

"I don't know. Just about anywhere, really. What about Lindsey's place?" Although I really didn't want to go to Lindsey's place. Not with Tom. With everything we'd been through tonight, there was a connection between us right now that I didn't want to risk ruining. I closed my eyes, feeling the warmth of him against my body, inhaling the musky scent of him through my father's shirt. I could get lost in him so easily . . .

"Do you really want to go there?" he asked quietly, as if reading my thoughts.

"No," I admitted. "No, I don't. Not tonight." I stared at the purple front door, which was flanked with two huge rosemary bushes—"for protection," my mother always said—with resignation. I needed to tell my mom eventually. She'd never forgive me if I kept Luc's arrest from her. I might as well get it over with. "I guess we should go in," I said finally.

We didn't even get a chance to knock on the door before my mother flung it open, wrapping her star-patterned chenille robe around her. "Sophie, darling! What's wrong?" Her dark eyes flicked from me to Tom, and then back to me. "Your hair . . ." she said, touching a blotchy strand. Then her eyes found the bloodstains on my shirt. "Oh, my, sweetheart. What happened to you? Are you okay?"

"I'm fine, Mom."

"But that blood . . . Come in, both of you. I think it's time you told me what's going on."

She led us through the shop, past tables dressed with lacy tablecloths and laden with love charms and candles and talismans, to the kitchen in the back. As my mother fussed over me—"Are you sure you're not hurt?" she asked me at least three times—I pulled up a chair at the same table I'd done my homework on all those nights growing up, fantasizing about my absent father and wishing Nair didn't smell so awful as I worked my way through long division and precalculus. The familiar smell of herbs, candles, and old house was comforting. As my mother poured hot water into a pot of wolfsbane for us, the green scent of the tea floated over to me, flashing me back fifteen years in a second.

Only Tom hadn't been sitting in the kitchen with me back then—and his wild animal scent, the raw maleness of it, created a constant buzzing throughout my body that I didn't quite know what to do with.

"What trouble has your father gotten himself into now?" my mother asked as she slid mugs of tea to both of us, then poured the remaining hot water over a chamomile tea bag for herself. Her armful of bangles jingled as she put the teakettle back on the stove, then pulled up a chair and joined us at the table.

"How do you know he's in trouble?" I asked.

"He's your father, isn't he?"

She *did* have a point. I wrapped my hands around my mug and looked into my mother's warm, dark eyes. It was now or never.

"He's gotten himself arrested," I said quietly.

Twenty-eight

I steeled myself for an outburst, but none came.

"By the police?" my mother asked, looking completely unfazed. Whether that was because of her psychic abilities or her personal history with Luc Garou, I wasn't sure.

"No. By the werewolves."

"Luc, Luc, Luc," she said, shaking her head. "He always was in trouble. What did they take him in for?"

I let out a long breath. "They accused him of killing an old rival, here in Austin, during the Howl."

Her face paled. "The cards are always right, aren't they?

Sometimes you wish they weren't, but the goddess knows . . ." She reached over and took my hands, clasping them tightly together. "Tell me the worst of it, Sophie. No matter how bad it is, I need to know. If he's convicted, what will they . . ." Her voice faltered, and my heart contracted in my chest. God, this was miserable. "What will they do to him?" she finished finally.

I knew she'd ask that. I took a breath to answer, but before I could form the words, Tom answered for me. "If he is convicted, the punishment is death," he said solemnly.

My mother sat motionless for a moment, digesting what he'd told her. I looked at her, the mother who had raised me alone for so many years. Her long, thick, dark hair was frosted lightly with white, and creases had begun to line the smooth skin of her oval face over the last few years. Why did she still care so much for the man—correction, werewolf—who had abandoned her and her child almost thirty years ago?

And why, for that matter, did I?

"I knew something was wrong," she murmured, staring off into the distance. Her eyes were shiny with tears. "The cards told me . . . I just couldn't see clearly." She withdrew her hands from mine, wiping at her eyes, and looked at Tom. "Has he been tried yet?"

"Not till tomorrow."

Then she turned to me. "Is he guilty?" she asked softly.

"No," I said quickly, and realized as I said it that I believed it. I was sure my father was innocent.

"Good," she said, leaning back. "Good." She was quiet for a moment, as if coming to some internal decision; then she leaned forward and clapped her hands together. "Well, then. What are we going to do to set him free?"

If only it were that simple, I thought. "That's the thing," I said. "I'm pretty sure the trial is going to be fixed."

"Fixed? What do you mean?"

As we sipped our tea, Tom and I filled my mother in on everything we had discovered over the last week.

"So in other words, the presiding judge, Wolfgang, wants to see Luc executed," she summed up.

"Yes," I said.

"That's not encouraging."

That was the understatement of the decade, in my opinion, but I held my tongue.

"Have you talked to the Paris pack?" she asked. "Maybe they can come and help him out."

"We tried," I said, "but we couldn't get in touch with them." I remembered the scene at the Driskill, and decided it was best to omit the gory details. And they *were* gory.

"But it sounds like there's plenty of evidence to indicate that someone else might have wanted this Grenier person dead. And no one saw your father commit the crime, so how can they prove it? There's plenty of . . . what is it called? Reasonable doubt?" She looked at me. "Too bad we can't call Marvin to defend him." Her face softened as she said the name of her beach-ball-shaped attorney boyfriend. They'd met while he was defending her against a murder rap, and they'd been hot-air ballooning and spelunking on weekends ever since. I was always afraid he was going to get wedged in a cave entrance somewhere, like Winnie the Pooh trying to escape Rabbit's house, but so far, he'd always managed to wiggle through okay. "Or if we could get that ex-boyfriend of yours to come and defend him," my mother continued, picking up her mug and taking a sip. "He wasn't your type, of course, but he was quite talented."

"Actually, Heath is working on the case right now," I told her. "I should probably call him, in fact."

She set her tea down so fast half the contents of the mug sloshed out on the wooden tabletop. For the first time in years, I realized, I had actually startled her. "What? I thought . . . didn't you break up with him because you didn't want him to know about . . . well, you know?"

"That wasn't the *only* reason Heath and I didn't work out," I said, glancing at Tom out of the corner of my eye. Of course, it had been rather a large factor. But there had been other things, too . . . like the stirring I'd felt when I kissed Tom that one time. And Mark. Speaking of Mark, how the heck was I supposed to get in touch with him tonight? Maybe I'd excuse myself in a few minutes and sneak upstairs to use the phone . . . "Anyway, Heath kind of, well, found out accidentally."

"Did he see you transform?"

"No, not exactly . . . "

"Catch you shaving?"

"No . . . "

"Well, then, what happened?"

"Lindsey told him," I said.

It was the second time in ten minutes that I'd managed to surprise her. "*Lindsey?* You're kidding me! Why?"

"Like I said, it was an accident—a misunderstanding. But it's a long story. Mind if I run upstairs and use the phone? I need to get in touch with Heath and Lindsey, let them know what we found out tonight, and see if Heath's found anything useful in the Code."

My mom blinked at me. "There's a written copy of the Code?"

"I'll let Tom tell you all about it," I said. "I'll just run upstairs and call them."

"Why not use the phone down here?" my mother said, narrowing her dark eyes at me just a little bit. Like I said, having a psychic mother can be a pain in the rear sometimes.

"I'm just more . . . comfortable upstairs," I said lamely. "Besides, I want to visit my old room. Back in a minute!" And before she could ask me one more question, I left the pentacle-clad kitchen and headed up the creaky stairs to my old bedroom.

As always, crossing the threshold of my childhood room was like stepping back in time. My mother left it just as I'd kept it—the sparkly scrunchies on the dresser, the ancient bottle of Vidal Sassoon hairspray, the extra razors in the top dresser drawer . . . even my Austin High letter jacket still hung in the closet. I'd always regretted not going out for the drill team, but I was always terrified we'd have a home game during a full moon, and I'd be the freak-show portion of the halftime performance.

As I rounded my bed and reached for the phone, the pain of my hidden childhood washed over me. I found myself wondering what it would have been like to be raised in my father's pack, to have known at least one other person who struggled with the excess hair growth, who was terrified a tail would sprout from her gym shorts as she spiked the final ball in the volleyball game. There would have been some comfort in knowing I wasn't alone in the world—even if I *did* disagree with pack policies on human-hunting.

Snap out of it, Sophie. I shook myself like a wet dog, trying to dispel my maudlin mood. Maybe being raised a werewolf in a human world wasn't exactly a Norman Rockwell childhood. But being raised among my own kind hadn't even been an *option*, so there was no use pining for a possibility that never existed. My half-human status, after all, was the reason we'd had to leave Paris—and my father—in the first place.

The truth was, I wasn't sure I'd ever be at home in either world. But if I wanted a chance to forge even a little bit of a relationship with the werewolf who had fathered me, I'd better quit mooning over the past and focus on finding a way to set him free.

I grabbed my pink princess phone and dialed Heath's loft. When no one answered, I tried his cell phone.

He picked up on the second ring. "Sophie!"

"It's me. How's it going?"

"Not so hot, actually." That wasn't good news. "Did you find anything out tonight?" he asked.

"All kinds of things," I said, and filled him in on what I'd learned.

"So there are other suspects," he said. "That's something.

In short, we have a witness who has promised to tell the jury that the victim was a traitor to the Houston pack, and there are no witnesses who saw your father commit the crime."

"Innocent until proven guilty, right? And reasonable doubt. We have a case then."

"In U.S. law, we certainly would. The problem is, in the *Codex*, it's all a bit hazy."

"What do you mean?"

"The packs are given pretty free rein in terms of trial methodology. There are references to the types of trials that can be done, but very few details."

"So?"

"So, the long and short of it is, I don't know whether cross-examination is allowed, or even whether witnesses can be called. If you ask me, the werewolf community could use a good lawyer to update some of these rules and put everything in some semblance of order. It's a mess."

"Does the *Codex* mention the Fehmic Court?" I asked. "Because that's where he's going to be tried."

Heath was quiet for a moment. "Are you sure?"

"That's what Tom told me."

"That's unfortunate," he said. "From what I've read, that wouldn't be my first choice. But all we can do is come up with the best case we can, right?"

I heard a woman's voice in the background. "Who's with you?" I asked. My stomach flip-flopped. Had he told Miranda about me?

There was a strangely awkward pause. "I'm at Lindsey's place," he said.

Thank God. "Better not tell Miranda you've been up all night at Lindsey's," I said lightly. I knew Heath and Miranda had spent some intimate "working" evenings together before Heath and I broke up. Even though I was the one who had ended our relationship, it still stung a bit.

He ignored my jab and returned to the matter at hand. Heath always had been a consummate professional. "Why don't you run through the facts one more time, and we'll meet in the morning and talk strategy. Is there any way you can get me in to defend him?"

"I doubt it," I said.

He sighed. "We'll have to rehearse the arguments tomorrow, then. I'm sure you'll do fine; you always talked a good game."

"Thanks, Heath." Although I wasn't sure it was a compliment. "I'll call you in the morning, okay? And get some sleep." I had decided to accept Mark's offer to free my father; since there wasn't going to *be* a trial tomorrow, I meant it. No sense trying to put together a case for a defendant who wasn't planning to turn up for his conviction.

"I will," he said, "in a few hours. Take care of yourself, Sophie."

"Thanks, Heath. For everything."

"Don't mention it."

I hung up, feeling torn in all kinds of directions. Heath was so . . . so blasé about my hairy revelation. Had I made a mistake by not telling him? Could we have worked it out after all? *Worry about it later, Sophie*, I told myself. *Once your father is free*. I took a deep breath, trying to clear my mind of the doubts that kept crowding in, and dialed Mark's cell phone. He picked up before it even rang.

"I knew you'd call." His voice was low, commanding, and—as always—shiveringly seductive.

"Mark. It's Sophie."

"I know."

I glanced at the door; I couldn't say why, but I knew my mother would have a conniption if she knew what I was doing. "Remember that offer you made?" I said in a low voice. "To free my father?"

"Of course," he said silkily.

"I think I'm going to have to take you up on it," I said, feeling my stomach turn over as the words left my mouth.

"I'm on my way," Mark said, a note of eager anticipation in

his voice. I chalked it up to a desire to be helpful—and a desire to have a few minutes alone with me again. "Where are you?" he asked.

I gave him directions to my mom's shop. "But don't come to the door. Can I come and meet you outside at about . . . " I glanced at my watch. "Say, one thirty?"

"How exciting. A secret assignation."

"We're meeting to break my father out of the garden cottage," I reminded him.

"Of course," he said. "I'll wait for you at the curb."

"One thirty," I repeated. "See you then. I've got to go now."

"Till then, my darling."

I hung up. Even though the plan was to go and break my father out of werewolf jail, I felt like a teenager planning to sneak out of the house for an illicit snog in the backseat of my boyfriend's car. Or limo, as the case may be. Before going back downstairs, I sat staring at the pink phone for several seconds, trying to clear my mind. I still had to spend at least an hour with my mother, and unless I was very, very careful, she'd be onto me in a heartbeat.

When my mind was as empty as it was going to be, I checked my hair in my white-painted mirror—big mistake, since it was a disaster—and headed back downstairs, praying I could make it the next few hours without tipping my hand about Mark.

Twenty-nine

"How's Heath doing on the case?" my mother asked when I walked back into the herb-scented kitchen a few minutes later.

"He's still working on it," I said. "Heath said the Fehmic Court wouldn't be his first choice—apparently there are several other trial possibilities he'd prefer—but that he'll put together as much of a case as he can." I looked at Tom. "There's no way he can represent my father at the trial?"

"It is forbidden," he said. "Humans are not permitted."

"But *I* can do it, right?"

He nodded.

"Well, then, I'd better get some shut-eye."

"Do you want to stay here?" my mother asked, eyeing me with a knowing look. "Something tells me you'd be safer here than at your place."

I glanced at Tom, who nodded. "That would be great," I said. "Can Tom stay in the spare bedroom?"

"Of course," she said. "It's right upstairs, across from Sophie's room. I just put fresh sheets on it the other day, and there are some spare toothbrushes in the drawer in the bathroom."

"Thank you," he said. A moment later, he followed me up the stairs.

After showing Tom the spare bedroom, which was only a couple of feet from my own, I closed my bedroom door behind me and slipped out of my bloody clothes, thankful to be out of them.

I waited until I couldn't hear Tom moving around anymore, then pulled on my old flannel bathrobe and slunk to the bathroom to clean myself up. Granted, I hadn't been at my best over the last couple of days, but that didn't mean he had to see me in my holey flannel, too. Thankfully, the hallway was empty of gorgeous werewolves, and a moment later I had locked myself in the bathroom and flicked on the light.

The vision that met me in the mirror was less than ravishing. My hair was beyond redemption—I might have to invest in a wig if the Midnight Satin didn't come out soon—and although I'd gotten my face clean, flecks of Boris's blood still stained my neck and chest. I turned on the hot water and stripped down, glad for a chance to shower. Not only was the idea of wearing someone else's blood completely disgusting—not to mention totally unhygienic—but I was meeting Mark in a few short hours, and wanted to be at least mildly attractive.

As I let the hot water cascade over my naked body, I tried not to think about the werewolf who was mere yards away from me. This was the second time I'd been naked in close proximity to him tonight, and I tried not to think about what he might be doing. Or thinking. The smell of my antique Clairol Herbal Essence wasn't enough to cover his wild male scent, and I was sure he was just as capable of picking up mine.

But he was Lindsey's. And although I didn't *belong* to Mark—his opinion to the contrary—I was certainly dating him.

I spent a good twenty minutes washing off the remains of the blood and black eyeliner. The water stung the bite marks that Boris had left on my tailbone, and I was happy to have a chance to get them clean. I turned off the water when it started to turn cold; then I dried myself off, combed through what was left of my hair (Herbal Essence hadn't gotten rid of the blotchiness either) and dug through the drawers, trying to find some makeup that wasn't completely desiccated.

After a lot of searching, I finally came up with some eye shadow and a tube of mascara that hadn't solidified. After doing what I could with those, I rubbed some of the old Revlon lipstick I'd found onto my cheeks and lips. When I was finished, the result wasn't exactly what I'd call glamorous, but since I didn't look like the bottom of a shoe anymore, it was a definite improvement. I wrapped my old flannel robe around me and crept out of the bathroom.

Tom's door was closed, but a sliver of light showed beneath it. So *he* wasn't sleeping yet, either. For the first time, I started to think about what Tom might be giving up in exchange for his association with me.

He'd long had an alliance of sorts with Wolfgang, and obviously they had family history. And Tom must have no love lost for my family.

Why, then, had he gone to such lengths to help me? And what was it costing him in the werewolf community to do so?

I paused outside his door. I was dying to knock, to talk to him. But I couldn't. I stood there a long time, listening to the creaks of the old house around me, before turning and heading across the hall to my room. I had just opened my door when light flooded the hallway behind me.

Tom stood in his doorway, looking at me. He was still wearing my father's jeans, but he'd taken off his shirt, and I caught my breath at the gleam of the light on his broad shoulders, and the hard planes of his chest.

I pulled my robe more tightly around me. "Hi," I said.

"Hi." We stood silent for a moment. The tension in the air was almost tangible. "I see you showered," he said finally.

"Yeah. Wanted to get the remains of Boris off me."

"Understandable," he said.

I took a breath, inhaling the sexy, musky scent of him, and found myself wondering what that tanned skin would be like under my mouth. Would he taste like he smelled? He was only three short steps away . . . "I want to thank you," I said finally.

"For what?"

"For standing up for me," I said. "And my father. I'm afraid you're making enemies on my behalf."

"Perhaps," he admitted, shrugging just a little bit.

"Why are you helping me?" I whispered.

He didn't answer for a moment. Time seemed to slow down as we stood there, in the upstairs hallway of my mother's house. Me, and a werewolf. Something I'd never in a million years have dreamed would happen.

Finally, just when I was beginning to think he hadn't heard me, he answered me. "Don't you know?" he said in a low voice.

"No," I said truthfully. "No. I don't."

He leaned against the doorframe, his eyes fixed to a point on the wall next to me. "After Beate died, I became numb to the world. There were women—there were too many women, honestly." He laughed a little, bitterly. "But there was never a connection." He gave his head an abrupt shake. "Never. And then I met you, downstairs in your mother's shop . . . "

I swallowed then, and my heart beat so hard I was sure he could see it. But I said nothing, waiting for him to continue.

"I felt something," he said. He looked up at me, and the pain and intensity in his golden eyes made my body turn to putty.

I took a step toward him, as if pulled by an invisible magnet. Now there were only inches of air separating us, and I could feel the heat of him, smell his desire. And my own. "What did you feel?" I breathed.

He looked like he was about to say something, but then he paused. "It doesn't matter," he said shortly.

Yes, it does matter, I wanted to scream. Instead I said, "Why not?"

"Because I am entangled with your friend. And you . . . " He trailed off.

"I'm with Mark," I said quietly.

He nodded.

I wanted to tell him that I'd stop seeing Mark immediately, if only he would end things with Lindsey. But common sense prevailed. First of all, Mark wasn't just the guy I was seeing; he was also the guy who, in about two hours' time, was planning to help me free my father. Second, he was my client. Third, Tom was a werewolf. And I was still deeply conflicted about the whole werewolf thing. And even if I did manage to get over my werewolf aversion, things still wouldn't be simple. If we ever chose to formalize the arrangement, we'd have to do the whole pack-approval thing, and I couldn't imagine asking the werewolf who had sentenced my father to death to rule on my romantic life as well. Of course, Wolfgang hadn't sentenced my father to death just yet—and if things went well tonight, he never would—but knowing he intended to was more than enough.

As my mind raced, the tension between us grew—I could almost feel the air crackle—until Tom broke it by taking a step back. "You should get some rest," he said, and I found myself wanting to close the distance he had opened between us. "Tomorrow will be stressful."

I paused for a moment, looking at Tom's silhouette, wanting with every cell of my body to wrap my arms around him and pull him into my bedroom after me. But he'd stepped back.

"You're probably right," I said. "See you tomorrow."

Tom nodded, and we retreated to our separate rooms—Tom to sleep, and me to wait.

I have rarely spent a longer two hours in my life. Even though I was relieved that we would be breaking my father out of the garden cottage shortly, and saving him from almost certain death, I was anticipating Mark's arrival with both excitement and dread.

I eased back into my jeans, traded my wrap top for an old

Madonna T-shirt I found in one of the drawers, and waited, trying to ignore the fresh blast of Tom's erotic scent that came through the vent every time the heat turned on. As I sat alone in the darkness, watching the red numbers on the digital clock as they crept toward the appointed hour, my mind kept going back to the name Mark had given me. *Ashmodei.* What did that mean? What was he, exactly? And why did he have such a hold on me?

Under normal circumstances, without my laptop and an Internet connection, it would have been impossible to do any research. But I was in my mother's house, with perhaps the most complete occult library in Austin. Since I wasn't going to be sleeping anytime soon, I decided, it wouldn't hurt to see what I could find out. Even if I couldn't find the name, I could at least research creatures with a tendency to catch fire and sprout wings, and had access to weird, removal-proof magic rings.

I cracked my door, checking for a light under Tom's. The hallway, thankfully, was dark, so I closed the door behind me and crept down the stairs to the office where I knew she kept her reference books.

Like my mother's filing system, the book collection in my mother's office was rather haphazard. If it had been my library, everything would have been organized, if not alphabetically, at least by subject, making things easier to find at a moment's notice, rather than stacked on every available horizontal surface. Then again, if it was my library, the subject matter would have tended toward accounting, not spells and herbs. And there probably weren't a lot of references to supernatural names in *Principles of Accounting, Volume Six.*

I found a couple of dusty volumes dealing with supernatural creatures, but while I found several fascinating entries in the A section, including Asdeev (a white Persian dragon) and Ashuaps (a distant Canadian cousin of the Loch Ness monster), there was no reference to Ashmodei.

An hour later, I had gone through every reference book I

could find, and had discovered all kinds of disturbing things about baboon gods, magical seals whose favorite food was human hands and feet, and an intriguing creature called the Skunk Ape, but nothing related to the name Mark had given me.

I had accidentally tipped a short stack of hardbound books over and was eyeing a book titled *Gods of the Ancient World* with interest when my mother appeared at the doorway in her star-clad robe.

"What are you doing in here, sweetheart?" She squinted at me through sleep-puffed eyes.

Damn. I cursed myself for not being quieter. "Looking for something to read," I said. "Having a hard time going to sleep."

"So you're up reading about magical creatures and ancient deities?"

I followed her eyes to the books that were open on the desk behind me, and blushed.

"They're all open to the letter A," she said, peering at the pages. "Are you looking for something specific, dear? I would have thought werewolves, of course, but we're in the wrong part of the alphabet."

"It's nothing," I said, reaching over to close the books. "Sorry I woke you—I'll head on up to bed now."

"What are you looking for?" she asked. "It involves your father, doesn't it?"

"Indirectly," I said without thinking.

"Tell me, Sophie."

I could tell by the tone of her voice that I wasn't going to get back upstairs without giving her *something*. And she'd know if I was lying. I decided to commit the sin of omission. "Someone mentioned a name the other day, and since I couldn't sleep, I figured I'd come down and see if I could find it."

"What was it?"

I hesitated for a moment—I'm not sure why—and told her. "Ashmodei."

Her eyes narrowed a little bit. "I've heard the name before, and I think I know what it refers to. Who mentioned it to you?"

"Oh, one of my clients," I said.

"Strange. I thought all you businesspeople talked about was money," she said, turning to scan the bookshelves. "Ah, yes. Maybe it's in here." She took down a thick, red-bound tome that was so well thumbed that all that remained of the gilt letters were a smattering of gold flecks. She cleared a spot on the desk and opened it, flipping through the onion-skin pages and bending down to study the type. "Let's see here. Amduscas, Apepi, Apopus . . . " She flipped another couple of pages. "Ashmodei." She ran a finger down the page and looked up at me, puzzled. "It's not here. Maybe I was wrong." She turned the page, then stopped. "Wait a moment."

"What is it?"

"I remember now—Ashmodei is a derivation. I just can't remember the original name—but it was pretty close, I think." She studied the page, slowly moving her finger down the text. Suddenly she stopped. "Aha."

"What?" I asked, trying to peer over her shoulder at the tiny print.

"Ashmodei is only one of this entity's names. Ashmedei is another, but the primary listing is under Asmodeus."

Entity. I wasn't sure I liked the sound of that. Not that I should have been surprised, really—from what I'd seen of Mark, he clearly wasn't your run-of-the-mill CEO. "But what exactly is he?" I asked, not sure I wanted to know the answer.

She sat back in her chair and looked at me with something like pity in her eyes. "Asmodeus, my dear, is a demon."

Thirty

My stomach contracted, and I felt the room spin around me. "A demon," I repeated in a faint voice.

"And not just any demon," she said. "His origin is unclear—some say he was originally of Persia, born of Zoroastrianism. But whatever his past, he is known as one of the kings of hell, and as the demon of lust."

The demon of lust. I thought of Mark, and his magical Duraflame properties. And the wings—the wings of a fallen angel? I closed my eyes, trying to wrap my brain around the whole idea. *Your client, and sort-of boyfriend, is the demon of lust.*

My eyes snapped open. "That's impossible." Because demons didn't exist. *Couldn't* exist.

Then again, werewolves weren't supposed to exist, either. And if Mark was the demon of lust, that would go a long way toward explaining my libido's ability to trump any and all rational thought whenever he was in the room.

My mother fixed me with a shrewd brown eye. "How exactly did this name come up in conversation, Sophie? Most people don't bandy around the names of major demons. Particularly not people who are entrenched in the material world, like most of your clients."

I stared at the hooked rug on the floor, focusing on the dust bunnies gathering near the frayed edges, afraid to meet my mother's gaze directly. "I . . . I don't remember, really."

My mother's eyes moved to the ring on my finger, the one with the iridescent moon on it. Then she turned back to the book on the desk, peering at the text. "I'd forgotten about this particular individual, but it's all coming back to me now. There are several stories about Asmodeus, you know. But two in particular that stand out."

"Which two?" I asked, although I wasn't sure I wanted to know.

She turned to the book. "The first story is from the Book of Tobit. In the Old Testament." She paused for a moment, scanning the text before she continued. "Apparently Asmodeus fell in love with a woman named Sarah, many, many centuries ago. And it was a very jealous love."

"How so?"

My mother looked up at me. "Asmodeus drove Sarah's suitors away. And he didn't just shoo them off. He killed them. Seven of them."

I swallowed, thinking of Mark, his deep blue eyes, his sexiness, the way he made me feel utterly wanton. Was he really the demon of lust? And had he once been so infatuated with a woman that he'd murdered his competition? My mind flicked to the medieval paintings I'd seen on his office wall. They'd always seemed out of place before, for a successful, young, hip CEO. I'd always chalked it up to a collector's interest in medieval art—after all, they'd all been of a woman in a weird-looking headdress. But was it possible that they were all paintings of his beloved Sarah? After all, if it was in the Old Testament, the monks probably did tons of illustrations of her . . . could he have somehow collected them, so he'd always have her with him?

No, Sophie. You're making assumptions. It's probably a coincidence.

"Not a very nice demon," I said, finally.

"No," my mother echoed. "Not very nice at all. Then again, demons aren't known for their kindness, generally."

"What was the other story?" I asked, anxious to move off the subject of jealousy-induced homicide.

"Ah, yes. There is another thing Asmodeus is known for."

"Other than dispatching problematic suitors?" I asked lightly. But my mind was reviewing the events of the last few days. Tom's motorcycle accident—and the limb that had fallen just as we were about to kiss. Had those been coincidence? Or was Mark somehow responsible?

Mark *had* been jealous of the time I was spending with Tom, I thought, even if it did concern freeing my father. But he also knew Tom was seeing Lindsey, so it's not like I was two-timing him. There was no reason for him to feel threatened. Besides, if Mark was this—this demon of lust—then why hadn't he tried to get rid of Heath, too?

"It's not so much a story as a legend, really," my mother began, "but in this case, it may be relevant." She took a deep breath. "According to some sources, Asmodeus bestows special rings on those who follow him."

I covered my ring with my other hand and swallowed the cantaloupe-sized lump that had developed in my throat. "Oh?"

"And do you know what those rings have on them?"

"I don't know. Diamonds?" I guessed, knowing it was hopeless. "Rubies? Giant emeralds?" *Shimmering moons?*

"Planets," my mother said quietly.

My eyes darted to my ring. It was the moon, not a planet, I told myself. And he'd given it to me because I was a werewolf, not because he wanted to turn me into one of his followers, or acolytes, or whatever you call them.

"Who gave you that ring?" she asked softly.

"Mark," I said. "You knew that. I told you."

"Mark's last name is Sydney, right?"

I nodded.

Her finger ran down the page. "Alternate spellings: Asmoday, Ashmodei, Asmodeios, Asmodeu, Chammaday, Chashmodai . . . " She looked up at me. "And Sidonay."

I leaned back in my chair and closed my eyes, feeling the world fall out from underneath me. "So you're saying my client is a demon," I said.

"He's more than your client, dear."

I didn't bother to contradict her. We both knew she was right.

The problem was, demon or no demon, Mark was my father's ticket out of jail. And he was going to be here in—I opened my eyes long enough to check my watch—less than fifteen minutes. "Mom," I said. "I know you're probably not crazy about me spending a lot of time with a demon. Assuming he is a demon, that is. It's all just speculation at this point—we don't have proof."

"The Devil card came up in the spread I did for you the other day."

"Tarot cards aren't proof, Mom."

"Well, then, shall we try to remove that ring again?" she asked.

I hid my hand from her. Whether Mark was what my mother said he was or not, the ring he had given me had some definitely weird properties. The last time she'd tried to get rid of it, by cutting it with clippers, there had been something like an explosion, and I was afraid a second attempt would leave me an amputee. But the ring *was* bizarre; even when I transformed into my werewolf form, it somehow managed to change size with me. It had not left my finger since the moment Mark slid it on.

"And you mentioned Mark made something of a magical entrance when you were at that werewolf compound last month. Didn't he do battle with one of the spirit allies?"

"Maybe he did," I admitted. "It still doesn't mean he's the demon of lust," I said stubbornly. "And even if he is, I need him."

Her eyes widened. "Oh, no. Sophie . . . has he already put you under his spell? How did I miss it? Oh, my darling . . . "

All the blood left her face. She looked like someone had shot her.

"No," I said, "I'm fine, Mom. It's nothing like that." Although I wasn't completely sure I was telling the truth. The way I felt when I was around him, as if I had no control . . . *could* I be under an enchantment of sorts? "The thing is," I said, "I need him. He's my only hope of getting Luc out of jail."

"How is he going to accomplish *that*?" she asked.

"I don't know," I said, glancing at my watch. "But he'll be here in about fifteen minutes."

"You can't let him do it, Sophie." Her voice was flat.

"But it's my only option," I said. "If I don't, they're going to kill him."

"What about the trial? Surely they won't condemn an innocent man . . . or werewolf."

"It's rigged, I'm afraid."

"We should call the French werewolves, then," she said, thinking fast. "Have you gotten in touch with the Paris pack yet?"

I swallowed hard. "I tried, earlier tonight. But they killed Luc's assistant before I got there." I omitted the fact that they'd tried to kill me, too—my mother had had enough surprises for one night. "And I have no way to get in touch with them." My mother paled, and I reached for her hands. "Mom, don't you see? It's the only way."

Her eyes welled with tears, but she shook her head resolutely. "You can't do it," she said.

"Once we've got my father free, I'll talk to Mark, tell him I can't see him anymore." I felt a wrench thinking of it—demon of lust or no demon of lust, I'd gotten rather attached to my sexy, witty client. Not to mention the fact that a breakup would probably mean my losing the Southeast Airlines account. And, potentially, the partnership I'd worked so hard to achieve.

My mother shook her head. "Sophie, this cannot continue.

I still love your father—I always have, and I always will—but he's not worth your life." She paused, her dark eyes boring into me. "Or your soul."

"Who said anything about souls?" I said. "You're jumping to conclusions here. All he said was he'd help me spring my father, that it would be a piece of cake."

"He won't do it for free, you know. He'll use it as leverage. Has he started talking about you belonging to him?"

Yes, he had, in fact—and it was more than a bit annoying—but I didn't say anything.

"He wants to own you, Sophie. Body and soul." She pointed to my finger. "You're already wearing his ring."

"I'll give it back," I said.

Her eyes were haunted. "If you can," she said. "If it's not already too late."

As she spoke, the purr of a car's engine sounded from outside. I peered through the blinds as the black stretch limo came to a stop outside the house.

"Don't go," she said. "Please, sweetheart, don't go. I'm sure Heath will figure something out for the trial. I can't let you walk into the arms of evil."

"Mom, I have to try. I promise I won't agree to anything. If he tries to make me, I'll just tell him to take me home."

"That's likely to happen," she said.

"He came to help me once, and didn't ask anything in return," I reminded her. "If he can get my father out . . . "

"Please," she said. The desperation in her voice was deeply unsettling.

"I have to try," I whispered, and headed for the door.

"Wait!" I paused, turning back toward her. "Before you go, I want you to take something with you."

As I stood in the doorway of her office, she hurried to the kitchen. She returned a moment later and pressed a small bag into my hand.

"What's this?" I asked, looking at the handmade drawstring

bag. It was tied with a red satin ribbon, and its cheery floral pattern made it looked like a sachet.

"Salt," she said.

"Salt?"

"It'll help you resist him, if you get into trouble. Demons hate it. If I had time, I'd put together something more thorough, but for tonight . . ." She bit her lip. "I wish you weren't going, but if you have to, just keep it with you." Her eyes were wet with tears. "If you need it, hold it against him. It should keep him at bay."

I took a deep, shuddery breath. Keep him at bay? Demon or no demon, Mark was one of the sexiest men I'd ever encountered; I wasn't sure I wanted to keep him at bay. And if I did, I would think dressing in flannel pajamas would be more effective than a bag of salt. I tucked it into my purse—whether I wanted to admit it or not, this talk of demons and souls had rattled me. As did my mother's obvious fear.

Still. What choice did I have? I couldn't leave my father to die.

"I'll take my cell phone with me," I said. "If I need you, I'll call." I stepped forward, giving her a big hug and a kiss. "Wish me luck," I said.

And before she could object, I stepped outside, closing the door firmly behind me, and went out into the night—and into the arms of the demon of lust.

Thirty-one

"I've missed you," he purred, pulling me into a hot embrace. His smoky smell was stronger than ever tonight—or maybe I was just hypersensitive.

"I've missed you, too," I said, perhaps a bit tentatively. Which was understandable, given the conversation I'd just had with my mother.

He released me, studying my face. "Is something wrong?"

I shrugged, trying to put aside my misgivings. Which was a challenge, because there were a lot of them. "Just worried about my father, is all."

"We'll have him out before you know it," he said, and ushered me into the back of his limousine. I tossed my purse into a corner and climbed in. The partition, I noticed, was now black, and despite the rather stressful nature of our errand, the moment Ben closed the door behind Mark, my demon lover had slid over beside me and was playing with the neckline of my T-shirt.

His fingers, as always, were hot against my skin, and they seemed to ignite a trail behind them. As worried as I was about what the evening would hold, I felt myself respond, and when he lifted my chin to kiss me, I melted into him. His hand reached for the hem of my T-shirt, sliding under it, and soon his fingers found my breasts, running slowly, teasingly, over the lace of my bra. I moaned with pleasure, leaning into him as his tongue traced a trail of fire down my neck, dipping into the crease of my neck; within seconds, he had lifted the T-shirt over my head and his tongue was slipping under the edges of my bra.

All of my concerns slipped away, things that seemed so important a moment ago as insubstantial as wisps of cotton, and I reached for him, my hand closing around his hard member. He tore down my bra with his teeth, mouth closing on one nipple, then the other, tracing a line of fire between them, then fumbled with the button of his slacks. His urgency was contagious; all I could think of was having him deep inside me, thrusting, filling me. I slid my jeans down my hips, opening myself to him, hungry for the feel of him inside me.

"Sophie," he said, his voice rough with lust. The sound of my name made me tingle.

"Asmodeus," I gasped as he reached down and slid a finger down my clitoris, sending a shiver of pleasure through me.

He paused, raising his head from my breasts, his blue eyes sparking in the dim light of the limousine.

"What did you call me?" he asked.

"Asmodeus," I repeated. "You're Asmodeus." For some reason, at that moment, it seemed perfectly reasonable.

"Yes," he said, reaching down between my legs. I shivered at his touch. He caressed me, touching lightly on my clitoris, then slowly reached lower and parted my lips. Then he pushed my legs apart and lowered himself so that the head of his penis just touched me. The heat of him made me shiver.

And then he plunged deep into me, filling me, withdrawing and then thrusting again. I growled, deep in my throat, and pulled him toward me, deep into me, feeling the slick sweat on his flat abdomen as it slammed against me. I was hungry for him—I wanted him inside me, all the way inside me. My mouth found his neck, his salty, smoky neck, and my teeth clamped down as he rode me, until the taste of blood mingled with the sweat. I was teetering on the brink of ecstasy when finally he thrust into me one last time and I tumbled over the edge, howling, heat rising in a ball inside me and spreading through me until I was limp.

I lay beneath him for a few minutes, watching the reflection of headlights on the roof of the limo, starting to feel somewhat human again—and wondering exactly what it was I'd just done. Other than having unprotected sex with a demon in the back of a limo, that was. If Mark really was the demon Asmodeus, I just hoped Sarah hadn't had the clap.

The lights of Austin were fading into the distance by the time I was feeling up to talking again. Mark and I sat in the back of the limo, fully dressed, stretched out next to each other. Although I was trying to play it cool, it wasn't easy.

"So," I said as we passed an Exxon station advertising Camel cigarettes and six-packs of Lone Star Light. I really wanted to ask him all kinds of questions about his demonic history—his crushes, the mortality rate of his crushes' close associates, why it was the ring he gave me seemed to be glued on with epoxy and have a direct line to Mark's brain . . . there were so many, it was hard to choose. But instead, I said, "What's the plan for tonight?"

"We go in and get your father out of the garden cottage," Mark said, as if it were as easy as picking up a pack of Camels at the Exxon we'd just passed.

"I *know* that," I said. "But the question is, *how*?"

"I have my ways," he said.

"Like sprouting flames and wings and walking past everyone?"

"I was thinking of something a tad more subtle," he said, and even in the dim light I could see his grin.

"But you won't tell me," I said.

"Of course not," he said, his voice mischievous. "I want it to be a surprise."

Great. Personally, I'd had more than enough surprises for one day—heck, maybe even my whole life—but something told me not to push it further. Funny how the power balance shifts when you realize your companion is a ranking member of the demon community.

We lapsed into silence for a few minutes, and his warm fingers encircled my ankle, making me shiver—both with a little bit of lust, and fear. I fingered the metal band on my hand, and finally couldn't contain myself anymore. "This ring you gave me—why won't it come off?"

"You don't like it?" he asked.

"No, it's not that. It's just, well, when I transform, it changes size with me. I've never had a piece of jewelry do that before."

"And your mother couldn't get it off either, could she?"

"Uh, no. How did you know she tried?"

"Another mystery, my dear."

"You're just full of mysteries tonight," I said.

"Do you really want to know?" he asked.

"I wouldn't have asked if I didn't."

"It's a magical ring," he said.

"I figured as much. How many of them have you given out?"

"Why do you assume there are more than one?" he asked. Something changed in the tone of his voice.

"It's just a hunch," I said.

"You used a name a few minutes ago," he said. "A name I didn't tell you."

"What name was that?"

"Asmodeus," he said.

Despite the heat Mark was emanating, I felt a chill of fear when he spoke the word. "You told me Asmodeus was your name," I said quietly.

"No, I didn't." His blue eyes glowed slightly in the darkness of the car. "I told you it was Ashmodei."

I shifted in my seat, trying to keep calm. "That's what I said, wasn't it?"

"No, my dear." He traced his finger up and down my calf. "It wasn't." He was quiet for a moment longer. Then he said, "Have you been talking to your mother about me?"

"Maybe," I admitted. "A little."

"She doesn't like me, does she?"

"It doesn't matter what she thinks."

"Perhaps. Perhaps not."

"Mark," I said. "What are you?"

"Why should I tell you?" he asked, his voice teasing, yet slightly dangerous.

"Why wouldn't you? You know what *I* am. Shouldn't we even things up?"

The limo was silent, except for the muted hum of tires on asphalt. The world seemed very dark outside, and fear prickled my skin. If Mark decided to hurt me, I realized, there was nothing anyone could do about it. "The reason I won't tell you," he whispered, "is that I think you already know." The limo seemed very small, all of a sudden, the walls pushing in at me, and Mark seemed very, very big. The smell of smoke was thickening in the air, and his eyes were sparking.

"You're a demon," I whispered.

He nodded, looking satisfied. "And not just any demon," he said, and he leaned forward, kissing me so hard and fast I felt my body tingling all over again.

"Wait a minute," I said, turning my head and gasping for air. "Tell me what happened with Sarah."

He stiffened slightly. Then he leaned down and kissed my neck, leaving a trail of heat that led to the hollow of my neck. "Sarah," he said between kisses, "is ancient history, my dear. The only thing that matters now is you."

I crossed my arms, pushing him away slightly. "Oh really? Then why are there so many pictures of her in your office?"

That stopped him. "Pictures?"

"The woman," I said. "The one in the headdress. The one in all those old paintings you've got on the walls."

"I have an interest in medieval art," he said curtly. "It stands to reason, since I was there when it was painted.

"So you *are* that old," I said. Even though I knew Tom and

Wolfgang were centuries old, I still wasn't used to people talking about events that had happened 500 years ago as if they had taken place just last week. "And Sarah was a real person."

"Yes, I am that old." He nuzzled my neck. "But I like to think I've aged pretty well."

"And Sarah? What about her?"

"She was a fling," he said. "Like I said, ancient history."

"And so were the suitors you killed. There were seven of them, I believe."

He shrugged. "Actually, only four—they exaggerate."

"But you *did* kill them."

He didn't answer, just continued to brush my neck with his lips. Now he was nibbling on my earlobe, and although part of me was happy to surrender to the heat of him, another, growing part of me was starting to set off the alarm bells.

"Did you have something to do with Tom's motorcycle accident?"

He ignored me.

"And what about that tree limb that almost crushed him the other day? Was that you, too?"

Again, nothing. And in this case, as far as I was concerned, his silence spoke louder than words.

"What I can't figure out," I said, "is why you didn't go after Heath. I mean, Tom and I are both werewolves, but he's dating someone else. But Heath—Heath and I were sleeping together, and you didn't do a thing."

He paused in his ministrations for a moment.

"What?" I asked.

"I must confess that I wasn't entirely blameless in your breakup with Heath," he said. The headlights of a passing car illuminated his face as he spoke. He looked thoughtful, like a CEO who has just learned of a potential takeover bid. But he wasn't just a CEO, I reminded myself. He was an ancient demon.

"What do you mean, you weren't blameless?" I asked.

"Miranda and I, well, we are associates."

"But she's *Heath's* associate," I said, confused.

"Miranda and I have a long, long history together. She has a way with men, so she agreed to help me distract your boyfriend. Worked like a charm, actually."

"Wait a minute. Miranda's a demon, too?" I thought about the faint smoky smell I'd often picked up from her, and with a sinking feeling, I realized it made sense. "I've smelled it on her," I said quietly. "I don't know how I didn't figure it out."

"Most rational people don't expect to find demons popping up all over town, so you can hardly blame yourself. Her real name is Lilith, by the way—she just likes the name Miranda." Mark said. "But all of that is beside the point. Heath wasn't right for you, anyway. You broke up with him because he's not a werewolf, remember? So I don't see why you're concerned."

I pushed myself up on the seat. Demon or no demon, I was pissed. "So let me get this straight. You got your friend to seduce my boyfriend, and then contrived accidents to kill another friend of mine?"

"I never said I did anything to your werewolf friend," he said. "And you and I both know he's more than a friend to you."

"What do you mean?"

Mark pointed to the ring on my hand. "It doesn't lie."

I looked from Mark's shadowy face to the silver band on my ring finger. "Wait a minute. You put this ring on me so you could *spy* on me?" I tried to tug it off. Of course, it didn't budge. "What does it do? Does it have a radio monitor? How much do you know?"

He gave me a sly smile. "It came in handy when you were in trouble with all those werewolves in Round Top, you must admit."

Just because he'd appeared out of nowhere last month and helped keep me from turning into an Aztec sacrifice didn't mean I thought spying was okay. "It doesn't matter. That's just . . . immoral!"

He smiled, a lazy, gorgeous smile that even in the dim light of the limo made me weak in the knees. "But darling, I'm a demon. I'm supposed to be immoral."

"I want the ring off," I said. "Now."

"But what about dear old dad?"

"What about him?"

"Don't you want to free him?"

"Of course. What does that have to do with the ring?"

"I am quite fond of you—you must know that—but you must know I can't just keep dishing out my assistance without any recompense, my dear."

A finger of ice ran down my back, and I leaned over to retrieve my purse. "What kind of recompense?"

His fingers slid up my leg, circling my kneecap. "A promise, of sorts."

I swallowed hard, my throat dry. "A promise," I repeated, trying to keep from squeaking. "How about, 'I promise to be deeply grateful for your assistance and to take you to dinner.'"

"Delightful," he said. "But I'm afraid I'm going to want a tad more than a kiss on the cheek and a steak dinner." The smell of smoke intensified, and his presence seemed to grow, somehow, so that there was hardly any air left in the limo. I'd had a lot of experience with client relations, but nothing quite like this.

"What do you want from me?" My voice was barely a whisper. I fumbled in my purse, reaching for the little bag of salt, feeling mildly comforted when my fingers made contact with the little cloth bag. The pressure in the limo was so great I thought I might scream.

Then, suddenly, there was a lightening, an easing in the air. I gasped for breath, feeling as if a spell had lifted. Mark was no longer a brooding presence across from me. He was just Mark. I shook myself, as if ridding myself of a bad dream. Only it wasn't a bad dream; Mark was still a demon. A demon who wanted something from me. And I still didn't know what.

"Let's not worry about that now, shall we?" he said. "We can talk about all this when we get there. It's a gorgeous night to be out in the limo, and I love these rural billboards. I've never understood why all these animals keep advertising the restaurants that serve them." He pointed to a lurid pink billboard with a poorly drawn rendition of Porky Pig. "I mean, look at that pig over there, advertising its own ribs for sale. Who came up with the idea of a cannibalistic pig? And people say demons are twisted."

Relieved that the pressure in the limo had abated, I let the whole demon thing go. Mark spent the rest of the ride pointing out weird billboards and adult video stores (the parking lots were always full) while I tried not to think too much about the fact that I was sitting just a few feet away from a thousand-plus-year-old demon with a reputation for murder. Or what I was going to do when Mark told me the true fee for saving my father.

And whether I'd have any choice but to pay it.

Thirty-two

All too soon, we were at the gate of the Graf Ranch. Ben rolled down the window at the intercom, but before he had a chance to push the call button, the gates swung slowly open. I shot Mark a questioning glance, but he just smiled enigmatically as we bumped down the dusty road.

"How are we going to do this?" I asked, hoping to gloss right over the whole 'promise' thing.

"We haven't decided we're going to do anything yet," he reminded me.

"Don't you think this might be a good time to talk about it?"

"What makes you say that?"

"We're in the middle of Werewolf Central here, Mark. They'll figure it out soon enough."

"Back to Mark again? What a shame," he said, touching my knee. "I liked it when you called me Asmodeus."

"What are the terms?" I asked.

"In good time," he said, refusing to budge. I mentally cursed him, which was probably pointless—I mean, how do you curse a demon?—as Ben pulled under a grove of trees not far from the compound.

"You can shield yourself, right?" Mark asked.

I nodded. For some reason, I was able to shield my scent—and my presence—from other werewolves. Weird, but handy.

"Good," he said. "You might want to start doing that."

"Thanks for the tip," I said, and a moment later, I grabbed my purse and slipped out the limo door into enemy territory.

As Mark whispered instructions to his driver, I stood next to the limo and scanned the territory. As far as I could see—and smell—everyone had gone to bed, and I wished I was there, too. The chilly night air passed right through my T-shirt, raising goose bumps on my arms and back. When Mark gestured for me to follow him, I wrapped my arms around myself, shivering, and padded after him.

Within moments, we were passing through the compound. Wolfgang's house was dark, but a lone light glowed on the second story of Elena's little farmhouse. Was she waiting for the pleather boys? I wondered. Had either of them managed to get in touch with her yet? Or would Boris turn tail and flee? He'd promised to testify tomorrow; would he go back on his word?

It doesn't matter, I told myself. *Luc won't be here tomorrow anyway*. At least I hoped not. I still hadn't heard the terms I'd have to agree to to secure his release.

Before I knew it, we were at the outskirts of the little group of buildings, and only yards away from my father's prison. There weren't any guards at the door, which I took as a hopeful sign, and I followed Mark right up to the front porch. I could smell my father inside.

When we were a few feet from the front door, Mark turned and looked at me. His blue eyes glowed in the darkness, and once again, I got that sense of him . . . growing, somehow.

His voice was low, seductive, almost playful, and edged with excitement. "It's time to decide, Sophie."

I swallowed hard. "Fine." My voice sounded about a thousand percent more confident than I felt. "Name the terms."

His blue eyes glowed brighter for a moment, and I sensed his presence, well, *unfurling* is the closest I can come to describing it. As I stood there in the darkness, the hot smell of smoke rose around me. I felt engulfed by him somehow, as if he was blotting out everything around me—the garden cottage, the spring grass at my feet—even the stars seemed to gutter in the sky and go out. I clutched my purse to my stomach, wishing my mother had had time to whip up something more powerful than a bag full of salt.

"Name the terms," I repeated, this time in a whisper.

Mark drew himself up, and for a moment—just a moment—I thought I caught a flutter of dark wings. His voice, when it came, was different—deeper somehow. Older. And scary as hell. "You will bind yourself to me, Sophie Garou," he said. "You will forsake all others but me, for eternity. My will will be your will, and you will be mine. In exchange for your loyalty, I will free your sire, Luc Garou, from captivity."

My throat dried up. Right behind that door was my father, who would almost certainly die tomorrow. I had the key to his survival in my hand, but to use it would be to shackle myself to this being, forever.

I stood there, rooted to the porch, trying to take this in. I knew there would be a price. But my eternal soul? I cleared my throat and tried for a light tone. "And here I was hoping you'd settle for a weekend getaway."

Mark was growing impatient; I could tell by the intensity of his smoke smell. "What is your decision?" he asked.

"I'm thinking," I said. "It's kind of a big decision, you know?"

"Do not think too long," he said. "Even now, I sense them stirring."

I glanced over my shoulder; sure enough, a light had gone on in the main farmhouse.

"If you do not choose to agree," Mark said, "your father will die a long and painful death."

"You don't know that," I said.

He chuckled then, a low, throaty laugh that, despite the heat emanating from him, chilled me to the marrow. "How are you going to defend him?" he asked. "You know the trial is fixed. Graf has wanted his head for centuries. Are you really willing to throw your father's life away?"

I thought of Luc Garou, whom I'd barely gotten to know, shackled to a chair inside the garden cottage. His reddish hair, his green-flecked eyes—just like mine. Granted, we hadn't exactly been close, but that didn't mean I still didn't care about him. Could I turn my back on Mark and let the werewolves consign him to death?

"They do more than just stake them, you know," Mark said, his voice silky smooth. "They dismember them, too. Just to be sure. Sometimes they do it before they stake them."

I glanced up again. More lights were coming on in the big farmhouse.

"Time is running out, my darling."

I looked at the door of the garden cottage, feeling wrenched in two. I turned to Mark. "I can't do it," I said.

His eyes sparked. "You refuse me?"

"I have to," I said. "It's . . . you're asking me for too much."

He seemed to grow larger then. The boards of the porch groaned beneath him as he advanced toward me, and I could almost see the flames flicker along his skin. I fumbled in my purse for the bag of salt my mother had given me, wishing I'd taken a few minutes to clean it out. Lipstick, compact, wolfsbane tea bags, hair brush—finally, my fingers closed on the little cloth bag, and I yanked it out and thrust it toward the advancing demon.

"Stay away from me," I said, my voice quavering.

He snorted, and I swear little flames escaped his nostrils. But he didn't come any closer. "Are you certain you're willing to condemn your father this way?" he asked. "It would only take a moment for me to free him."

"Go away," I said, more firmly this time.

The heat on the porch blazed suddenly, and my face burned. I turned my head to the side—it was like being inches from a bonfire—but didn't lower the bag of salt. The band of metal on my finger was suddenly hot as a brand; I gasped in pain.

"Last chance, Sophie," he said.

I turned my head toward his, squinting, and almost dropped the salt. Gone was the handsome CEO of Southeast Airlines; in his place stood the flame-covered creature I'd glimpsed in the cave in Round Top. Even under the mantle of fire, I could still see the magnetic blue flicker of his eyes, drawing me in. The ring on my finger burned, and I could hear a seductive voice in my head, telling me to surrender, promising me all manner of delights, a life of ease . . .

"No," I croaked, and it took all of my strength to utter it.

"That was a mistake, Sophie Garou," he said, and the malice in his words shocked me to the core. "We will meet again, soon. I promise you." He blazed blindingly bright, and I shut my eyes again, waiting for him to burn me alive. Then the light and heat dissipated. I opened my eyes a hair, still brandishing the bag of salt like a weapon. But I was alone.

Well, not entirely alone.

Light flooded one of the windows then, illuminating the porch in front of me, and I heard voices from inside. Turning to flee, I spotted three werewolves loping toward me. I might have just saved my immortal soul, but the mortal part of me wasn't out of the woods yet.

Thirty-three

Tucking the bag of salt into my purse, I sprinted off the porch into the brush, praying the werewolves hadn't seen me, although that was highly unlikely, considering Mark's little bonfire display of a few moments ago. Still, they were in human, not wolf form, which was at least a little bit of an advantage. They moved more slowly as humans, and they couldn't smell as well.

About a hundred feet into the woods, I found a little hollow in the trunk of an oak tree. I pressed myself into it and thought invisible thoughts, then peered around the bole of the tree at the garden cottage.

The front door had opened, and five werewolves now populated the porch. Two of them trained a flashlight on the porch floor where Mark had stood a few minutes earlier, looking at scorch marks, probably; the other three, unfortunately, were training their lights into the bushes around me.

"It's the daughter, I'll bet," one of them said.

"She can't be far."

"Let's go," another growled. They were just advancing into the brush when a car engine growled from the parking lot, and a pair of headlights cut through the night. Mark's limo—I could tell by the hum of the engine.

"They're heading for the gates," one of the werewolves said. In an instant, all five of them were sprinting toward the parking lot, leaving me alone in the woods.

A second later, I glanced around the tree trunk toward the garden cottage, which was silvery in the light of the waxing moon. The smell of Luc Garou was stronger now. Was it possible they had left the front door open?

As a second car engine roared from the parking lot, followed by the screech of tires, I crept through the brush toward the garden cottage, sniffing for other werewolves. But except for Luc and the three made werewolves, which I could now smell as well, I appeared to be alone.

I hurried up onto the porch, excited to discover the sliver of light leaking from the open door. I slipped inside and hurried toward the back of the house—and my father.

"Dad," I whispered as I entered the room where they were holding him.

He looked totally nonplussed by my arrival. "Sophie," he said. "*Chérie*. Why have you come?"

"I've come to get you out," I said. Even though he still looked haggard, his eyes were bright, as if he'd been waiting for something. Me, probably, I realized. Could he smell me? I'd had my shielding on, though. I certainly could smell *him*—and the made werewolves, who I could tell were somewhere else in the little building.

"What happened to your *ami*?" he asked.

"My what?"

"Your little friend," he said. "The one who smells like a fireplace. It was very strong, the odor. I could not detect you, but I suspected you were somewhere nearby."

"You mean Mark?" I shrugged. "We had a little disagreement. He went home."

"Why are you here?" he asked. "And to bring him . . . what was your purpose? It is *trop dangereux*."

"I'm here to get you out," I said.

He nodded sagely. "Ah. I appreciate your loyalty. Admirable."

"Where are the keys?"

"Is not Armand en route?" he asked.

I took a deep breath, feeling guilt wash over me. "I'm sorry. I couldn't reach him."

"Georges?"

I paused for a moment, not wanting to break the news. Finally, I said, "They killed him."

My father looked stunned. "*Les animaux*," he whispered. "Georges. *Le pauvre* . . ."

"I'm sorry," I said, feeling racked with guilt. If only I'd listened to Luc, and tried to reach Georges earlier . . .

"Sophie," my father said then, his voice urgent. "Georges is—was—a warrior. It is a waste, a terrible waste, but it is not your fault."

"If I'd gotten in touch with him earlier, though . . ."

He gave another of those Gallic shrugs, making his chains jangle. "That is past. Presently, though, unless you want to be imprisoned by those Teutonic *animaux*, you must leave. *Immédiatement*. If they find you here . . ." he began.

"They won't," I said, with more confidence than I felt. "The keys. Do you know where they are?"

"Wolfgang's *animaux* carry them with them always. I doubt you will find one."

"There must be some way to get you out of here," I said, hurrying over to examine the padlocks that held the ends of the chains together. They were distressingly bulky, as were the chains they linked. As I fingered the heavy metal, my father's scent—gamey as it was at the moment—brought up a mix of old emotions. Emotions I couldn't afford to examine at the moment, to be honest. *Concentrate on the problem at hand, Sophie*. If I could get the biggest lock loose, he would at least be free enough to run. It would be tough—unlike mine, my father's scent was rather powerful—but if we could get out of the compound, we could deal with the manacles on his hands later. If only I'd brought my mother's hedge clippers with me . . .

"You must leave this place," he said.

"I can't," I hissed, my eyes rising from the padlock to my father's wrenchingly familiar golden eyes. "If I leave you, they'll execute you. The trial's fixed."

"*Peut-être*," he said. "But I have a plan."

"So do I," I said. "If I don't get you out tonight, I'm going to defend you tomorrow."

"Sophie, *ma chérie*. I appreciate your attempts at assistance, but I assure you, it will not help."

I sighed. "I know it probably won't. But I've got to try."

"You must not attempt to free me, my darling. I would not have them attack you as well."

"But . . ."

His eyes glowed in the dim room. "You must leave me be tomorrow."

"How about we get you out of here now? Then we won't have to worry about it."

Before he could say another word, I ran to the kitchen to see what I could find that would help me pick the lock.

I returned to the little room a moment later bearing a steak knife.

Luc Garou raised an eyebrow. "What are you planning to do with that?"

"I'm going to try to open the big padlock," I said, and jammed the metal blade into the lock while my father looked on mildly.

"It's too big," he said. "Perhaps something more slender would be better?"

"There isn't anything," I said. And it was true; the kitchen was almost completely bare. "Unless you think a corkscrew would work."

He chuckled. "Not unless there's a good Côtes du Rhône along with it."

I paused in my knife-jamming to glance up at him. How could he be so cavalier?

"After all," he added, "why die sober?"

Die sober? "I thought you said you had a plan!"

"I did not lie. I do have a plan."

"Then why are you talking about dying?"

He raised his shoulders a fraction. "I said that I had a plan. But I never said that it would work."

"I'm coming to defend you tomorrow," I said as I jabbed the lock fruitlessly.

"No you're not."

"I am," I said, "and there's nothing you can do to stop me."

"That's my girl," he said quietly. I looked up at him again to see a proud smile on his face. "Even if tomorrow is my execution, I die a happy *lupin*. Tell your mother she has done well."

"No, Dad." The word felt so strange on my tongue, but right, somehow. "You're not going to die tomorrow. You're coming with me. Tonight."

"No, *chérie*," he said sadly. "They are coming, I am afraid. You must leave this place." As he spoke, I heard the murmur of voices outside, and caught a whiff of werewolf.

Damn.

"Go, my daughter," he whispered. "Flee this place. Send your mother my love."

"But . . ."

"And you have mine as well," he added, eyes burning into mine. "Now go."

I was about to protest, but the footsteps on the front porch, and the smell of several hostile werewolves, made me decide that he was right. "I'll see you tomorrow," I whispered, reaching for his hand. He grasped mine and squeezed it hard, only for a moment.

Then he released me. "Go," he whispered, and I did. Tears

stung my eyes as I stumbled to the kitchen and let myself out the door. I'd spent my entire life without my father; now that I'd met him, I had only a few hours before we'd be parted forever.

As I shut the door behind me, I could hear the thunder of boots in the garden cottage. Where my father remained shackled to a chair, awaiting his execution.

Thirty-four

I took a few moments outside the garden cottage to get my emotions back into some semblance of control, which was a challenge. After all, not only had I just deserted my father, but I'd barely escaped being burned to cinders by a demon who until recently had been my lover, and my client. *Adele will be so pissed*, I thought, then snorted out loud. Of all the things I had to worry about, my boss's concerns were pretty low on the list.

Once I'd manage to collect myself, I looked around and tried to get my bearings. Obviously I wasn't going to be leaving in the style in which I had arrived—Mark's limo was long gone—but after considering my options, I decided my best bet was to follow the main road and hop the fence near the entry. With a last look at the garden cottage, which was now chock-full of werewolves, I skirted the compound and cut a path through the scrubby oaks about fifty feet away from the main road, trying not to think too hard about everything that had just happened.

The presence of large stands of cactus lurking at regular intervals was a mixed blessing. It distracted me from my worries, but I ended up with a few dozen spikes embedded in my jeans. Aside from a few botanical entanglements, though, I made it to the front gate unscathed. I guess because Mark had left in the limo, the werewolves presumed the intruder had left the compound, so there wasn't a lot of focus on internal security. Once I cleared the fence, sporting only a couple of injuries from barbed wire, I reached into my bag for my cell phone to call my mother, only to discover it wasn't there.

Brilliant.

What kind of an idiot walks out of the house with a demon in tow to try to save her werewolf father without even carrying a cell phone?

Oh, well. There was nothing I could do about it now. And although I hadn't been packing technology, at least I'd had a bag of salt. Which had come in remarkably handy.

Since my only other option was to walk to a gas station or go back into the ranch and ask to borrow a phone, I started hoofing it down the shoulder of the highway, hoping I was moving in the right direction. It was slow going, since every time a car came roaring down the highway I had to hide in the gully in case it was a werewolf. Every time I lay down in a patch of burrs I cursed Mark—redundant, I know, but I couldn't help myself—and by the time a Kwik Stop came into view two hours later, I found myself experimenting with ways to tell my soon-to-be-former-client to go to hell. Literally.

Light was starting to color the sky by the time I located the gas station's lone pay phone and dialed my mother's number. It wasn't the best sunrise I've ever experienced—after all, my father was still on line to be condemned to death and I'd narrowly escaped eternal damnation—but at least there weren't any werewolves hanging out in the parking lot and threatening to rip my throat out.

My mother answered before the second ring, her voice breathless. "Sophie—you're okay." It came out as more of a statement than a question.

"I'm fine," I confirmed, even though I'd never been closer to despair in my life. All I wanted to do was curl up in a ball and forget about everything that had happened. But I couldn't. My father's trial was scheduled to start in mere hours, and if I didn't show up to defend him, who would?

"You didn't get him out, did you?" she asked in a low voice.

"No," I said, and the feelings I'd been trying to hold off all rushed in. I felt hollow, and hopeless, and ashamed that I hadn't been able to help my father. Or that I hadn't been brave enough to sacrifice myself to free him.

"But you held off the demon," my mother said.

"He's gone," I said, wiping my eyes. "You were right about him, though. The salt—if I hadn't had it, I don't know what would have happened." I closed my eyes, wishing I could rewind the evening and replay it. The problem was, I couldn't think of any other way it could have gone. Unless I had somehow managed to smuggle in a locksmith. And maybe an exorcist or two.

"I'm sorry, Sophie." The pity in my mother's voice made it worse somehow.

"Thanks."

"Did he at least take his ring back?"

I looked down at my hand. Until now, I hadn't even thought about it. As if aware I was thinking of it, a little flash of heat emanated from the silver band, which made my skin prickle with fear. I tugged at the ring, anxious to erase any last trace of Mark. But it was still stuck fast. "No," I said. "It won't come off."

She sighed. "We'll still have to deal with it then. But we can talk about that later. Where are you, sweetheart?"

I glanced up at the front of the Kwik Stop and read off the address.

"I'll be there as soon as I can. Take care of yourself."

I hung up and went back inside the store, where I grabbed a king-size Snickers bar, a bag of Doritos, and a Diet Coke. By the time my mother pulled up in her ancient Volvo, I was so full I felt sick—but my heart was still hollow.

"Thank the goddess you're okay, Sophie. Sending you out with that creature was one of the hardest things I've ever had to do. I've been trying to keep tabs on you all night," my mother said when I'd relayed the night's events to her.

"I think that's the last we'll see of Mark. Or Asmodeus, or whatever you call him," I said, wondering exactly how I was going to explain my client's sudden change of heart to my boss. I twisted the ring on my finger; it had become uncomfortably hot again.

"Don't name him," my mother whispered, her hands gripping the wheel so hard her knuckles turned white.

"What? Why not?"

"It draws them," she said quietly.

I glanced down at the ring. The heat had subsided, but clearly my mother was right. The ring had responded to the name. And the last thing I wanted to do was draw any more attention from Mr. Demon from Hell.

I might be much better off without Mark in my life—at least on a personal level—but what was I going to tell Adele? That the CEO of Southeast Airlines, my star client, was a full-fledged demon who had demanded I turn my soul over to him in exchange for helping my werewolf father escape execution for murder? That would fly about as well as a Greyhound bus.

I pushed morbid thoughts of packing up my office and moving to a cubicle next to Sally's out of my mind. After all, my career trajectory really wasn't the top priority on the agenda right now. The rising sun glared through the windshield, flashing on the mirrored pentacle dangling from my mother's rearview mirror and making me wish I had my sunglasses.

"Yes, your demon friend is gone—for now," my mother said. "But we're going to have to do something about that ring."

I closed my eyes against the glare and took a swig of warm Diet Coke. "To be honest, I'm more worried about the trial right now." I hoped Heath had been able to work some magic with the Code.

"I thought your father said he had a plan."

"He did," I said, "but even he isn't too confident about it."

My mother reached over and patted my hand. "All you can do is your best, my dear. But I'm glad that you've had at least a little time with him."

Something about her tone of voice scared me a little bit. "You sound like it's a done deal already," I said. "Did the cards tell you something bad?"

My mother pursed her lips, which was not a good sign. "The spirit world is unclear regarding your father's situation," she said.

I studied my mother's rounded face. "What did the cards say, Mom?"

She kept her dark eyes on the road, which was also not a good sign. I was perpetually having to remind my mother that when driving, focus should remain on people—and objects—*outside* of the automobile. Now, though, she wouldn't look at me. "Like I said, my dear. It's impossible to tell." She reached over to pat my hand again. "Why don't you rest, or try to get some sleep?"

"Fat chance," I said, leaning my head back. But staying up all night warding off demons and trudging along highways is hard work, and the thrum of the car lulled me to sleep before we even made it to Johnson City.

* * *

I woke to a knocking sound.

"Who is it?" I said, sitting bolt upright in bed, disoriented. I was in my childhood room, with its familiar smell of old house, hairspray residue, and a base note of herbs from the shop downstairs, but I had no recollection of getting here. Then last night's events came rushing back, and panic set in. I was supposed to meet with Lindsey and Heath this morning. Had I overslept?

"It's me," my mother said, stepping into the room. "I wish you could sleep more, but Lindsey just called, looking for you. She said you and Heath have a meeting scheduled?"

"What time is it?" I asked again.

"Half past ten," she said.

"I'm late," I said, pulling on the shoes that someone—my mother, probably—had lined up neatly on the side of the bed.

"Can I make you a cup of wolfsbane tea?" she asked. "The moon will be full in about twelve hours, my dear, and the equinox is in just a couple of days." I couldn't understand my mother's relaxed tone of voice. Didn't she realize that my father would probably be condemned to death in a matter of hours?

"Sure," I said, even though the last thing I wanted right now was wolfsbane tea. A triple-shot latte would have been far preferable. "But only if you can make it really fast—I'm already late." I ran my hands through my hair and winced as they stuck on something small and sharp. I examined a chunk of hair—dead grass and burrs. Lovely.

"Oh, and I meant to tell you: Tom left an hour ago, but wanted me to tell you to meet him here at four."

To go to the trial, I thought with a sinking heart. God, I hoped Heath had come up with something good.

"I'll let you get ready now. There'll be tea downstairs for you, sweetheart." My mother gave me a quick, patchouli-scented hug and headed back downstairs. I sat on the bed for a moment, tempted to burrow back under the covers. But I was already late to Heath's office, so instead I grabbed a brush from my old dresser and began removing bits of vegetation from my hair. When I'd de-grassed myself, I repaired to the bathroom for a quick shave.

It was almost eleven by the time I made it to Heath's office, dressed in a fresh T-shirt and the jeans I'd worn last night. I hadn't gotten around to calling Adele to explain my absence, but I figured with the whole Mark blowout, it wasn't going to matter; my job was probably toast anyway. "Sorry I'm late," I said as I closed Heath's office door behind me. Heath and Lindsey were sitting at a conference table, heads together over a xeroxed copy of the Codex. Heath's familiar smell of CK1 and fresh laundry sent a twinge of longing through me. Not just for Heath, but for my former life.

"How's it going?" I asked, afraid to hear the answer.

"I think we've made some progress," Heath said, and he and Lindsey exchanged an unreadable glance.

"What happened last night?" Lindsey asked.

"I tried to get Luc out," I said. "It's a long story."

"Did it work?" Lindsey asked.

I shook my head. "Unfortunately, no. And Mark and I . . . well, we parted ways."

Lindsey sat back in her chair, eyes wide. "You're not seeing each other anymore?"

"Nope." I blushed a little bit. I wasn't comfortable discussing my romantic life with my very recently ex-boyfriend in the room. "And I'm probably going to be short a client soon. But that's not important right now," I said, sliding into one of the unoccupied chairs. "Did you come up with any way to defend my father?"

Heath ran a hand through his silky brown hair and sighed. "It's a bit sketchy. Trial procedure is left to the packs' discretion, which makes mounting a legal defense a challenge, to say the least."

"But you came up with something?"

He let out a long sigh. "All we can do is raise doubts, I'm afraid. Show that others had motives." Flipping through the xeroxed pages, he said, "It's difficult, Sophie. I'm not a criminal lawyer by trade, which makes this a challenge in and of itself."

"But you've done a lot of trial law," I pointed out. "That should help."

"That will help, but it won't make it easy. Because of the unusual situation, I can't cross-examine witnesses, can't do discovery—my hands are tied. All I have to work with is what you've told me, and I can't even present the case myself."

"Do we even have a chance?" I asked, afraid to hear the answer.

"You're sure there's no way to get me in to defend him?" he asked.

"Not unless you turn into a werewolf," I said. "Heath, tell me the truth. Do you think there's any way we can get him off?"

"Honestly? With a hostile jury?" Heath looked me directly in the eye, and I could see the pity in his expression. "I wish I had better news, Sophie, but probably not."

"Wait a minute," Lindsey said. "Sophie—that's a brilliant idea!"

I turned to look at her. "What?"

"You could make him into a werewolf," she said, "and then he could defend your father for you."

Make Heath into a werewolf? "But Heath doesn't want to be a werewolf," I said once I'd finally located my voice. "And even if he did, I don't really know the details on how to do it. Besides, there's no way to know if the Houston pack would let him in."

But Lindsey was like a dog with a bone. "How could they turn him down? It's the Howl, right?"

"I don't know the rules . . ." I protested.

"But I do," she said, tapping the stack of copies on Heath's desk. "All werewolves are allowed at the Howl. Made or born."

"Oh."

"Seriously, Sophie. Heath's probably our only hope, and the only way we can get him in is if he's a werewolf. You've got the blood. You just need to give him some of it."

"But that's a huge, life-changing decision," I said. "And it's almost impossible to live with—trust me. You don't know what you're asking me to do."

Lindsey rolled her eyes. "Sophie, don't get so preachy. You may think it's awful, and life-changing, but I'll bet a lot of werewolves would hate to lose their powers."

"But what about blood types?" I was desperate now.

Lindsey shrugged. "It can't take that much blood. I'm sure it will be fine."

"But—"

"But nothing." She waved my objections away. "It's not a life sentence, anyway. If Heath didn't want to stay that way, Tom could always unmake him. Right?"

"I suppose that's possible," I said. "But what about the Code? Isn't it illegal?"

"It's at pack discretion," Lindsey said. "And since you're not part of a pack, you're not bound by any pack rules. You could turn half of Austin into werewolves if you wanted to."

As I pondered that unpleasant thought, Lindsey whipped out her cell phone and started dialing.

"Tom," she said into the phone a moment later. "It's Lindsey. I have a proposition for you." And before I could protest, she launched into her plan, concluding with, "If he wanted to change back, you could unmake him, right?" She paused for a moment. "Great. Now, what do we need to do?" She grabbed a piece of paper and scrawled something. "Okay. Got it. See you at four then."

As she flipped the phone shut, Heath and I stared at her. "It's all arranged," she said. "We just need to get some syringes and do a blood transfusion."

"But you haven't even asked Heath if he's willing to do it!" I protested.

She turned to Heath. "Are you game?"

"If it's the only way to get me into the trial," he said, "and if your friend is certain he can reverse the process, I'm willing to try it."

"But it's a blood transfusion!" I protested. "It's so dangerous!"

"You don't have tuberculosis or anything, do you?" Lindsey asked. When I shook my head, she said, "Well, then, I think we're safe. I'll just run down to the CVS on the corner, and we'll get started."

"But what if someone comes into the office?" I asked.

"I told the secretary I'm in a strategy meeting all day," Heath said.

"See? I told you we were covered," Lindsey said.

Before I could object, she was gone.

Thirty-five

Heath and I looked at each other. Now that we were alone together, closeted in his office behind a closed door, the room seemed incredibly small. "So," I said, trying not to sound as awkward as I felt, "it looks like you're going to be a werewolf for a day."

"It's certainly been an interesting week." He shook his head and straightened his silk tie. "All this is kind of hard to believe, isn't it?"

Since I'd spent the last year or two trying to hide the fact that I *was* a werewolf from him, I had to agree. "Are you sure it's okay with you?" I asked. "It's a lot to ask. And I know we're not really, well, dating anymore."

He reached out to touch my arm, and I caught a whiff of Miranda's smoky smell. *Miranda*. I had to tell him to watch out for her! "It doesn't mean I don't still care for you," he said.

"Likewise," I said. I looked into his chocolate-brown eyes, breathed in his familiar smell. This wasn't going to be fun, but it was necessary. "Heath. There's something I need to tell you."

"Another revelation?" He cocked an eyebrow. "I'm kind of afraid to ask. Are you going to tell me you're half vampire, now, too?"

"Of course not!"

"Good," he said, fingering his collar. "Because I'm having enough difficulty with the whole werewolf thing as it is."

"Actually, it has to do with Miranda," I said, not sure exactly how to proceesd. I mean, exactly what was I going to tell him? That his current girlfriend was not just an attorney, but the supernatural henchwoman of Asmodeus the demon, who had sent her to seduce him away from me?

"What about her?" he asked.

"Have you ever noticed anything . . . I don't know. *Strange* about her?"

"Don't tell me *she's* a werewolf, too."

"No," I said, thinking, *she's a demon, actually*. "But I'm being serious. Ever notice anything a little weird? Like a higher-than-normal body temperature? Or a smoky smell?"

He shook his head. "Not that I can think of. Why?"

I sighed. "If I tell you, you're not going to believe me."

"I believe you're a werewolf," he pointed out.

"True. But this is different."

Heath's brown eyes widened. "Is Miranda a *vampire*?"

"Actually, no," I said, hedging.

"Come on, Sophie. Spill it."

"Okay," I said. "As long as you won't think I'm crazy."

"You forget, Sophie. I've spent the last twenty-four hours trying to come up with a defense for a centuries-old werewolf. I think I can handle it."

I took a deep breath and blurted, "I think she's a demon."

Heath blinked. "A *demon*?"

"Yeah. Like an incubus, or a succubus, or something." I took a breath and kept going. "She knows Mark—my client, the one I broke up with last night? Well, it turns out he's a demon named Asmodeus, and he's been around for forever. Since medieval times, and earlier, even. And she, well, he told me they—he and Miranda—work together a lot."

"You're telling me I've been dating a *succubus*?"

I nodded. "I think so. Her real name is Lilith."

"Lilith," he said thoughtfully. "Interesting. Isn't there a Lilith in the Bible?"

"I don't know," I said. "I don't think I've ever read it. My mom isn't exactly Catholic, you know. But the point is, you have to be careful with her." I reached over and gripped his arm. "This is serious stuff, Heath. Mark tried to entrap me into selling my soul last night, in exchange for him setting my father free. I'm afraid Miranda—or Lilith, or whatever her name is—might do the same thing to you."

He shrugged. "I doubt it. After all, my father's not in werewolf jail, so she wouldn't have the leverage."

I resisted the urge to kick him. "Heath. I'm being serious here."

He gave me a wry smile that tugged at my heart. We'd had some good times together, Heath and I. "I know, I know. It's just a little hard to swallow. Demons? I mean, werewolves are bad enough . . ."

"Watch out. You're going to be one in a few minutes, if Lindsey has her way."

"About Miranda, though . . ." He shrugged. "It doesn't matter anyway."

I couldn't believe what I was hearing. "What do you *mean* it doesn't matter? You're dating a demon, and they're incredibly bad news. Just ask my mom. She'll tell you."

"Miranda and I broke up a few days ago, actually. It wasn't working out. I mean, the sex was great, but there wasn't much more to it."

More information than I needed, thank you. "Ah," I said in kind of a choked voice. "Well, then. I guess that's taken care of."

"Anyway, she's going to transfer to a firm in Seattle."

"Then why do you still smell like her?" I asked.

"I *smell* like her?"

"Yeah. Kind of smoky. Mark has the same scent."

"We were in a client meeting together this morning. Maybe that's it."

I relaxed a little. "That makes sense."

Heath pulled his arm from my grip and leaned forward, looking suddenly serious. "While we're talking, Sophie, I've got something I'd like to ask you, too."

"I'm all ears," I said.

But before he could say another word, Lindsey burst in, brandishing a red-and-white plastic CVS bag. "Got the syringes," she said, closing the door behind her and turning the deadbolt. "The woman in the pharmacy did give me a funny look, though. I guess people don't usually come in asking for the biggest syringes they've got."

"Wonderful," I said faintly as she plopped the bag down on the table and pulled out a box of syringes, a bottle of rubbing alcohol, a bag of cotton balls, and a box of Lorna Doone shortbread cookies. "What are the cookies for?" I asked.

"For after you give blood, silly. Just like at the blood bank. I thought about Chips Ahoy, but these were on sale. Now," she said, consulting her notes, "According to Tom, we need to transfer at least a hundred milliliters of blood, but more would be better—up to about five hundred milliliters."

"How much is five hundred milliliters?" I asked.

"About a cup," Heath said.

I eyed the box of syringes. "And how much does each of those hold?"

"About sixty milllileters," Lindsey said.

Only sixty? To me, the syringes looked like sharp nails attached to gallon jugs. Then again, I've never been a big fan of needles in general. "How about we stick to the low end?" I asked. "Otherwise, we're going to look like pincushions."

"You'll be fine," she said. "Now, let me think. Do you have any rubber bands in here?"

"In my top drawer," Heath said, walking over to his desk and pulling out a handful of brown rubber bands. "What do you need them for?"

"To make one of those tourniquet thingies, like they do at the blood bank." She grabbed two thick ones, doubled them up, and turned to face me. "Ready, Sophie?"

"Does it matter?" I asked, holding out my arm and feeling like I was about to face an executioner. Which is how my father would feel shortly if I didn't find a way to free him, I realized.

I closed my eyes as Lindsey slid the two rubber bands up my arm, to just above the elbow. "It's not as tight as they make it, but it will do," she said.

"Let's just get this over with," I said.

"It'll be a cinch, Sophie. Now, alcohol first," she said, ripping open the bag of cotton balls and dousing a few with alcohol, which she then applied to my arms. "And we're supposed to look for a vein. Heath, what do you think?"

My ex-boyfriend peered down at my exposed arm. "That looks like a big one there, don't you think?" he asked, pointing to a small blue blotch on my inner elbow.

"Great. Hand me the syringe, will you?" she said. Heath passed her a plastic syringe with what looked like a six-inch needle on it. She popped the cap, and I closed my eyes tightly. God, this was *so* not a good idea.

"Am I supposed to push the needle in straight down, or slide it in sideways?" Lindsey asked.

"I think they kind of go in sideways," Heath said, "but I usually don't watch."

"Well, let's try it that way, then," she said. "This will only hurt a bit, Sophie," she said, and then plunged the thing into my arm, missing the vein by a mile.

"Drat," she said, and I yelped as she stabbed me again. And again, and again, and again.

"This is a lot harder than it looks," Lindsey complained after what seemed like the thirty-ninth jab, and I was about to grab the syringe and tell her to try a kitchen knife instead when she gave a sharp exclamation and I felt an unpleasant pulling sensation. "We got it!"

"Here's the second syringe," Heath said, and a moment later there was a second jab, and then a third, until I started feeling light-headed.

Finally, instead of the pricking sensation, I felt cool pressure, and opened my eyes to see Lindsey pressing a cotton ball to my arm. Lined up on the table were six syringes filled with my blood. The cotton ball was rapidly turning red, as well.

"Lorna Doone?" she asked brightly.

I took a cookie grudgingly. "Whatever you do," I said, "I'd recommend you steer clear of the health professions, Lindsey."

"Oh, come on. I didn't do too badly for the first time out! I've heard they usually practice on oranges first."

"I can understand why," I said, lifting the cotton ball and peering at my hole-riddled arm.

Lindsey ignored me and turned to Heath. "Are you ready?" she asked.

"I guess so," he said, rolling up his sleeve. As Lindsey dabbed him with alcohol and raised the syringe, he looked at me. "What does it feel like?"

"What does what feel like? If you mean having Lindsey poke a needle into you, imagine pissing off an entire hive of African bees."

"Not that," he said. "I mean changing. Becoming a werewolf."

"The change to werewolf form?" I thought about it for a moment. "It's an amazing sensation, really. Like coming to life in a new way." Out of the corner of my eye, I could see Lindsey staring at me with hunger in her eyes. "But I've always been a werewolf," I said, "so I don't know what it's like receiving werewolf blood for the first time. Did it say anything in the *Codex*?"

"No," he said. "It didn't."

"Well, then. I guess we'll have to find out," Lindsey said. "Ready?"

"I guess so," he said, sucking in his breath as Lindsey plunged the first needle into his arm. I watched as she emptied first one, then two, then three syringes into him.

Then she stood back and looked at him. "That's one hundred and eighty milliliters, which should be more than enough, according to Tom."

"Feel anything?" I asked.

He shook his head, and for the next twenty minutes, we just sat there, waiting. I was about to suggest we abandon the project and run through the defense Heath had come up with, just in case I had to present it myself, when he gave a little grunt.

Lindsey was on her feet in a flash, peering at Heath as if he were a laboratory mouse. "What is it?" she asked breathlessly.

"I thought I felt something," he said, and a moment later a growl erupted from him.

"Is it just me, or are his hands getting hairy?" Lindsey asked.

"It's not just you," I said. Heath was changing; his chocolaty eyes had taken on an iridescent shimmer, and his body was responding to the call of the almost-full moon. I had been through it often enough to recognize it, but it was jarring to watch someone else transforming. Particularly when it was Heath who was doing it.

"Get his shirt off, so he doesn't destroy it," I told Lindsey as I leapt to my feet to help, feeling a little dizzy from the lack of blood. Between us, we managed to get his tie, shirt, and pants off before the change finished rippling through him.

Then we sat back in quiet astonishment. Where my ex-boyfriend had stood a moment before was a dark brown wolf with shimmery brown eyes, dressed in a pair of red-striped boxer shorts.

Thirty-six

"Heath?" Lindsey whispered.

He growled a little, low in his throat, and then he dropped his nose to the floor, snuffling the carpet.

"Heath," I said, but he was engrossed in an olfactory examination of the room around him, and didn't look up. "Heath," I repeated, trying to catch his attention. "We'll have plenty of time to try out the werewolf thing if you want to, but can we do it later?"

He took another long sniff of the baseboard and looked up at me.

"Can you change back now?" I asked. But nothing happened.

"What do we do if we can't get him back?" Lindsey asked. "We're at his office! How are we going to explain that there's a wolf in the building?"

"We'll get him back," I said with more confidence than I felt. "It's close to the full moon is the problem." Not only was Heath unfamiliar with controlling his animal impulses, but he hadn't had any wolfsbane to assist him. "Can you go get me a cup of hot water?"

"I'll be right back," she said, and vanished out the door, leaving me alone with Heath, who had gone back to sniffing things again.

"I know you can't answer me right now," I said, "but when she gets back, I'm going to have you drink some wolfsbane tea. And then you're going to concentrate on your human form until you transform back."

He gave me a little bark, which I interpreted as assent, and continued doing his rounds of the room, tail poking out of the leg of his boxer shorts. He was a good-looking man, and it translated to his wolf form, I noticed. Maybe I had made a mistake in hiding my wolfie nature from him. What if I'd told him from the outset? We could have had romantic full-moon weekends together, and raised our pups together.

But as I watched the chocolate-brown wolf pad through his office, I realized that ultimately, it wouldn't have lasted. Even though Heath was a werewolf now, he wasn't of the same magnitude, I guess you'd call it, as Tom. There was something mysterious about Tom, something alluring that I couldn't quite pin down. Maybe it was that he'd been around for 600 years, and knew so much more than I did. Maybe it was his faint European accent, or his tall, broad-shouldered Viking frame. Or maybe it was the look I'd caught in his shimmery eyes once or twice—a look that sparked a longing in me so intense I hadn't known what to do with it but ignore it.

But it didn't matter. He and Lindsey were already an item, and I would never betray my best friend. And in any case, my romantic life—or what was left of it, after last night's fiasco with Mark—wasn't the top priority right now. I hadn't turned

Heath into a werewolf to date him. I'd done it so he could help save my father.

My ex-boyfriend was snuffling his leather chair and I was flipping through the xeroxed *Codex*, looking for something we could use in my father's defense, when Lindsey slipped through the door again with a mug of hot water.

"Great," I said, fishing two wolfsbane teabags out of my purse. "We'll let these steep for a couple of minutes. Once it's strong enough, Heath can drink it down and think human thoughts, and we'll be back on track."

After a bit of coaxing, we finally managed to get Heath to slurp down eight ounces of double-strength tea, and although he wrinkled his nose a bit at the smell—and the taste—after much coaching from yours truly, he was back in human form, the boxer shorts still in place.

"What was it like?" Lindsey asked breathlessly as he flopped into one of his chairs, breathing hard.

"It was incredible," he said, turning to look at me. "Sophie. I had no idea the world could be so . . . intense! The smells! There are billions of them, and the colors are so bright . . . it's amazing."

"So you don't mind the extra fur and the tail?" I asked.

"It just felt so . . . *natural*, somehow. Like I said, it was an incredible experience."

Lindsey's eyes strayed to the three remaining syringes on the table, then to me.

"You really want to try it, don't you?" I asked.

She nodded.

"It's not all great smells and colors, you know. I know Heath said it was incredible, but it can also be a royal pain in the ass." Like when you were trying to schedule meetings around moon phases.

"Tom will change me back if I decide I don't want it," she said.

"I won't stand in your way, then." Before the words had left my mouth, she was already dabbing her arm with a cotton ball and grabbing the closest syringe. Her eyes were bright with excitement, and she licked her lips as the needle bit through her skin.

"I'd better get some more hot water," I said wearily, slipping through the door and closing it behind me just as Lindsey injected herself with the second syringe. Twenty minutes later, yet another sleek wolf was standing in Heath's office, her fur a golden brown and her eyes silvery gray.

It was a good thing I'd tucked some extra wolfsbane tea into my purse before leaving Sit A Spell that morning.

It took almost an hour for me to get everyone off the thrill of discovery and back to the subject at hand, namely, finding a way to get my father out of werewolf jail. Once everyone was human again, dressed, and no longer sniffing the carpet, I reviewed everything I knew about the case for Heath and asked him what the plan was.

"Well, I looked for a loophole, but the rules governing the proscribed time are pretty strict," Heath said as I sipped my wolfsbane tea. He and Lindsey were abstaining for now; Tom had warned Lindsey not to have more than four cups a day, since made werewolves are more susceptible to its rather lethal side effects, and the transformation was still pretty recent. Even so, after years of keeping my tea habit undercover, it was strange being so open about everything and fielding all kinds of questions, from average hair-growth rates to my favorite hunting spots.

"Are there any other loopholes?" I asked, glad to be back on topic. "Like special circumstances for traitors or something?"

Heath shook his head. "If we were in France, on your father's home territory, perhaps. But here? He's in hostile territory."

"So what do we base the defense on?"

"We can't prove your father wasn't there," Heath said. "A witness places him there, there was a scratch on his cheek, and he certainly had motivation."

"The fact that Charles double-crossed him?"

"Exactly." He looked at me over steepled fingers; once we started talking law, he easily slipped right back into lawyer mode, which was very comforting. "A witness placed him at the scene, but no one actually saw the murder. And I think we can demonstrate that other werewolves had a reason to want Charles, and your father, out of the way."

"So we're looking to establish reasonable doubt," Lindsey said. "And that Sophie's father wasn't the only one who wanted Luc dead."

Heath nodded. "I don't know if that's enough to get your father off in the werewolf world—like I said, it's a bit sketchy, and there's nothing in the Code indicating that reasonable doubt is at all a factor in these trials—but we'll give it a shot." He grabbed a legal pad from his desk and turned to me. "Just to make sure we're ready, let's go through it one last time."

For the next few hours, I ran through everything I had learned as Heath crafted his defense.

Finally, at three-fifteen, Heath flipped his legal pad closed and looked at me. "I think we've done all we can do here," he said.

"You think?" To me, the defense sounded far from ironclad—in fact, it was about as substantial as dryer lint—but if Heath thought we had done our best, who was I to say otherwise? Besides, we were out of time.

"I guess we'd better head over to Sit A Spell," Lindsey said, standing up and smoothing down her dress.

"What do we do if Boris doesn't show up?" I asked, voicing the fear that had hounded me all afternoon. Without Boris to back the assertion that Charles Grenier had been in Elena's room that evening, and that Elena was plotting against Wolfgang, we didn't have much of a case.

Heath looked at me. "I don't know. Wing it, I suppose."

I tried to respond, but the lump in my throat had grown so big I couldn't.

* * *

When we pulled up outside Sit A Spell at just a few minutes before four, Tom was waiting on the front porch, dressed in faded jeans and his black leather jacket and oozing werewolf masculinity. The afternoon sun gleamed on his gold hair, which was slicked back in a ponytail, and made his amber eyes glow.

Heath, in contrast, had a masculinity of his own, but despite his dark hair, athletic frame, and the excellent cut of his Brooks Brothers suit, he didn't even seem to be in the same species as Tom. Even though, now, technically, he was—if werewolves can be called a species, that is.

We headed up the walk to the porch, where the two men shook hands; I could almost see the tension crackling in the air between them.

"It looks like the transformation went all right," Tom said, giving Lindsey a light kiss on the forehead. "The shimmery eyes are nice. Is it as wonderful as you hoped?"

"I think so," she said. "But I haven't had much chance to find out. We've been a bit busy with legalese this afternoon."

My mother met us at the door draped in her customary flowing silks. I was still in the jeans I had worn last night, dirt smudges at all. My mother gave me a huge hug, then drew me aside and began telling me what to do if I was having trouble with demons.

"Mom, I'm going to a werewolf tribunal, not the seventh level of hell," I said. Not that there was a big difference, actually.

"You can never be too safe," she said. "And something tells me we haven't seen the last of . . . *him*."

"You mean . . ."

"Don't say his name," she said, holding up a hand. "*Never* invoke his name."

Goose bumps rose on my arm. I glanced down at the ring on my hand, which had flashed hot several times that day, and thought with a hint of dread that she was probably right. "But the salt worked fine yesterday."

"It wasn't enough to drive him off so completely," she said. "I doubt he'll give up that easily. Demons can be quite persistent, you know. And crafty. A lot of people think they're stupid, but they're anything but."

"Just what I need," I said.

"I wish I could come with you," my mother said.

"Me, too," I said. "But you're not a werewolf." And unlike Lindsey, she thankfully had no interest in becoming one.

"Be safe, darling. It's hard enough losing one of you," she said, and there was a note of fear in her voice I hadn't heard before. "I couldn't bear to lose both."

"Mom . . ." I began.

She seemed to shake off her thoughts. "Now then," she said. "This is oil of frankincense. It will help repel him." As I stood there, she anointed my forehead, neck, and arms with the stinky stuff. "I've made you a salt amulet to wear, and here is a bag of things to take with you, just in case. I don't know if they'll help, but better safe than sorry."

I opened the mouth of the cloth bag she had given me and pulled out a crucifix. "You're kidding me. A crucifix?" Since my mother favored pentacles, it was a bit of a surprise.

"I know it's unorthodox, but I'm not sure what will work with this one, so better safe than sorry, darling. I've got a vial of holy water in there, too."

I looked up at my mother, who to my certain knowledge had never before darkened the doorstep of a church. "*Holy water?* Where the heck did you get *that*?"

"I visited Saint Mary's while you were at the office," she said.

Wow. She was definitely worried about Asmodeus if she was off collecting holy water and crucifixes.

"Once you get back, we'll do a proper exorcism, of course," she said, "but I don't want you to go out unprepared."

"Thanks," I said, returning the crucifix to the bag before tucking it into my purse. Then I gave my mom a big hug, which she returned fiercely, as if she was afraid to let me go. I closed my eyes for a moment, letting her clean, spicy, patchouli scent surround me. For a moment—just a moment—I was a child again, safe in my mother's arms. "I'll be careful, Mom," I said. "I promise."

"Do you have to do this?" she whispered.

"You know I do," I said.

"Whatever happens," she said throatily, "I want you to come home. Even if it means . . . leaving him behind." She released me, brown eyes awash in unshed tears. "Promise me you'll come home, Sophie."

I hugged my mother tightly once more, feeling the comfort of her soft body. "I promise," I whispered.

I just hoped it was a promise I could keep.

Thirty-seven

The sun was hovering low in the western sky when we entered the gates of the Graf Ranch, and I could already feel the pull of the full moon. Lindsey sat beside me in the M3, and Heath had somehow managed to fold his six-foot frame into the back. Tom followed behind on his Harley.

A burly guard I didn't recognize stood at the gate. I rolled down the window and announced myself, and his gold eyes widened a little bit.

"And the other two?"

"They're friends of mine," I said.

The guard sniffed at the windows, evidently checking for werewolfiness. Even though the switch was fairly recent, evidently Lindsey and Heath passed olfactory muster, which didn't surprise me—I could smell the change in them, too. Which was a little unsettling. "Pack affiliation?" he asked.

"They're still, uh, shopping around," I said. The guard raised his eyebrows.

The werewolf's voice was suddenly stern. "These two are fresh. Who made them?"

"I did," I said.

"*You* did?" He smirked. "Did you have pack authority?"

"She doesn't *need* pack authority," Tom yelled from behind the limo. The guard glanced at him, then back at me, evidently deciding not to pursue it further. He gave me a sharp nod, gruffly asked Lindsey and Heath to restate their names, and recorded their names in a black, leather-bound book. Then, with another glance back at the Harley behind us, he opened the gate and waved us through. Tom followed a moment later, revving the engine as he passed the guard post.

"Well, that was relatively easy," Heath said, shimmery eyes scanning the landscape rolling by.

"I'm afraid that may be the only thing that's easy," I said.

"Where do we go from here?" Lindsey asked.

"There's a long road, and then a parking area. The ranch is really a bunch of farmhouses; they hold all of their big events in clearings. At least from what I've seen."

As we pulled into the gravel parking lot, which was already mostly full, the smell of Lindsey's excitement, and Heath's apprehension, was stifling, and I practically jumped out of the car. Tom pulled in and parked beside us.

Heath and Lindsey were silent as they climbed out of the M3 and looked around at the farmhouses—and the werewolves. There certainly was plenty to look at. As usual, despite the formality of their ceremonies, the werewolves were all in jeans. I scanned the crowd, looking for Boris. Would he be here? If so, what had he told Elena? And if he wasn't, did we have any chance at all?

As we prepared to walk into Werewolf Central, Lindsey stepped up and adjusted Heath's tie; Heath checked his briefcase one last time, then turned to Tom. "Any protocol I should be aware of?"

"They expect deference," Tom said. "Keep your head down and say as little as possible, would be my recommendation."

"Anything I should know about the jury?"

"As I am sure you are aware, they are not kindly disposed toward Sophie's father. Most of the American alphas are here because they were forced out of the old country, and Sophie's father was instrumental in making that happen in at least two cases."

"And the rest of them?" Heath asked.

Tom gave him a wry smile. "Have recently agreed to alliances with the two he helped relocate."

Heath grimaced. "Is there any way we can convince the court to require a jury of Garou's peers?"

Tom smiled, exposing his gleaming canines. "The problem, Heath, is that they *are* Luc Garou's peers; they are all high-ranking werewolves. Besides, this is the Fehmic Court. The judges were selected and sworn in years ago."

"I did some research on that," Heath said. "It got a pretty bad reputation back in the middle ages. Traditionally the court is secret; is that the case here?"

"No," Tom said. "It is hidden from humans, of course, but all werewolves may attend."

"At least that's something," Heath said. "From what I read, I was afraid it would be a closed court. Still, I'm guessing there's not much chance of getting a reduced sentence."

"I plan to discuss that with Wolfgang," Tom said, with an edge of iron to his voice. I started to break into a cold sweat. Was all of this for nothing? Were we just here to attend my father's execution? Luc had said he'd had a plan . . . but what would he do if Heath failed?

"It's hopeless, isn't it?" I said.

"Can we have a little optimism here?" Lindsey asked. "This is a trial, not a funeral."

"Just trying to get the lay of the land," Heath said. He turned to Tom. "Can you take us to the courtroom? Or whatever passes for a courtroom here?"

Tom nodded and led the way across the gravel parking lot and through the throngs of werewolves gathered among the farmhouses. There must have been food inside somewhere; I saw a few people with plates of fajitas, and I could smell the smoky aroma of grilled steak, but my stomach was too churned up to consider eating. I scanned the crowd for signs of the pleather boys—my nose was attuned to the slightest whiff of synthetic textiles—but there was nothing. Conversations dwindled to silence as we passed through the clearing, only to be replaced by a buzz behind us. I could smell the hostility in the air.

"They don't look too friendly," Lindsey murmured to me as we met with yet another group of stony-eyed werewolves. Heath smiled winningly at them, which usually worked wonders—at least on the women—but tonight, it only seemed to piss them off more.

"You can say that again," I whispered back, feeling the hackles rise on my neck. Why were they all so angry with us? Had Elena and Wolfgang been whispering poisonous rumors about me?

Or had my father somehow managed to turn everyone against not just him, but me?

My mind whirled with dark thoughts as I trudged through the woods after Tom and Heath. Although sunset was still an hour off, the night animals were starting to stir—I heard a cricket in a dark corner of the wood—but the world seemed removed, somehow. It wasn't long before we broke through the scrubby oaks and cedars and stepped into the clearing where they'd condemned the made werewolves just last night. The tents still stood proudly, their flags fluttering gaily in the evening breeze, and were filling up with werewolves already. Tonight, though, in addition to the granite slab where the pack's earlier business had been conducted, the clearing boasted a long table draped in black cloth. The letters *SSGG* were embroidered on the front of it in a red, Germanic-looking style, and atop the table, quite ominously, lay a long, vicious-looking knife, a rope, and worst of all, a big wooden stake.

I swallowed hard and turned to Tom. "What are those for?"

"You mean the objects on the table?"

"Yeah. The weapons, actually."

"It is part of the tradition," he said. "If your father is found guilty . . ."

"They'll be used in the punishment," I said, feeling the world shrink around me. *This couldn't be happening.*

But it was. Tom put a hand on my shoulder. The warmth of his hand, and the weight of it, steadied me, but his words didn't. He said, simply, "Yes."

"And the red letters?"

"They're abbreviations for old German words. *Stein, Strick, Gras, Grün*: stone, rope, grass, green."

"What the hell does that mean?" I asked.

He chuckled bitterly. "If Hubert were here, I'm sure he'd be able to give you the entire history of the words. All I know is that for the Grafs, it's always been that way; it's the sign of the Fehmic Court. It's been that way for centuries."

"So I'm guessing there aren't any court reporters," Heath joked, but his voice was strained.

"There will be a scribe," Tom said. "But I think you will find the proceedings very different from what you are accustomed to."

Heath glanced at his watch. "When does it officially begin?"

"Two hours before moonrise," Tom said. "In about fifteen minutes, give or take a few."

As we positioned ourselves at the fringe of the clearing, a short distance away from the nearest tent, the werewolves quietly began filling the clearing, repairing to their packs' tents. When five minutes remained, I heard a jangle from the side of the clearing, and my skin prickled as I turned to look.

Four burly werewolves were leading my father into the center of the clearing. Despite the less-than-ideal circumstances, my father held his head high, and even with his scruffy, unshaven appearance, there was still something handsome and regal about him that made my heart swell. Maybe he *had* been a terrible father, but he was still my father. And right now, I was proud of him.

"Is that him?" Lindsey whispered.

I nodded, scanning the crowd for Elena's henchmen. *Where were they?* We were sunk without Boris.

"He looks just *like* you," she said.

"He does," Heath echoed as the guards came to a halt next to the slab of granite, pulling my father up short; he stumbled a little, and I found myself growling at them. Beside me, Tom bristled, too. The skinniest guard pulled a thick padlock out of his pocket, attaching the end of a chain to a ring in the rock. Once my father was secured, like a slave chained to the auction block, they moved to the edges of the clearing, leaving my father alone.

I leaned against Tom, feeling light-headed all of a sudden, and glad to have him with me. I was about to pull away—after all, Lindsey was just a few feet away—when he put his arm around me and squeezed. It was a relief that Heath was here to defend my father, but there was something about Tom's strong, magnetic presence that was much more reassuring. "Can I go to him?" I murmured into his ear, taking strength from Tom's masculine scent. I was longing to talk to him one last time.

"No," he said firmly. "Not now. But whatever happens, I

will make sure you have time together. Wolfgang owes me that much."

My father's eyes scanned the throngs, as if searching for someone, and I willed him to look toward me. Finally, his gaze reached our little group, and I could swear I saw his eyes light up a little. I gave my father what I hoped was an encouraging smile; he winked back at me.

"Boris isn't here," I whispered to Tom. "What do we do if he doesn't turn up?"

Tom, who had been scanning the crowd, suddenly stiffened slightly beside me. His arm slipped from my shoulders, leaving me feeling very alone. "Stay here. I will return shortly," Tom said.

I caught his arm as he turned to go. "Where are you going?"

"Wolfgang is here," he said, turning to look at me. He suddenly seemed very large and very powerful; there was something about him that made me shiver. In a good way. "There is something we need to discuss."

Before I could ask for details, he was walking toward the edge of the clearing, moving with the litheness of a predator.

Thirty-eight

The tents continued to fill, and the sun dropped lower in the sky, but Tom still didn't return. Boris was conspicuously absent, as well, which worried me. My eyes kept returning to my father, who stood with his chin high, seemingly oblivious of the crowd around him. The three made werewolves who had been condemned the other night had been brought to the clearing, too; they huddled in chains, on the side of the clearing. Tom had told me they would be released for the wild hunt when the moon rose, about two hours after sunset. Why hadn't I gotten in touch with Georges earlier? Then I could have avoided all of this . . .

It's too late to worry about that, I told myself, and glanced at Heath, hoping for reassurance. But the blankness of his face didn't help.

Suddenly, there was the low, mournful clang of a bell, and the murmur of voices fell silent. Tears prickled my eyes as a procession of torches entered the clearing, followed by several figures in black robes and hoods. As the toll of the bell echoed around the clearing, the robed werewolves took their seats, and Isabella took her place on the slab of granite, a mere yard from my chained father.

"Tonight, the Fehmic Court is convened to decide the fate of Luc Garou, alpha of the Paris pack."

There was a murmur from the crowd. The robed figures sat silent.

"I now cede the floor to the *Freigraf*, *Stuhlherr* Wolfgang Graf, chairman of the court and reigning alpha of the Houston pack."

With a deep bow to the figures at the table, Isabella stepped down from the granite slab. She hadn't reached the edge of the clearing before the tall werewolf in the center stood slowly and began speaking in a low, gravelly voice.

"The court has convened, for the first time in almost fifty years, to hear the case against Luc Garou." He paused for a moment, and I caught the flicker of his eyes beneath the hooded robe. They burned cold, with barely suppressed hatred. "He is charged with the murder of Charles Grenier, beta of the Houston pack, during the proscribed time." Wolfgang turned to my father, whose chin thrust out.

At that moment, Tom appeared at my side, his warm hand grasping my elbow.

"What happened?" I asked.

He put a finger to his lips and directed my attention to the proceedings in the clearing.

"The accused has requested he be permitted a representative to defend him in this matter," Wolfgang said. My father blinked in surprise, and he wasn't the only one. Evidently this was not traditional procedure for the Fehmic Court, because there was a murmur from the crowd—and the black-robed judges. "As *Freigraf*, I have elected to accede to his request."

My father's head jerked up, and again, the murmurs swelled, becoming so loud that Wolfgang was forced to call the proceedings to order. "Silence!" he barked, and was obeyed immediately.

"The court calls Heath Thompson to act as Luc Garou's representative in this matter," Wolfgang said.

I glanced at Heath, whose face was white as milk in the flickering torchlight. Lindsey squeezed his arm, and after a moment's hesitation, he strode to the center of the clearing with a jaunty step that belied the fear I'd seen in his eyes.

"Ladies and gentlemen," Heath said, with a small bow to the assembled werewolves, "and distinguished judges of the court," he continued, addressing the robed figures. "I am honored to be called to represent the accused in this matter."

"Thank you," Wolfgang said. He snapped his fingers. "Chair," he barked, and within seconds, a skinny werewolf hurried out to the clearing with a wooden chair for Heath.

"We will begin with hearing the details of the case," Wolfgang said.

Heath, I noticed, chose to remain standing tall instead of sitting in the proffered seat.

"*Freischoff* Hartfinder," Wolfgang said. "Will you present the evidence against Mr. Garou?"

A werewolf whose voice I didn't recognize stood up, and in a rough, dry, voice, went through the details. Grenier had been found dead on Fourth Street a mere twenty minutes after two witnesses observed him arguing with Luc Garou. Hartfinder went through all the reasons Garou would want him dead, including the fact that Grenier double-crossed him centuries ago. He then pointed out that the accused bore a scratch on his face that was consistent with a scuffle. Throughout, my father stood motionless.

As Hartfinder concluded his recitation, Heath raised his hand. "Excuse me, sir," Heath asked. "But were there any actual witnesses to the murder?"

Hartfinder was silent for a moment. Then he said, "There were not."

"Well, isn't it possible that someone else may have committed it, then?"

Wolfgang leaned back in his chair. "Who are you suggesting, Mr. Thompson?"

Heath shrugged. "Any number of people, sir. Or, in this case, werewolves."

"Do you have any evidence to support this theory?" Wolfgang asked.

"Actually, I believe I do have someone who will testify that there were other alternatives." He turned and addressed the assembly. "I'd like to call Boris Krepinsky, member of the Houston pack, to the stand."

I held my breath, waiting. Tom was rigid beside me.

Another murmur tore through the crowd—but no pleather boy appeared. Heath kept his jaunty stance, but I could see his face turn even paler. "I call Boris Krepinsky to the stand," he repeated. Again, nothing.

"Mr. Krepinsky appears not to be in attendance," Wolfgang said lightly. "Is there anything else you have to present?"

"I will testify."

I turned in shock as Tom strode forward into the clearing.

As the entire assembly looked on, he slung himself into the wooden chair that had been brought for Heath. Lindsey clutched at my hand, and I tried to remember to breathe. What was Tom *doing*?

"What is your involvement with this case, Mr. Fenris?" Wolfgang asked coldly.

"As I had a detailed conversation with Mr. Krepinsky last night," he said, "I felt that in his absence, I should contribute my understanding of the situation. I believe what he told me is relevant to the proceedings."

"You spoke with Mr. Krepinsky last night?" asked Heath, who had recovered his sangfroid.

"Yes," Tom said, radiating an air of effortless command—and utter sexiness—that, were it not for the fact that I was already a little unsteady due to the fact that my father's life was on the line, would have made me weak in the knees. I glanced at Lindsey, but her eyes were fixed on Heath.

"Under what circumstances?" Heath asked, looking cool and collected and quite handsome.

"I accompanied Miss Sophie Garou to visit her father's assistant last night, at the Driskill Hotel in Austin."

"How does this relate to Mr. Krepinsky?" Wolfgang asked sharply.

"Mr. Krepinsky met us at the door, along with his associate, Mr. Ludovic."

"They were in conference with Garou's compatriot?" Wolfgang asked.

"Not exactly," Tom said. "They had murdered him. We found him with a stake through his heart."

There was a gasp from the crowd, and my father's face screwed up in pain.

Tom continued. "They proceeded to attack Miss Garou and myself upon our arrival."

There was an outburst from the spectators; when the uproar had died down enough to hear, Heath addressed Tom. "But you say you spoke with Mr. Krepinsky last night."

Tom nodded. "That is correct."

"What was the nature of that conversation?"

Tom leaned back in his chair. "After Miss Garou and I neutralized the situation, Mr. Krepinsky explained to me why he was present at Mr. Garou's hotel."

"Why was that, exactly?"

"He had been sent by Miss Tenorio," Tom said, glancing at Elena, who was standing stock-still in the Houston tent. "I suspect his failure to appear tonight may have something to do with Miss Tenorio's reluctance for him to share his testimony, in fact."

"Why had she sent them?" Heath asked.

"She sent them to kill both Georges Lemuet and Sophie Garou," he said simply. "Which constitutes," he added, glancing at Elena, "a murder during the proscribed time. And is punishable by death, unless I am mistaken."

"They were going to call the Paris pack!" Elena burst out, striding into the center of the clearing. "I didn't tell them to kill anyone. I told them to stop her from contacting the Parisians."

Wolfgang stared at her coldly. "You arranged this without my knowledge?"

"That is not the only thing she arranged without your knowledge, Wolfgang," Tom said quickly before Elena could respond.

Elena started talking, but Wolfgang cut her off with a wave of his hand. "What else did he say?" he asked Tom, leaning forward in his chair.

"Evidently, Miss Tenorio had made an arrangement with Mr. De Loup," Tom said in a languid voice. Despite the relaxed tone of voice, I could see the tension in the muscles of his shoulders.

"What was that arrangement?" Wolfgang asked coldly.

"According to Mr. Krepinsky, once Miss Tenorio had been made co-alpha," Tom said, "with the help of Mr. De Loup, her plan was to depose you and replace you with Charles Grenier."

"That is a lie!" announced one of the other judges, who stood up and ripped his hood back.

"Why would Grenier offer his assistance?" Wolfgang asked.

"It seems that in exchange for his assistance, Miss Tenorio would cede Beaumont and the surrounding territories to the Louisiana pack."

There was a shocked silence; then everyone started talking at once.

"Silence!" Wolfgang roared. The talking stopped.

Then he turned to Tom. "How does this relate to the case against the accused? If, as you say, Elena planned to involve Grenier in her future plans, why would she kill him?"

"Perhaps he became a liability," Tom said. "After all, you did see him leaving her hotel room."

Wolfgang's face became very still.

"Perhaps, Wolfgang, you were the one who killed Grenier," Tom said, his voice deadly calm. "Because you knew he was planning to depose you, and because by killing Grenier and framing Luc Garou, you could finally wreak your revenge on the werewolf who evicted you from your home territory all those years ago."

"It's only a theory," Heath said hurriedly, trying to salvage the situation. "Miss Tenorio could have disposed of Grenier, as well. After all, she certainly had no compunction about ordering the death of Mr. Garou's assistant. Or his daughter."

But I could tell it was too late; the damage had been done. I stared at my father, feeling sick to my stomach. Unless I was mistaken, Tom had just signed his death sentence.

"Do you have anything else to add?" Wolfgang asked coldly.

"Only this," Tom said, standing up so that he towered over the black-robed *Freigraf*. "Wolfgang Graf, if you put Luc Garou to death, I will do everything in my power to draw the gods' wrath down upon you."

Thirty-nine

"You dare to threaten me?" Wolfgang said in a dangerous voice.

"I am simply encouraging you to make the right decision," Tom said, but with an edge of menace in his voice. Again, I felt that ripple of power through the clearing. Tom then turned to Heath. "Do you have any more questions?" he asked.

"The questioning is over, Mr. Fenris." Wolfgang turned to his fellow judges. "I move we determine the verdict."

"But I haven't made my closing arguments," Heath protested.

"They will not be required," Wolfgang said, looking over to Isabella. "The bag, please."

Isabella strode to the table holding a black bag, stopping at each chair as the judges wrote their verdicts on slips of paper and dropped them in. When they had all dropped their papers into it, Isabella presented the bag to Wolfgang, who examined the judges' statements in silence.

Tom remained standing a few feet from my father, a menacing look on his face, as Wolfgang stood and faced my father.

"Luc Garou," he intoned. "The Fehmic Court has tried you in accordance with the court's laws for the crime of murder during the proscribed time." I stared at my father, praying that Tom's threat had worked. My father had said he'd had a plan, but so far, he hadn't said a word. Had he somehow managed to get in touch with the Paris pack? Would they be descending on the Howl at any moment?

I squeezed my eyes shut, and Wolfgang's next words came to me as if in a dream. "Luc Garou," Wolfgang said, "I regret to inform you the court has determined that you are guilty."

Tom stepped forward, and a dark cloud scuttled in front of the waning sun. "I warned you, Wolfgang."

"The penalty for said crime is to be drawn and quartered," Wolfgang intoned. I almost doubled over from shock. "Followed by staking and decapitation."

Oh, my God. I looked at my father, wishing I could do something—anything—to free him.

"No," Tom said, seeming to grow as I watched him. "You will not do this thing."

"Wolfgang," said my father, his voice taunting despite the terrible sentence Wolfgang had just declared. "Are you such a coward, then?"

Wolfgang's eyes blazed, but he didn't respond.

"Are you afraid you will lose again?" he asked. "Is that why you won't face me?"

Wolfgang said nothing.

"You were weak in Alsace. If you hadn't been, I'd never have been able to topple you and send you to this hole on the other end of the earth." My father's eyes burned as he faced down Wolfgang. "If you kill me now, everyone will know that you are weak," he said. "And it will be only a matter of months before someone stronger takes your place."

Luc then looked around at the crowd. "Wolfgang has proven nothing against me," he said. "And if he murders me, he can never prove his own innocence."

There was a swell of something—agreement?—from the crowd.

"There is another way, though," Luc said. "We could let the gods decide." Luc turned to Wolfgang. "There are no witnesses," he continued. "There was no confession. This trial is nothing but a sham. The judges are determined to wreak revenge on me, not to dispense justice." He paused, focusing on Wolfgang. "If you're convinced of your innocence—and my guilt—why not put all doubt aside?"

Wolfgang stiffened.

"You know what I mean," Luc said, with a voice of firm authority that made me understand why he was alpha of the Paris pack. "Ladies and gentlemen, Madame Murano, distinguished members of the Fehmic Court . . ." he delivered a mock bow to the hooded figures—" . . . I propose a trial in the old ways. A duel before the eyes of the gods, to establish innocence or guilt." He turned to address the crowd ringing the clearing. "Did I kill Charles Grenier? Or was it the threatened alpha of the Houston pack?" Despite the shackles and the rather scruffy wardrobe, his presence was commanding. "Shall we dispense with jaded juries and turn the verdict over to the gods?" He turned to the crowd. "What say you?"

There was a moment of excruciating silence. I could tell the crowd might go either way. I stared at my father; would his sally work?

Then, finally, somebody yelled, "Duel!" A moment later, another voice joined in, and within seconds, there was a low chant echoing through the clearing.

Luc turned to Wolfgang. "The clan has spoken, Herr *Freigraf*," he said, drawing himself up like a king. Which I suppose he was. "Will you accede to their request?"

Wolfgang stood there for a moment, motionless, rigid with anger. Then, brusquely, he nodded. "I should have torn your throat out the day you attacked Strasbourg," he growled, his voice thick with barely repressed hatred. I hardly recognized him; his cool demeanor was gone, replaced by a fury that made him look, well, animal. "Since I did not, I will do it now." He threw off his cloak. "Ten minutes. Here, in the clearing." He jerked a hand at Garou. "Free him, and allow him to prepare," he spat. "But do not let the coward escape."

As Wolfgang strode off, the rest of the cloaked Fehmic Court falling in behind him, Tom went to my father, whose guards were releasing him from his shackles. I ran across the clearing to join them.

"Dad," I said. "That was incredible. Are you sure you can win?"

His eyes blazed as he turned to me. "You doubt me?"

"No," I said. "I'm just worried about you, is all."

"You did call me dad," he said with a smile. He reached out and kissed me on the head. "You were right about Fenris, my dear," he murmured.

"I know," I said.

My father turned to Tom. "Thank you," he said. "You risked much to save me, and I know your family and mine have not always been on the best of terms."

Tom nodded gravely, and the sight of him—his strong Nordic face silhouetted in the firelight, the gleam on the gold of his hair—made something inside me quiver. He'd been so strong, so masterful just now. "Will you be needing a second?" Tom asked. He was offering to be my father's backup.

Luc's gaze was piercing. "Are you offering?"

"I am," Tom said.

"Then I accept," my father said, shaking off the shackles and gripping Tom's hand. "Forgive my earlier suspicion. Clearly, I was wrong in my estimation of you."

"Thank you," Tom said simply.

"Now," my father said, clapping his hands together with anticipation. His golden eyes gleamed in the torchlight. "Where do we go to prepare?"

"I will lead you to the changing tents," Tom offered.

"Wait," Luc said. He turned to me, and put his hands on my shoulders. "Sophie. I do not anticipate any trouble, but should, by chance, something happen . . ." He gazed at me with tenderness in his eyes, and ran one finger along my cheek lovingly. I realized with a pang exactly how much I'd missed having a father all these years. And that now, if things didn't go perfectly, I might lose him again. Forever.

"Sophie, my darling, I am delighted with the werewolf you have become. And meeting you . . ." He swallowed hard, and if I didn't know better, his eyes started looking moist. "Meeting you has been one of the highlights of my life," he said huskily, pulling me into a hug. The smell of him, unwashed as he was, triggered a wave of emotion in me.

"But . . ." My eyes started to fill with tears.

"If I do not emerge victorious, tell your mother I thank her. She has done a wonderful job raising you."

"After all I've been through," I said, wiping my eyes, "you'd better not die."

"I'll do everything in my power to prevent it," he said, eyes gleaming. "Besides, I've known Wolfgang a long time. I'm not too worried." A grin that could be described as slightly maniacal crossed his face. "It will be just like the battle of Colmar. He'll be skulking off with his tail between his legs."

I glanced over toward Wolfgang, who had shed his robe and was stalking off to the side of the clearing, radiating fury. He didn't look ready to skulk off, in my opinion, but I kept it to myself. The entire assembly was abuzz; apparently this was one of the most exciting events to happen at a Howl in some time.

As the dark woods swallowed Tom and my father, Lindsey and Heath hurried up to where I stood, alone.

Heath looked stricken, his face still pale. "I'm so sorry it came to this, Sophie. I did what I could."

"You were wonderful, Heath—you did everything you possibly could," I said, trying to smile. "The jury was fixed; unless we could produce the murderer and make him or her sign a confession, there was no way they were going to let him go."

"Still. I'm sorry I wasn't able to avoid . . . this," he said, pointing to the center of the clearing, which was currently being cleared of the long, cloth-clad table.

"Is your father going to be okay?" Lindsey asked, her gray eyes disturbingly shimmery. I wasn't used to her werewolf scent, or Heath's, really.

"He seems to think so," I said. "Let's just hope he's not wrong."

Lindsey glanced around at the crowd, which was focused rather intently on our little group. "I think we should move out of the way," she whispered, and when I looked up at all the fiery eyes focused on us, I let her guide me out of the clearing, where we stood in the shelter of a gnarled oak tree.

"How does a duel work?" Lindsey asked when we'd drawn into the shadows a bit.

"I don't know," I said. "But they don't use swords, I don't think."

"So they'll be fighting as . . ."

"As wolves," I finished for her.

Lindsey reached over and squeezed my arm, and Heath flashed me a sympathetic look from his strangely iridescent brown eyes. We stood in silence among the buzz of excited werewolves. A few minutes later, two massive wolves, one reddish, with slightly matted fur, the other pure, sleek gold, padded into the clearing. The reddish wolf raised his head and let out a howl that curdled my blood, then trailed off into a mournful dirge that raised every hair on my body.

A moment later another huge golden wolf entered the clearing, followed by one as black as night, and let out an answering howl.

The seconds moved to the edge of the ring then, leaving the two alphas to face each other.

The two wolves' eyes locked, and the growls emanating from their throats seemed to make the ground vibrate around me. Adrenaline pulsed through me; combined with the pull of the soon-to-rise full moon, I had to struggle to retain my human form. Then Wolfgang leaped forward, white teeth slashing, and my father darted to the right, teeth snapping at the Houston alpha's hindquarters.

My fingernails bit into my palms as the two turned to face off a second time, hatred rolling off of them in waves. The duel had begun.

Forty

Both werewolves were experienced fighters— that much quickly became clear—and Luc Garou's estimation of Wolfgang's courage and fighting prowess appeared to be rather optimistic. Or else Wolfgang had been practicing over the last hundred years.

The two of them lunged at each other again and again, teeth snapping in the air—and occasionally, on the other's body. The crowd watched, excitement in their iridescent eyes—it was almost as if they were watching gladiators, back in the Colosseum—but for me, every lunge was pure torture.

Luc made a series of grabs for Wolfgang's powerful neck, but was rebuffed each time. After circling the clearing, Luc lunged again, but Wolfgang was ready for him. He darted to the side, but before Luc could retreat, the Houston alpha leaned in and grabbed hold of the red wolf's neck. I could hear the rip of raw flesh, a yelp of pain. My heart rose to my throat as Wolfgang's paws slid on the grass and he maneuvered to get a better grip.

But just as I was sure he was going to clamp his jaws down for the last time, Luc shook him off. The blood stained his matted fur, and the breeze brought me its coppery smell. The others could smell it, too. I could sense the bloodlust rising, and the fear of the three made werewolves huddled together on the other side of the clearing. Their turn would come soon enough.

Things went downhill fast from there. The wet stain on Luc's pelt grew, and instead of attacking, he found himself on the defensive, fighting off Wolfgang's increasingly aggressive lunges. The Houston alpha managed to grab my father's throat again, and I impulsively moved to help; Lindsey held me back as my father shook free a second time, obviously in trouble.

As the two circled each other again, my heart folded in on itself. Luc was obviously fading—the blood was all the way down his front now, and he was slower to dodge Wolfgang's offensive. Luc had just managed to escape another attack when I heard my name, softly, from the woods behind me.

I turned; there, in the darkness, I could make out the blue flicker of a familiar pair of eyes. The ring on my finger burned suddenly.

Mark.

It's not too late, he said. But Lindsey and Heath didn't hear—it was as if he spoke the words in my mind. I fumbled in my purse for the bag of amulets, feeling my fingers close on the holy water my mother had gotten me. *He's going down fast*, Mark said. *He's weak, and wounded. He doesn't have a chance. But you can save him.*

I can't!

The demon moved out of the shadows a little bit, so I could see the torchlight on his silky dark hair, make out the handsome planes of his face, the seductive curve of his lips. *Would it be so bad, to spend the rest of eternity with me?* he asked, his eyes imploring me. I remembered the feel of his lips on me, the heat of his tongue. *Look*, he said, pointing into the clearing behind me. I whirled around and pulled in a sharp breath; Wolfgang had my father pinned to the ground. *If you don't do something soon, your father will die.*

"No!" I moaned.

"It's okay," Lindsey said, totally unaware of the demon ten feet behind us in the trees.

"I . . . I can't," I said, feeling like my heart was being torn out of my chest. Wolfgang had both front paws on my father's chest now, and looked around the ring with a fierce growl that made me sick. He was going in for the kill—I could tell.

Leave this place, came yet another voice. It was Tom's, I realized. While everyone else was watching the battle in the clearing, Tom's eyes were fixed on the creature behind me.

So be it, Mark said. Wolfgang's head dove, mouth open, jaws prepared to rip out my father's throat. The ring suddenly seared my finger, making me cry out; at the same time, I felt a pulse of energy, and a flash of light and heat from behind me. I glanced over my shoulder. Mark had vanished.

Startled by the commotion in the woods, Wolfgang jerked his head up a split second before making contact.

In that instant, my father whipped his head around, stretching toward Wolfgang; before the Houston alpha realized what had happened, his throat was firmly clamped in Luc Garou's jaws.

The crowd gasped at the sudden turnaround. In seconds, Luc was on his feet again, his teeth still embedded in Wolfgang's hairy neck, fire blazing in his eyes. *God*. Was my father really going to rip his throat out?

I was hoping maybe he'd let him go, now that everyone knew my father had won the duel. But Wolfgang wasn't done fighting yet. As my father shifted from paw to paw, Wolfgang started flailing, pushing against my father's chest, using his muscular hindquarters to try and free himself. With his paws firmly braced on Luc's chest, he jerked backward, and my father clamped down harder.

A moment later, Luc Garou was still holding onto Wolfgang's throat, but the rest of the Houston alpha was sprawled on the ground beneath him, twitching in a puddle of blood.

"Oh, God," I whispered, feeling vomit rise in my throat as the wind brought a whiff of blood to me. My father had ripped Wolfgang's throat out.

I raised my hands to my face, unwilling to look.

"He did it," Lindsey said. "I can't believe he actually did it."

The next voice I heard was my father's. "The gods have spoken," he bellowed. I looked up; he was standing, naked and bloodstreaked, over Wolfgang's twitching body. As delighted as I was to see him alive, it was a tad embarrassing having him starkers in front of God and everyone. He, on the other hand, didn't seem to have a problem with it. Wolfgang's second had transformed, too, into a dark-haired burly man I had seen but didn't recognize. As I watched, he took the stake that had sat on the table earlier—the one intended for my father—and, looking like he was about to be sick, buried it in Wolfgang's chest. The furry body twitched once, violently, and was still.

"So that's what a second does," Lindsey murmured. "Ugh."

"As the gods have shown, I am innocent," my father proclaimed, breathing hard—he had won, but he was still injured. "And now that I have vanquished the alpha, the title falls to me."

There was a murmur in the crowd.

"As you know, however," he continued, "I have duties of my own to attend to, in my home territory of Paris. After I have avenged my assistant's death, I will be returning." He turned to me, and his golden eyes locked on mine, pride burning in them. "But my genetic heir, Sophie Garou, will take my place as the new Houston alpha."

All eyes turned to me then.

"Oh my God," Lindsey said. "You're alpha!"

"But . . ."

My father held out a hand to me.

"Go on," she said, pushing me forward. I stumbled across the clearing toward my naked, blood-slicked father. My eyes caught Tom's; he regarded me impassively.

My father took my hand, eyes bright with excitement. "It's what I wanted for you, Sophie," he said in a low voice. "Your birthright."

But before he could make any more formal announcements, Elena's cold voice cut through the night air.

"She will not be alpha."

Elena strode into the clearing, head high, face dark as a storm. "It is my right. I will not relinquish it."

"It has not been made formal, Elena. Things have changed." My father faced her down. "Step aside, Elena Tenorio."

"I will *not*." What happened next occurred so fast I didn't have time to react. One second, Elena was pulling at her dress. The next, she was barreling into me—half-transformed, teeth bared, aiming for my throat.

Forty-one

The change tore through me as I hit the ground, Elena's weight like a truckload of bricks, her jaws snapping at the air above me. My legs ripped through the fabric of my T-shirt as I rolled, trying to escape the onslaught of her jagged teeth.

Finally I wriggled out from under her, scuttling over to the side of the clearing and shaking off the remains of my jeans. She growled again; I looked around, waiting for aid. My father was watching closely, but seemed not at all inclined to leap into the fray. Tom, too, stood on the sidelines, watching me.

Do you want my assistance?

I blinked; it was Tom's voice. Only it was in my head. He was still in wolf form, prowling at the edges of the clearing.

I will aid you if you need it. But to show your supremacy, you must eliminate your rival once and for all.

I stared at the sleek black she-wolf, who even now was looking for a weakness in my defenses, and let a low growl rip from my throat. *Do I have to kill her to end it?* I asked.

No, he answered. *But you must show that you could.*

Before our little mind-think conversation could go any further—and I had lots of questions, like, Why didn't you tell me we could do this a year ago? And, Are you the only one who can talk in my head? And, Does this only work when we're in wolf form?—Elena hurled herself at me at top speed. I rolled to the side just in time, quickly righting myself.

What should I do? I asked as I faced Elena yet again, wondering how I was supposed to get past all those angry teeth.

Do what Wolfgang did. Tom's voice echoed in my mind. *And your father.*

You mean go for the throat.

Exactly. I glanced at Tom for a millisecond, afraid to take my eyes off of Elena any longer, and he nodded his head a fraction. *Bite down hard, just not too hard. You bested Anita, you can best this one, too.* I glanced at him again. *Eyes on Elena, Sophie. Focus. Lose it for a moment and she will kill you.*

As my eyes flicked back to Elena, I realized too late that Tom was right; she was on the move again, and already mere inches from my head. I jumped to the side, but not fast enough—her teeth clamped onto my back leg, throwing me off of my feet and onto the ground.

Now I was on my back as her teeth bit into my leg. I could feel the crunch of bone, and a searing pain shot through my body. Elena's eyes were hot on mine, aflame with long-suppressed rage, as she bore down with all of her strength. I could feel the bone breaking beneath her teeth, and let out a howl of pain.

Satisfied that I was subdued, she let go her grasp and reached for my throat.

At that moment, something rose inside of me; I could feel it coalescing behind my breastbone, gathering its strength. Then, as she closed on me, it contracted into a tiny ball and—I don't know how to put it, exactly—but it kind of hurled itself at her. I could feel the hollowness where it left me.

Elena's teeth snapped shut inches from my throat; there was a breeze on my face, and a yelp as if Elena had been punched, and then she was on the ground, ten feet away from me.

I pulled myself to my feet, right hind leg dragging, and closed the distance between us, my thoughts lost in a red cloud of pain and anger. She lay on the ground, winded; all predator now, I focused on the black fur of her neck, judging the angle, already tasting her blood on my lips. I lunged; but she flailed to her feet, and my aim went wide. My teeth missed her neck, burying themselves in her shoulder. At the same time, hers tore down my side, ripping through the flesh and making me yelp in pain.

As I tightened my grip, she snapped at me again, this time grabbing my front leg. I yanked, feeling the tearing as her teeth slid down the leg bone to my paw. I jerked back, feeling the agony as her teeth ripped through the flesh of my paw. Just for a moment, I found myself wondering how I was going to explain all this to a plastic surgeon.

Then the thread of thought was lost in instinct again. As Elena snapped at me, my teeth dug deeper into her shoulder, drawing blood. I felt a crunch between my teeth, and she let out a howl of pain; I could feel it radiating from her, along with her anger, which still burned hot. I was beyond thinking—all I wanted was to sink my teeth into her, to vanquish her before she vanquished me. As she lowered her dark, sleek head, preparing for her next attack, Tom's voice rang in my head again. *When she comes after you, let go and go for the throat.*

I had only a moment to react; within a split second, she was coming at me again, teeth gleaming in the torchlight. I released her shoulder and feinted to the side, throwing her off balance. She fought to shift gears, but she couldn't stop the momentum. As she stretched her long black neck, I went for the kill.

The moment seemed to play out in slow motion. I saw the stark fear in Elena's eyes as she realized what had happened, but it was too late for her to pull back. I felt the fur in my mouth first, then the firmness of muscle, then the hot spurt of her blood as my jaws closed tighter. I started to squeeze harder, consumed with pain and vengeance, but as her body flailed, Tom spoke again. *Hold, Sophie.*

If he hadn't stopped me, I would have killed her.

I'm not terribly clear on what happened next. Once Tom told me I could let Elena go, I succumbed to the pain. Although I vaguely remember being carried off in Tom's arms, and hearing my father's voice somewhere in the distance, the next actual moment I can recall is waking up in my bed in my childhood room, looking up at a werewolf who was a dead ringer for Gloria Steinem.

"She's awake!" Gloria said, smiling.

"Sophie!" It was Lindsey, who I now realized was sitting, along with Heath, in chairs that had been set up alongside the bed. They were holding hands, I noticed in a detached sort of way, and wondered what Tom thought about it.

"You did well, Sophie." It was Tom's voice, only not in my head this time. I turned to look into his amber eyes; he was perched on the side of the bed. A smile curled his lip, giving me a glimpse of those long white canines.

"You're not in my head anymore," I said. "Why not?"

"I don't know," he said, his golden eyes burning. "The connection seems stronger when we are in our animal forms."

"Why?"

"What's she talking about?" Lindsey asked.

"I could hear him," I said. "When I was out there . . ."

"Shhh," Tom said, laying a finger on my parched lips. "We'll talk about it later."

Despite my rather reduced state, his touch still ignited a response in me. I glanced at Lindsey, feeling guilty.

"It's okay," she said. "I'll explain later."

Suddenly, I sat up straight. Or tried to—it didn't work out very well, and only resulted in excruciating pain. "My mother . . ." I gasped. "We need to call her."

"She knows everything. In fact, she's barely left your bedside," Lindsey said. "She just went to get something to eat. We're at Sit A Spell now. Your father's here, too."

"Is he okay?"

"He's fine," she said. "Well, maybe not fine. He's in about the same shape as you are."

"What's the damage?" I asked, looking down at my bandage-swaddled body. I noticed the fur coverage on my unbandaged arm was rather heavy, and panicked for a moment—then realized that everyone else in the room was in the same boat, and there was no need to worry.

"Broken leg, and your arm and hand got torn up pretty well," said Lindsey. "Your dad's in the guest room, recovering. He wanted to come see you, too, but she gave him something to help him rest. Fortunately, we didn't have to take either of you to a hospital. You're both in excellent hands here." She nodded toward Gloria Steinem. "Dr. Stenger trained at Johns Hopkins."

I looked at the kindly looking woman—werewolf, actually, based on the glowing amber eyes—with the long hair and big glasses. "You're a doctor? That's amazing! How did you manage med school? I mean, the full moons . . ."

She grinned. "It was a challenge, but not an insurmountable one. I just had to dodge a lot of blood tests. And drink a lot of wolfsbane during my residency." Her eyes glinted behind the heavy glasses. "But right now, it's time for everyone to leave. You need to rest if you're going to mend."

Lindsey smiled at me, looking gorgeous as always, even with the little bit of extra sideburn I noticed was starting to develop. "She managed to get you fixed up before moonrise. It was touch and go, but we made it."

"Your first full moon," I said, realizing it had been Lindsey's, and Heath's, first experience with compulsory transformation. "How did it go?"

"It was a little hectic, after everything that happened. But it's amazing, Sophie." Her eyes sparkled. "Everything smells so incredible. Even the wind has a scent! And the feel of running through the woods . . ." She shivered. "Heath and I had a wonderful time. Thank you so much for sharing with me!" I knew she meant it on both counts; both the blood and my ex-boyfriend. I smiled up at her, glad to see her so happy.

"So, are you guys going to switch back?" I asked.

"I don't want to, but Heath's kind of on the fence. We agreed we'd try it out for a few months and then decide."

"I hope you like wolfsbane tea," I said.

"I know there's a lot to catch up on, but Sophie needs rest," the doctor said reprovingly.

"You're right—I'm so sorry, Doctor." Lindsey turned to me. "You're in good hands, like I said. Just relax and get better now, okay, Madame Alpha?"

I blinked at her. "What did you just say?"

"You're the big cheese now. Remember?"

I'd been so focused on saving my father's skin—not to mention my own—that I'd forgotten about the other implications of what had happened. Like that I was now supposedly an alpha.

It was too bizarre to even think about. After twenty-eight years of avoiding werewolves, suddenly I was in charge of a bunch of them?

My thoughts drifted to the made werewolves who had been scheduled for execution. "The made ones—the ones they were going to hunt. Are they still alive?"

Lindsey nodded. "They postponed the final ceremonies because of what happened. You were in no shape to preside."

"I want to free them," I said. "Immediately. Can I do that?"

"You can do pretty much whatever you want to, based on what I've read of the *Codex*," Heath said. "That's what Wolfgang did. Evidently he's the one who killed Grenier. Your friend Tom was right."

I turned to stare at him. "What?"

"He decided to kill two birds with one stone. Kill Grenier, who he knew was seeing his future mate, and then pin the crime on your father."

"We can discuss all of this later," Dr. Stenger said. "When she's better."

"Lindsey," I said. "What time is it?"

"It's nine a.m."

"And it's a weekday." I winced. "I need you to call Adele for me. Tell her . . . tell her I was in an accident, I guess."

Lindsey gave me a doubtful smile. "Sophie, I'll call her, but to be honest, I don't think it will matter much. You're going to have lots of new duties now that you're the alpha."

"But I haven't decided to take it. I'm an auditor, not an alpha. And I've worked hard for that partnership."

"Hard enough to continue serving a client who's a demon after your soul?"

Tom looked at her, startled.

"Okay, folks. It's time to go," Dr. Stenger said, herding everyone toward the door.

"One last thing," Tom said. With Lindsey, Heath, and Dr. Stenger looking on, he bent down and kissed me, his gold stubble brushing against my cheek. I was about to melt into a puddle of goo—or rip his clothes off, audience or no audience—when he lifted his head, and I gasped for breath.

And looked at Lindsey, feeling horrified.

To my surprise, she was grinning. "It's okay," she said. "Heath and I—well, if it's all right with you . . ."

I glanced at Heath disbelievingly. He and *Lindsey*?

"When we started working on the case together," Heath explained, "we realized we had a certain chemistry."

"And it's obvious that you and Tom are cut from the same cloth," Lindsey said. "I've known you were stuck on each other for ages. I just didn't want to admit it."

"But . . ." I stammered.

"Everybody out," Dr. Stenger ordered. "There will be plenty of time later." When they had filed out of the room, she turned and pressed a cup to my lips. "Drink this," she said. "It will help you mend faster."

I drank, letting the syrupy liquid coat my throat. It tasted sweet, and slightly medicinal, somehow. I had barely handed the cup back before my eyelids started to droop.

"Rest now," she said.

Since there really wasn't another option, I did.

Forty-two

The next time I woke, instead of Gloria Steinem, it was my mother who was sitting next to me, peering at my hand.

"Mom?" I croaked.

"Sophie!" My mother's dark eyes were bright. "You look just awful. I'm so sorry you got banged up. But you did it!" She beamed at me proudly. "And now you're alpha, I hear. I just knew you needed to be with your kind." She leaned down and folded me into a hug, and I relaxed just breathing in her familiar smell. She released me after a long moment, then whispered, "What happened with the demon? Did the bag help?"

"You were right," I said. "He did come back."

"And?"

"I think the bag may have helped; I grabbed the holy water when he turned up. It was when Wolfgang and Luc were fighting it out. But Tom did something also. It . . . repelled him somehow."

My mother nodded sagely. "I've spoken with Tom a bit; he seems to have some of the same powers that run in our family. Sometimes they manifest themselves most in periods of extreme stress."

"Like having a werewolf try to rip your throat out," I said.

"Or something along those lines," she said.

"Something really weird happened. During the fight, I was able to talk to Tom. Mentally."

She nodded. "You both have some talent in the psychic department, and you and Tom have a strong connection."

"But I couldn't, before. Even when we were in the cave in Round Top. Except . . ." I remembered the episode in the Driskill Hotel with Boris and Dudley, and the way Tom had turned up just in time. Had he heard me then?

"The ability may come and go," she said. "It's not reliable, unfortunately."

I sighed. What *was* reliable? Other than my—and my family members'—ability to get into trouble, that was.

"There was something else, too," I said. "In the middle of the fight, there was this weird sensation—it just kind of built up in me, like a ball of energy. I don't know how, but it kind of, well, hurled itself at Elena. And it seemed to have an effect on her."

She smiled. "I've been talking with Tom about that incident," she said. "He sensed it, too. Between that and the conversation the two of you shared in your minds, it seems you and he share some unusual powers. Unusual even among werewolves."

"Really?"

"Part of the reason he is so well respected in the werewolf community—or at least this is what I gather from your father and from Tom—is his special abilities, which are evidently quite rare. I don't know whether you inherited them from me or from somewhere in your father's background, but it appears you have been gifted in the psychic department, too. Perhaps Tom can train you when you're better; he had some instruction in Norway, when he was younger."

"So I heard," I said. So much for being average. Even among the werewolves, I was abnormal. On the plus side, at least I was in good company; although I wasn't sure how I felt about Tom being able to read my mind. I was starting to wonder what he might have discovered about me during our little connection when there was a sudden pain in my arm. My mother was poking at my bandages. "Mom!" I yelped. "What are you doing?"

"I was trying to see about that ring," she said, "so we can get rid of him once and for all. But it's all covered up."

"What are you going to do to it?" I asked, glancing around nervously, looking for hedge clippers.

"I brought a few spells I thought might work," she said.

"You're not going to cut it off, though?"

"Of course not!" she said, as if she'd never gone after me with a giant pair of shears in the past.

"You can look," I said grudgingly, wincing as she carefully unwrapped the bandages. I couldn't bear to watch.

Suddenly, she gasped.

"Is it that bad?" I asked.

"No—I mean yes—but . . ."

"What?"

"Your hand is a mess. I mean it's *awful*. But the ring is gone!"

"Gone?"

"Unless I've got the wrong hand." She glanced over at my intact hand, but my fingers were unadorned.

"Where did it go?" I asked.

"I'm guessing maybe Elena tore it off of you," she said, wrapping my hand back up. "That's a pretty nasty slice she gave you, though. I hope it heals well."

"So, I guess that's that," I said.

"It's odd, though. I couldn't pry or even cut that thing off. Maybe when you experienced that power you directed at Elena . . ."

"I also knocked off the ring?"

"It's a possibility," she said.

"Well, however it happened, he's gone."

My mother checked her watch. "He may be, but I decided to invest in a little insurance policy."

"An insurance policy?"

Before she could answer, someone called up the stairs for my mother. She disappeared, returning a moment later with a short, chubby man wearing a priest's collar.

"Hello there, Sophie," he said, blue eyes twinkling in a ruddy face.

"But . . ." I stammered, confounded at seeing a priest in Sit A Spell.

"Yes, Father Roland is a priest, dear. I told him what the situation was, and he's agreed to perform the exorcism."

"She looks pretty good," he said, eyeing me critically.

My mother smiled at him. "Like I said, Father, she's not actually possessed. She's just been targeted. We just want to make sure he doesn't come back."

"And you're certain of the entity's name?" he asked my mother.

"Positive," she said, nodding vigorously.

"But . . ." I said again.

"Hush, dear," my mother said, patting my unbandaged hand as Father Roland set what looked like a small suitcase on the bed and snapped it open. "It's just a precaution."

I was about to protest, but decided against it. If my mother was scared enough to press a Catholic priest into service, it wouldn't hurt to go along with things. Even though I was pretty sure any connection between Mark and me had been severed at the Howl.

Once Father Roland had set up shop on my dresser—he laid out a vial of holy water, a cross, and a Bible—he turned and looked at me, his voice lowering as he chanted in Latin. A whole hour passed, during which I was showered repeatedly with droplets of spit and holy water. Father Roland was nothing if not enthusiastic. About halfway through, my mother had to offer him a cough drop, as his voice was becoming hoarse.

Finally, just as I was about to request an iPod and an umbrella, he stopped and closed his book, panting heavily and mopping his beet-red brow. "I think she's fine," he said.

My mother squinched her face. "Are you sure?" she asked. "I didn't feel anything."

"That's because there was nothing to feel," he said. "If there was a connection before, there doesn't seem to be one now." He turned to me. "Did you feel anything?"

Other than the constant shower of moisture, I hadn't. I shook my head.

He smiled and popped another cherry cough drop. "Well, then. I think that's that."

"Thank you, Father," my mother said, not looking entirely convinced.

"My pleasure, Ms. Bianca," he said, packing up his case. "In cases like this, it's better to be safe than sorry."

"Absolutely," she said.

He fixed her with a bright blue eye. "And I'll look for you in church this Sunday. I'll be giving the sermon this week. It's one of my favorites, all about dedicating one's life to God. I think you'll find it most absorbing."

"Sounds riveting," she said feebly. "Perhaps, if my daughter's feeling better, I'll look in for a bit. But I do want to thank you for taking the time," she said, escorting the father and his little case from my room. As they headed downstairs together, still talking, I thought back over the last hour. I hadn't felt a thing, even when the priest was at his most strident.

My eyes strayed to the hand that no longer held Mark's ring. Did the absence of feeling mean he was truly gone?

Or just that the exorcist wasn't up to snuff?

About an hour later, I was staring out the window at the trees and wondering if I should hobble over to my father's room and say hello when the roar of a motorcycle sounded outside. My heart leapt when it stopped outside Sit A Spell.

As footsteps sounded on the stairs, I reached up to rake my hair into place, wishing I could reach the mirror on the dresser.

Then he was in the doorway, and it just didn't matter.

"Sophie," he said, stepping inside and closing the door softly behind him.

He was dressed, as usual, in faded jeans and a T-shirt that molded itself to his muscular chest. His gold hair spilled over his broad shoulders, and his golden eyes burned.

My body quivered at his nearness. Now that Lindsey and Heath were together, I knew, there was nothing to keep us apart. Except, unfortunately, for the cast on my right leg.

"Tom," I said quietly. He closed the distance between us and sat down on the side of my bed. I could feel the heat of him, and his smell . . . I struggled to catch my breath.

"Have you had any time to think about things?" he asked.

I swallowed, my mouth suddenly dry. "What things?"

"The pack," he said levelly, his eyes fixed on mine. "The position is yours by right."

"If I took it,"—I sucked in my breath, trying not to think of what his skin looked like under that T-shirt—"wouldn't that mean I'd have to leave Austin?"

The light from the window gleamed on his blond hair as he shook his head. "You can organize it however you like," he said.

I thought about that for a moment. Tom was saying I could run the pack from my loft in Austin if I wanted to. I'd probably have to give up my job at Withers and Young. Then again, since Adele was doubtless going to rescind my partnership as soon as she found out I'd exorcised my star client, perhaps that wasn't such a big deal.

"The question is whether or not you want to," he said.

"What does an alpha do?" I said, still struggling to keep my thoughts on track, even if my eyes kept straying down his exceedingly fit body. His smell was getting stronger, it seemed, or maybe I was just hyper-sensitive to it.

He chuckled throatily. "The alpha runs the pack," he said. "It's not a democracy. You're the queen."

"And if I don't take it?"

He sighed. "Then the betas battle it out until there's a successor." He eyed me. "I think you would make a very good alpha, if you want my opinion."

"I just don't know," I said. "This is all so sudden."

"Think about it," he said. "You can close the Howl tonight as the acting alpha. You don't have to be sworn in until you're ready."

"So I don't have to decide immediately?"

He shook his head. "I wouldn't wait too long, but I think you can take a couple of weeks." He reached out and brushed a stray bit of hair from my cheek.

"Have you thought about . . . other things?" he asked in a low voice. His eyes found mine. "Like us?"

"It depends," I said, thinking of all the rumors I'd heard about Tom's love life. And his relationship with Lindsey. "Do you still have feelings for Lindsey?" I asked.

"I care for her," he said slowly. "But my feelings for you are in another league altogether."

Could I believe him? I wondered.

"I think the important question," he said, "involves you. What are your thoughts? Now that Lindsey and Heath are together, and your client . . . well, his mask has been removed."

"I'm relieved, I think."

He leaned closer, and his scent intensified.

"Surprised, of course, but also . . ." Before I could say another word, his mouth was on mine, his right hand cradling my head.

My body surged in a way I had never felt before, as if an animal that had been caged up for years had finally been set free. I reached for him, clawing at his T-shirt, desperate to remove all barriers between us. His mouth was hungry on mine, and a low growl escaped him as his fingers tore at my nightshirt, ripping it from my body, until I was naked beneath him.

The feel of his skin against mine was electric, and as his tongue blazed a hot trail down to my breasts, I fumbled with the button of his jeans. He was hard against me, and he groaned as I closed my hand around him.

"Sophie," he said, his voice rough. His hand dropped to the moist cleft between my legs, and I arched my back, moaning with delight as he touched me. He paused as his fingers grazed the plaster cast. "Your leg," he whispered.

"Don't care," I mumbled. I felt nothing but the heat of wanting him. He spread me apart on the bed then, his mouth engulfing first one nipple, then the other, then blazing a hot, wet trail farther down. When his lips touched me, I almost dissolved into a million bits. His tongue was hot on me, and I felt myself rise to the top of the wave, moments from cresting. Just before the peak, I reached down and gently pushed his head away.

"I want you inside me," I said.

He paused, his eyes fixed to mine, pupils dilated with lust, only a thin ring of gold surrounding them.

"Are you sure?" he asked.

"Yes," I said roughly, and he got to his knees on the bed, spreading my legs farther, and gently, slowly, thrust himself into me.

I pulled him down to me, biting into his shoulder, growling with pleasure. He tasted like he smelled—exotic, male, all animal. The touch and smell of him, even his taste, was incredible, and unlike any man I'd ever been with. It was as if Tom was something my body had been craving my whole life; now, I couldn't imagine how I'd survived without it.

Tom thrust deeper, filling me again and again, his mouth lapping hungrily at my mouth, my neck, my breasts. I groaned in pleasure, loving the feel of him inside me, the reverberations shuddering through my body, driving me to the brink of ecstasy. I was in my element now—all animal, all instinct, lost in a jungle of pure lust. Just before I succumbed, I heard his echo through me.

I love you, Sophie Garou.

A second later, everything dissolved around me. The

orgasm that ripped through my body was like every pleasurable feeling I'd ever experienced, distilled and poured into one single moment. *This is what you've been waiting for,* I realized; there was a rightness, a connection between us that I'd been longing for since I was born, only I hadn't known it.

A second later, Tom's body tensed above me, and he emitted an animal groan that made me shiver.

I'm not a hundred percent sure, but I think I may have howled.

Forty-three

It felt strange returning to the Graf Ranch knowing that it no longer belonged to the enemy, and that my father, instead of being chained up in the garden cottage, was in the backseat of my M3 with my mother, chatting about all of my relatives in Provence and Auvergne and replaying the highlights of my battle with Elena. "We'll have to change that name," my father said as we passed through the gate. "Garou Ranch sounds so much more melodious, don't you think?" Tom was in the driver's seat, his hand on my cast-free leg, his mouth twitching as he suppressed a grin.

"You were incredible, *chérie*," my father continued from the backseat, picking up the monologue that had been going almost since we left Austin. "Particularly for one who has not had any training."

"All the same, I'm glad I wasn't there," my mother said.

"Oh, but she was spectacular, Carmen. You've done a fantastic job raising her. Just marvelous." I glanced in the rearview mirror at my father, who was already practically healed from his encounter with Wolfgang. He and my mother had spent most of the afternoon catching up, and he would be in Austin another week or so, trying to track down Boris and Dudley. And what remained of Georges, so he could be shipped back to France.

"You can't just kill them, you know," I'd told him.

"Why not?"

"Because I'm the alpha, remember? And they need to be tried."

His eyes twinkled. "Oh, so you've decided to take the position?"

"Since I'm no longer employed at Withers and Young, I thought I might." I had called Adele just before five that afternoon, back at Sit A Spell. After listening to a five-minute harangue, during which she upbraided me for disappearing without calling and told me that our star client, Southeast Airlines, had canceled its contract, doubtless due to my less-than-professional behavior, I had calmly informed her that I was resigning.

"What?" she barked.

"I've been offered another position," I said.

"But . . ."

"Thank you for everything you've done for me," I said. "I'm sorry for the short notice, but I'm going to have to resign effective immediately." This wasn't how I wanted to leave the job I'd worked so hard to earn, but I couldn't risk another encounter with Mark. "I'll be in to clean out my office next week."

Adele started backpedaling. "Sophie. I may have been a bit harsh. You're still a valuable employee. I was thinking, maybe if we went down and visited Mark Sydney together . . ."

A shiver ran through me at the sound of his name, and I almost thought I caught a whiff of his smoky smell. Goose bumps rose on my arms as I said, "I'm not sure he's the kind of client you want."

She sighed. "I can't say I agree with you, Sophie. I mean, Southeast Airlines—one of the country's top companies." She was quiet for a moment, thinking of the billing opportunities she'd just lost. "Well, it's a good thing Sally passed her CPA exam," she said. "It looks like we're going to have a vacancy to fill."

I clutched the phone. "What?"

"Didn't you know? She's been taking night classes for the last year or two. She just got her results in; she passed with flying colors."

"I don't believe it," I said. No wonder she'd been dressing more conservatively; she'd been angling for a job. *My* job.

"We'll miss having someone of your experience and caliber, though. I always viewed you as a bit of a protégé." She paused for a moment. "Are you sure you won't reconsider?"

I looked over at Tom, who was sitting on the end of my bed watching me. "I'm sure," I said.

"Well, if that's your decision, I guess that's it," she said as he got up and walked over to me.

She said something else, but I'm not sure what. Tom hung up the phone and wrapped his arms around me. After years of working to get to the top at Withers and Young, suddenly the partnership I'd just given up was the very last thing on my mind. We'd spent the next half hour exploring possibilities that I'd only ever fantasized about. It had been a most pleasurable thirty minutes.

Now, as we bumped down the road to the ranch, Tom squeezed my leg, reminding me that in a few minutes I'd be doing my first stint as the new Houston alpha. One of the first things I'd do, I'd decided, would be to move the headquarters to Austin. I glanced over at Tom, suppressing the thought that had kept surfacing since I'd made the decision to try out the alpha thing.

It's too soon to think about that, I told myself, hoping his mind-reading skills weren't in full operation.

In deference to my broken leg, Isabella had moved the ceremony to the clearing where the original bonfire had been held, in the center of the farmhouse compound. Just as it had been the first week, the clearing was full of werewolves, all of whom watched our little caravan with a look of curiosity and suspicion. You'll have to be strong, Tom had told me. You've won the position, but you have to show them you can hack it.

"I never knew there were so many of them!" my mother breathed as we got out of the car. Lindsey and Heath, who had been following in Lindsey's Miata, parked next to us and joined us as we headed toward the gold and blue tent that until yesterday had been Wolfgang's.

A hush fell over the group as we made our way through, and I didn't think it was just because I'd brought my human mother along. Even though I hadn't officially been consecrated, or crowned, or whatever it was that made the whole alpha thing official, I made my way directly to the big wooden chair and plunked my bottom down on it, trying to look like I belonged there. My father took the throne next to mine, beckoning for chairs for my mother and for Tom. Wolfgang's former underlings hurried to do his bidding.

It seemed an eternity before Isabella took the center podium and got everyone to quiet down, and after several minutes of the entire group staring at me with an unsettling mixture of curiosity and hostility, I was starting to wonder whether I'd made the right decision. My father, seeming to sense my concern, leaned over and whispered, "Have no fear. You're a natural."

Tom, too, gave me an encouraging smile. And a moment later, thankfully, Isabella got down to business.

"Thank you all for extending your stay at the Howl," she

said. “As you know, due to unforeseen circumstances, there has been a regime change, and we are here to ratify it tonight.”

There was a murmur among the crowd. The other alphas were watching me intently; I could feel their eyes like holes burning into me.

“Luc Garou, alpha of the Paris pack, has bested former Houston alpha Wolfgang Graf in a duel. Although the throne by rights belongs to him, he has ceded it to his daughter, Sophie Garou, who then bested Elena Tenorio, who was a contender for the position.” I suddenly wondered what had happened to Elena and the pleather boys. Were they still here somewhere? Tom had told me not to kill Elena, and I was glad I hadn’t. But if she was still at large, I’d have to watch my back.

Then again, as alpha, that came with the territory.

Isabella turned to me. “Sophie Garou, will you please step forward?”

I didn’t exactly step forward, but I managed to gather my crutches and hobble over in what I hoped was a regal manner.

Isabella stared at me with impenetrable eyes. “Sophie Garou,” she said solemnly. “Do you accept the mantle of alpha of the Houston pack?”

“I do,” I said. Since I no longer had a job, I’d decided to make it official—and, hopefully, permanent.

“Have you selected a consort?”

My eyes darted to Tom, who was watching me impassively. “No,” I said, feeling my stomach flutter. “Not yet.”

“Will you lead and protect your pack, and swear to abide by the Code?”

No one had told me I’d have to swear to abide by the Code. Although I didn’t think it would be too hard to limit myself to two murders per month. “I will,” I said.

Isabella turned to one of her underlings, who handed her a document, a fountain pen, and a knife. She took them and then held them out to me. “Sign the document, and it will be done.”

I took a moment to review the document, which pretty much summed up what she'd just said, and glanced around, hoping someone would offer me a nice rollerball pen. Unfortunately, however, rollerballs hadn't been around when the Code was written. So I took the knife, reflecting that I'd donated a whole lot of blood to the werewolf cause over the last couple of days. Closing my eyes, I ran the sharp blade down my forearm, just as I'd seen Wolfgang do.

The pain seared me for a moment, then faded to a dull throbbing. I grabbed the pen as best I could with my bandaged hand and dipped it into the welling blood. Then I started to sign my name at the bottom of the document. By the time I finished a clumsy rendering of my name, it had taken four returns to the well, so to speak, and the cut was already starting to close.

Isabella examined the document, then rolled it up and handed it to me. She turned to her underlings again as they handed her something small and gold. It was a ring, suspended from a long chain.

"By the power of this assembly, I name you, Sophie Garou, alpha of the Houston pack, with all the powers and property associated with that rank." She lifted the chain over my head, so that the ring came to rest against my breastbone.

"Congratulations," she murmured, her eyes twinkling, and then the silence was broken by a burst of applause from the Houston tent. I glanced over to see my father, who had risen to his feet and was clapping loudly, accompanied by my mother, Lindsey, Heath, and Tom.

A moment later, the rest of the werewolves followed suit, and soon the applause thundered around me, accompanied by a chorus of loud, haunting howls.

I was now alpha of the Houston pack.

When everyone had gone, except for Lindsey, Heath, Tom, and my parents, who were snacking on leftover barbecue in the main farmhouse, I hobbled out to the porch and sat down on a rocking chair, examining for the fortieth time that day the ring Isabella had given me. I'd pardoned the three made werewolves, who had immediately petitioned to join my pack, and after meeting with the other alphas and the members of my new constituency to receive their congratulations—except Jean-Louis, who felt the need to leave immediately—I was exhausted.

My father had spent the rest of the day filling me in on all the family history I'd missed and begging me to come visit him in Paris. While what he had to tell me was fascinating, and finally filled in the yawning void that had been his side of my family, I found myself having a hard time focusing. I was dog-tired, and I still hadn't come to terms with everything that happened.

Now, as I rocked on the porch, I stared at the gold ring Isabella had presented me. It was a signet ring, and on the face of it was a wolf with golden eyes and fierce, ivory teeth, which glowed slightly in the light of the waning moon. I shivered to look at it, and let it fall from my fingers. It came to rest on my breastbone again, feeling strangely heavy. As soon as I got home, I decided, I would head to the bank and put it in the safe deposit box. I didn't want to lose it, but I didn't like wearing it, either.

As the crickets chirred around me, the screen door slammed shut. I could tell by the change in the air that it was Tom. He sat in the chair next to mine, and we sat in silence for a few minutes, staring at the moon.

"How are you doing?" he asked finally.

"I'm okay, I guess," I said. "Tired."

"That's to be expected. It's been a long week." He was silent again for a moment. "Are you still comfortable with your decision?"

"I think so," I said, turning to look at him. His eyes gleamed in the pale light of the moon, and I felt a stirring at the sight of him. "My father killed an old friend of yours yesterday. I'm sorry."

He shrugged. "My sister loved Wolfgang. I felt I owed him a debt for being a good husband to her, and we have been allies in the past. But when he turned on you . . ." He trailed off.

"Thank you," I said after a long moment. The question I wanted to ask bubbled up inside me, but I pushed it down. Instead I said, "I've been wondering about the ring Elena ripped off of my hand. Will you go with me to see if it's still there?"

"It's a long walk on crutches," he said. "And with your hand wounded . . ."

I hoisted myself to my feet. "I'll manage."

And manage I did, but not without a good bit of discomfort. Even with Tom's help, my hand was throbbing and my armpits were bruised from the pressure of the crutches by the time we reached the clearing where my father had killed Wolfgang the day before. I could still smell the coppery scent of blood.

"It was over here," he said quietly, walking over to the grassy knoll where Elena and I had battled. I couldn't see the blood, but I could smell it.

"I should have brought a flashlight," I said, bending down to peer at the ground.

"If it's here," he said, "we'll find it."

We searched the area for a good half hour, pushing the bunches of grass aside and sifting through dry leaves, but the ring was nowhere to be found. Finally, after the fourth time through, I decided I'd had enough.

"He must have taken it back," I said.

"Good riddance," Tom growled.

I was glad it was gone, but worried that I couldn't find it. Privately I resolved to come back when it was light. If Mark hadn't somehow retrieved his magic ring, I needed to know it wasn't where someone else would discover it.

The pain was so bad I was gritting my teeth by the time we were halfway back to the main farmhouse. "Let me carry you," Tom said softly.

"But the crutches . . ."

"I'll come back for them," he said, gently removing them from me. When he'd leaned them up against an oak, he gathered me into his arms, and I let my head rest against his chest as he carried me back to the farmhouse.

We had almost reached the porch when the question burst out of me.

"Tom," I said. "Will you be my co-alpha?"

He stopped, looking down at me. Then, without answering, he kissed me.

"Is that a yes?" I gasped when he released me.

"It's a definite maybe," he said, and although his rejection stung, the glint in his eyes made my heart leap with hope.

"Will you at least think about it? And stay awhile?"

"Of course," he said, and kissed me again.

I woke in Tom's arms, sometime in the middle of the night, feeling like something had brushed against me. Disentangling myself from him, I sat up, eyes scanning the room, adrenaline rushing through my veins.

Nothing.

I considered waking Tom, then decided against it; instead, I reached for my crutches and hoisted myself to my feet. I hobbled to the window, sniffing hard, and caught a whiff of smoke.

My body on full alert, I glanced back to the bed, where Tom was sleeping, and followed the scent to the bathroom, where I closed the door and flipped on the light.

The light was harsh, and I shielded my eyes, but not before I caught a glint of something on the bathroom counter.

It was the moon ring Mark had given me.

I pulled back the shower curtain, half expecting to find a demon there, but the bathtub was empty.

I stared at the ring for a long moment, pulled by the pearly sheen of the inset moon, the gleam of the silvery band. Using a washcloth, I gingerly picked it up, afraid to touch it with my own skin. I flipped open the lid of the toilet and held the ring over it.

I don't know how long I stood there, alone in the bathroom, holding the washcloth-wrapped ring over the basin of the toilet. Finally I stepped away, closing the lid and bundling the ring more tightly in the rough terrycloth. I stared at the bundle for a moment; then I wound a rubber band around it and tucked it into the back of my toiletry case, zipping it closed.

Then I turned my back on it, flipped the light off, and hobbled back to my bed.

And Tom.

Acknowledgments

Thank yous go first and foremost to my family—Eric, Abby, and Ian—for all their love and support; also to Dave and Carol Swartz and Ed and Dorothy MacInerney, for everything. Thanks also to Bethann and Beau Eccles (and Mara and Sam), who are such dear friends I consider them my adopted family; to my sister and the rest of the Potters; and to my fabulous grandmother, Marian Quinton (and Nora Bestwick).

Many thanks to Jessica Faust, agent extraordinaire, who has been my partner throughout. Thanks also to Kate Collins, Kelli Fillingim, and the rest of the team at Ballantine for all their work to bring Sophie to the printed page; and to Thea Eaton for all her help on the Internet front.

My deepest gratitude, of course, goes to the friends who help keep me sane—particularly Dana Lehman, Susan Wittig Albert, Michele Scott, Debbie Pacitti, Leslie Suez, Njambi Wanguhu, Mary Flanagan, Melanie Williams, Jo Virgil, and all my friends at the Westbank Library and my local coffee shop and bookstore. Thanks also to Austin Mystery Writers for their support and critical eyes: Mark Bentsen, Janet Christian, Dave Ciambrone, Judy Egner, Mary Jo Powell, and Manfred Reimann.